Advance praise for
The Path From Regret

"For fans of fantasy and adventure stories, J.G. Gardner's *The Path From Regret* will soon be among your favorites. His weaving of human nature and mythologically conjured creatures is sure to enchant. Can we cross into The Void and return? Can we amend our regrets? This novel asks these questions while bringing us endearing characters we won't soon forget."

   — Nancy Burke, author of *Only the Women are Burning*

"High fantasy at its best, *The Path From Regret* immerses the reader in a colorful world full of outlandish creatures, rough-and-ready mercenaries, and mysterious mages capable of wielding terrible power for good or evil. Steeped in lore and brimming with compelling characters that are complex yet relatable, J.G. Gardner shares with us an epic story about one man's quest to free himself from the ghosts of his past. With a fast-tempo plot teeming with action and intrigue, it's easy to get lost in its pages."

   — Mark Reefe, author of *Spindle Lane* and *The Road to Jericho*

The Path From Regret

A novel

J. G. Gardner

Apprentice
House Press
Loyola University Maryland

First Edition

Library of Congress Control Number: 2022950444

Hardcover ISBN: 978-1-62720-462-0
Paperback ISBN: 978-1-62720-463-7
Ebook ISBN: 978-1-62720-464-4

Design by April Hartman
Editorial Development by Sam Dickson
Promotional Development by Shanley Honarvar

Typset with Palatino Linotype

Published by Apprentice House Press

Apprentice
House Press
Loyola University Maryland

Loyola University Maryland
4501 N. Charles Street, Baltimore, MD 21210
410.617.5265
www.ApprenticeHouse.com
info@ApprenticeHouse.com

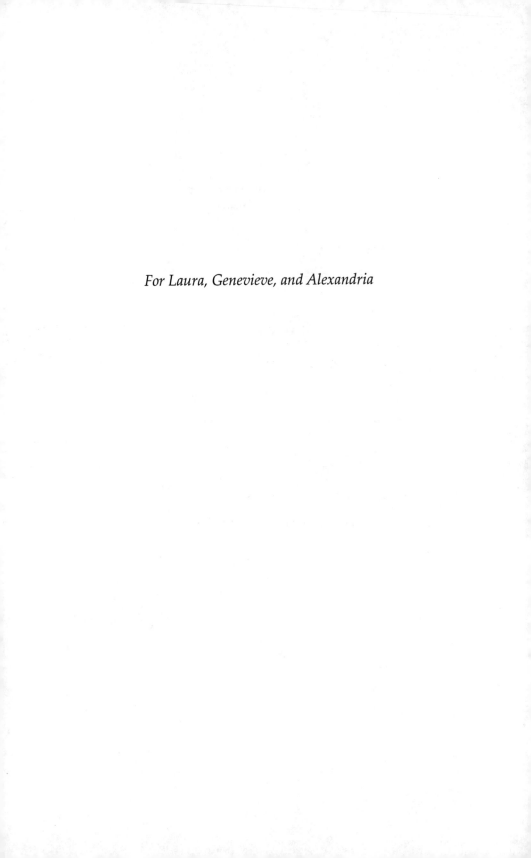

For Laura, Genevieve, and Alexandria

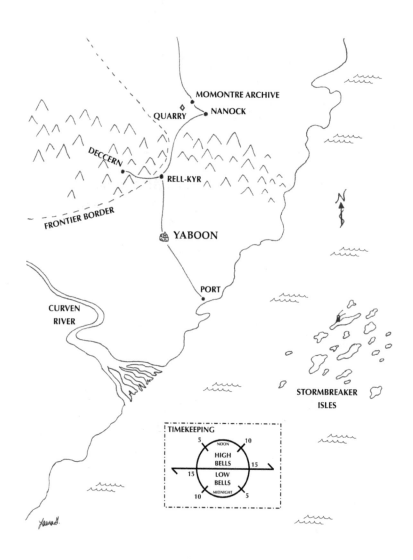

MOMONTRE ARCHIVE

NANOCK

QUARRY

DECCERN

RELL-KYR

FRONTIER BORDER

YABOON

PORT

CURVEN
RIVER

N

STORMBREAKER
ISLES

TIMEKEEPING

5   10
     NOON
HIGH
BELLS   15
15
LOW
BELLS
10   5
     MIDNIGHT

CHAPTER ONE

THORNE

The obsidian sand in the hourglass was trapped. There was plenty in the top bulb, but the glassblower had drawn the neck too narrow and the fine granules were unable to pass through. In its current orientation the bottom bulb would always remain empty. As a consequence, time stood still.

Standing in front of the table, Thorne reached out and turned the hourglass over. With a single movement, the perspective changed from one of infinite time to one where it was exhausted. In years past Thorne had often kept the hourglass with the sand forever in the top chamber. These days, when the hourglass wasn't hidden in a drawer, it sat on the table with the sand on the bottom. Thorne thought it was appropriate, given that he was now late for a meeting. His time had run out.

Warm afternoon sun entered through his apartment window and pulled long shadows from the furniture across a thick rug. It was only after Thorne had finally attained the rank of Master that he'd stockpiled enough favors and influence to secure a private room of his own. Looking from the window to the wall, Thorne scanned the large continental map that hung above the table. The teardrop shaped land mass was annotated with the borders and capitals of the five Sovereignty provinces, along with their Archives and major cities. As his eyes traced the path from Sunrock to the capital city of the Yaboon province, he remembered the dusty and uncomfortable journey in the back of a wagon when he traveled the only major road that took him from the merchant city where he grew up to his current home at the Archive.

The memory of his escape from a mundane life made Thorne slowly turn away from the map. On the opposite wall, next to a large bookcase, was a painting of a young girl. She was standing near a solitary willow tree growing close to the bank of a wide river. At the base of the tree was a small shrub that had flowered with a single white rose. The title of the painting, *Rose*, was etched on a small brass nameplate at the bottom of the frame.

Thorne turned and studied his reflection in a small mirror that rested on a bookcase shelf. The creases across his brow deepened as he ran a few fingers though the grey hair at his temple. Some would have said he had the appearance of a distinguished man in middle age, but at the moment he just looked tired. He stared deep into muted blue eyes and attempted to strengthen his resolve for what was coming.

Knowing that he couldn't procrastinate any longer, Thorne left his room and walked down the residence wing of the Yaboon Archive. The floor of the long hallway had a large rug running down the center to soften footfalls, as there was activity at all hours of the day and night, especially near the laboratories. Glass spheres that glowed with a warm light were affixed at evenly spaced intervals high up on the walls. Soon a small team of apprentice mages would stop by to change the color and intensity of the light to a low blue, indicating the change from day to night in the windowless interior hall.

Thorne tried to muster up a level of confidence he hadn't felt in some time and compelled his legs to move with purpose. As it was nearing time for the evening meal the corridor was empty save for a pair of scribes whose whispered conversation stopped when he walked past. They recognized him, but their expressions were grim. Giving the pair a polite nod that went unreturned, Thorne made his way to the central stairwell. Having left the apartments, the floor was now bare and Thorne's boots clicked on the stone steps as he crossed the second-floor landing and entered into another long hallway.

Walking down the corridor, Thorne knew that if his prolonged use of magic had not robbed him of his sense of smell and taste years ago he would have detected the unmistakable scent of ozone as he approached the alchemy labs. Down the hall there were doors on one side, as the laboratories were built only along the outer walls of the Archive so they could be properly ventilated. Even when the bellows were active inside the labs some fumes would inevitably escape into the hallway. Walking past the alchemic labs, Thorne's left wrist began to throb with pain. Clenching his teeth until his jaw ached, he veered to the far side of the hallway and near the display cases of successful material syntheses. The pain lessened, but did not completely dissipate.

As he approached the end of the hall, Thorne saw an apprentice mage stationed outside an ornate door. She was organizing loose sheets of paper that were spread across her lectern. Her eyes flicked up in annoyance initially, but then became timid when she saw Thorne's unsmiling face.

"They're expecting you. Please wait here," she said.

Getting off of the high stool she sat on, the apprentice knocked softly on the door. A muffled call came from behind it, and she opened the door and stepped inside. She didn't close the door completely, and although Thorne could not see inside from where he stood, he recognized the voices of everyone who spoke.

"Excuse me council members, but Master Thorne is waiting

outside," the apprentice announced.

A harsh masculine voice, one that Thorne recognized as Tarbeck said, "The Beast finally graces us with his presence."

"You know he doesn't like that name," replied Erica's tired voice.

"I've called him worse," Tarbeck said. With only a slight increase in volume he added, "Come in, Master Thorne." There was little respect when Thorne's title was spoken.

Thorne pushed open the door. The room was a large semi-circle with the arc made entirely out of floor to ceiling windows. Black velvet curtains were pulled to the side, letting the afternoon sun reach to the lowest portion of the back wall. The detailed maps that ran along the wall were yellowed with age and exposure, but Thorne knew that they were primarily for aesthetics. The ceiling was domed and painted with an accurate representation of the constellations on a dusky blue background. Furniture cut from thick beams and lacquered to a smooth and shiny finish was centered in the room, with everything resting on a thick woven rug. The apprentice quickly showed herself out, closing the door as Thorne stepped near to the table that was the focal point of the room.

The mage scowled at the three members of the Archive council, who were all wearing matching black hoodless robes with three quarter length sleeves. He had expected Tarbeck since he was the chair of the Yaboon Archive, and the powerfully build Sehenryu male's feline features were fairly bristling in annoyance. Tarbeck's golden fur contrasted sharply with the brilliantly white whiskers over his eyebrows. Thorne knew that Tarbeck would use the empath abilities innate to all Sehenryu to scan his emotions, so the mage tried to maintain a calm and neutral demeanor.

Thorne had also expected Erica to be present as well. A tall human with dark skin and braided black hair, she was a severe woman with little patience for things she found unpleasant. Erica had been the chair of the Archive in Momontre province before it was destroyed, and had taken residence here for the time being.

Olaf was an unwelcome addition. The demeanor of the oldest serving human council member was considerably more relaxed than everyone else in the room. Olaf's pale skin was spotted and wrinkled with age. The few wisps of white hair he still had formed a sparse crown around his head, but this was nearly compensated for by expansive eyebrows.

"Thank you for coming, Thorne. We all know you are very busy," said Olaf as he half stood up from his seat. He rested his hands on the large table that separated Thorne from the remaining council members for a moment before he slowly sat back down.

The empty platitude was the usual opening gambit of the shrewd council member. Despite his friendly and open demeanor, he was a master of the shadow games, peddling influence secretly within the Archive. Thorne had his suspicions that his own spies were feeding information to Olaf's agents, but at the moment he was likely going to need the old man's support. The mage glowered, as he wasn't interested in polite discourse and wanted to get to the heart of the meeting.

It appeared that Erica shared the same sentiments. "You are making an already long council meeting longer, Master Thorne," she said irritated. "Please save the preamble and be plain with your arguments."

Thorne gave her a single nod in agreement and replied, "I'm here to petition taking Erza's internal bounty in exchange for removal of my binding mark." The mage pulled up his left sleeve and showed the council a blue tattoo on his wrist of a five-pointed star with arcane runes at each point and in the center.

"Out of the question," Tarbeck said fiercely.

"Erza was an extremely gifted alchemist and a highly respected instructor, but there have been no volunteers to search for her since her disappearance," Thorne said, trying to maintain an even tone. "I will not speculate here why that would be, but my network has recently reported that her apprentice is in Rell-Kyr. That's at the edge of the frontier and in contested B'nisct lands. Wouldn't you agree that a Paragon's skills would be appropriate to successfully complete an investigation?"

"Even if your information was accurate, the council does not bargain for internal bounties," Tarbeck said. "Especially when you're asking to end a punishment that was meted out less than two weeks ago. Your ill-designed, and might I add unsanctioned, experiment turned an entire research laboratory to slag. You're fortunate that we voted just to restrict your access within the Archive and not completely bind your Awareness."

"Tarbeck, please," Olaf said. "Despite Thorne's rather poor timing, he does have a point." Looking to Erica he added, "And I can confirm his report. My own agents learned the same information about Erza's apprentice. However, we both know that particular internal bounty will languish, given the rather meager incentives for completion."

"I'm inclined to agree with Olaf," Erica said, after taking a minute to consider. Looking at Thorne she added, "And I agree that Thorne's past association with the Paragon program would be an asset. If you are able to successfully bring Erza back, then we can continue this discussion about resuming your use of the alchemic labs."

Thorne was about to leave when Olaf raised a staying hand. "This may be presumptuous, but I believe in all your travels that you have not yet been to Rell-Kyr. You may want to hire a guide. I've no doubt that someone from the mercenary guild would be suitable," he said smoothly. "Who knows, you might even see a familiar face there."

Giving Olaf a probing look, Thorne waited to hear more, but the council member remained silent with a practiced smile on his face. Olaf did not give advice for free, so there must have been a reason why he hinted that Thorne seek help. He turned his back on the council and left the room. There was a different apprentice at the lectern, but he didn't even look up from whatever document he was copying to acknowledge Thorne.

Despite the meeting going as well as it could have, Thorne felt restless instead of relieved. Without thinking, the mage went to the first-floor concourse and then down the eastern hallway, descending several flights of stairs into the bowels of the Archive. The temperature grew noticeably colder and the air became damp. Despite sustained engineering efforts, the lower levels of the Archive always felt like a crypt. The glow globes along the wall had been changed for the evening and bathed the hallway in soft blue light. Walking through a large arched entryway, Thorne stepped into Masters Hall.

With a casual gait down the wide central path, Thorne looked to either side to find several large recesses. Entering a specific niche, he approached one of the chrysalises housed there, which looked like a combination of its namesake and a sarcophagus, sitting on a raised stone platform. Although many mages had used this particular chrysalis over the history of the Archive, Thorne always thought of this one as belonging only to him. Thorne ran his hands over the resin folds of the capsule and traced the seams where it peeled backwards to open. The resin that was used to construct the chrysalis had an orange pearlescent color that contrasted starkly with the surroundings in the blue light.

"Is there something that I can help you with, Master Thorne?" came the polite query. One of the Vigil Keepers had crept up on him and now stood very close at his side. She was dressed simply in a light grey robe with the hood pulled over her head, but down so low you couldn't see her face.

"No, thank you, Inge. I was just remembering," Thorne said, recognizing the voice.

"I haven't seen you down here since the accident," she said.

"I thought it best that I stay away and not cause you any more trouble, considering your favor moving that chrysalis up to my lab," Thorne said.

She waved the thought away, "Don't talk to me about favors. I don't play the shadow games, Master Thorne, as you well know. I just liked the thought that someone had an interest in the work being done here for a change."

Thorne looked down at the chrysalis and said, "I still do. There's considerable potential in the chrysalises beyond astral projection into the Void, if only the council would grant a little more access for research. But as you've no doubt heard, I'm now being punished for thinking I could beg forgiveness rather than ask permission."

"For what it's worth, I think the council's judgment was too harsh. I can't remember the last time they forbade someone from a part of the Archive. It's fundamentally against our mission."

"I was told that the damage was extensive," Thorne said absently.

"That may well be, but no one was hurt and labs can be rebuilt. In fact, more than a few of us tried to support you in private. But it seems the council is out to make your life miserable, despite your past contributions as a Paragon," Inge replied.

"The work of one mage is remembered or forgotten when it suits them," Thorne said with a sad smile. "They view things on a scale grander than most of our own personal desires." He paused and took his hands off of the chrysalis lid. He looked down at his left wrist and the binding mark the council put on him. The pain he felt when he passed the alchemy labs was gone, but would instantly amplify if he went close to that part of the Archive again. Unconsciously covering the binding mark with his other hand, Thorne added, "I normally appreciate the company, but I actually just came from a meeting with the council and I was hoping for a quiet place to collect my thoughts."

"Say no more. I will leave, but visiting hours are ending soon. Please be mindful of the time," she said before silently departing.

Given the purpose of Masters Hall, Thorne had always thought it strange that it kept the same hours and staff changes as the Archive infirmary. Deciding he still had time left to follow Olaf's advice, Thorne returned to the main floor concourse and left the Archive, taking the stone paved street into the heart of Yaboon. Thorne turned onto Manor Road, so named because it was the primary artery of Yaboon that ran from the main gate to the estate of the Sovereign prince. The majority of the buildings that lined the street were single story and could easily be differentiated as either home or business, the former painted in dull browns or greys while the latter were more garish depending on what was being sold.

As he walked, Thorne watched the people in the street as they went about their late afternoon business. It had been rainy and cool recently, so the gutters that ran along the edge of the street were clear. He liked the larger cities of the continent, especially the ones with an Archive, because he could walk the streets and not feel like he was going to get a stone thrown at him for being a heretic or demon worshipper. There were still regions of the world beholden to superstition about what it meant to be a mage and Aware of the arcane elements.

The mercenary guildhall was a simple but sturdy single-story building painted a dirty yellow. Thorne pushed open the heavy wooden door and walked to the counter in the back.

The interior was sparsely furnished and equally as populated. When Thorne passed a small table where some mercenaries were playing cards, they glanced up from their game and greeted him with an expression that made it obvious he was intruding. The mage ignored them and continued to the back of the room where the guild secretary was reviewing a series of documents. A burly man with a thick black beard and shaggy hair, he only looked up from his work when Thorne rapped his knuckle on the counter.

"What is the nature of your request?" the guild secretary asked formally.

"Escort," Thorne replied. "Might I see your roster?" It was not an uncommon thing to ask as mercenaries, like any other profession, had reputations that followed them from city to city.

The guild secretary shuffled his papers and handed one to Thorne. The mage scanned the list of names of guild members in good standing and not currently under contract. When Thorne reached the name Trinity he stopped. "When did he arrive here?" the mage asked, laying the paper on the counter and pointing to the name.

The guild secretary looked at the paper and grunted. Thinking for a moment he replied, "A few weeks ago. He came as part of a three-man crew. His transfer papers were in order from the Granick guild, so he was granted license to work here for the next six months. Do you want to set up a meeting with him tomorrow?"

"No, I want to talk to him now. Where is he boarding?" Thorne asked, trying not to sound too eager.

The guild secretary gave him an inquiring look. "He's lodging at the Red Dragon, so he's probably there for drinks and dinner."

"Thank you. I appreciate your time," Thorne said.

"Are you sure you don't want to wait until tomorrow

morning when he reports in? The Red Dragon has a reputation for being a rough place," the guild secretary said.

"It'll be fine," Thorne answered. "I've been there before."

"If you say so, sir," the guild secretary replied with forced politeness and returned to reviewing his handful of documents as Thorne left the guildhall.

CHAPTER TWO

CARLION

Carlion clapped a stack of coins onto the counter with a metallic thump. His thick fingers slowly revealed the money as he continued to glare at the man behind the counter. The moneylender on the other side was a thin man with a pockmarked face and a too thin neck. When he cleared his throat and swallowed Carlion was able to see every muscle contract with effort. The man's eyes flicked down at the stack of coins for a second, but Carlion knew the moneylender had precisely counted the coins and knew their exact value.

The sun had disappeared behind the houses of the city and the ambient light that came through the windows in the front of the banker guildhall gave the room a greyish hue. Carlion had made it inside just as the moneylender was about to turn the sign that hung in the window to "Closed." All the bookkeepers behind the counter were finishing their notations for the day and looked annoyed at the sight of one final customer. The two City Watchmen near the entrance looked bored and Carlion guessed they were counting the minutes until they could return to the barracks for a hot meal.

"There won't be any problems with delivery this time," Carlion said. It was a threat as much as a statement.

The moneylender shook his head vigorously. "No, sir," he said with a voice like a crow. "We would have severed ties with that particular courier for theft, but he was not seen for several days and then I heard a rumor that he was found murdered in a back alley not far from here. Dreadful for business all around, if you ask me."

"I wouldn't know anything about that," Carlion said with a brief glance over his shoulder to the City Watchmen. They weren't paying attention to the conversation, but instead looking outside towards their barracks and the dinner that was waiting for them. Carlion saw the moneylender's hand twitching at his side and knew that the greedy little toad could barely wait to get his hands on the money. Carlion jutted his chin towards the coins and said, "That should be twenty-five."

"Oh!" the moneylender said, instantly in good spirits. He deftly scooped up the coins and Carlion heard them jingle into a tray underneath the counter. As Carlion suspected, the moneylender didn't need to count the coins to know their value. As he retrieved a slip of paper and a clean stylus to write a receipt, the man said absently, "Will that be all Sir Cantra?"

"Don't call me that!" barked Carlion.

The moneylender started and scratched a jagged black line on the note. Carlion saw him give a worried glance towards the City Watchman. Turning around, Carlion raised a hand in apology at the two men near the front of the lodge who were now watching him more carefully. One of the Watchmen rested his hand on the pommel of his short sword and Carlion understood the unspoken message to conclude his business quickly. Reaching into his belt pouch, Carlion produced a tightly folded letter sealed with orange wax. Holding it up in the rapidly fading light of evening, he made sure the seal remained unbroken.

"I have this to go along with it," Carlion said, holding out the letter. "I want your assurance that the contents will only be seen by the recipient in Deccern."

"Of course," the moneylender replied and placed the letter on the counter before he resumed writing the receipt. Finishing quickly, he handed the slip of paper to Carlion and said, "Any correspondence that returns will be forwarded to the mercenary guild secretary."

"See that it does," Carlion said.

"If we have no other business, I will bid you a good evening," the moneylender said with a forced smile.

As Carlion closed the bank door on his way out, he heard laughing and looked up the street to see a small boy running towards him. The child was looking backwards at two people Carlion surmised were the boy's parents. Casually strolling along, the mother and father were well-dressed and walked arm in arm. They looked happy. Carlion felt a pang of jealousy, and then instantly guilty for it. He had no one to blame but himself for being in this wretched predicament. He could never buy back what he'd lost despite regular payments.

With a final look at the bank façade, Carlion started to make his way home. Several pairs of City Watchmen were lighting lanterns that hung from tall poles just far enough away that the circles of yellow light cast on the ground barely touched. One of the churches a few streets over sounded the fifteen high bells for the transition from day to night. It wouldn't be much longer before the large main gate would close, shortly followed by the two smaller secondary gates behind the Sovereignty prince's manor.

Quickening his stride, Carlion walked down a side street that led to a less affluent part of the city. The glow from the main street faded quickly and now only slits of light escaped from shuttered windows to help Carlion avoid tripping over the uneven ground. He knew that there were eyes watching from tight gaps between buildings, but he felt little concern. Carlion had been accosted only once by a trio of would-be thieves when he first arrived in the city, but the only thing they got from him was a beating.

He approached a tiny dwelling just as the door opened. Backlit by an interior lantern, a stooped figure stood in the doorway and asked, "You make it in time, my boy?" The old man's drawl made Carlion smile. That accent wasn't common on this side of the continent. Carlion walked up to the doorstep and could now see the owner of the house covered in sawdust from the day's labors.

"I was able to sneak in just before the doors were locked, Oskar," Carlion said. "Looks like you just finished yourself."

"Just put my tools away," the old man pointed to the two-story building connected to the tiny house that was part barn and part workshop. "It sounded like the lads were hungry when I was in there, so I'd appreciate it if you made the climb for me. I already lit a lantern for you."

Carlion nodded and smiled. "I'm on my way," he said.

Oskar patted him on the shoulder and then went back inside his house. Carlion turned and opened the unlocked door that led to the cartwright's workshop. He walked through a short hallway that had a collection of tools hung on the walls before entering the large adjacent room. From the lantern light in the next room over, Carlion saw a partially assembled cart next to a pair of large pens containing two draft oxen. The placid animals watched him enter and one of them snorted, which Carlion took as a statement of displeasure while waiting to be fed.

When the mercenary guild captain posted this job along with other local requests from the city's residents, Carlion pursued it immediately. Having just arrived in town, he negotiated with Oskar to include private lodging in the workshop's loft for a reduced payment. The cartwright agreed quickly, and Carlion soon found that the lonely old man was just as happy for the company as he was for the help caring for his animals.

The draft oxen groaned and shuffled as Carlion climbed the ladder to the loft and retrieved a bale of hay. With the fodder slung across his back, he climbed back down and began filling the long troughs in front of the pens. As the animals began eating Carlion closed his eyes and for the briefest of moments he could trick himself into thinking he was in a Barnterc province stable. He could almost feel the smooth leather of a finely tooled saddle when an agitated bellow from one of the oxen broke his reverie and reminded him that he wouldn't be riding a horse anytime soon.

With the animals fed, Carlion returned to the loft and the stacked hay bales that were the makeshift walls framing his sleeping space. The blanket he slept on was still laid on the floor and the pack that contained all his worldly possessions was tucked in a corner with the contents carefully organized. Next to the pack and propped up against a hay bale were his long sword and cuirass. Carlion knelt down and ran his hand over the surface of the blackened and marred breastplate. It had been about five years since the beautiful etchings on the armor were scrubbed away by acid.

With a sigh, Carlion reached down and opened his pack. The first thing he saw was a bundle of letters carefully bound together with a thin cord. He gently ran a few fingers over the wrinkled envelopes as he counted them to make sure they were all there. Next to the letters was a small dagger, and after allowing his fingers linger a moment longer on the bundle of letters, he took the weapon and slid it into his belt before closing the pack. Giving a resigned look at his meager accommodations, he absently spun the steel ring that he wore on the middle finger of his right hand. It was another memento from his life before becoming a mercenary. Despite being not worth much money, the ring was something he valued greatly nonetheless. After climbing back down the ladder, Carlion extinguished the lantern and quietly closed the workshop door as he left to find his dinner.

Even though it was a clear night, the alley was dark and Carlion heard the tavern before seeing it. Walking inside, Carlion's stoicism was pushed aside with an honest grin. The Red Dragon Inn was charged with the energy that men-at-arms brought wherever they gathered to drink, boast, and occasionally brawl. Carlion had spent many hours in places like this, and when he shared good company he was at ease. The room was well lit by chandeliers made from wagon wheels and by lanterns lining the walls. Opposite the long bar counter was a huge hearth that warmed the entire inn. Between the bar and hearth were many heavy oaken tables and chairs, and now that it was well into the dinner hour most of them were occupied with rough looking men eating and talking loudly.

Scanning the room, Carlion smiled when he saw his two comrades sitting at a table. Trinity was a solidly built man of middle age, but the smooth skin of his recently shaven face and long black hair made him appear youthful. Originally from the southern continent, Trinity's dark brown eyes had epicanthic folds that betrayed his foreign origin, but having spent considerable time on the continent he could speak and read the language of the region better than most.

Amos was a Venhadar, a race that looked little different than humans other than being about half as tall and twice as thick. Though he had never said his age explicitly, Carlion guessed that Amos was somewhere between one and two hundred years old, which was about middle age for a Venhadar. With dark skin, a shaven head, and a preference for wearing brightly colored bandanas or caps, Amos looked like he belonged on the deck of ship. Since he often cursed like a sailor, Amos sounded like he belonged on the seas as well.

As he got closer, Carlion's expression soured at the sight of a third man at the table who was slouched low in his seat. A long scar across his cheek stretched taut against a clenched jaw as he straightened up at the sight of Carlion. The scarred man sneered and abruptly stood up. With a look of contempt at Carlion he said, "Take care, you two."

Amos slapped the table and replied, "What's the rush? Have another with me!"

"Another time," the scarred man said tersely. "The room just got too crowded for me." The scarred man roughly brushed past Carlion and left the tavern.

Carlion sat down in the now vacant seat. Amos turned to him and said, "He still doesn't like you."

"He's a military washout, Amos," Carlion replied. "Hopefully, we'll be getting another decent job soon so I don't have to look at his ugly face in the guildhall."

"We just got back!" Amos exclaimed. "Escorting pilgrims is the worst! I mean the money's fine, but they won't let you drink or smoke on the trip! Those pious fucks take all the fun out of living!"

"Tobacco and beer cost money. Don't be so lazy. Tell him Trinity."

"I'm not taking sides in your debate tonight," Trinity said. "I'm actually glad we're off the road for a while. I'm tired of trying to fall asleep in a wet ditch while listening to a dozen people sing hymns out of tune."

Carlion called out to one of the Sehenryu females who were serving drinks and food. She wore a sleeveless shirt tucked into breeches, with an apron covering her from neck to thigh. Her fine black fur looked glossy in the firelight and her feline features were swept up in an inviting smile.

"Good evening, sirs. How may I serve you?" Her voice had an accent that indicated she hadn't been raised in this region.

"Beers for me and him," Amos said pointing to Carlion. "And water for the babe," he added mockingly as he pointed at Trinity. Amos reached into one of the pouches on his belt and put three coins on the table. "And food for everyone." The tavern maid deftly swept up the coins and said in a soothing tone, "Of course, good sirs. Our finest coming to you."

"That remains to be seen," grumbled Carlion under his breath as she slinked away.

Amos barked out a laugh and then said, "Look what the cat dragged in." The Venhadar pointed his mug at the door and Carlion turned to see a man who clearly looked out of place in the Red Dragon. First of all, he didn't have the feral aggression that was common to the men who were regulars there. Second, this man walked with an authority that came from a privileged upbringing. Graying hair at the temples and an appraising expression on his face further gave the man an aristocratic appearance.

"You know him?" Carlion asked.

"Oh, you're in for a treat," Trinity said with a wide smile and a twinkle in his eye. He shouted at the man, "Thorne, over here!"

CHAPTER THREE

THORNE

Even without his sense of smell, Thorne knew that dining room of the Red Dragon Inn stank of piss and blood. The former would be coming from the floor near the bar, and the latter from the back of the kitchen that doubled as a slaughter-house. A butcher's family ran the tavern, so the combination of fresh beef and cheap beer meant that each night the tables were full. The crowd was comprised mostly of laborers and merce-naries and the tavern had a reputation as a rough establishment. It was the type of place where the City Watchmen regularly had to break up fights that spilled out into the street. The majority of mages from the Archive, as well as the civil folk of the city, avoided the place altogether.

When Thorne entered, most of the patrons didn't pay any attention to him and those few that did were simply sizing him up as a threat. Given his plain clothes and fit but non-threaten-ing physique, he was quickly forgotten. Scanning the crowded room, Thorne wasn't keen on the prospect of walking around gawking at every table searching for Trinity. Thankfully, the mage only took a few steps away from the crowded bar when he heard a familiar voice shout across the room.

Trinity was standing near a table at the back of the room and waving so hard his black ponytail was swinging erratically behind him. Thorne raised his hand and Trinity grinned the whole while as the mage moved towards him. As he got closer, Thorne could see Trinity was sharing a table with a dark-skinned Venhadar who had a shaved head covered by a maroon bandana. He smiled when he recognized Amos. It had been a long time since he'd seen the old corsair.

Thorne didn't recognize the third occupant at the table, but he was a young man that looked just outside of his teenage years. With the sleeves of his linen shirt rolled up to the elbows, the man had large hands and thick forearms that hinted at great strength. Dirty blond hair hung over his ears and sunken cheek-bones covered in stubble betrayed that he did not care much for appearances. However, his light blue eyes watched intensely as Thorne approached the table.

Trinity seemed to be oblivious to his companion sizing up Thorne, and stepped around the table and wrapped the mage in a hug that crushed the air out of him. Thorne returned it with genuine warmth, but about half the vigor.

"What are you doing here?" Trinity asked after he let the mage go.

"Looking for you, actually," Thorne said. Glancing down at the Venhadar he added, "Captain Amos, good to see you again. How have you been doing?"

"Can't complain just yet. The night is young, and I still have beer in my mug," Amos said taking a drink. "And you don't need to call me 'Captain,' son. I appreciate the respect, but you were never under my command. And for that matter, I don't have my ship back yet."

After Thorne found an empty chair and sat himself down at the table, Trinity returned to his seat and gestured towards him. "Carlion, this is an old friend of mine," he said. "Meet Thorne, Master mage of the Yaboon Archive." Trinity gave a mocking flourish with his hand towards Thorne.

"A mage," the blond man said with disdain.

"Charming. Who's this?" Thorne asked Trinity, not trying to hide the annoyance in his voice.

Trinity gave a brief lopsided grin before he said, "May I introduce Sir Carlion Cantra."

Thorne narrowed his eyes, and then frowned when Trinity laughed. The mercenary had gotten the reaction he had wanted. There was little love lost between the arcane Archives and the Sovereignty military. Any actual bloodshed between the two factions had mostly stopped decades ago, but the political warfare to influence the provincial princes raged as intensely as ever.

Trinity continued, "Don't worry Thorne. Carlion is good people. The Barnterc military cashiered him some time ago. Joined the guild a while back and we've been working as a crew."

"How does a Darkman feel about doing mercenary work?" Thorne asked looking directly at Carlion, using the colloquial term for an expelled soldier.

Carlion shrugged, "It doesn't matter where the coins come from, just that it keeps coming. You don't dress like a mage."

"And how's that?" Thorne asked as he looked down at his outfit. For decades he had eschewed the traditional alchemist robes for durable leather boots, a linen shirt, and canvas pants with a matching vest. It was attire for people more accustomed to travel and adventure than to contemplation and study.

"Robes and pouches with bits and baubles hanging from your belt," Carlion said.

Thorne shook his head. "We're not all like that. My Awareness is of a more practical nature."

Carlion gave him a questioning look and said, "Awareness of what?"

"The arcane elements," Thorne replied. When he saw Carlion's confused expression, Thorne sighed audibly and then said, "Magic." A boorish word at the Archive, he disliked using it if possible.

"Why didn't you say that in the first place?" Carlion asked, irritated. "That's why regular folk don't like wizards. You make things intentionally hard to understand. People think you're hiding something."

"You're rather blunt," Thorne said.

"At least you know where I stand. If you can, I'd like you to act in kind," Carlion said, crossing his arms across his broad chest.

Amos belched loudly and put his empty mug on top of two others on the table to make a small pyramid. "Now that we're all friends, let's get this started," he said pointedly, looking at Thorne and Carlion.

Thorne thought Amos was referring to why he was here, but then felt someone close behind him. Turning around he saw a Sehenryu tavern worker with three plates of food balanced on top of three large clay mugs. Placing everything in the center of the table, she looked at Thorne and asked, "Did you want something, kind sir?"

"No, I won't be staying long," the mage answered and then watched her weave her way back into the crowd.

When Thorne turned his attention back to the table, he saw that Amos was nearly finished with his meal, and the other two were not far behind. Even when not on a job, the tendencies of a soldier were to wolf down as much food as fast as possible since they never knew when or where the next meal was coming from.

Despite the rather unseemly table manners, seeing Trinity again put Thorne's mind at ease. Maybe he found the apprentice in Rell-Kyr or maybe he didn't, but if he convinced Trinity to come with him he'd be in good company. Given Amos' lust for life, the Venhadar would keep moral high if he came along too. However Thorne had some reservations about traveling with a disgraced cavalier.

"How did you know we were here?" Trinity asked as he licked his fingers.

"Guild secretary told me. He said you've been here a few weeks," Thorne said. "You could have stopped by the Archive."

"We had back-to-back contracts after coming in from Granick," Trinity said. "In fact, we just returned yesterday, so you'd have seen me later this week. What were you doing at the guild anyway?"

"I'm heading to Rell-Kyr and was looking to find a guide," Thorne said.

"That's it? Escort?" Carlion said with a tone indicating that the job was unimpressive.

However, Trinity had a more thoughtful and serious expression. The mercenary looked at Carlion and said, "It's never that simple with him." Looking back at Thorne, Trinity asked, "What's the rest of the story?"

The mage leaned forward and said, "For a number of reasons, the Archive doesn't like losing track of their members. It's most common for apprentices who go missing during their traveling education. In those cases, a bounty is sent to the local mercenary guild to go find them."

"A sad business," Amos said with a shake of his head. "We did one of those not too long ago. The job certainly paid well, but we returned with a corpse dug up from a shallow grave."

Thorne nodded and then continued, "On rare occasions there are special bounties that are offered at the discretion of the Archive council to retrieve mages that have disappeared under suspicious circumstances. These are usually only posted internally to keep things quiet and prevent any panic or accusations from the Sovereignty military or any of the guilds."

Carlion looked incredulous and said, "How do you tell the difference between a mage being up to no good versus one that just went missing? I suspect there isn't much difference between the two."

Thorne gave a dismissive gesture and said, "That's for the council to decide."

"Why are you going after this one? I doubt you're doing it for the reward," Trinity said.

"Not as such, but I have a vested interest in being successful," Thorne replied. Before another question could be asked, he changed the subject and said, "The trail's been cold for a while, but one of my contacts recently found a lead. Have any of you been to Rell-Kyr?"

Amos nodded, "It's up in the mountains and on the edge of the frontier. I've been there once or twice. It's surprisingly well fortified for being a little mining city. Taking the Princes' Highway we'll get there in a couple of days with good weather. Travel will be easy across the plains."

"Then we should make good time with some luck," Thorne said with a nod of approval.

Carlion leaned back in his chair and asked, "What's so important about a missing mage again? If he's gone up to the frontier then he's probably dead."

The mage shook his head slightly, "This mage, Erza, is important because she was a protégé of an Archive councilman and a well-respected alchemy instructor. There's a personal interest in her return by the powers that be. It was recently discovered that one of her apprentices was seen in Rell-Kyr. The Archive very much wants to know what happened to her and so I'm going to chase down this lead."

"It sounds like you're chasing after wild geese," Carlion said. "What happens when this Erza woman isn't there, or doesn't want to talk?"

Amos stroked his chin and said slowly, "To track down one person alone would take longer than you would like, right?

Hiring a mercenary crew would accelerate your search."

"If you've assembled into a crew, I've no problem hiring all three of you," Thorne said reasonably. He had come into the Red Dragon just for Trinity, but he was certain that the other two could be useful as well. Thorne had learned a long time ago the virtues of traveling in a group.

"Would this little adventure pay us the standard fee?" Carlion asked.

"I'm sure," Thorne said, but then realized that he didn't know what the Archive paid mercenaries these days.

"Then in the morning let's sign the contract so the guild gets its cut and we can be on our way," Amos said.

"As I said before, the bounty is internal so there's no contract," Thorne said more defensively than he intended.

"So, where's the guarantee that we're going to be paid?" Carlion asked.

"Don't worry about it," Trinity said. "This sounds like a good time for me. I'm in."

"Me too," Amos said quickly.

Thorne looked to Carlion, who had a sour expression. Thorne guessed the Darkman was weighing the costs of being in a mage's employ. "If money is your concern I will give you a payment in advance," the mage said. "I highly doubt that most clients who put in jobs at the mercenary guild would do such a thing. Will that buy me some trust?"

"Trust is earned, not bought. That being said, we have to start somewhere," Carlion said. "So do we prick our fingers and sign our names in blood?" Carlion said, still trying to goad him.

"I suppose I could ask for an oath," Thorne answered. He could see the word still had an effect as both Carlion's jaw and hand on the table clenched tightly.

"I said I would do the job. That's as close as you're going to get from a Darkman," Carlion said sorely.

"Then I believe it is still guild custom to shake hands at the conclusion of a deal between two new parties," Thorne said.

Carlion gave Thorne a critical look. For a moment the mage thought he would refuse, but then the Darkman wiped his large hand on the front of his shirt and thrust it out across the table. Thorne reached out and grasped Carlion's hand, and suddenly two of his fingers exploded in pain. With a yelp, Thorne jerked his hand away and clutched it close to his chest. He felt his face flush and he began to sweat as the throbbing sting raced from his fingers up his arm.

"Your ring!" Thorne hissed through clenched teeth. "What metal is it?"

Carlion had a confused look on his face as if he did not understand the question. The Darkman looked down at his palm and examined the thick band on his middle finger. "It's steel," Carlion said. "Recast from a dagger taken at the battle of Jaeger. It was a gift from my patron when I became a cavalier." The Darkman's eyes widened in realization of what just happened. "My apologies," he said retreating back in his seat. "I heard stories about mages' weakness to iron, but I've never seen it firsthand. Will you be alright?"

Thorne stood up, still nursing his hand. "I'll live," he grunted. Looking to Trinity he said, "Tomorrow, at five high bells, meet me at the main gate."

Trinity nodded, "Sure, we'll be there." He looked concerned, but said nothing more.

Thorne excused himself and quickly made his way back to the Archive. As he walked he felt a rapid pulse in the palm of his hand, each heartbeat pumping fire up his arm. Taking the most direct route to the infirmary, Thorne pushed open the door and found an Archive physician sitting with an initiate medic in the midst of a quiet conversation. Seeing Thorne nursing his hand, the physician asked in a brusque tone, "Broken or burned?"

"Iron burn," Thorne said walking over to them. Opening his hand to show the physician, Thorne saw that his entire palm was red with two large blisters near his middle finger. The blisters were black and under his inflamed skin he could see the veins underneath were an unhealthy dark color.

"What'd you do, grab a key ring?" the curious medic asked.

The physician gave him an admonishing look and said, "It's none of our business." She looked up at Thorne and asked, "Any vision problems, difficulty breathing?"

Thorne shook his head, "No, it was only a brief contact. I don't think it broke through the skin."

The physician grunted and then said to the medic, "Take him back and drain the blisters."

Nodding obediently, the medic turned to face the mage. "Follow me," he instructed. They walked behind a series of curtains hung from the ceiling near the back of the room. Thorne didn't see any other people being treated, which suggested the evening was starting off quietly. He supposed that was better than the alternative.

Taking a seat on a wide bench, Thorne watched the medic pull a small table close and gather up a few materials. After lighting an oil lamp, the medic held a long needle in the flame until it glowed red. He lanced the two blisters, which deflated and oozed dark blood into Thorne's palm. Carefully mopping up the blood with gauze, the medic then used a small wooden spatula to spread a white paste over the burn. Thorne's hand tingled for a minute and then went numb.

"You won't be writing anything tonight," the medic said, wrapping Thorne's hand with a strip of linen.

"No, I suppose not," the mage said, instead thinking that he still needed to pack in preparation for travel in the morning.

Quietly thanking both the medic and the physician on his way out, Thorne walked slowly back to his apartment. After he entered, the mage kept the door open wide so the blue light from the hallway would help him navigate to his desk. A small glass sphere was resting on a ring of darkly stained wood in one corner. Gently placing his uninjured hand on the sphere, Thorne focused a small amount of his mana into his palm and then slowly transferred it into the sphere. The glass absorbed the energy and began to glow with a warm yellow light. Once the room was comfortably lit, Thorne went and closed the door.

Reaching under his bed, the mage pulled out a large leather satchel. The bag looked like it had seen considerable use and was scratched and stained, but otherwise in good repair. Over the next quarter of an hour he opened drawers and pulled from shelves the various items he would need for the journey. He had learned long ago to pack only essential items he couldn't procure outside of the Archive, and in one of the small inner pockets he put a glass lens that was his fire starter. A dagger with a rigid resin blade synthesized in his alchemical lab was slid into another pocket. With care, Thorne packed a small chest that contained alchemical glassware and reagents, making sure the stoppers were secure. Finally, he layered a thick wool blanket on top of everything and buckled the flap tightly. He would fill his water skin on his way out of the Archive and stop by a couple shops he liked on his way to the main gate to pick up enough food to last him until he reached Rell-Kyr.

With packing completed, Thorne undressed and climbed into his bed. He reached over to the glass globe and retrieved the mana within it, feeling a faint rush as the arcane energy raced through his body. Thorne lay in the dark and took a moment to truly appreciate the feel of clean sheets on his skin and a pillow under his head. He never assumed he would be returning soon to these comfortable arrangements when he left the Archive. With some effort, he was able to clear his mind of the day's turbulent events and fell asleep.

CHAPTER FOUR

CARLION

Carlion woke when the angle of the morning sun filtered through the gaps in the barn siding and hit his face. Bits of hay stuck to his hand as he rubbed the dust from his eyes and sat up. Normally, he'd fold the blanket next to his pack before climbing down to feed the oxen, but today Carlion spent some extra time brushing the hay and dust off before putting it in his pack. He checked to make sure his bundle of letters were all accounted for, and then closed his pack.

The Darkman slid into his cuirass and tightened down the leather straps until it fit snuggly across his chest. He ran his fingers over the blackened and scratched surface and remembered what it looked like before being ruined. With a sigh, he donned his grey tabard and then threw his matching cloak around shoulders, both of which effectively hid the armor from view. Finally, he fastened his sword belt around his waist to complete the garb of a mercenary ready for travel.

After tossing two bales of fodder down from the loft, Carlion quickly checked to make sure he had not lost anything in the loose hay on the floor. With such meager belongings, he was both satisfied and saddened that there was nothing to be found. Carlion took care as he climbed down the ladder carrying all of his possessions, and then spent the next quarter of an hour feeding and caring for the pair of oxen. Once the animals had their needs attended, Carlion took the unused bale of hay and set it next to the door that led into the workshop. Walking out of the barn, the cool morning air still had a refreshing crispness that would eventually fade as the sun rose higher in the sky.

"Looks like you're dressed for the road," drawled Oskar from the open door of his adjacent house.

Carlion looked over and saw that the old man held a mug of coffee in each hand. As Carlion approached Oskar offered one. Taking the mug, Carlion raised it in a small salute of thanks. He took a sip to gauge the temperature and then a big swallow, enjoying both the warmth and bitterness of the brew.

"What time is it?" Carlion asked.

"Four high bells rang out a while ago," Oskar replied. "Are you in a hurry to get somewhere?"

Draining the mug Carlion said, "Not until I eat something." He tried to give back the empty mug, but the old man refused it.

"Come inside. You can tell me where you're going," the cartwright said. Offers of breakfast were rare from him, so Carlion smiled and followed the old man inside the small house.

The interior was hazy with tobacco smoke, and as Carlion took a seat at the small table near the hearth he saw Oskar pick up a pipe and light it. Taking a few puffs, the cartwright hummed quietly as he went to the larder and retrieved some biscuits, dried venison, and several eggs. Placing a large skillet on the trivet that hung over the fire, Oskar quickly cooked a simple, but filling meal for them both.

Leaning back in his chair, Carlion said to his breakfast companion, "I should be back in about a week. Going to Rell-Kyr."

"Ah, north towards the mountains," Oskar mused. "Take care on the frontier."

Carlion waited for the old man to ask about the reason for the trip, but the question never came. He realized then that Oskar wasn't really interested in why he was leaving, just that he would return. This was confirmed when the cartwright went to the larder once again and returned with a large linen handkerchief holding more dried meat and biscuits.

"Here's an advance on your next board," the old man said, wrapping up the food. "I'm thinking of adding to your duties once you get back. How well can you handle a saw?"

"I've already got a guilder to work as a mercenary. I don't think they'd take kindly to me moonlighting as a cartwright," Carlion said with a smile as he took the parcel.

The old man gave a dismissive grunt, and then said, "As long as you don't go advertising it, you should be fine." He extended a hand, "Providence go with you."

After shaking Oskar's hand, Carlion left the small house and walked down the alley in the direction of Manor Road. He stopped to fill his water skin and wash his face at the pump near the City Watch barracks, but had to wait his turn, as there was already a line. He had just finished at the pump when he heard the ring of five high bells echo through the city. Jamming the stopper tightly into his water skin, Carlion walked briskly towards the main gate.

Carlion found that he was the last to arrive. Amos was leaning against the wall talking to Trinity, though both stopped and turned in his direction as he approached. The Venhadar was wearing a shirt and vest, with baggy trousers tucked into heavy boots. Amos' travel pack was on the ground near him and his heavy mace rested against it. Trinity looked the very part of a mercenary escort, wearing studded leather armor, a short sword slung on his hip, and a small pack strapped securely on his back.

The mage was standing nearby with his arms folded across

his chest. His clothes looked to be the standard travelers fare of grey canvas pants with a lightweight white shirt under a dark blue cloak. Carlion could see no weapons hanging from Thorne's belt, but the mage did have a pair of leather gloves tucked into it. With only a small bag slung over one shoulder, Carlion thought that Thorne was going to be ill prepared for the road, and said as much when he stopped in front of the mage.

"We're only going to be outdoors a night or two each way. Unless we get caught in a storm, what I brought will be sufficient," Thorne said, adjusting the strap across his chest.

Carlion saw Thorne's bandaged hand and pointed at it. "I take it you were able to get patched up last night?" he asked.

The mage flexed his injured hand and replied, "I'll be able to manage. Let's get going."

Trinity walked over and clapped Carlion on the shoulder as he passed to stand next to Thorne. Amos drew alongside Carlion, and the four walked out the open gate. The morning was spent walking north along the Princes' Highway. It was easy travel going north as they traversed the plains with the mountains rising in the distance. Passing a farm around midday, Carlion saw two men in a field trying to coax a bull to drag a plow in a straight line, but the animal had other plans in mind. Carlion heard Amos bark a laugh at his side and looked down at his Venhadar companion.

"Not going to get much work done today," Amos said with a chuckle.

"It's hard enough being a farmer," Trinity said over his shoulder. "Don't make light of their struggles. It's not like the bull knows it's time to work."

"A horse would," Carlion said wistfully. "They're incredibly intelligent animals."

"Speaking of horses, does it still feel strange hoofing it with the common folk?" Amos asked.

The Darkman grunted before he replied, "Clever, but yes. Even after years as a mercenary it's still strange seeing the plains so close to the ground."

"It's a shame they're so rare," Thorne said. "You'd have thought any of the Sovereignty princes would put more money into breeding them instead of importing them."

"Don't think they haven't tried," Carlion said. "The current theory is that the climate of the continent is too cold, even in the southern regions."

"I take it you had one?" Thorne asked.

"I did. She was beautiful," Carlion said.

"What happened to her?" the mage said intrigued.

Carlion was struck by a pang of loss. "She was probably given to another cavalier. Horses are worth a small fortune so only commissioned military officers get them."

"Was it the same with your armor?" Amos asked casually. Carlion had not previously discussed the specifics of his past with either of his mercenary companions.

"Most armor can be used by anyone with the same body type, but a cavalier's cuirass," Carlion said tapping his chest, "is custom etched. No one would want to wear armor from someone like me. When I got cashiered, they marred it with acid and gave it to me as a memento of the life I threw away."

"You must have lost comrades, friends. Whatever happened to them?" Thorne pressed.

"I was run out of Barnterc, so I never got a chance to ask," Carlion said bitterly. "Since I joined the guild, I've been content to live by my sword. It's a much less complicated life." He sighed and then continued, "That being said, it might be nice knowing how some of my company is doing under a new commander."

The morning passed, and after a brief stop for a drink of water and bite of whatever they had brought with them for lunch, the four travelers were about to continue onward when they heard a shout back from the road.

"You were wondering about your old comrades. Well, here's your opportunity to ask," Amos said.

Turning, Carlion saw a cavalier atop a warhorse and two spearmen on the road moving purposefully towards them. The horse was massive and even at a relaxed trot the spearmen had to nearly run to keep pace with it. All three were lightly armored and dressed in the green and silver livery of the Yaboon Sovereignty. Carlion instantly recognized that they were an advance party sent to scout ahead of a larger force.

"Where do you think you're going?" the cavalier asked after pulling the horse to a stop a short distance from the group. The spearmen kept moving until they were behind the group and could cut off any attempts to flee. Carlion saw they held their spears casually at their sides, but his body tensed all the same. The Darkman rested his hands on his belt in a feigned display of annoyance, but it was just an excuse to have his hand next to the hilt of his sword. If they weren't careful, things could get dangerous very quickly.

"North to Rell-Kyr. Is there a problem?" Thorne said with pointed looked at the spearmen now flanking him.

"What's your business there?" the cavalier asked, clearly not taking too well to the mage's tone.

"Archive business," Thorne said and pulled out a medallion on a chain from under his shirt. Stamped on the silver metal disc was the insignia of a Master from the Archive. Carlion quietly sighed at the stupid mage. It was almost like he was begging the cavalier to have an excuse to question them further or arrest them on suspicion of wrongdoing. Carlion quietly cursed Thorne, all mages, and every other fool who wasted their life in some cloister, academy, or Archive.

"The forest at the base of the mountains can be dangerous.

It's known to be a hideout for bandits and a hunting ground for B'nisct," one of the spearmen said.

"Good thing I hired three bodyguards," the mage replied with a sweeping gesture to indicate Trinity, Amos, and Carlion. The cavalier locked eyes with Carlion and his expression darkened.

"Bodyguards aren't much good if one stabs you in the back," the cavalier said, staring directly at Carlion. "Wouldn't you agree, Cantra?" Before Carlion could reply the cavalier looked at Thorne and said, "Maybe it's for the best that you're headed for an out of the way town, given what's coming. The days are numbered for the privileged status of the Archive."

"What are you talking about?" Thorne asked angrily.

"We can't waste any more time on mages and other undesirables," the cavalier said. "Onward to the city." The spearmen jogged to the cavalier's side and the three of them slowly continued towards Yaboon.

"What the hell was that all about?" Trinity asked baffled. "Did you know him, Carlion?"

"And what about that thinly veiled threat to the Archive?" Thorne added.

Carlion realized that he now had his hand resting on the hilt of his sword. He flexed his fingers and then dropped both arms to his sides. "I don't know him, but he certainly recognized me," he said still watching the soldiers retreat down the Princes' Highway.

"But what about the Archive?" Thorne asked again.

"I don't know what that was about, but once we finish your little quest in Rell-Kyr, then you can go ask him," Carlion said.

The mage glared at him, but said nothing and resumed walking. Carlion saw Amos shrug and trotted to follow Thorne, with Trinity following. Bringing up the rear and watching the backs of his three companions, the Darkman wondered if there would be an unpleasant surprise waiting for them when they returned.

They walked mostly in silence for the remainder of the day. As they entered the forest a few hours before sunset, Carlion was struck with an uneasy feeling. He continually scanned the surrounding trees trying to see anything amiss. Suddenly, he realized that what was out of place wasn't something he could see, but hear.

"The birds have stopped calling. Something has frightened them," he said sweeping his cloak away from his hip and pulling out his sword. Trinity and Amos followed suit and readied their weapons.

"Maybe the cavalier was right about bandits," Amos said, hefting his mace.

Carlion looked at Thorne, "Make sure you stay at my back when the fighting starts."

The mage was about to say something when a series of loud vibrating sounds cut through the forest. Carlion spun around to see four B'nisct fighters hurtling straight towards them.

An indigenous race that lived in the frontier regions of the continent, the B'nisct were known for their insectoid appearance and matriarchal clan organization. Each hive of B'nisct was ruled by a queen that commanded a swarm of fierce fighters known to attack frontier settlements and push back on the ever-expanding boundaries of civilization. Sovereignty soldiers-in-training had to perform a tour of duty on the frontier, but more than a few never returned due to fatal encounters with B'nisct swarms or scouting parties. Despite often only being armed with short spears, B'nisct were agile fighters and once commanded to attack would continue to do so until either they or their enemy were dead.

The fighters were running in such a tight formation that Carlion could hear their chitinous armor clicking against each other. As the B'nisct churned up the leaves from the forest floor in their frenzied advance Carlion dug his foot into the ground preparing his own charge. He was about to leap forward when out of the corner of his eye the Darkman saw Thorne's hand emit a yellow glow before he pushed an open palm at the B'nisct. Carlion felt and heard a powerful gust of wind in front of him, and his jaw dropped when he watched all four fighters get blasted off their feet. The B'nisct tumbled back as they fell, their flailing limbs tearing up the forest floor along the way.

"Trinity, go!" Thorne shouted.

Trinity seemed to know what Thorne meant and dashed towards the prone B'nisct, veering off to attack one that fell further to his left. Amos was a step behind but went to the right, his mace raised at the ready near his thick shoulder. As Trinity and Amos engaged their foes, the two remaining fighters quickly clambered to their feet and sprinted towards Thorne.

"Stay behind me," Carlion commanded as he moved past the mage. Thorne made a quick sidestep of his own to stand at Carlion's shoulder. "Stay out of my line of fire," he retorted.

Carlion reached out to pull the mage back, but felt something powerful jerk him sideways several steps. The Darkman saw that Thorne's hands had an eerie amber glow and it looked like the mage had pantomimed a pushing motion at him.

Regaining his balance, the Darkman watched Thorne plant his feet and with arcing swings sent two spears of light towards the B'nisct. The streaks of energy pierced the B'nisct fighters in the chest with devastating impact. Carlion saw hemolymph spray from the back of the fighters as if a heavy lance had impaled them. Both B'nisct staggered from the blasts and tumbled forward a step before collapsing. Wisps of smoke and the smell of burnt meat wafted into Carlion's nostrils. It reminded him of what a battlefield smelled like after all the fighting was done.

Carlion looked past the B'nisct corpses to see Amos and Trinity standing over their own adversaries' bodies, neither looking particularly winded. Trinity was wiping hemolymph from his short sword with a handful of leaves and Amos was leaning on his mace examining his handiwork, the skull of the fighter completely caved in. Carlion was about to call out to them when Thorne stepped in front of him.

"Listen, I want Trinity with me because he's a friend," Thorne said sternly. "Amos is here because he knows the way. I extended the courtesy to you because you were part of their crew, but let's get one thing very clear. I do not need the protection of a disgraced cavalier. From now on, you do what I tell you." Without waiting for a reply, the mage spun on his heel and walked towards Trinity and started talking quietly to him.

Carlion sidled up to Amos and said, "Did you know he could do that?"

Amos looked up at the Darkman. "Yup," he replied. "You don't need to worry about him. Thorne can hold his own in a fight."

Thinking back to his assessment of the mage at the main gate earlier in the day, Carlion shook his head and said more to himself than to anyone, "I thought he'd get eaten alive out here, but I was wrong. He's a demon."

"Beast," Amos said.

"What?" Carlion shook his head confused.

"It's what people used to call him," Amos said. "When it suits him, Thorne has no problems killing."

"I'll keep that in mind," Carlion said pensively as he started helping Amos pull the slain B'nisct off of the road.

CHAPTER FIVE

THORNE

Rell-Kyr was known as a relatively safe frontier town, so it surprised Thorne when they approached the main gate and observed new stone and mortar work from a recent repair. Two men-at-arms stopped the group as they approached the open gate and looked visibly more at ease after Thorne showed his Archive guilder and asked for entry.

"Finally, some Archive help for that damn swarm," one of the guardsmen said. "We figured all of our pleas were going to be ignored."

"What swarm?" Amos asked idly. The Venhadar had kept his word and led them here in two days, but he had pushed the pace after the mid-day meal to make sure they were inside the city walls by dark. There was no sense in camping unnecessarily on the frontier.

The guard pointed at the repaired section of wall behind them and replied, "About a month back a B'nisct raid punched a hole in the wall. A few of the bastards made it into the town and damaged a couple buildings. The crazy thing was that we never found any of them after searching every square inch of the town. It was the strangest thing I've seen in twenty years as City Watch and it's left some of the folks here on edge."

"Are you worried about another attack?" Trinity asked. "Is

that what you meant by Archive aid?"

The other guard nodded and said, "Shortly after the attack we lost our last remaining Archive mage. Just up and left, the coward." The man spit on the ground in disdain before he looked up at Thorne and continued, "If you're not here to help us, then what's your business on the frontier?"

Thorne made a placating gesture then said, "I will help where I can after I complete my investigation. Where is the proprietor of your alchemic shop?"

"What do you need him for?" the City Watchman asked suspiciously.

The mage smiled but shook his head, "Sorry, but I'm not allowed to talk about Archive business. Need to follow the rules." The mage gave Trinity a dirty look when the mercenary choked back a laugh.

The sentry appraised Thorne and the mercenaries a moment before pointing down the street. "You'll find what's left of Ulrich's old shop three buildings down on the left."

"What's left?" Carlion asked.

The guard was apparently uninterested in talking to the group if they weren't there to help and just waved vaguely down the street. "Take a walk, you'll see what I mean," he said, not looking at them.

As Thorne walked down the street, he saw that the town seemed to be doing very well despite the recent raid. While he didn't notice any obvious damage to the buildings they walked past, he could sense a slightly uneasy atmosphere amongst those he passed. However, what was more troubling to the mage was what the guard had said about an Archive mage leaving. It seemed that his information about Erza's apprentice was at least a month old, and perhaps his investigation was about to hit a frustrating dead end.

"Here it is," said Thorne as they came up to the façade of

the alchemy shop. The front part of the shop looked to still be in good repair despite the windows being shuttered. On closer inspection the mage saw that the windows had a few glass panes shattered and brown paper had been put up to seal the openings. Along the side wall of the shop there was a huge hole that had been boarded up with wide, roughly hewn planks. The ground around this part of the building looked like it had been torn up not long ago and had bits of charred wood mixed in with the soil.

Thorne returned to the front and pulled on the door, but found that it was locked. Banging on the door and calling out did not get a response. From across the street, a window on the second floor opened up and a woman of middle age poked her head out.

"You're not going to get anything from that shop today, strangers," she said in a raspy voice. "The old boy's closed up early again."

Carlion looked up at the woman and gave small wave. "Is he inside?" he called up. "We've traveled from Yaboon to talk to him."

The woman shook her head and replied, "You'll find him in the tavern at the end of the street, but I doubt he'll be in any state to talk with you. Good luck if you try, though."

The Darkman gave a half-bow and the woman retreated inside and closed the window. Turning to Trinity, Carlion asked, "Fancy a drink?"

The tavern was nearly empty, and the few ongoing conversations inside only died down for a moment when the group entered. Scanning the room, Thorne did not see anyone that matched the description he was given by his contact in the Archive. A woman in a stained apron approached them and said, "Sit where you want, I'll get you drinks in a minute."

"Wait," Carlion said quickly, "We're looking for the alchemy shop owner. Is he here?"

The woman frowned as she pointed to a drunk at the end of the bar before sliding past the barkeep on her way back to the kitchen. The man she had gestured at was seemingly passed out, his head was resting on the bar and both arms hung limply at his sides. He had a mop of greasy hair and a sallow complexion, and his clothes looked rather threadbare. Overall, Thorne was skeptical that this was the correct person based on appearances. Even out on the frontier, he doubted that an Archive mage would end up in such a sorry state.

Amos rubbed his eyes and took another look, "You sure that's the shop owner?"

Thorne shrugged and replied, "One way to find out."

As the mage walked past, the barkeep said, "You won't have much of a conversation with Hank, if that's what you're after. I was about to carry him home. Every town needs its drunkard, I guess." He said the last part with a sad half-smile.

"A City Watchman told us the owner's name was Ulrich," Trinity said.

The barman nodded absently still looking at Hank. He turned to Trinity and replied, "It was until about a month ago. He just packed up and left after the B'nisct raid. Hank here was his assistant and Ulrich left everything to him."

Thorne looked to the barman, "This drunk is a mage? An apprentice?" His tone was skeptical.

The barman shook his head and replied, "No, Ulrich was always strangely specific to call Hank an assistant, not an apprentice. I guess to an Archive mage that term means something special?"

The drunkard at the end of the bar groaned loudly as he lifted his head up from the bar. Bringing his hand into view from under the bar, Thorne saw he was holding a large clay mug. Hank slammed the mug so hard on the bar that it shattered and sent pieces of crockery spilling to the floor. "Quit your yammer-ing and give a man some peace!" he bellowed, looking angrily in the direction of the conversation.

After a moment of trying to focus his eyes on the people near him, Hank then looked down at the shattered remains of the mug before he roared at the barkeep, "Get me another grog!" As the barkeep poured another drink, Hanks's head fell onto the bar with a heavy thump and he had passed out again by the time the barkeep brought the new cup to him.

Looking at the barkeep, Thorne asked, "Why'd you let him get in such a state? Can't be good for business."

The barkeep waved his hand at the mostly empty room and answered, "He is the business, as you can plainly see. His money is just as heavy in my pocket as the next man who walks through that door, though I doubt there will be many after word of the B'nisct raid gets to the surrounding towns. Just leave him here with me. I'll see that he gets home. Try his shop in the morning when he's sobered up. He keeps it open until midday, around seven or eight high bells."

"I appreciate it," Thorne said, reaching into his satchel. After finding the correct pocket, he pulled out a single rubium token and placed it on the bar. While not the official currency for any of the Sovereignty provinces on the continent, most merchants were just as happy to accept the hexagonal discs that Archive mages carried in lieu of metal coinage. The Archives had the reputation of being wealthy institutions and debts paid with rubium were always honored in any major city.

The bartender slowly picked up the rubium and brought the translucent red token close to his eye. "Don't see much of this wizard money out here on the edge of civilization," he said. "But I thank you kindly all the same."

As they were walking out of the bar, Amos told Thorne, "I think I know a place where we can get a decent meal and a warm bed for cheap."

"Lead the way," the mage replied.

• • •

The next morning Thorne led the mercenaries to the alchemic shop, which they were surprised to find open. As they entered, Thorne could see that part of the front room was soot stained, particularly where the walls and floor met. There were also long splinters sticking out from the jagged edges of the boarded up wall. Along the same wall were broken shelves and the mage saw where liquid had discolored the wood in long dark streaks where it had dripped to the floor.

A loud groan, followed by a curse, erupted from the back room. Sweeping a curtain aside, Hank took an unsteady step to the counter and it appeared he was going to accost whoever had entered the shop, but stopped short when he saw Thorne and the mercenaries. He dragged the back of his hand over his mouth and said irritably, "What do you want?"

Thorne approached the counter and pulled out his Archive medallion. Holding it up he said, "I'm an Archive mage and I wanted to talk to you about the old proprietor."

"Propri-who?" Hank stammered, clearly still hung over.

Thorne frowned and said shortly, "Your old boss. The last owner."

Hank grunted as he sat down on a stool. "Oh him. Ulrich gave me the shop after the B'nisct swarm blitzed the town. After the fire and the looting," he indicated the boarded-up hole in the wall. "He said that he didn't feel safe here anymore even though the governor sent a formal request for help to the capital." Hank belched crudely and asked, "Are you here to collect taxes or something?"

Thorne ignored the question and asked, "Where'd he go?"

Hank glared at the mage and said slowly, "He didn't say,

and it's none of my business. Why are you so interested in him anyway?"

"It's Archive business and wouldn't interest you," Thorne said dismissively. "Any other people work with him, any friends or family here?"

Hank scrunched up his face as if he were thinking hard. With a quiet grunt and a nod he replied, "There was the woman he first came to town with when he set up the shop."

"Woman?" Trinity said with a raised eyebrow. "Did she have a name?"

"It's hard to forget with it being so strange. It was Erza," Hank answered. "Just the type of name you'd expect from a wizard."

Thorne tried to act casually when he asked, "She not around here anymore?"

"Nope," Hank said. "One day she was just gone. I overheard Ulrich tell somebody that she got called back to the capital on urgent business and he was supposed to stay here and run the shop."

"But then he left not that long ago, right?" Carlion asked, but it sounded like an accusation.

Hank's eyes narrowed at the Darkman and he replied tersely, "Yup."

"Just like that?" Carlion pressed.

"Yup," Hank said and folded his arms across his chest. It was clear that he was tired of being questioned.

Thorne tried to give Hank an understanding expression and said, "It's very important to the Archive that we find Ulrich, but it sounds like you don't know where he went. I'd like to take a look at his transaction ledger and inventory reports. We might find a clue there."

Hank's hangover seemed to abate at this point as his eyes sharpened their focus and he forcefully slapped a palm on the counter. "I'm not showing you a damn thing!" he said raising his voice. "This shop is mine now, so if you aren't buying then get out."

Amos took a step forward and said, "Easy mate, we're just trying to find a friend. No need to get angry."

Thorne rested a hand on the Venhadar's shoulder and gave a very slight shake of his head. Looking at Hank the mage said, "Sorry to bother you, sir. We'll be going now."

Thorne could feel Hank staring daggers at them until they left and closed the door. Once they were a safe distance away from the shop and standing in the street Thorne said, "Not going to get anywhere that way." He then quirked an eyebrow at Trinity and asked, "Midnight special?"

Carlion shook his head confused. "What's that?" he asked.

"You'd be amazed at the skullduggery you can get into when you have a mage helping you," Trinity said with a smile.

"Yeah, fine, but what's a midnight special?" Carlion asked again.

Thorne replied, "All you and Amos have do is buy some drinks at the tavern tonight while Trinity and I go for a walk."

"Sounds good to me," Amos said.

With a scowl aimed at Amos, the Darkman said rhetorically, "Why do I get the impression that it's not that simple?"

• • •

"City Watch is on the far side of street, so we should be clear for about a quarter of an hour," Trinity said.

Thorne had been loitering in the back alley behind their lodgings waiting for Trinity to report on the current position of the patrol. Now that the mercenary had returned Thorne was ready to initiate his plan.

"Hold still," Thorne commanded and knelt down next to Trinity. He hovered a hand over each of Trinity's boots and focused his mana into his hands. Spreading his fingers wide, Thorne could acutely feel subtle air currents around the boots. Using his Awareness, the mage shifted the air away from the Trinity's feet until there was a small pocket of vacuum surrounding each of the boots maintained by his mana to keep the bubbles from collapsing.

Standing up, Thorne gave a nod towards Trinity's feet, and then said, "Check it."

Trinity stomped his feet several times and then gave a few short jumps in complete silence. Satisfied, Thorne crouched down and repeated the elemental manipulation around his own boots. With both of their footfalls silenced, Trinity and Thorne walked casually to the edge of the boarding house and peered around the corner to the main street. There were no regularly spaced lampposts, so the patches of light that pushed back the darkness came from homes that had hung lanterns outside of their doors.

"Let's go," Trinity whispered over his shoulder, and without waiting darted across the street.

Thorne was only a step behind, and the pair moved from shadow to shadow in staccato dashes until they were pressed up against the damaged exterior of the alchemic shop. The mercenary stayed close to the corner next to the street, looking outward for any passersby that might spot them. After a moment, he looked back at Thorne and gave him a thumbs up.

The mage placed his palm on the wall and focused his Awareness into a board. The wood responded to his touch and warmed under his fingertips. Thorne's tactile sensation spread throughout the board and he could feel the nails holding the board in place. Rearranging the tough fibers of wood around the nails, Thorne enlarged the holes until the board wobbled loosely. Carefully pulling the board free and setting it gently on the ground, Thorne repeated the process with two more boards.

With an opening to the shop exposed, Thorne quietly snapped his fingers twice. Without looked at the mage, Trinity walked backwards keeping his eyes on the street until Thorne rested a hand on his shoulder. One after another, the pair ducked inside the alchemic shop.

With the shutters closed the interior of the shop was a collection of dark amorphous shapes. Reaching into his satchel, Thorne pulled out two small spheres. Made from the same glass-like resin as the glow spheres that lined the halls of the Archive, Thorne charged them with a small amount of mana and they began to radiate with a pale blue luminescence. Silently handing one to Trinity, Thorne then pointed to the front of the shop. The mercenary understood and began to search the shelves.

Keeping the arcane light hooded in his hand, Thorne walked behind the counter and crouched down to examine the bank of drawers underneath. In one of them he found several leather-bound ledgers that contained all of the transactions and inventory for the shop written in a small tight script. The records were carefully annotated with what was sold, the amount, and who made the purchase. There were nearly daily entries for several years, but then abruptly they stopped. Thorne surmised the lack of records was the result of Hank taking over the business.

Abruptly, the front door rattled. Thorne snapped his fist closed to extinguish the light in his hand and peered over the counter. Trinity had pressed himself flat against the wall and held a bottle he snatched from a nearby table ready to strike whoever entered the shop. Through the oiled parchment that covered the window Thorne could see the silhouette of someone standing in front of the shop. The handle rattled again and the door wiggled as whoever was outside tried to force it open. From outside the mage heard a voice call out, "At least he remembered to lock the shop today. Don't know why I'm doing him the favor."

From the street came a reply, but it was indistinct and Thorne couldn't make out what was said. The mage surmised it was either the City Watch making the rounds or one of Hank's friends that was here to make sure the drunkard had properly closed up the shop. The silhouette faded away when who-ever was outside left and took their lantern with them. Thorne started to sigh in relief, but the breath caught in his throat when he remembered the gaping hole in the side of the shop. After a few tense minutes of waiting, the mage realized that the cur-sory security check of the front door was all that was going to happen.

Moving in a crouch, Trinity joined Thorne behind the counter and both men sat down on the floor. The mage opened his hand again to release a bit of light and he could see the sweat on Trinity's brow. The mercenary still had the bottle in his hand, but in a more relaxed grip. "Skulking around in the dark, danger around every corner, and the threat of a fight with every breath. Just like back in the old days, right?" he asked with a touch of irony in his voice.

"Thankfully, no," Thorne answered. "Anything useful up front?"

"Everything is just for show. There's nothing of real value out here," Trinity whispered and wiggled the bottle in his hand. Setting the glassware down on the floor he said, "I think we got lucky that Hank's not as well liked as Ulrich or we might have been in a tight spot just now. You want to keep flirting with Lady Luck?"

Thorne nodded and replied, "I do. There's got to be some-thing here. It's nearly impossible to hide your tracks if you're fleeing in a panic. Let's look in the stockroom."

Both men brushed aside the curtain to enter the back of the shop. Taking a chance and opening his hand to let more light escape from the glass sphere, Thorne slowly scanned the room.

Shelves tightly packed with boxes and jars of every size lined the walls. A series of floor to ceiling cabinets cut down the middle of the room. The mage pointed to the left aisle and Trinity slid past him to investigate.

Slowly walking down the right aisle, Thorne was reading the labels on the containers at eye level when he heard a scuffling sound near the back of the room. Shining his light in the direction of the sound, Thorne saw a shimmering box on a lower shelf. "Trinity, I found something," Thorne said quietly as he approached the box and knelt down.

The mercenary quickly joined him near the floor and peered at the box. "What's that sparkle from? Is it sand?" Trinity asked.

"I don't know for certain, but it looks like pixie dust," Thorne said.

"Pixies are so rare they're practically a myth these days," Trinity said incredulous.

"As are most elemental sprites," Thorne explained. "But the dander they leave behind only shimmers like this for a couple days before the mana in it fades away. Then it just becomes ordinary sand."

"Well, what was this one doing? Taking a nap on that fancy box?" the mercenary asked.

Thorne reached out to touch the edge of the ornately colored lid, and felt faint tingling on his fingertips. Jerking his hand back, Thorne said surprised, "This is a lockbox."

"There's no latch," Trinity said picking up the box. As he did so, a folded sheet of paper underneath it fell to the ground.

While Trinity struggled to open the lid, Thorne picked up the paper. The mage saw it was a map of the region. Opening it up completely Thorne saw that there were extra creases in the map. The previous owner appeared to have wanted to only view a section of the map and folded it to fit in one hand. Using the creases as a guide, Thorne re-folded the map and found that he was looking at a small section of the mountains on the eastern side of the continent. Near one edge of the exposed area was Rell-Kyr. There were no other cities shown on the map, save one near the top.

Looking up from the map Thorne saw that Trinity was about to use his dagger to pry the lid off. The mage grabbed Trinity's wrist and said, "It's got an arcane lock on it. Only an application of mana from the owner will open it. You stick a dagger in that seam and I guarantee you'll burn your hand."

Putting his dagger away, Trinity handed Thorne the box. "Can you force it open?"

"I could, but I have a better use for it." Flashing the map in front of the mercenary's eyes, Thorne continued, "And now I have an idea where Ulrich went. Let's get back to the tavern."

Stuffing both the box and the map into his satchel, Thorne and Trinity quietly made their way back to the side of the shop. Exiting as they came, the mercenary carefully set the boards back in place. Once this was done, Thorne sealed the nail holes and collapsed the vacuum around their feet. The pair then casually stepped out onto the street and walked to rejoin their companions.

It took a few minutes for Thorne and Trinity to find Carlion, Amos, and Hank in a booth along the wall opposite the entrance of the tavern. From the empty mugs on the table, Amos seemed to have passed the time pleasantly, but Carlion was glowering at the mage as he sat down. Between the Venhadar and Darkman, Hank was wedged between them apparently sleeping.

"Are we done babysitting?" Carlion asked, clearly agitated.

Thorne brushed the comment away with a wave of his hand and replied, "I'm sure you've been paid to do worse things."

"What did you give me to put in his mug?" Carlion asked.

"Papaver leaf extract," the mage said. "It's a powerful sedative. Sometimes a diluted dose is given to the sick to help them sleep. I gave you concentrated syrup. He'll be fine in the morning and won't remember much of tonight. But forget him for now. I know where we're going."

Thorne took out the map and put it on the table and jabbed a finger on a point near the top. He looked over at Amos and asked, "Do you know how to get to Deccern?"

Amos wiped the beer out of his beard and nodded. "Sure," he said. "Deccern is a decent sized frontier city that is actually mentioned from time to time in the capital. Despite being up in the mountains I think it used to have a garrison there, but that was a few years back."

Thorne nodded and added, "There's no major Archive influence there, and if there's still a military presence then that's even better."

"How come?" Trinity asked with a confused expression.

"Because that would be a good place to hide from other mages," Thorne replied. "I'm guessing that no one from an Archive would want to be that deep in the frontier, let alone with a company of Sovereignty soldiers breathing down their neck." Looking at Amos, Thorne eagerly asked, "Any guess how long it'd take to get there?"

"Even taking the mining roads, the terrain will get rough in the mountains," Amos said. "It'll take another couple of days, assuming we don't get caught in a storm."

"Then it's settled. I think Hank will be fine here by himself for the rest of the night. Let's go," Thorne said. Retrieving the map from the center of the table, the mage noticed that Carlion had a distant, almost fearful expression. "Something on your mind?" Thorne asked.

The Darkman's eyes refocused and he looked up at Thorne. "No," Carlion said quickly getting up and walking out of the tavern.

"Come on," Trinity said. "We need to catch him before he

walks back to the flophouse we slept in last night. I'd rather camp outside the city than go back there."

As Thorne got up to follow Trinity, he couldn't shake the feeling that the Darkman was hiding something connected to their next destination.

CELESTE'S MEMORY OF

AN UNFULFILLED PROMISE

"**N**ow Barrow, do you promise not to antagonize him?" Celeste rested her hand on the pump handle and looked from the large glass bowl she had just filled to the pixie standing next to it. Barrow had begged her to go swimming and Celeste thought now should be the time to remind her retainer of the condition for the filled washbasin.

Barrow was currently in a form that looked like a tiny human woman a hand's length in height with long violet hair that matched her eyes. The pixie gave a non-committal grunt as she wiggled out of her trousers and shirt to stand naked on the table. Her skin had an unnatural shimmer that contrasted starkly with the dull black tabletop. Reaching up to the rim of the bowl, Barrow gracefully pulled herself over the edge and slipped headfirst into the water.

Celeste watched the pixie backstroke for a lap around the bowl before she looked up to survey the rest of the room. The trappings were clearly of an alchemist's workshop, but the cold hearth and thin layer of dust on the mostly empty shelves suggested it had not been used in some time. Celeste had opened the shutters and windows upon entering to allow some fresh air and light into the stale room. Early afternoon sunshine now streamed into the laboratory and made it feel less claustrophobic.

Celeste looked down at the washbasin when she stopped hearing Barrow's rhythmic splashing. The pixie was at the edge and resting her arms on the side of the bowl. Small waves of water crested the rim and dripped to the tabletop.

"I think it was unnecessary for you to take that form," Barrow said critically. "An Archive would welcome being called on by a dragon. You look so plain as a human, especially an old one."

Celeste gave her retainer a playful smile and twirled in place, flaring the hem of her dark green robes. The dragon had wanted to blend in with the residents of the Archive and had chosen a somewhat dated but still appropriate dress for a mage. With crow's feet that radiated out from slate grey eyes and matching hair wound tightly in a large bun, Celeste looked every part an elder of the arcane profession.

"Not all of us are able to hide so easily," Celeste said, jiggling one of the pouches attached to her belt. "Besides, most people think dragons are gone from this world, even here in the Archive. I don't want to give them false hopes of a return to the old days."

"If we're in such a hurry, you could have just sent him a letter," the pixie said, pulling strands of wet hair away from her face.

Celeste sighed and shook her head. "No," she answered, "that would've been a cowardly departure. I still have to keep my promise to him."

Barrow slapped the surface of the water and sent a tiny shower cascading to the tabletop. "What that fool asked for is cowardly," she said angrily. "Having served as your retainer for almost two hundred years I've seen you take your fair share of lovers, but I still can't fathom why you waste your time on him. He's a broken man."

"You're too hard on him, Barrow," Celeste said more

severely than she meant. Softening her tone she continued, "I know the two of you have never seen eye to eye, but you're both so stubborn. I've told you this before, what I see in him is exactly what I found so attractive in my previous companions."

"And what's that?" asked a male voice from the laboratory entrance.

"Potential, Thorne," Celeste replied as she turned to watch him enter the laboratory.

Celeste was relieved to see that the mage looked much the same as when they had last parted several months ago. Dark brown hair greying at the temples and deep creases across his brow gave Thorne the distinguished features of a man in the middle decades of his life. The mage had fair skin that was common to the people from the middle of the continent, and his face was clean-shaven. Thorne's eyes were a faded blue and could, by a turn, be welcoming and relaxed, or cruel and piercing. A man that took his health seriously, Thorne was the opposite of what most people thought a mage looked like and appeared neither frail nor weak. Dressed more like a mercenary than a mage, Thorne's face showed happy disbelief when he stopped in front of Celeste.

"What are you doing here?" the mage asked. "The message I received only said that there were visitors in my laboratory and that it was urgent. I thought you were halfway around the world."

Barrow scoffed and resumed swimming around the perimeter of the bowl.

Thorne's expression soured when he saw the pixie. "Get out of there," he commanded. When he was ignored, the mage looked back at Celeste and asked, annoyed, "Why is your familiar in my washbasin?"

Before Celeste could answer, Thorne reached out and snatched Barrow's clothes from the table. As he lifted up the garments, a small amount of what looked like shimmering sand fell from them and scattered across the table. Glaring down into the glass bowl Thorne said, "Get out, or I'm throwing these out the window."

The pixie stopped swimming to tread water in the center of the bowl. She gave the mage a contentious scowl and said, "You are a villain, Thorne, and I curse the day I met you."

"Barrow, please," Celeste said in a tired voice.

With a conciliatory look at the dragon, Barrow swam to the edge of the glass bowl. The pixie climbed out of the washbasin and stood dripping wet on the tabletop. She looked up indignantly at Thorne as the mage dropped her clothes at her feet. Barrow reached down and grabbed them with one hand before she took a few steps away from the washbasin.

The pixie's naked body suddenly radiated warm yellow light. It was only visible for a moment and then quickly receded, replaced by what appeared to be a miniature cyclone that whipped her hair and the shimmering sand on the table upwards. The wet footprints she had left behind her instantly evaporated and tiny ripples raced along the surface of the washbasin.

As the wind died down, Celeste heard Thorne exhale a frustrated groan. "You're making a mess," the mage said looking down at his feet.

Now that she was dry, Barrow began to dress and replied, "It doesn't look like you were too concerned about that before. Your laboratory seems to have been collecting dust for some time now."

"Which is why I wanted to meet here," Celeste said, trying to stop the two from further squabbling, "I knew we'd get some privacy."

Celeste clasped both of Thorne's hands in hers, turning his attention away from her retainer. She took a moment to study his face. They had met when the mage was a much younger man, and while the years had been kind to him, Thorne's eyes always betrayed a hint of weariness when he looked at her.

"I won't draw things out, Thorne. I've been called back to the conclave in the Void," Celeste said.

"Why? Is something wrong?" The mage asked with a look of concern. "What happened?"

"The message wasn't very long," Celeste replied, "but it was clear that the conclave wants the few dragons still here to complete any personal business and return immediately."

"I don't understand," Thorne said.

"She's going back to the Void and likely won't ever see you again, you clod," Barrow said from the tabletop.

"Is that true, Celeste?" the mage asked, voice already pained.

"I don't know, Thorne," the dragon replied. "But that possibility is why I'm here. I've never forgotten what I promised you all those years ago and now I'm here to make good on it. I know this is all very sudden, but I'm here to erase your childhood memories."

The mage drew back as if hit. His expression withered and left him looking much older than he had a moment ago. Celeste watched Thorne's posture slouch, as if being reminded of his past had put a heavy burden across his shoulders.

"We've talked about this before," Thorne said, tired. "As much as I want that, it has to be after my father is dead. He's the last thread holding me to my past. Erased memories aren't really gone if they're shared by someone still living."

"This isn't some Venhadar favor we're talking about," Barrow said with renewed irritation. "You don't get to decide when a dragon fulfills a promise." Looking to Celeste the pixie said, "See, I told you he doesn't really want his memories erased. He just likes to wallow in this self-imposed misery. Can we go now?"

Celeste ignored Barrow's outburst and looked tenderly at the mage. "Are you sure I can't persuade you to do this now?" she asked.

"I can't do it, not now," Thorne whispered. "I'm sorry."

"I honestly don't know when I will be able to return," Celeste said.

Thorne seemed to be struck by a thought and his posture straightened. "What if I could come to you?" the mage asked. "Would I be able to find the conclave in the Void?"

"Perhaps," the dragon answered. "I'm not sure what my duties will be after I arrive so I might not be with the others."

"When do you have to leave?" Thorne asked.

"As soon as we've finished saying good-bye," she said. Celeste tried to give a genuine smile, but she knew it looked pained. "Thorne, I don't want you to suffer any more. I might be able to help you in the Void, but I can with certainty help you now if you let me."

The mage drew in close to Celeste and the dragon could see the tumult of emotions in Thorne's eyes. He opened his mouth to speak, but then pressed his lips tightly together again. Thorne did this once more and Celeste's heart ached to see the mage struggle to express what he wanted to say.

Finally, Thorne seemed to pull himself together and simply said, "Good-bye, Celeste." There was a hitch in his voice that betrayed how difficult it was to get those few words out. He gave her a quick kiss on the cheek and one last long look before he quickly turned and walked out of the laboratory.

Celeste stared at the door until she heard Barrow's voice, startlingly loud in her left ear, "Now that we have that unpleasant business done, can we go now?"

The dragon craned her neck so she could see Barrow sitting on her shoulder. Celeste hadn't noticed the pixie move from the table to her usual perch. "I thought things might have gone differently," she said.

"Well, things being what they are, he's going to have a hard time finding you in the Void if he changes his mind," Barrow said. "He left in such haste that you couldn't even tell him that he'd have to physically enter the Void, not just use an astral projection."

"Thorne will figure that out very quickly and give him a reason to use his laboratory again," Celeste replied with a furrowed brow as she looked around the room.

"Or maybe you weren't keen on telling him in the first place," Barrow said. The pixie crossed her arms and added, "It's not lost on me that you didn't answer his question about why you have to leave for an unknown duration."

Celeste looked back to where Thorne left the laboratory. "That was for his own good," the dragon said. "He's suffered enough and I didn't want to add to his troubles by telling him that we had to be separated because of another Paragon."

CHAPTER SIX

CARLION

While the first day of travel after leaving Rell-Kyr had been sunny and pleasant, on the second when the forest gave way to more rocky terrain the sky became overcast and the air colder. Despite being well below the timberline, the ground was mostly barren rock with pockets of brush. With nothing to break the wind, Carlion and Trinity walked with their necks shrugged into their cloaks. Thorne had pulled his cowl over his head, and Amos had switched out his bandana for a brightly dyed woolen cap.

As promised, Amos had skillfully led them up the narrow mining trails after leaving Rell-Kyr, and they only occasionally had to make way for a wagon transporting the mineral wealth of the mountains back to the capital. Trinity, being the genial and approachable man that he was, had exchanged pleasantries and even had a couple short conversations with the miners and guild members who were driving the carts pulled by teams of oxen. The transporters brightened in the presence of Trinity's earnest enthusiasm, but Carlion saw that it quickly faded when the conversation ended. To the man, they seemed to be burdened with something other than what was in their wagons.

The Darkman sympathized with those riding in the opposite

direction, as he was also struggling with inner turmoil. He hadn't spoken much since leaving the tavern in Rell-Kyr, but Trinity and Amos seemed content to leave him to his thoughts. However, he occasionally caught the mage watching him. Carlion's instincts told him that Thorne knew something was amiss, and he wondered how long it would be until the mage approached him about it.

It was during one of the last meetings with a mining wagon that Carlion took a step away from the others and dug into his pack. He carefully pulled out his bundle of letters and shuffled through them until he found the most recent one. His eyes jumped down to the last few lines and as he read the pit of his stomach roiled with a mixture of heartache and guilt.

"What have you got there?" came Thorne's voice over the Darkman's shoulder.

Clutching the letter to his chest, Carlion spun around. "None of your damn business," he said angrily.

"You've been awfully quiet since we left Rell-Kyr," Thorne said. "At first, I thought it was because you were reconsidering our employment arrangement and I burned my fingers for nothing. Now I think that letter is the source of your reticence. Is it too much to ask you to stay focused while we're in Deccern?"

"Keep your needless sarcasm to yourself," Carlion retorted. "I'm as good as my word."

"Then what is that letter about?" the mage asked.

"It's a private affair," Carlion growled. Kneeling down he put the bundle of letters into his pack and then tightly buckled down the straps. Slinging the pack over one shoulder as he stood, Carlion gave Thorne a defiant look that dared him to ask again about the contents of the letters.

The mage took a step back and smirked. "You can keep your secrets, I doubt I would find them of much interest anyway." He pointed up the road at Trinity and Amos, who had put some distance between them, "They called out to you a couple times after the cart left, but you were too absorbed in whatever is written on those pages."

"Well then, we better catch up," Carlion said, brushing past the mage.

With long, angry strides the Darkman quickly caught up with Trinity and Amos. Once Carlion was at Trinity's side, the mercenary looked over his shoulder. Carlion copied the movement and saw that Thorne was lagging behind and walking at an unhurried pace.

"I'm going to drop back and see if he has a plan once we get inside of the city. You two keep going," Trinity said before stopping.

For a time the only sound Carlion heard was the crunching of boots on the gravel road as he and Amos continued walking, albeit now at a slower pace. After a while Carlion glanced down at the Venhadar and wondered if he would have any sage words for him.

"Back in your corsair days, how did your women greet you after returning to port?" the Darkman asked in a measured tone.

"Depended on the port," Amos said with a grin, seeming to enjoy a private memory.

"No, that's not what I meant," Carlion said. "Did the time away change things?"

The Venhadar's expression grew more serious and Amos gave Carlion a probing look. "Sometimes," he said. "Given your uncharacteristic silence since we left Rell-Kyr, I take it something similar is on your mind?"

Carlion looked up the road, not wanting to meet Amos' gaze any longer. "I've been thinking about someone that I left behind when I was put out. I haven't seen her in years," he said.

"And you're wondering if she still holds a candle for you,"

Amos said. "You finally going to tell me something of your sordid past?"

"Some other time. It's complicated," Carlion said, looking away.

Amos scoffed, "Doesn't have to be."

"What do you mean?" Carlion asked, still refusing to look at him.

"When we're done with this job, just go see her. Stop being such a fucking coward," Amos said harshly. "How far away is this thus far nameless woman?"

Carlion gave Amos a frustrated look and then said, "Julia. Her name is Julia, and she's not too far away."

● ● ●

Despite being isolated halfway up a mountain, Deccern was known as a growing and prosperous city thanks to the rich veins of silver and copper in the mountain. The city was arranged in a semi-circle, with the flat face built into the mountain where the mining operations took place. The stone that was excavated during the early mining days of the city was used to erect an imposing wall that protected the city from the dangers of the frontier and the occasional blizzard that blew down from the higher elevations.

Near the end of the drab, cold afternoon, Carlion found himself staring up at the imposing barrier that surrounded Deccern and felt very small. Rising several stories, the Darkman craned his neck up and noticed that there were no sentries watching the road from the ramparts. Where the bulwark met the road a heavy wooden gate was constructed from thick timbers and banded together with wide iron straps. Cut into the gate was a smaller door for foot traffic during the night when the city was asleep.

With no indication that their approach was noticed, Carlion

stepped in front of Amos and pounded a fist on the metal hatch that was built into the door near eye level. A few seconds later the panel slid aside and a pair of suspicious eyes were staring at him.

"State your business," the voice behind the door said with a mixture of formality, authority, and suspicion.

"We're here to see the alchemist Ulrich," Amos said. "We set out from Rell-Kyr two days ago."

"No alchemist here by that name," came the terse reply behind the door.

"Just let us in, mate," Carlion said shortly. "It's cold out here."

"The governor isn't letting any non-guild business in the city until we get things under control here," the sentry said.

"What are you talking about?" Carlion asked.

The metal panel door slammed closed.

Trinity and Thorne, who had been in conversation a few steps behind them, finally started paying attention and stepped closer to the door to join Carlion and Amos.

"What's this about?" Trinity asked.

"Fuckers aren't going to let us in," Amos said.

The sound of other voices must have piqued the interest of the sentry on the other side because the hatch slid open again. Seeing two other cold-looking men didn't seem to change his mind, and said, "Now listen here…"

"That's enough out of you," Amos cut him off. "We just walked half-way up this damn mountain to get this wizard here," he motioned to Thorne, "so he can talk to your wizard. If you don't want your door blown off of its fucking hinges, you'll open it now."

"Nion sent for you?" the sentry asked with an abrupt change in tone, now sounding almost hopeful. He looked back to another person who Carlion couldn't see and said, "Captain, maybe Nion sent for some help." Getting some sort of reply the sentry looked at Thorne and asked, "Is this true, sir? Did Nion send for your aid?"

"He did," Thorne lied underneath his cowl. The mage pulled out his Archive guilder from his satchel and held it out for the sentry to see. "I am an Archives mage. These men are my escorts from the mercenary guild and I will vouch for them. We request entry into Deccern."

The sentry slid the hatch closed. Nothing happened for what felt like a long time, and Carlion saw that Amos was about to start kicking the door when it slowly opened. They wasted no time entering the city and the door was slammed shut and barred behind them the instant they were through. Behind the door the Darkman saw that there were more guards standing there who watched them with curiosity.

"If you can just direct us where to find Nion, then we'll be on our way," Thorne said.

"He's most likely at the governor's manor right now," the sentry said. "I'll take you there."

The sentry ushered them down the street towards the center of the city. There were few people outside, but those that were going about their business moved with a nervous energy. Carlion could feel a tension envelop him as he left the barrier wall and walked amongst the multi-story buildings of the merchant district. Coupled with his own apprehension about being in Deccern, Carlion began to have serious misgivings about his decision to accompany the mage here.

"What's the trouble here?" Trinity asked the sentry as they turned off the main road onto an avenue that was populated with affluent looking houses and shops. "There's been no ill talk about Deccern in the capital and we passed several wagons coming from here that didn't mention any trouble."

"Transporters have been," the sentry paused to find the

right word, "compensated, to remain quiet about the situation here. We're recovering now, but for the past several weeks a terrible disease has ripped through the city. It seems to have burned itself out, mostly, but if the Sovereignty found out about it they'd send the garrison back here to blockade the city until we could prove any pestilence is gone. I suspect they'd just as soon stay anyway and starve us out so the prince could wrest control from the guild and have direct access to the mines."

"You give the Sovereignty too much credit. I doubt that the prince is that clever, given the state of affairs in the capital," Carlion said. "I do agree with your assessment about a city blockade, though. Nothing good ever comes of it. I take it the garrison is no longer here?"

The sentry cast the Darkman a wary look, but then nodded. "This is a precarious time for Deccern, and not only from this recent bout of disease," he said. "Our transporters and couriers have been asking for more protections and higher fares given the increased B'nisct activity over the past year."

"Was there a reason that the governor did not send for Archive aid?" Thorne asked. "We might have been able to help on both of those accounts."

The sentry gave a weak smile. "I'm sure that Nion will be better able to explain. He was working mostly out of his new shop, but then the governor's daughter fell ill and he was taken to be her personal physician. He's done his best to help the rest of the city during a couple of small flare ups, but there's only so much one man can do."

"What did we just walk into?" Trinity asked no one in particular, but loudly enough to elicit a sidelong glance from Thorne.

Carlion hoped the mage was a quick thinker and could come up with a plan during their short walk to the governor's manor. It looked as if Thorne had been paying careful attention to his surroundings as they walked to their destination. Carlion didn't know what he was looking for, but his expression darkened the further along they walked.

The Darkman was about to ask the mage if something was amiss when Carlion saw a large hanging sign over a building to advertise that it was the regional office of the mining guild. Stepping out of the guildhall was a sturdy looking man with a thick mustache and piercing eyes. A jolt of fear raced through Carlion an instant after he recognized the man. Slouching deeper into his cloak, the Darkman turned away from the guildhall. He didn't realize he had been holding his breath until his chest started to burn and he exhaled loudly.

"Just breathe easy," the sentry said looking back at Carlion. "People have already tried holding their breath when they walk outside to avoid the disease, but it never works and just leaves them gasping in the streets."

CHAPTER SEVEN

THORNE

Thorne was the only one who seemed to listen to the sentry's abridged history of Deccern as they walked from the barrier wall. The guardsman explained that over the years the city had built itself up into a prosperous settlement as the mountain continued to have easily accessible metal ores. It wasn't long thereafter that the guilds began to establish a presence, and the town grew to become a point on the map. Regional government was established, and with it a trade-off where the residents hated the new taxes but welcomed the protection of the Sovereignty military. There was no shortage of danger on the frontier. Raids on the town by B'nisct swarms remained a common threat, as were attempts by highwaymen to rob ore wagons on their way to the capital. Still, while Deccern was no stranger to disease, the recovery of the city this time had been slow for reasons that the sentry could not explain.

After making their way through a small and sparsely populated merchant square, the sentry led Thorne and the mercenaries up a wide avenue. Rising before them was a stately mansion with sculpted hedges and a tall fence constructed from thick iron bars. The gate to the manor was currently open and the group walked though unchecked, but as they took the first steps up onto the large veranda, a servant dressed in tan colored livery exited the house to greet them.

"Welcome to the governor's manor," the servant said with a slight bow. "How might I serve you gentlemen?"

The sentry escort replied, "These good souls are from the capital and are here to aid Nion in eradicating the disease."

The servant looked genuinely happy. "That is wonderful news," he said. "I am sure that Nion will welcome the assistance. Please come inside and I shall retrieve him."

Thorne saw Carlion roll his eyes as they entered the manor. Apparently the Darkman wasn't fond of the aristocracy, even one from such a remote city in the Sovereignty. Standing in the foyer, Thorne watched the servant ascend a large staircase leading up to an open second floor and disappear around a corner. Taking in the space around him, Thorne surmised the current governor was a man of restraint. The rug they stood on was simple and durable, though showing some signs of wear at the edges. The walls had a few paintings on them, but they were mostly plain looking portraits. From behind a set of doors to his left Thorne could hear work going on in the kitchen, but otherwise where they were standing was quiet.

"How long have things been like this?" Trinity asked the sentry who had remained in the foyer with them.

The guardsman replied, "It started with a couple miners a few months ago and slowly spread through the boarding houses and taverns. Before we knew it, the City Watch was in a bad way and only until just recently the barracks were basically an infirmary. I still wouldn't say we're at full strength, though."

The man looked back towards the door, "I'm glad you're here to help, and that you got here safely. B'nisct activity around the area has also increased. No one knows what got the swarms so riled up, but the attacks have gotten a lot more serious of late. The captain has done his best to keep morale high, but with the reduced roster of soldiers everyone is pulling double patrol rotations. It's starting to put a strain on us, but you didn't hear that from me."

A voice from the top of the staircase drew everyone's attention. "Though I respect the captain greatly, I have argued rather vehemently that the resources of the city should be focused on combating the disease first, and then we can worry about any perceived external threats."

Thorne looked up to the second-floor landing and saw a thin man standing alongside the servant who had left a few minutes ago. Dressed in traditional alchemist's robes dyed a dark maroon, the man had a pale complexion and a tired look on his clean-shaven face. After descending the stairs the man stopped and gave a slight bow to the group, "I am Nion, independent mage and herbalist for the city of Deccern. I was told that you gentlemen are here to help eradicate the disease afflicting the city. I am certainly grateful for your aid, though I wonder how you came to know of our troubles."

Thorne realized that this man was already wary of them. He would have to be restrained in this opening discourse and not reveal his true intention for coming to Deccern. Unfortunately, the mage never got the chance.

"Here you are called Nion, but perhaps that is a family name. Are you not also Ulrich, previously from Rell-Kyr?" Carlion asked, though it sounded more like an accusation.

The mage ground his teeth in anger, knowing that any attempt at subtly was now gone. He silently cursed Carlion as a fool who was doing little to lessen the reputation of the Sovereignty military as nothing more than loutish bullies. Thorne shot the Darkman a venomous glance, but Carlion didn't seem to notice.

"I've never been to Rell-Kyr," Nion said with a slightly confused expression. "I left the Barnterc Archive during my traveling education, but never returned. Technically, I'm still an apprentice, but my Awareness is certainly sufficient to help the miners and their families here with most of their daily needs. My travels brought me here a little more than a month ago, but the city enchanted me so completely that I decided to stay and try my hand as an apothecary."

"Surely your mentor must have tried to contact you?" Thorne asked, trying to salvage the conversation.

"We weren't on the best of terms," Nion said, shaking his head sadly.

"Is that Erza? Where is she now?" the Darkman demanded.

It was only for an instant, but Thorne saw an expression of recognition on the man's face when the name was mentioned. Quickly recovering, Nion cocked his head and furrowed his brow before addressing Carlion, "Who is that, sir? My mentor's name was Delaney."

Thorne was about to interrupt Carlion again, but a woman wearing a simple white dress quickly descended the stairs and whispered something in Nion's ear.

The herbalist nodded slightly, looked towards Carlion, and then said, "Forgive me gentlemen, but I must tend to the governor's daughter. I'm afraid this might take some time, so I must bid you goodbye." With a forced smile Nion turned from the group and ascended the stairs as the servant ushered Thorne and the others out the door.

"Are there any places that are still safe to board?" Trinity asked the sentry as they stepped onto the veranda. The servant was quick to shut the door after them to keep the warm air from escaping the foyer.

"The Phoenix hasn't had too many people get sick," the sentry said, rubbing his hands together. "The tavern is still mostly open, so you can also get your meals there."

"So we're just supposed to wait until we're called on?" Carlion asked. "It doesn't sound like that he's that interested in our help."

Thorne finally lost his patience. "You damn fool!" he said hotly. "Asking him about Erza so brazenly was the absolute worst thing you could have done. We already know she never returned to the capital, so what he told Hank back in Rell-Kyr was a lie. You have all the subtlety of a cow. I thought cavaliers were supposed to be educated in the art of discourse and etiquette."

"Did you think he was just going to volunteer a confession to you?" Carlion shot back. "He wasn't going to tell you anything. We would have wasted all afternoon talking circles around one another."

"That wasn't your decision to make," the mage said. "Let's get one thing very clear, you are working for me. That means you do what I tell you, and unless the situation calls for it, you will keep your mouth shut."

Carlion took a menacing step towards the mage, but stopped short touching him. Getting right up into his face, the Darkman said, "Don't talk to me like I'm some idiot stable hand."

"Or what?" Thorne challenged, a feral gleam in his eye.

Before Carlion could reply, Trinity slid in between the two men and gently pushed the Darkman back a few steps. "Easy there, mates," the mercenary said in an attempt to deescalate the situation.

"Maybe we should take a walk to cool off some," Amos suggested, his eyes shifting between Thorne and Carlion.

"The Phoenix. I'll meet you there later," Carlion said and stormed down the stairs and through the manor gate before anyone could reply.

"Later? Where the fuck is he going now?" Amos asked, looking up at Trinity.

The mercenary shook his head and replied. "Something's been weighing on his mind the whole trip here. Did he say anything to you?"

"He seemed to be pining for an old girl of his from back in his chivalrous days," Amos replied. "He never struck me as the sentimental sort, though."

"It's not important now," Thorne said. "We're not going to learn anything more here, not today. Whether called Nion or Ulrich, the Darkman's impromptu inquisition was not the best way to meet him."

"I never said he was clever," Trinity said, watching Carlion rapidly retreat down the street.

"No, you did not," Thorne replied, following the mercenary's gaze.

"You can put your dagger away now," Amos said. "You're quicker than you look. I didn't notice it in your hand until Trinity pushed Carlion back. Where are you hiding it?"

"The sheath is sewn into the underside of my satchel flap," Thorne replied, showing Amos as he returned the dagger to its case.

"Would you have really cut him?" Amos asked.

Trinity answered for him as the group started to walk down the stairs and away from the manor, "Why do you think I stepped between them? Carlion owes me now."

Ignoring the mercenaries, Thorne turned to the sentry and asked, "Where is Nion's shop?"

The sentry coughed awkwardly, and then looked over his shoulder back at the manor. He didn't return Thorne's gaze when he replied, "It's actually only a few buildings from the Phoenix. The outside is painted green, with a large sign hanging over the door. It should be easy to find."

As the group left the manor property, sentry stopped and said, "I reckon that you gentlemen can make your way on your own. I need to report back to my post. Please conduct your business with the peace of the city in mind. I don't want us to meet under less cordial circumstances." He then left the group quickly on a route back to the city wall.

"That wasn't exactly encouraging, was it?" Amos asked rhetorically.

"It was a warning," Trinity said, casting a concerned look at Thorne. The mage only gave a dissatisfied expression for a reply.

The group marched quickly to Nion's shop as the overcast sky steadily grew darker. Entering the shop, a portly young man introduced himself as Nion's assistant. There was no one else in the shop, and the mercenaries took the opportunity to have a seat on a pair of stools near a small heating stove while Thorne began to inspect the herbs and other contents of the shop's shelves. After a few minutes of browsing the mage pulled the arcane sealed box they recovered from Rell-Kyr from his satchel.

"Does Nion keep special herbs in a box like this one? Could you check in the back? I'm looking for Papaver leaves," Thorne asked the clerk.

The young man nodded and replied, "I can look for you." Nion's assistant slid off his stool and drew aside the curtain. He could be heard shortly thereafter rummaging through the shelves. After a few minutes he came back with a box of similar dimensions, and said, "We don't have any Papaver, but this one has Argemone. It's supposed to do the same thing."

Thorne looked to the ceiling for moment as if in thought, then looked the young man and said, "Not quite, but it should be fine for what I need it for. I'll take it all."

The clerk's jaw dropped a bit and replied, "But that's twenty-five ducats!" He looked down at the box then back up at the mage, "Since you're not from here, I can't give you a line of credit. You have to pay for it all now. I'm sorry."

Thorne shook his head, "No, it's fine. The Archive granted

me some funds." He pulled out a pouch from his satchel, counted out a number of coins, and placed them in three tidy stacks on the counter. After collecting the money the clerk pulled out a cloth bag and opened the box, but the mage stopped him. "For twenty-five, you could at least let me keep the box," Thorne said.

"I don't know, Nion never said anything about selling the boxes," the clerk replied, looking down at the small container.

Thorne took few more coins from his pouch and slid them across the counter close to the young man. "How about now?" he asked with a small smile.

Nion's assistant looked down at the coins, thought a moment, and then scooped them up. "It's just a box," he said more to himself as he handed the container to Thorne. The box quickly went into the mage's satchel and with a nod good-bye, Thorne led the mercenaries out of the shop.

"Why'd you ask about Papaver leaves?" Amos said when they were back on the street. "You gave me a vial full of extract from your little chemistry kit when we drugged Hank back in Rell-Kyr. What do you need more for?"

"The contents were irrelevant," Thorne replied quickly. "I needed the box."

"What for?" Amos asked.

"My next gambit," the mage said. "Let's go to the Phoenix and try our luck at not getting whatever disease is in this city. I could use a cold drink and warm hearth right now."

CHAPTER EIGHT

CARLION

Carlion walked away from the manor with his neck and shoulders rigid with anger. He had not been dressed down like that since before he was cashiered. It was just as humiliating now as it was then, perhaps even more, coming from a mage. It was a good thing that Trinity had stepped between him and Thorne. He wouldn't have felt bad about beating the mage to a pulp, but he would have had to answer to Trinity later.

With his head just starting to cool, Carlion realized that he was approaching the mining guildhall. Perhaps the argument with Thorne was a blessing in disguise because now he was unsupervised and not expected to return to the tavern until much later. If he was going to take Amos' advice he needed to get some information from the mining guild and the man he saw earlier. Using the remnants of anger from the argument to keep his momentum towards the guildhall, Carlion jerked the door open.

"Bold actions are worth the risk of regret," he growled to himself as he lowered his shoulder as if to storm through a mob.

The interior of the mining guild felt like old wealth, but it was devoid of people as Carlion closed the door. Two oblong tables with matching pairs of chairs were polished to a high shine and sitting on a thick rug. Hung on the wall to Carlion's left were several portraits of stern-looking men in expensive regalia. As the Darkman walked over the rug towards the counter at the back of the room, the floorboards creaked loudly, which elicited a call from the room behind the counter.

"Be with you in a minute!" rang a sonorous voice.

"Looking for the guild master," Carlion replied loudly, with more bravado than he felt as he approached. Resting his forearms on the darkly stained wood, Carlion leaned over the counter and could smell the faint odor of pipe tobacco. As he counted the tree rings in the wood, the Darkman quickly came up with his cover story.

Emerging from the doorframe behind the counter was a stocky man with shock of white hair and a wrinkled face. He smiled at Carlion and said, "Guild master was summoned to the capital and left not an hour ago. You just missed him. Can't say when he'll return, but I'm in charge until he gets back. I'm the guild secretary."

The Darkman tried to keep a neutral expression, but inwardly was relieved. He couldn't believe his luck. Carlion relaxed and gave an amiable smile. "That's just as well, because I'm actually looking for his niece, Julia," Carlion said. "My name is Carlion Cantra. I am a commissioned cavalier in the service of the Yaboon Sovereignty."

"You don't look like one," the clerk said. "You got any orders from your commander? Or a writ from the prince?"

Carlion pulled his tabard to the side and exposed his ruined breastplate. "Only this."

The man gave him a sideways look and said, "I thought only expelled cavaliers had that done to their armor."

"I'm on a covert assignment," Carlion lied. "There were," he paused searching for the right word, "irregularities, in the governor's quarterly ledgers and the accountants in the capital thought it prudent to have a subtle approach for once. Plus, sending a contingent of footmen up here would be expensive. My cover is of a Darkman trying to find work as a miner."

"If it's so secret, why are you telling me? And what does Julia have to do with any of this?" the secretary asked.

"I was informed that the mining guild would welcome any reports of corruption and would aid me. As for Julia, we're old acquaintances and I just wanted to see a friendly face. It's rather bleak here, and witnessing the aftermath of a plague isn't making it any better."

"A rather unconventional approach for revealing graft, especially for the military," the man said. "Take care, friend, with everyone so skittish you're not going to be well received if the governor catches on to what you're about." The secretary took a step back to appraise Carlion more carefully, "The guild master's house is just across the street. Once you leave, look to your left. It's the red two-story."

"I appreciate your help," Carlion said, pushing back from the counter. He rapped his breastplate and added, "And also for you keeping this a secret. It's best that folks here don't know I'm a Sovereignty agent."

"Who are you again?" the man asked. "We get a lot of people drifting through here looking for work." He gave Carlion a sly grin.

Carlion left the guildhall pleased with himself, and felt vindicated after Thorne's accusation about his inability to be clever. The Darkman had the information he had come for and covered his tracks. He quickly found the correct house, but as he stood in front of it Carlion's arms suddenly became very heavy and he couldn't bring himself to knock on the door. A sudden fear gripped him, much stronger than the vague feelings he experienced on the march to Deccern.

The words he uttered before entering the guildhall echoed

in his mind and mocked him as he stood in the cold. He was so close to having what he had wanted for so long, but was now afraid to take the final action. Carlion closed his eyes and pushed out the breath he was holding. With what felt like considerable effort, he reached up and knocked on the door.

After a moment a woman opened the door. She wore a simple blue dress, with an apron around her waist. Her brown hair was tied up behind her head and her face had small wrinkles around the eyes and at the corners of her mouth. Those wrinkles were what he had loved best about Julia's face because they were the result of life full of laughter. He was happy to see that their years apart hadn't added creases to her brow from worry. For a moment the two of them simply stood there, then tears began to well in her eyes, but she quickly wiped them away.

"You're finally here," she said quietly. As more tears slid down her cheeks Julia laughed. It was the most beautiful thing Carlion had heard in a long time.

Julia grabbed Carlion's hand and pulled him inside the house. Once the door was closed she wrapped her arms around his neck and kissed him.

"Carlion, you're finally here," she said breathless. "After all this time, you're finally here. You never mentioned anything in your last letter. Did something happen in the capital? What about your men?"

The Darkman stepped back and gently took both of Julia's hands and guided her to a chair. He knelt down next to her. "I thought I'd be able to tell you the same lie I just passed off at the guild, but I can't," Carlion said. His tongue felt thick in his mouth and he struggled to get the words out. "Something bad has happened. It's about my commission."

"They found out about us, and expelled you," Julia replied. When Carlion went to pull his hands away she grabbed them tightly and said, "It's alright. I've known for a while now."

"What?" Carlion gasped, now thankful for the support that Julia's grasp gave him. He felt unstable on his knees and wobbled slightly in shock. "If that's true, then why did you play along in your letters?"

Her expression grew serious. "I knew it would be devastating if I told you," she said. "I wanted to give you some hope that we could still find a happy life together someday. I knew your return had to be on your own terms, but I never doubted that you'd come back to me, even as the years went by."

"How did you find out?" Carlion asked, a lump growing in the back of this throat. Julia's devotion to him was something he had hoped for but didn't think he deserved.

"Uncle got a letter from Father," she said. "Father wished you ill and cursed you to die a miserable death for your betrayal of a cavalier's oath and hoped he never heard of you again. He still forbade me from returning to the capital. I'm an embarrassment to him and he needs to set a stern example for his command."

"And how did the guild master react to that information?" Carlion asked hoarsely.

"The same as when I first arrived," Julia replied with a smile. "He is happy for the company now that his wife has passed on. We bring excitement to his house and joy to his life." Julia stood up and finally let go of Carlion's hands. "And speaking of 'we,' it's time that you meet the reason I was banished to the frontier, unmarried, and bearing a bastard child," she said in an ironically playful manner. Walking to the doorway near the back of the room she called down a hallway, "Natty, come out here!"

Carlion heard a door open and small feet running down the hall. "What is it, Mum?" a child's voice said. Julia reached out and wrapped her arm around the child and ushered him into the room. Standing in front of his mother was a boy of about five years. Julia wrapped her arms around the boy's shoulders and hugged him close.

"Natty, I have a wonderful surprise for you," Julia said looking down at the top of his head. "Your Papa has come home." Julia looked up and Carlion saw tears in her eyes again when she said, "Carlion, I want you to meet your son, Nathaniel."

Carlion had read the name many times in the letters that Julia had written, but now seeing the boy in person was too much for him to bear. Still on his knees, Carlion wept.

• • •

It was several hours past dinner when Julia said, "I never gave you the chance to answer my question from before. What finally got you to come here?"

Carlion leaned back in his chair, full and warm and happy. He had felt the first two many times in the intervening years separated from Julia, but now he could genuinely add the third. Since sitting down to eat the only thing Carlion had thought about was the future he had with his family, but Julia's question brought him back to the present and his expression fell slightly. "Well, there's not much honest work a Darkman can get that doesn't rely on his sword," he said.

"So mercenary then?" Julia said evenly. "I hope you're at least a member of the guild and not a freelancer."

"No, I have my guilder," Carlion said. "I was based out of Granick at first, but now I'm working in Yaboon. Actually, right now I'm here as an escort." He could see that she was going to ask more, but Carlion put up a hand and continued, "It's well paying and relatively safe work, but I don't want to trouble you with it because it's not important. I'm going to quit tomorrow morning. It might take me a little while to find work here, but if your uncle is sympathetic to our plight, then we'll be fine."

"You're going to stay, Papa?" Natty asked.

The boy looked tired. Before and during dinner Natty had

tried to catch Carlion up on everything he could remember, the stories tumbling out of him in an excited stream of consciousness manner. Julia let the boy stay up later than normal if he promised to slow down and take a breath between stories.

"Escorting who?" Julia asked, seemingly not deterred by his declaration.

"An Archive mage," Carlion said. "He's here to investigate Nion."

"A mage?" Julia said, surprised. "What did Nion do? He's been nothing but a boon to us here. Given the climate and rough living, there hasn't been a mage here in any capacity for years. The church was our best source of medical care before he came. To be honest, the shepherd was happy to have the burden lightened."

"I don't know his story," Carlion admitted. "I don't usually ask a lot of questions when I'm on a job. I just do the job."

"I don't like it," Julia said, her expression darkening. "We need Nion now more than ever in case the number of people getting sick goes up again. Don't quit just yet. Stay close to that mage and make sure he doesn't do anything to Nion. Let him ask his questions, and when he's ready to leave then you should quit."

"Calm down, Julia," Carlion said with a placating gesture. "I'll keep the mage in line. I promise." He paused and continued, "Speaking of which, he and my companions are at the Phoenix tavern. I need to return there. If I stay out much longer, they might get suspicious."

"Suspicious of what?" Julia asked, then her eyebrows jerked up in realization. "You didn't tell them about me or Natty. They don't know you're here." For a moment her expression grew angry, but she looked down at Natty and relaxed. Placing a hand on the boy's head, she said, "Well, I suppose they'll find out when you don't leave with them."

Promising Natty that he'd return tomorrow and giving several good-bye kisses to Julia, Carlion left the house and walked the cold dark streets back to the Phoenix. There were lampposts only at the intersections of the streets and the diffuse spheres of light did little to push back the night. Carlion spent the walk trying to decide how he would tell his companions that he was going to leave the group the day after tomorrow. He would have to make an opportunity to thank Amos in private. The Venhadar had given him the push he needed and for that he was grateful.

Stepping into the Phoenix tavern, the Darkman found the dining area mostly empty. A few miners were drinking and engaged in quiet conversation, but they didn't even look in his direction as he walked past them. There was a heavyset woman standing behind the bar who looked up from staring at the fire on the opposite side of the room. Carlion raised his hand in greeting, but the woman turned back to the fire when he didn't stop to request a drink. He frowned at the less than warm welcome.

On a table in the center of the room Amos had collected a set of empty cups in front of him. The Venhadar was sitting slightly slouched in his chair and looked glassy eyed as he puffed on a little stump of a pipe.

"Where are the other two?" Carlion asked as he slid into a chair opposite Amos.

The haze that surrounded Amos was pungent and smelled like the ocean. The Venhadar exhaled through his nose and sent two jets of smoke streaming onto the table. He blinked lazily and replied, "Already retired. Didn't even make it to seven low bells. Been here by my lonesome for a while now waiting for you."

The woman from behind the bar approached the table and looked down at Carlion. In a scratchy voice she said, "You need something? Kitchen is closed."

"He's with me," Amos replied, his speech slightly slurred.

"That's all fine and good, but I'm telling you to get out. You can come back and eat breakfast at four high bells," the woman said. She rested her hands on her hips and flicked her head towards the door. "I trust you still remember what room you paid to sleep in?"

Amos puffed a final time on his pipe before tapping the bowl's contents into one of the mugs on the table. Ignoring the woman's scowl at his rude behavior, the corsair said, "It's been a pleasure, madam."

Walking outside and behind the tavern, Carlion followed Amos along the long single-story building, passing regularly interspersed doors. It looked like old miners' barracks that had been repurposed to be lodgings for travelers. Amos approached a door about halfway down the building's length and banged on it. He called out loudly, "Hey! Trinity, open up!"

After a minute Carlion heard a bolt slide and Trinity opened the door looking like he had been asleep. "Glad you could make it," he grunted to the Darkman as they were ushered inside.

As Carlion's eyes adjusted to the near complete darkness inside, the Darkman noticed that Trinity had his blanket on the floor next to a potbelly stove that was heating the room. There was no furniture in the room and Carlion guessed the only reason the stove was still there was because it was bolted to the floor. Along the back wall there was a solitary window that had all the glass smashed out, so it was shuttered tightly to keep any warm air from the stove inside. It was the most austere of accommodations and made their stay in Rell-Kyr seem opulent in comparison.

Amos pulled out a blanket from his backpack, laid down on his back next to the stove, and was asleep almost instantly. The corsair snored occasionally as Carlion readied his own sleeping area and sat down next to Trinity, who had already returned to his blanket.

"Where's Thorne?" Carlion asked quietly.

"He paid for his own room," Trinity said. The mercenary wrapped his blanket tightly around his shoulders and curled onto his side with his back to the stove. "Said he was going to stay up late and get ready for whatever he's planning tomorrow."

"He sure has deep pockets," Carlion mused. After a moment of silence he said, "We need to talk."

"It can wait until the morning," Trinity said irritably. "I'm tired. Roll Amos over so he doesn't choke on his own tongue."

Carlion leaned on his side to reach Amos and pulled on his shoulder until the Venhadar was splayed out on his belly. The Darkman then reclined on his own blanket and stared up at the indistinct blackness of the ceiling. His mind was still busy processing the events of the past few hours, but he eventually dozed off with the comforting thought that tonight would be the last time he would be sleeping on an unfamiliar floor.

CHAPTER NINE

THORNE

Thorne was already awake when the sound of three high bells filtered through the shuttered window of his shabby lodgings. He had a restless sleep and had spent the past half hour simply sitting near the stove, waiting for it to be light enough to walk the streets without suspicion by the City Watch. As the echo of the last toll rang out, the mage got up and quietly gathered up his belongings and left the room. He was glad that he would not be returning.

The mage had decided that his next plan to question Nion would be best attempted alone, and took care to remain silent as he walked past the door to the mercenaries' room. After he entered the tavern the proprietor immediately accosted him.

"No food until four high bells!" she said irritably, wiping her hands on a stained apron. Then realizing she wasn't addressing a miner, her tone softened some. "I'm still cooking. You and your friends will have to come back in an hour."

"I'm not here to eat," Thorne said somewhat reluctantly. "But I would like for you to relay a message to my companions. I have some business at the governor's manor this morning and I would like you to let them know that I have gone ahead without them. Once they have eaten they should come meet me there." He reached into his satchel and pulled out a rubium coin and placed it on the bar. "For the trouble," he said.

The woman looked down at the money and back up at him. Her sour expression lessened and she asked, "You want something to eat before you leave?"

"What do you have ready?" Thorne asked.

"Only bread leftover from yesterday," the woman replied as she looked back towards the kitchen.

"That will be fine, thank you. A cup of water would also be appreciated," Thorne said.

The woman grunted and said, "A meal fit for a prisoner. You're easy to please."

The mage gave a mirthless smile as she went to the kitchen and brought out the meager breakfast. Once the food was on the bar, the proprietor snatched up the token and retreated to the kitchen. Thorne swallowed the tasteless food quickly. He sometimes lamented that his use of magic had eroded his senses and fully robbed him of the ability to taste and smell, but other times Thorne thought it a blessing as he worked to chew the obviously stale bread. Draining his cup in a single long draught, he gently placed it on the bar as he exited the tavern.

As he walked the nearly empty streets Thorne pulled his cowl over his head and tucked his fists inside the sleeves of his shirt in an attempt to keep the mountain air from chilling him. The mage's fast stride further warded off the cold, but also betrayed his eagerness to confront Nion unhindered by the mercenaries. While he appreciated the companionship of Trinity and Amos, he regretted allowing Carlion to come along. The Darkman had proven himself to be unreliable and unable to follow directions. Thorne surmised those qualities were what got him cashiered and they wouldn't help if he wanted to stay employed as a mercenary.

The gate to the manor was closed when Thorne arrived. An armed sentry gave the mage a critical eye through the iron bars.

Thorne did not recognize the man, but could plainly see that the guard did not welcome the intrusion to his early morning reverie. "The governor's estate is closed until seven high bells," the man's thick tongue seemed to chew the words rather than speak them.

"Nion is expecting me," Thorne said. It was true, if only as a statement of fact and not context. "He asked that I arrive as early as I could this morning," he added.

"Is that so?" the sentry asked unconvinced. "What's your name?"

"Thorne. I'm an Archive mage," Thorne said. He retrieved his guilder and held it up for the guard to inspect.

The man didn't seem to be impressed by the medallion. "Wait here," he grunted. The guard walked at an unhurried pace up the path and entered the manor. A few minutes later, the mage was surprised to see that a servant exited the house alone and quickly walked down to him. The woman had an expression of someone compelled to perform an unpleasant task.

"Master Nion has forbade you entry. I'm very sorry," she said not quite apologetically.

The mage did not ask why, or what had happened to the sentry. Neither of these questions would get him any closer to Nion. Instead Thorne decided tried to play on her loyalties. "I see. How long has Nion served the family?" he asked.

"Not long," she replied. "Perhaps a month."

"But you have served them longer?" the mage said.

"For five years," the servant answered proudly.

"And has the governor treated you well?" Thorne asked, trying to sound earnest.

The woman nodded and replied, "As good as you can get for a mining town."

"And his family is a good one to serve?" the mage asked.

"The lady is kind and her daughter a joy," she said as her expression grew sad. "To see her suffering now breaks my heart."

"So you'd want to do everything you can to help her?" Thorne asked.

"Yes of course, but what Nion said..." the servant's voice trailed off.

"It's because he's proud," Thorne replied gently and then continued, "He wants to serve the governor like you do, with distinction. But he doesn't know the family like you do and this disease can be very dangerous. Please let me help. Be the one who had the courage to give an Archive mage from the capital a chance to help your master's daughter."

The servant seemed to struggle with the decision, but then pulled a key from inside her heavy cloak and opened the gate's lock, allowing Thorne to enter. They walked in silence up to the manor. Entering the foyer Thorne saw the sentry from before with his hands wrapped around a steaming mug. Seeing the mage, the sentry gave a disappointed look, but the mage didn't know if it was because Thorne was admitted to the manor or because he would have to return to his post at the gate again.

Quickly ascending the staircase and walking down an ornately decorated hallway, the servant guided Thorne to a closed door. The mage heard voices on the other side and stilled the servant's hand when she raised it to knock. The woman opened her mouth to protest, but then leaned closer to the door to hear the heated exchange better.

"I didn't send for any Archive help," a voice said, which Thorne recognized as Nion's. "These men are no doubt confidence artists trying to get in your good graces, selling snake oil. Your daughter's life is at stake! You should have the City Watch run them out of the city immediately."

A baritone voice replied, "I would hear what they have to

say before resorting to such measures. It strikes me that a plot to travel from the capital just to fleece a few coins from a minor governor is rather implausible. Perhaps one of the other merchant guild members sent for them. They probably feel shortchanged a physician since I have taken you from your shop. Unless you want the city blockaded by the Sovereignty military, we must prevent this disease and information of it from leaving the city. If this mage and his retinue are here to help, then we should be thankful for our good fortune and accept it. However, if things are as you say, then they will be met with frontier justice."

With a gleeful sense of poetic timing, Thorne bade the servant to now knock on the door. Hearing a command to enter, Thorne followed the servant into a large bedroom. Thick curtains were pulled back from a bank of windows on the opposite wall, lighting the room well despite the overcast weather. Along the left wall was a bed with several blankets layered over it. Lying underneath all those covers was a young woman. Her blanched complexion and greasy hair were clear indicators of illness. Her eyes were wide open and starting blankly at the ceiling. Occasionally her breath came out as a wheeze, and when this happened an older woman sitting near her head wiped the girl's brow with a handkerchief. Near a small writing desk on the opposite wall stood Nion and a stern looking man.

Everyone, save the daughter, turned to watch Thorne and the servant enter. Nion's expression grew angry when he saw the mage. "Who sent for you? I did not." Nion demanded.

"I come from the Yaboon Archive with the council's blessing," Thorne said. He walked into the center of the room and turned around just in time to see the servant leave and shut the door behind her. He was about to address Nion's companion when the herbalist spoke first.

"The Archive council does not send unrequested aid," Nion

said, his hands in fists at his side.

"You told me yesterday that you have not been to an Archive in some time," Thorne said calmly. "Things change."

"Or you are a liar," Nion accused as he stabbed a finger at Thorne. "You said you are an Archive mage. Prove it."

Thorne reached into this satchel and retrieved his guilder. Holding it out to Nion, the mage said formally, "I am Thorne, Master mage from the capital."

Nion snatched the medallion from Thorne and inspected it closely. Turning it over in his hand, Nion scowled.

"What can you do to help my daughter?" the older woman sitting at the bed asked. Her voice sounded tired.

Taking back his guilder from Nion, Thorne turned to the woman. He smiled gently and said, "The Archive prepared a package of medicines that Nion and myself could use to aid the sick in town. I will use it to help your daughter, if you will allow me."

The governor's wife gave a vigorous nod and Thorne swung his satchel around to his front. Opening the catch and reaching inside, he pulled out the wooden box purchased from Nion's shop the previous day.

Nion took a glance at it and said, "That's from my shop, not the Archive. And it contains Argemone, which can help with pain, but it was ineffective as a treatment for her."

Thorne put the box on the nightstand and produced a second box from his satchel. "That may be true, but here are some more potent and rare ancillary herbs and extracts that were given to me by the Archive," he said.

Nion scoffed, and then replied, "Since when does the Archive dispense alchemic components? That's ridiculous!" He reached for the second box in Thorne's hands, but then seeing the patterns on the top of the box jerked his hands back to his chest. "Where did you get that?" Nion demanded.

Thorne didn't answer the question, but looked to the governor and said, "For reasons of security, the Archive thought it prudent for this one to have an arcane lock. I'm afraid only Nion can open it."

Seeing Nion hesitate too long the governor thundered, "What are you waiting for, Nion? Open the box!"

Thorne smirked when Nion realized he was trapped. Giving the mage a hateful glance, Nion reached out and placed his hand on top of the box. There was a faint hum followed by the sound of a latch clicking open. With a quick motion Thorne pulled the box to his chest and flipped open the lid. Inside the velvet lined container were a few vials of a hazy blue liquid that sloshed viscously when examined. There was also a thin leather-bound notebook and an Archive guilder on a silver chain.

Holding up one of the vials to the light Thorne guessed it was not any type of reagent that would help the young girl, so he lied. Looking at the governor Thorne said, "This looks like a potent restorative draught. It will need to be carefully diluted, but I don't think we have the alchemic apparatuses here. We will begin preparing it at once, but I want to first make sure your daughter will be able to rest more comfortably while we work."

Thorne moved to the girl's bedside and opened his satchel. He put Nion's box inside and slowly took out a small vial from his own chemistry kit. Removing the cork stopper, the mage let a few drops fall on the girl's lips. She instinctively licked the liquid and swallowed. After a moment her breathing slowed and became more relaxed. The pained look on her face eased and slowly closed her eyes in a restful sleep.

Seeing the effect of the mage's ministrations, the governor's wife let out an audible sigh of relief. "What did you give her?" she asked.

"Diluted Papaver leaf extract," Thorne said truthfully.

"Nion's shop did not have any yesterday when I inquired, but thankfully I was able to bring some from the Archive. I have only a limited quantity with me, but I think it will ease the suffering of the most ill in the city. It seems you only have one church, so I will give it to the shepherd to distribute as needed."

"Your aid is most welcome, Master Thorne," the governor's wife said to the mage. She reached out and touched his hand.

Before the mage could reply, Nion made an angry sound and swept out of the room. There was a soft exclamation in the hallway and a moment later a servant peeked her head inside. "Excuse me, your grace," the servant said. "The Master mage's companions are in the foyer."

"Very well," the governor said with a dismissive wave. The servant looked at Thorne, and the mage took the cue and followed her back to the manor entrance to meet his companions.

"Did you pass Nion on your way here?" Thorne asked Trinity once they all were together.

"We did, but he looked none too happy," Trinity replied. "What happened?"

"He opened the box from Rell-Kyr," the mage said.

"So, he is our man," Carlion said. Looking to the servant he asked, "Young miss, does Nion keep a residence here as your physician?"

"Indeed, he does," the servant said. "It's in the servant's quarters on the first floor. It's the corner room that looks out onto the garden. Perhaps you should go and speak with him. I found his behavior just now rather confusing. He is usually a more cordial man."

From outside there came a series of bells clanging. It was not the sonorous tolling that indicated the time, but was higher in pitch and the next strike sounded before the previous one had finished reverberating.

"Alarm bell!" Carlion exclaimed before darting out of the

manor. Thorne and the others gave chase and only caught up to Carlion because he had stopped the sentry from closing the manor gate.

"What the fuck is going on?" Amos asked the panicked guard as Carlion pushed the gate back open.

"We're being attacked!" the sentry said, not hiding the distress in his voice. "I need to close this gate!"

Rushing through the gate and into the streets of Deccern, Thorne saw people running for shelter. Two City Watchmen came from around the bend and were sprinting past when Carlion grabbed one and commanded, "Report, soldier!"

The man panted, "A B'nisct swarm is attacking the city barrier! They're in a frenzy, trying to scale it and break it down at the same time. Maybe twenty made it over before we could push the rest back down. They're running loose in the streets and cutting down anyone they can catch. I need to get to the guild district!" A scream punctuated the soldier's assessment, and he broke free of the Darkman's grip and ran towards it.

"The guild district? No!" Carlion said wide-eyed and took off sprinting after the soldier.

"Go after him," Thorne commanded Trinity. "And keep him out of trouble. I'll take care of the wall."

Thorne watched Trinity and Amos chase Carlion. Once the mercenaries had disappeared around the corner the mage turned and ran in the direction of the city wall.

CHAPTER TEN

CARLION

As he ran, Carlion's training took over and he tried to calculate battle logistics. With Deccern recovering from disease the number of fighting men would be lower than normal, which the Darkman had already seen when he entered the city the day prior. Deccern was wedged into a mountain and consequently the city had grown by building up instead of sprawling out. Racing past the closely packed multi-story buildings, Carlion knew that if one caught fire an entire block would be reduced to cinders in a matter of minutes.

Wheeling around a corner, Carlion saw a single B'nisct fighter hacking at the door of the butcher shop. Carlion pulled his sword free and stalked towards the fighter. The B'nisct spun to face Carlion and emitted a sound almost like speech, but with an unnatural buzzing quality. Whatever the fighter said was unintelligible to Carlion, but the savage axe swing that attempted to remove Carlion's head from his shoulders was a language that the Darkman instantly understood.

With the B'nisct fighter's next attack, Carlion found an opening to counter. The fighter tried to dash forward with an upward slash, but Carlion quickly dodged the whistling axe and stabbed his blade between a pair of armored chitin plates.

Quickly jerking his sword free, Carlion retreated a step and watched dark ichor spurt down the B'nisct fighter's carapace. The axe fell to the ground with a clatter, followed by the thump of the dead fighter.

Only taking enough time to make sure his adversary did not rise again, Carlion broke into a run down the street once more. The Darkman caught the faint smell of something burning, but couldn't tell where the scent had originated. As he approached Julia's house the tense fear he felt dissipated when he saw that the dwelling was thus far untouched. He skidded to a stop in front of her door and began pounding it with his fist. "Julia, Julia! It's Carlion! Open the door!" he shouted.

Julia opened the door and embraced Carlion. She pressed a closed fist into his back and Carlion pulled back from her and saw that she was tightly gripping a large kitchen knife. "Are you alright?" the Darkman asked.

Julia nodded and then asked, "What is going on?" She looked over his shoulder towards the sound of the alarm bells. "The City Watch alarm only sounds if we're under attack. Who is it?"

"A B'nisct swarm has breached the barrier wall," Carlion answered.

Still looking over Carlion's shoulder Julia sharply drew in her breath. The Darkman spun around and saw a pair of B'nisct fighters running down the street at them. They must have heard him shouting and were drawn to the noise. "Get inside and block the door!" he said pushing her though the doorway. Carlion then turned and ran to engage the two new enemies, trying to meet them well before the front of Julia's house.

The Darkman's charge took an angle where he would engage a B'nisct fighter that held a short sword. The other fighter wielded an axe and quickly pulled away from its comrade when it was clear whom Carlion was targeting. The sword bearing B'nisct braced for the charge while its companion began to circle and flank the Darkman. Jerking backwards, Carlion pulled from his advance and then lunged with his sword, using its longer reach to his advantage. The move took the B'nisct fighter by surprise but its parry deflected Carlion's sword enough to prevent a killing blow. The Darkman's blade slid along the fighter's armored flank, and as a consequence Carlion took a staggering step forward to regain his balance.

Instinctively, he swung his sword in a vertical arc at his side just as the second B'nisct fighter's axe came crashing down on him. The metal clang of sword against axe reverberated down the empty street, followed by the clatter of the blade as it was torn from Carlion's grasp and thrown to the ground. The heavy impact of the blow knocked the Darkman on his back. As Carlion looked up the B'nisct fighter filled his field of view. He expected the creature's buzzing speech to be the last thing he heard as the B'nisct raised its axe high, but was surprised instead to hear the sharp smack of something heavy hitting the fighter in the back. Stumbling forward and tripping over Carlion's body, the dying B'nisct fighter crashed to the ground and sprawled out next to him.

Carlion looked up just in time to see a pair of boots dash past him, followed by the sound of the second B'nisct shrieking in pain. Suddenly, rough hands pulled him up from behind to a sitting position and twisting around he saw Amos. Behind the Venhadar, Carlion saw the sword-bearing B'nisct fighter dead on the ground. Hemolymph from a deep wound filled the narrow channels between the paving stones of the street.

"What the fuck did you think you were doing?" Amos asked angrily. He reached up to his forehead and adjusted his cap to mop up the sweat above his eyebrows.

Slowly getting to his feet, Carlion looked over to Trinity. The mercenary snapped his sword hand down to flick the residual

B'nisct ichor off the blade. Keeping a firm grip on the weapon he asked Carlion, "Where is your head at, man?"

With the immediate danger past, Carlion realized that he needed an excuse for his seemingly strange behavior. However, before he got the chance a voice called out from across the street. The Darkman turned and saw Julia running out of her house to towards him. Ignoring the mercenaries, she flung her arms around him and pulled him close.

"Who's this?" Trinity asked with a sharp rise of his eyebrows. "Wait, was this what you wanted to talk about last night?"

"What is this about?" Amos asked. He stabbed a finger at Julia. "Who's she?"

"You remember what we were talking about when we first entered the city?" Carlion asked Amos. Without waiting for a reply, he continued, "Julia is the mother of my son. She's the daughter of an influential cavalier commander. When she wouldn't tell him who got her pregnant, she was sent here to live with her uncle. The whole scandal is what got me kicked out of the Sovereignty military."

"Why didn't you come here straight away?" Trinity asked.

"We were able to keep it secret for years," the Darkman replied. "The salary I got as a cavalier was passed along to her via the moneylender guild. We were also able to exchange letters." He looked at Julia with a guilty expression. He was now admitting things to her as much as Amos and Trinity. "Things took a sour turn when Julia's father finally found out I was the reason he had a bastard grandson. He got me cashiered and run out of Barnterc. I was so ashamed. I couldn't come here in disgrace, so I used the few friendly contacts I had left and was able to get accepted into the mercenary guild in Granick."

"We can talk about this later," Trinity interrupted. "We need to get back to the barrier wall and help Thorne."

"I'm staying here. You two go. I'll meet you at the Phoenix later," Carlion said.

Amos looked at Julia and then Carlion before he said simply, "Stay safe." The Venhadar then took off down the street with Trinity at his heels. The Darkman watched the mercenaries for a minute as they ran towards the city entrance before looking at Julia. "Where's Natty?" he asked as he ushered her back to her house.

"He's hiding in the cellar," she replied.

"Go join him. I'm going to keep watch up here. I'll call for you when it's safe," Carlion said.

Julia crossed the threshold and then turned around. "Is another of your mercenary companions at the barrier wall?" Julia asked

"No, it's actually our employer," Carlion said. "The mage I was telling you about last night went to reinforce the City Watch. He must have sent Amos and Trinity to come find me."

"You left a mage to face a B'nisct swarm?" Julia asked alarmed. "What can an academic do against those savages? He'll be killed for sure."

"It's not Thorne you need to be worrying about," Carlion said remembering how the mage had easily killed a pair of B'nisct on their way to Rell-Kyr. "Now please, go keep Natty safe," he added.

Julia nodded and closed the door. Carlion heard a table being pushed on the other side as Julia used it to make a barricade. The Darkman took a few steps into the street and retrieved his sword. As he did, he glanced at the bodies of the B'nisct fighters in the street. He had killed more than his share of men, but until today he had never killed a B'nisct. They were a frontier problem and never threatened cities along the major Sovereignty highways.

Returning to rest his back on Julia's door, Carlion noticed

again the sound of the alarm bell. He listened to it for what felt like a long time, but then it abruptly stopped. For some reason the Darkman could not explain, the silence felt ominous. He hoped that Trinity and Amos had gotten to the barrier wall in time.

CHAPTER ELEVEN

THORNE

Thorne scaled the stairs two at a time as he ascended to the fighting terrace of the barrier wall. When he reached the landing, the mage took a moment to assess the state of Deccern's defenses. There were a dozen archers shooting arrows down the wall, but their rate of fire was slow. Thorne surmised that these men were volunteer citizens acting as reserve troops and not regular City Watch. There were five additional soldiers with swords or spears shuffling between the archers to support them in case an attacker crested the wall. The bodies of several slain B'nisct fighters and city defenders had been pulled to the back of the terrace.

The center of activity was a soldier who looked the part and was barking orders over the clamor. "Fill in the gap at position three!" the man shouted. A sword-bearing soldier shuffled to the indicated position, but shrieked as a B'nisct fighter leapt atop the parapet next to him.

Thorne spread out his fingers and focused his Awareness on the breeze brushing past his palm. Feeling its weight, he pushed a column of air towards the B'nisct fighter with a burst of his mana. The fighter took the blow in the chest and tumbled off the wall with a surprised shriek.

The City Watchman whose life Thorne just saved flinched

backward and then looked at the source of the powerful wind gust. Seeing the mage he pointed and shouted, "A wizard!"

The soldier in command was instantly at Thorne's side, his expression intense. "Do you have something bigger up your sleeve so we can wipe these bastards out?" he grunted.

"Stay out of my way," Thorne said tersely as he took a position at the center of the battlement wall. Looking down the mage saw a writhing swarm of B'nisct fighters, each one trying to climb over its comrades in a race to ascend the wall. The fighters were using chitinous barbs that protruded from the underside of their wrists to dig into the mortar. On the ground were pairs of B'nisct with slings who were haphazardly firing stones at the top of the battlements.

Thorne sneered in disdain at the lack of sophistication to this assault. The swarm was simply trying to overwhelm the barrier wall with a brute force frontal attack. Placing both of his hands on the top of a crenel, Thorne focused his Awareness and pushed his arcane energy into the stone. The mage concentrated on keeping his body from sagging from exertion as his mana interfaced with the barrier wall. With a labored breath, Thorne finally felt the stone acquiesce to his command and become pliable. With his jaw set and perspiration beginning to bead on his forehead, the mage thrust his palms down and his hands sunk into the stone as if it were fresh clay. With shout that was magically amplified, Thorne commanded the barrier wall to become a weapon.

Instantly, a wave of stone spikes burst forth from the crenel and raced down the wall impaling B'nisct fighters along the way before being reabsorbed into the wall. After being impaled, the B'nisct fighters slid off the spikes and toppled down the wall and amassed in great heaps of gruesome corpses. The spikes then burst forth on the ground just before the wall, impaling the already dead attackers a second time, but also shredding the feet and legs of any B'nisct fighter that had not started their ascent. These non-lethal wounds elicited sharp buzzing noises from the B'nisct fighters, who then scrambled away from the wall and retreated back down the mountain.

At the sounds of his enemies' screams, a vicious smile appeared on Thorne's face. As he grew older the mage had been able to check his violent impulses, but at rare times like this he reveled in the carnage he was capable of creating. However, Thorne knew not to let his reach exceed his grasp now that he was no longer needed here for defense of the wall.

Taking a slow and cleansing breath, Thorne pulled his mana from the barrier wall. While this wasn't required, as over time the mage's arcane energy would slowly regenerate, it would speed along his recuperation after such a taxing exertion of his Awareness.

Feeling slightly less fatigued, Thorne looked back along the wall and finally noticed the eerie silence upon the battlements. The alarm bell had stopped tolling. Thorne looked to see the sentry who was ringing it now staring at the killing field with his mouth agape in disbelief. The mage saw all of the gathered City Watch, the solider in commander included, staring at him at a loss for words. He had wiped out almost an entire B'nisct swarm in a single frighteningly powerful display of magic.

Pulling his hands from the impression in the stone, Thorne turned towards the captain. "Finish it," the mage said brusquely as he walked past.

"There are barely any left," the solider said astonished. "And they're fleeing. There's nothing to finish. How did you do that with the wall?"

Thorne did not respond as he quickly descended the barrier wall stairs, now uncomfortable with the gawking looks from the city's defenders. As his blood cooled Thorne was able to return his thoughts back to his morning confrontation with Nion at the governor's manor. The mage turned onto the main road and was walking to the Phoenix tavern when a familiar shout from a side street made him stop. He saw Amos and Trinity hurrying to join him at the intersection.

"The alarm bell stopped and you're not at the wall, so I take it things are well in hand?" Trinity asked when he stopped in front of the mage.

Thorne nodded and replied, "The wall is secure." Looking past the mercenaries and down the street he asked, "What took you so long to get here?"

Amos held up his mace, which still dripped with B'nisct hemolymph. "Just mopping up," the Venhadar said.

"I'm sure the City Watch will be appreciative," Thorne said. The mage then realized that Carlion was not with them and creased his brow. "Where's the Darkman?" he asked.

"About that," Trinity began. The mercenary told Thorne the secret Carlion had been hiding from them about Julia and his bastard son.

"Only the young," Thorne sighed in disappointment after Trinity finished. Shaking his head he said, "That's a distraction, and we need to focus on Nion. Go back to the governor's manor and make sure he's still there. I don't want to have to go searching for him if the City Watch is going to increase patrols to find any stray B'nisct fighters."

"What about Carlion?" Trinity asked. "He's standing guard outside of Julia's house. Should we just leave him there for the time being?"

"No," the mage replied. "After you find Nion, then go collect the Darkman. I want to know if this is going to further complicate things."

"That's fine, but where are you going now?" Amos asked.

"Back to the Phoenix," Thorne said. He patted his satchel and continued, "I want to examine some of the items from

Nion's lockbox now that it's opened. I'll meet you in the tavern for dinner and we can plan our next move."

Thorne parted with the mercenaries and walked quickly back to his room at the tavern. The mage opened the shutters and sat on the floor in a slanted patch of sunlight. He shivered as what little warmth fled out the window, but was too eager to examine Nion's belongings to start a fire in the stove.

Pulling the box from his satchel, Thorne opened it and carefully laid its contents out on the floor in front of him. He would have to wait until he was back at the Archive to determine the contents of the vials. Picking up the guilder, Thorne looked along the thick edge for the identifying marks that were cut into each medallion when presented to a Master mage. Near the small loop that held the silver chain Thorne found stamped into the metal a date and the name *Erza Uffani*.

The mage set the Archive guilder back on the floor and picked up a small leather notebook and turned it in his hands. Thorne's fingers got the same faint tingling sensation as when he handled Nion's lockbox in Rell-Kyr. The journal had an arcane lock on it as well, which the mage confirmed by a series of unsuccessful attempts to physically unbuckle the strap that bound the front and back covers. Nion must have wanted to be extra cautious with the contents of the journal if he sealed both the book and the lockbox.

Thorne was thankful at this point that he had taken a few extra moments to retrieve his mana from the barrier wall. If he had not, then he would have needed to rest and eat a hearty meal to have the strength to force the sealed book open. However, even in a fatigued state the mage knew the seal, like that on the box, was weak. Nion was only partially Aware and his enchantments didn't have significant mana bound to them.

There were more subtle ways to pick an arcane lock, but Thorne was impatient. Disdainful of Nion's ability to secure his belongings, the mage prepared to force the book open. He placed his palm flat over the buckle of the journal. Thorne felt a prickling across his hand as the mana Nion had pushed into the book reacted violently against the mage's competing arcane energy. With a grunt Thorne shoved a wedge of his mana into the lock, which ruptured it. The sensation felt like a soap bubble bursting against his skin.

The journal flopped open and Thorne began scanning the pages. Early entries were about various tasks that Nion had to complete under Erza's tutelage. It wasn't uncommon for mages to keep journals to reflect upon their work as they progressed through their training, however Nion's effusive praise and naïve excitement for Erza as a mentor was embarrassing to read. Flipping to the end Thorne found that the last two entries were from several months ago. The short sentences seemed to be written in staccato bursts and were of a completely different tone. He read a curious passage about Nion charging several stones taken from Rell-Kyr and then shipping them south to an unnamed destination. The next passage Thorne read made his eyes widen in shock.

"It is done. Erza is in the Void and unlikely to survive in such a crippled state. U and R said they were pleased and would contact me again soon."

The final journal entry was longer and more plaintive. One particular passage that caught Thorne's notice read, "It has been some time since U has contacted me. I sent what R asked for, but I have not gotten a reply as to my request. I am growing restless and now believe this conspiracy is leading nowhere."

Closing the book, Thorne took a deep breath. He had found out the fate of Erza, and while not technically part of the internal bounty, the mage felt duty-bound to bring her apprentice back to Yaboon for further interrogation. Not forgetting that regaining access to his laboratory was his primary objective, Thorne now also felt that he had stumbled onto something more ominous. Why did Ulrich feel the need to rebrand himself Nion when he came to Deccern? Who were the other conspirators only known by the initials U and R? He sat on the floor deep in thought as the sunshine on the floor shifted across the room, and then eventually faded as night approached.

• • •

When Thorne entered the Phoenix tavern that evening it was nearly full with townsfolk celebrating the successful defense of the city. The mood of the room was upbeat but still felt reserved, no doubt due to the aftermath of the city still recovering from disease. Nevertheless, repelling the B'nisct swarm had buoyed the spirits of some of the town's miners and City Watch, and they had come out to drink and make merry.

Thorne found the mercenaries at a table near the bar and slid into the empty chair flanked by Trinity and Amos. The men had already been served drinks, in Amos' case several, and were conversing but stopped abruptly when they saw Thorne's grim expression directed at Carlion.

"Glad you could join us," the mage said, but his voice had little warmth.

Before the Darkman could say anything a young Venhadar male approached the table. "Can I get you four some food now?" he asked warily. Thorne couldn't tell if the server's timidness was from something said to him by his companions earlier or if his exploits on the barrier wall made some of the Deccern residents fearful.

"Yes," Thorne answered. "And another round of whatever is in their cups. I'll just have water." The mage pulled out some coins from a pocket and asked, "How much?"

"Um, six ducats," the Venhadar replied, nervously watching the mage's hand.

Thorne thumbed the coins onto the table and they rested there a moment before the server hesitantly collected them and quickly left for the kitchen. The mage then retrieved Nion's journal from his pocket and placed it in the center of the table. "Erza is dead," he said flatly. "Nion killed her."

"It says that in there?" Trinity asked. "He was foolhardy enough to write a confession?"

"Not in so many words," Thorne replied, "But more than enough to implicate himself in her disappearance."

Trinity took the book and scanned the last few pages. Putting it down, he looked at Thorne and said, "Sounds vague, but definitely suspicious. Who are the letters U and R referring to?"

"I don't know," the mage admitted. "What I do know is that we need to take him back to Yaboon. If he killed Erza, then he's a liability to the Archive and potentially dangerous to the people of Deccern."

The Venhadar returned to the table balancing four large bowls on his arms. He deftly placed them in front of everyone and then dug wooden spoons out of his pocket. Without another word he made another hurried retreat.

"He didn't bring our drinks," Amos complained.

"He might come back," Trinity said, but didn't sound hopeful.

Thorne picked up his spoon and peered inside the bowl. It was some sort of brown stew. He could see what looked like carrots and potatoes, maybe some onions, but the meat was a mystery. However, judging by the satisfied slurps coming from Amos, it must have been something good. With his mind still mulling over the contents of Nion's journal, Thorne began mechanically shoveling food into his mouth.

"You're eating this like you can't taste it," Carlion eventually said to the mage.

"He can't," Trinity replied.

"What?" Carlion said confused.

"It's one of the prices paid for being able to use magic," Trinity said looking at Thorne, who hadn't stopped eating. "Single instances of strong magic or using weaker powers for sustained periods of time damages a mage's body. Eventually their nerves give out and every mage starts to lose their senses."

"That's insane! Why would you willingly cripple yourself?" Carlion asked astonished.

"You heard what he did on the barrier wall," Trinity said. "That's why."

"Is the power you gained worth more than what you lost?" the Darkman asked, lowering his head in an attempt to establish eye contact with the mage.

"For certain," Thorne replied between bites.

Carlion leaned back in his chair and ate the remainder of his dinner in silence, though at times he cast questioning glances in the mage's direction. Thorne ignored him and finished eating, as did Amos and Trinity.

"Even if apprehending him is the right move, I doubt Nion will come quietly," the mercenary finally said, pushing his empty bowl to the center of the table. "And given his reputation as a healer, I imagine the governor won't be too keen on relinquishing him either. When we went back to the manor we were kept in the foyer, but a servant told us that Nion hadn't left his room. I got the impression that he wasn't going anywhere."

"Then we'll have to extract him," Thorne said.

Amos swallowed his beer with a grunt, and then said. "Kidnapping a grown man, and a wizard no less?"

Thorne looked at Amos and replied evenly, "His Awareness is weak, so that won't be a problem. Not getting caught while taking him from the manor will be the challenge."

Amos frowned and replied, "What about the town? It

sounded like the church is ill equipped to handle whatever disease is being passed around here, even if it is in decline."

The mage shook his head. "The faster we get Nion back to the Archive, the faster I can dispatch someone here, a real healer who is fully Aware and not dependent on herb lore," he said. "In my opinion, the town will be ridding themselves of a charlatan and getting something of real value."

Carlion had been silent up until this point, but Thorne could see him grow increasingly agitated. Finally, the Darkman blurted out, "You can't do this!"

Thorne glared at Carlion's outburst.

"I made a promise that you wouldn't take Nion from the town," Carlion continued. "Look, you found Nion. He might have done something unscrupulous, but Deccern needs him right now. You should return to Yaboon, report what you know, and then come back here with another mage. Then you can take him into custody if that's what has to happen." The Darkman straightened in his seat as if struck by an idea. He said quickly, "I will stay here and keep an eye on him."

"Unacceptable," Thorne said with a shake of his head. "We need to act now. The council needs to know about Erza's fate and Nion's involvement immediately." The mage didn't add his very personal reasons for why such haste was required.

"Why? How can it be more important than what is going on here?" Carlion said angrily. Crossing his arms across his chest, he growled at the mage, "I won't let you do this."

Thorne's eyes grew hard as he leaned across the table. "You can't stop me," he said slowly.

Carlion looked down at his hand and made a show of the steel ring. "I think I can," he said menacingly.

"Hold it a minute, mates," Amos said trying to ease the tension between the two men. Looking at Carlion he said, "If you want to stay here with your family, that's all well and good. But

I still want to get paid, and Trinity and me have guilders that we value."

"We'd get this done a whole lot faster if you helped us," Trinity offered. "If we push the pace we can be back to the capital in four or five days and you'll be back here in not quite two weeks. You've made her wait years, what is a few more days?" Looking at Thorne, the mercenary asked, "Do you have a plan to apprehend Nion?"

The mage nodded. "We're taking advantage of tonight's revelry. We're getting him and leaving tonight, so Amos stop drinking after that one."

Carlion remained silent, and it was clear to everyone at the table that the Darkman was weighing his options, considering the consequences trying to stop the mage versus breaking his promise to Julia. Carlion's features hardened in angry resignation as he shoved his bowl to the center of the table. He stood up and looked down at Thorne. "Come with me. I want you there when I say good-bye. I want you to have to look her in the eye and tell her that you aren't dooming the town."

Thorne slowly stood up. "Lead the way," he said.

CHAPTER TWELVE

CARLION

Leaving the Phoenix, Carlion had the impulse to knock out Thorne on their way to Julia's house, but thought better of it. Part of him didn't want to have to explain any incident to Trinity and Amos, and although he didn't want to admit it, part of him was afraid that he wouldn't succeed. While Carlion's ring had injured the mage's hand, it could not be denied that Thorne was immensely powerful. Walking down the street in an unfriendly silence, Carlion hoped that Thorne would change his current course of action when Julia confronted him. Perhaps she would be able to succeed where he failed.

Once they arrived, Carlion quickly knocked on Julia's door. A few seconds later Natty threw it open. The boy must have been sitting close by, waiting for his father to arrive. Looking at the dour man next to Carlion, Natty asked bluntly, "Who are you?"

"Stop blocking the door Natty, and let your father get in out of the cold," came Julia's voice from inside the house. She stepped into view and her smile vanished upon seeing the mage. "Hello," she said without warmth. "Carlion, who is this?"

"Let's talk inside," Carlion said as he stepped over the threshold. Thorne followed silently and closed the door behind him. Once everyone was seated at the table Carlion said, "This is Thorne, he's the wizard from the capital that hired me as a part of a mercenary crew."

"And what are you doing here, exactly?" Julia asked Thorne in an accusatory tone.

Thorne appeared to be unfazed by her direct manner and replied, "An inquiry into Nion. He was the apprentice of a prominent alchemist," he emphasized the last word and looked at Carlion pointedly before continuing, "who had gone missing. I am investigating what happened."

"I don't know anything about that," Julia said just as intensely as before. "What I do know is that Nion has been a blessing to Deccern since he arrived."

"That may well be, but he is also a murderer," Thorne said.

"So you say, Master Thorne," Julia replied. She looked to Carlion with an expression indicating she wanted him to speak up and support her. The Darkman did not respond quickly enough and Julia scoffed before saying, "I assume you have some strong evidence for this alleged crime?"

Thorne inclined his head in an affirmative. "Yes, and I need to bring him back to the capital immediately."

"But he's helping all the sick people in the town," Natty said confused.

"Maybe not as much as everyone thinks, Natty," Carlion said, finally finding his voice. By the look of derision that Julia gave him, it wasn't what she wanted to hear.

Julia shifted her disapproving look to Thorne. "Even if what you say is true, it doesn't need to involve Carlion," she said. "Leave with Nion if you have to, but let Carlion stay here. Release him from the guild contract. You don't even have to pay him for the work he's done."

"It's not that simple," Thorne said. He rested his arms on the table and continued, "The governor has no doubt by now found out that I brought mercenaries with me and that Carlion is working for me. If I take Nion without the governor's permission and Carlion stays, then he'll be arrested. I don't know what type of man the governor purports to be, but I can imagine he won't be kind, given that Nion was the personal physician to his daughter. To keep Carlion safe he needs to come with me."

"Thorne has assured me the Archive will send another healer to Deccern as soon as we return," Carlion said. Carlion knew that any more of Julia's entreaties would fall on deaf ears. Thorne wasn't going to change his mind. Trying to salvage something positive from the conversation he said, "I will probably be the one to escort him here. As soon as Nion has been delivered to the capital, I'll return to you in haste."

"Do you promise?" Natty asked, sounding hopeful.

"Yes, I won't let us be apart again," Carlion said, smiling at the boy.

"I suppose that is the best we can hope for now," Julia said resentfully. "When will you arrest him?"

"As soon as we have access to the governor's estate," Thorne said.

Carlion silently appreciated the mage's clever wordplay. Standing he looked at the mage and said, "Thorne, why don't you go back to the Phoenix and make sure the others are prepared. I'll meet you there shortly."

Thorne stood up and tried to look accommodating. "Of course," the mage said and turned towards the door.

It was just for an instant, but Carlion saw an unexpected expression on the mage's face as he left. As the mage reached back to close the door after his exit, Carlion glimpsed the mage's composed features shift to reveal a profound sadness. When the door closed and Thorne was gone, the Darkman turned back to his family.

Julia looked to Carlion and sighed. "You're not making it

easy for us," she said, shaking her head.

"A healer that has the full support of the Archive is going to be more of an asset to the town than Nion," Carlion replied. He stood up and took Julia's hands into his and said, "I've got assurances from Thorne that he has enough influence at the Archive to dispatch someone to come back with me. I'm sure the governor will forgive all when he realizes what he's gotten in exchange for Nion. I'll be back next week. I promise."

"Don't say that if you can't keep it," Julia warned, but squeezed his hand before wrapping her arms around him. "Travel safe."

"Is Papa leaving again?" Natty asked as he watched his parents.

Julia looked at the boy and smiled. "He's just going to finish his work for the wizard and then come right back home," she said.

"I need you to take care of your Mum while I'm gone," Carlion said, resting his hand on the boy's shoulder. Not wanting to draw out the farewell, Carlion gave Julia a kiss and then left the house. The cold night air stung his face and he resisted the urge to look back as he quickly walked away.

Carlion was a few houses down the street when he felt he was being followed. The Darkman turned around and saw Thorne walking casually towards him. "Didn't trust that I'd go back?" Carlion asked cynically when the mage stopped in front of him.

"We're on a tight timetable," Thorne said. "Just wanted to make sure you didn't take too long."

Falling in step with the mage Carlion said, "That was quick thinking about the governor's retaliation. I hadn't thought of that before."

"I know," the mage said in a clipped manner. Carlion glanced over and caught a strange look on Thorne's face. What was it that he saw? Grief, anger, loneliness, it was hard to tell in the dim lamplight, but something was weighing heavy on the mage's mind.

"What's your problem? You're getting what you want," Carlion asked irritated.

"Broken families," Thorne said as if the two words were a complete explanation. Before the Darkman could ask more Thorne pulled his hood over his head to hide his face. Thinking it best not to provoke the mage anymore tonight, Carlion said no more and they walked back to the Phoenix with only the sounds of Deccern falling asleep to fill the silence.

CHAPTER THIRTEEN

THORNE

Thorne tried to stand and stretch from his crouching position only to have Trinity's hand roughly pull him back down. The mage gave the mercenary a sharp look that went ignored as he rocked on his haunches. Thorne, Trinity, and Carlion had been hiding near the wall of the governor's manor on the southern edge of the garden for two hours, waiting for the light in Nion's room to go out. The city tower had just rung out eleven low bells and the mage was growing restless.

Surprisingly, there were only a few City Watch patrols in the streets so the mage reasoned that all of the B'nisct that had made it over the wall had been killed. Coupled with much of the city in celebration at the successful defense of the barrier wall, it was relatively easy to skirt detection on their way to the governor's manor. The iron fence that formed a perimeter around the estate was no trouble for the mercenaries to scale, but Thorne had to be more careful. He had used his blanket to carefully cover the iron bars as he climbed over. Now, the three men hid behind a pair of ornately trimmed shrubs that were near a decorative fountain in the garden.

"Quit moving," Trinity whispered without taking his eyes off the window to Nion's room. The mercenary had been scanning the area in front of them for the past hour trying to find the optimal approach to the window that would keep him in the shadows. There were shrubs lining the entire manor, which would make gaining entry a challenge. A servant with a hound had made a regular circuit around the grounds, but the timing was not uniform and Trinity had been trying to determine if there was any pattern to the patrol.

"Finally," the mercenary thrust his chin in the direction of herbalist's window. Nion was pulling the thick velvet drapes closed after he checked the latch on the window. It was not long before the light that bled around the drapes was extinguished and the window was left completely dark.

After waiting for the next patrol to pass Trinity pulled a dagger from his belt and handed it to Thorne handle first. Wearing a thick leather glove, the mage took the handle carefully and poured a few drops from a tiny bottle onto the blade.

Letting the liquid slide down to the tip before handing it back to Trinity, Thorne said, "You have to move quickly. The toxin is only effective while the blade is still wet."

Taking the dagger back from Thorne, Trinity asked sarcastically, "You think I'm going sightseeing first?"

Without waiting for a reply, Trinity dashed in a low crouch to the window and slid silently behind a bush. The mercenary was obscured from view momentarily, but then Thorne saw Trinity reach up and deftly slide a rigid wire under the frame of the window that released the latch. With one hand the mercenary opened the window and pulled himself up onto the ledge. He sat couched there a moment while he carefully pulled the velvet curtains back a few inches to peer inside. With a look back in the direction of Thorne and Carlion, Trinity gave a little wave and then disappeared underneath the curtain. A few minutes later Trinity came back to the window, pulled open the curtain, and made a beckoning gesture.

"Go," Thorne commanded Carlion.

The Darkman quickly approached the window and only had to wait a few seconds before Trinity set a body-shaped parcel on the window ledge. The mercenary had wrapped Nion up in a bed sheet, and rolled him out the window into Carlion's waiting arms. Trinity pulled the window shut as he climbed down and closed the shutters. It would be hard to tell that Nion's room had been breached from the outside, at least until daylight.

A bit more slowly than before given the cargo they now carried, Trinity and Carlion moved carefully across the lawn to rejoin the mage behind the fountain. The Darkman had slung the herbalist over his shoulder like a sack of grain and now propped the bundle against a shrub. Thorne pulled the sheet down just enough to expose Nion's head. Trinity only nicked Nion near the base of his neck, which was all that was needed for the toxin to work, but the touch of iron on the herbalist's skin left a burn that had blossomed into angry black veins that spread out several inches round the small cut. Despite his incomplete Awareness, Nion was still susceptible to the iron toxicity that afflicted all arcane practitioners.

"He won't wake up?" Carlion asked softly.

Thorne pulled the sheet over Nion's head after making sure the herbalist was breathing regularly. The mage shook his head and replied, "Not for at least half a day, unless I administer an antidote. Now we just need to get out of here and meet up with Amos."

"Quiet!" Trinity whispered and pointed in the direction of Nion's window. The servant and hound on patrol were searching the area and the dog was sniffing and growling. Suddenly, the hound let out a series of loud barks and began to strain on the leash in the direction of the fountain.

"What did the dog find?" a voice shouted. From the front of the house a City Watchman that was guarding the manor gate approached the servant with his lantern held high. The servant said something, but it could not be heard over the baying of the hound. The City Watchman pointed at the front of the house and the servant handed over the leash to the guard and left. The sentry drew his sword and held it and the leash in one hand while holding the lantern in the other. Pulling back on the leash, the guard followed the aggressive hound into the garden.

Trinity looked at Thorne, "I'll distract them. Go out the front gate. Wait for me at the last switchback before you can see the city from the road." He dashed along the wall away from them. Carlion and Thorne lost sight of the mercenary as he slipped around the side of the manor. The dog caught the movement and jerked the City Watchman after Trinity, barking loudly.

"Go!" commanded Thorne and ran towards the front gate without looking back to see if Carlion was following. At the now unguarded front gate, Thorne quickly examined the lock as the Darkman caught up to him.

Carlion set Nion against the wall to the right of the gate. "Quickly," the Darkman said, "magic that lock open."

Thorne shook his head while digging in his satchel. "It's an iron lock, so unless you want an explosion I can't use my Awareness. But I have another solution." He pulled out a small vial and unstopped it.

When Carlion's nostrils filled with a sharp scent he jerked back a step. "I recognize that smell!" he exclaimed.

The mage rapped a gloved knuckle on Carlion's chest, his tabard and cloak muffling the sound against his breastplate. "You should," Thorne said. "Acidum salis is the primary component of the solvent used to raze the decorations on armor."

Wearing his leather glove again, the mage carefully poured the caustic liquid into the keyhole, and then stepped quickly back as a hiss of steam and a jet of heat erupted from the opening. It only took a few seconds for the concentrated acid to dissolve the inner mechanism of the lock. With a rough shove, Thorne forced the gate open. With their human cargo, the two men walked down the street towards the barrier wall.

They found Amos in the guardhouse near the main gate standing over a sentry slumped on the floor with a cup still in his hand. Amos gave Thorne a dirty look when they entered the shack. "I fucking hate that Papaver extract," the Venhadar said. "I thought I had killed the poor sod for a while."

"I'm sure you would have gotten over it," Thorne said callously. "Open the door."

"Where's Trinity?" Amos asked as he unbolted the heavy door and pushed it open.

"Buying us some time," Thorne said. "Things didn't go as smoothly as I wanted, and he's going to meet us down the road." Thorne then looked at Carlion and pointed at the drugged guard. "Strip him," the mage said. "We need his boots, trousers, shirt, and cloak."

"What for?" Carlion asked.

"Unless you plan on carrying Nion the whole trip back, the old man is going to need clothes and shoes if he's going to walk with us," Thorne said. "Under that sheet he's only wearing a nightgown."

"What about the guard?" Carlion asked.

"Roll him close to the stove," the mage replied. "Someone will find him in an hour."

Thorne could tell Carlion found the task distasteful, but the Darkman issued no further complaint. While Carlion was taking the unfortunate City Watchman's clothes, Amos had slung Nion over his shoulder and taken him outside. Carlion was next to leave the city, while Thorne lagged behind to complete one last task to help cover their escape.

Thorne tied a plait of braided paper to the bolt handle that locked the heavy door. The makeshift rope wrapped around the door as Thorne closed it, but still could be moved easily due to the gap between the doorjamb cut into the barrier wall. When the door closed the mage slowly pulled the braided paper rope tight. He felt the bolt slide into place and secure the door. Laying the paper plait against the door, Thorne then put on his leather gloves again before taking thick rings of flint and steel from his satchel.

"You can't make fire with magic?" Carlion asked, watching the mage fling sparks at the paper.

"No mage can," Thorne answered. Finally the flint threw a spark that landed squarely on the paper and ignited it. The mage then reached out his hand and nearly grabbed the flame and felt the heat on his palm. He charged his fingers with mana and began to manipulate the space around the burning paper. Carefully guiding the flame up the paper rope, Thorne burned it completely until he felt the flame puff out on the opposite side of the door when it ran out of material to burn. "We can only indirectly control fire that already exists," Thorne said before turning away from the door.

After a cursory inspection of the city wall battlements from their vantage point on the ground and finding them to be bereft of City Watchmen, Thorne led Carlion and Amos down the road leaving the city. The nearly full moon shone brightly on the path and made navigation easy. The mage was more than a little surprised when Trinity called out from behind an outcropping of rocks well before they reached the rendezvous point.

"What kept you?" the mercenary asked as he joined the group.

"How did you get out of the city ahead of us?" Thorne asked, impressed.

"More importantly, are you hurt, mate? You're covered in blood," Amos said as he pointed at the dark stains that stood out sharply on Trinity's clothes.

"It's not blood. It's hemolymph from a mess of B'nisct," Trinity said. "I ran to the top of the barrier wall and then jumped over."

"The fall would have killed you," Carlion said.

"I looked before I leapt," Trinity replied. "There was a massive pile of dead B'nisct fighters at the base of the wall. I didn't have to drop very far before I hit something relatively soft. You left one hell of a body count today, Thorne."

"It'll give the City Watch something to do tomorrow instead of look for us," Thorne said.

Carlion grunted, "Let's go. Nion's not getting any lighter."

Trinity looked at Thorne, "Wake him up and make him walk."

The mage shook his head and replied, "If he stays unconscious he's not a flight risk. I'll rouse him at daybreak when we've put some distance between Deccern and us. I suspect that twelve low bells will be rung soon, so you'll only have to carry him a few hours."

"What if Nion had been fat?" Carlion asked Thorne as he began to lead the descent down the mountain.

"Then I would have gotten you a wheelbarrow," Thorne said dryly.

• • •

Dawn was on the horizon when Thorne stopped the group and told Carlion to put Nion down. It was time to wake the herbalist so he could walk under his own power. They were far away enough from Deccern that Thorne thought it was safe to march their captive to the capital. He could also tell that Carlion was starting to fatigue from carrying the herbalist, but Thorne was impressed with the Darkman's strength. He had carried Nion for several hours without complaint and at only a slightly slower pace than the rest of the group.

Carlion propped Nion against a sickly-looking tree and quickly dressed the herbalist in the clothes stolen from the City Watchman. He then bound Nion's hands behind his back before pouring the sour smelling contents from an ampule that Thorne handed him down the herbalist's throat. Nion's eyes slowly opened and focused on the Darkman in front of him. The herbalist tried to rise only to be shoved back down.

"What is the meaning of this?" demanded Nion.

Carlion backed away and Thorne squatted down next to Nion. "You!" the herbalist exclaimed. "What are you doing?"

Thorne reached into one of his pockets and retrieved Nion's leather bound journal. The mage opened the book and showed Nion the final page before closing it again and putting the book away.

"What was this last entry in relation to?" Thorne asked. Seeing the shocked expression from Nion, Thorne said, "Your protection wards are not very powerful."

"Then why make me open the box at the governor's manor? Why the spectacle?" Nion asked sullenly. "You could have forced it open at will. Did you enjoy my humiliation?"

"Not at all," Thorne answered. "I needed to confirm that the box belonged to you. It is a bold accusation to say you were Erza's apprentice, given the time that has passed."

"Was that the whole point, then?" Nion asked. The herbalist continued condescendingly, "Come to fetch me for the council? Not good to have a rogue mage running around, right? That would look bad if it became common knowledge. Can't afford to lose any political capital with the guilds or Sovereignty, yes? Took you long enough to find me."

Ignoring Nion's goading, Thorne asked, "Who are the people you mentioned? U and R?"

At the mention of the letters, Nion bared his teeth in disgust. "They're the reason I had to leave Rell-Kyr. The construct they sent crashed out of my shop before vaporizing itself along with a chunk of the town's wall. I'm sure you saw the damage and what repairs have been done when you were there."

"Construct?" Thorne said confused. "The townsfolk said it was an B'nisct raid."

"Because that's what I told them," Nion said. "It was sent in the middle of the night so no one saw what really happened, but it would only be a matter of time before someone found the damage was inconsistent with a B'nisct attack. Before anyone could start asking questions I decided it was time to leave."

"Never mind that," Thorne said. "How did a construct get into the town without anyone noticing?"

Nion smirked, "Magic."

"Being evasive won't help you," Thorne said with increasing agitation. He stood up and spat out a series of questions in rapid succession, "Who are these other people? What are you doing? Why did you kill Erza?"

"Just because you caught me doesn't mean you can stop what is happening," Nion said looking up at the mage with an unpleasant smile.

At this point Trinity rested a hand on Thorne's shoulder. "We need to keep moving," the mercenary said. "You'll be much more effective at getting information out of him when you are back at the Archive."

Thorne glanced at Trinity and gave him a short nod in acknowledgement. Frustrating as it was, the mercenary was right. Trying to extract a confession from Nion now, especially by force, was a bad idea. They didn't know if there was any pursuit from Deccern, or if any well-meaning travelers passing by would try to intervene. It was best to get back to the Archive as fast as possible.

Thorne pulled Nion to his feet. "Start walking," the mage said.

CHAPTER FOURTEEN

CARLION

The march back to the capital was thankfully uneventful and Nion was a docile prisoner, though the herbalist had little choice given that Carlion walked a step behind him with his sword drawn the entire time. Despite his best efforts to keep the grim face of a professional mercenary, Carlion couldn't help feeling an anticipatory excitement as they passed through the Yaboon main gate and walked up the street that led to the Archive. He had seen the Archive from a distance many times, but as he drew nearer to the sprawling two-story brick building Carlion wondered what he was going to find inside.

A few strides from the large wooden double door of the Archive, Thorne stopped and turned to address the group. Holding up his hand to shield his eyes from the midmorning sun the mage said, "If you're coming inside with me, then you'll need to leave any iron you have outside."

"What for?" Carlion asked, instinctively gripping his sword tighter.

"All the outer doorways of the Archive are lined with alchemically enhanced lodestone," Thorne said. "Anyone wearing steel armor would get stuck to the wall or have their sword ripped from their hand."

"Clever anti-infantry defense," Carlion said impressed. "Does the Sovereignty know about this little trick?"

"I would imagine so," Thorne replied. "The Archives are open to anyone for study. That being said, it would not surprise me if the rank and file are ignorant of what is common knowledge elsewhere."

"I'll take our gear back to the guild," Amos offered quickly before Carlion could respond to the oblique insult. "Maybe have a rest while I'm at it."

Carlion grinned as he looked down at the Venhadar. Amos wasn't fond of the open road. The former corsair was much more comfortable in the city, particularly a crowded tavern. Carlion suspected that Amos would drop their belongings at the guild, then immediately go to his favorite bar and relax, eat, and drink until the money in his pockets was gone.

Keeping watch on Nion out of the corner of his eye, Carlion returned his blade to its scabbard and unbuckled his belt. He released the clasps on his shoulders and pulled his cuirass over his head. Wrapping the belt around his armor, Carlion pushed the bundle into Amos' outstretched arms. The Darkman then looked at his hand and with more than a little reluctance pulled off his steel ring and placed it into Amos' waiting palm.

After Amos collected Trinity's weapons and iron-containing gear, the Venhadar slowly walked away from the Archive and back towards the mercenary guild. After watching Amos depart for a minute, Carlion then rested a firm hand on Nion's shoulder and guided him to the Archive entrance behind Thorne. The herbalist was still bound and gagged, but had otherwise been treated well on the journey. He didn't appear particularly concerned as they passed through the doorway. Carlion wasn't sure if it was a trick of his imagination or something authentic, but he thought he felt a tingling sensation through his body as he entered the Archive.

The Darkman took in his surroundings as they walked slowly into the main atrium of the building. There was little difference in the trappings here than with what he would see in a Sovereignty great hall. The only thing that seemed out of place was the faint odor of burned varnish. The people that he saw walking through the atrium were also dressed in common fashion, with only one or two people wearing what he would have considered wizard robes. Carlion was a little disappointed to find that after the years of lectures from his superiors about the strange and dangerous people at the Archives, the truth was much more mundane.

A dignified woman with short grey hair stepped around a large lectern situated along the wall opposite the entrance and approached them. Her expression grew wary when she saw the state that Nion was in, but before she could say anything Thorne quickly stepped up and intercepted her. The mage whispered in her ear, and after hearing what Thorne said the woman drew back in shock and her gaze darted between Thorne and Nion.

"I just spoke with his apprentice so I know that councilor Tarbeck is currently in his study. He will want you to report immediately," the woman said. "Your companions can wait here."

Thorne turned to the mercenaries and said, "You can either wait here or go back to the guild."

"I'm not leaving until you get Deccern another healer," Carlion replied.

"Fine," the mage said with dismissive shrug. Grabbing Nion's arm, Thorne ushered the herbalist down a hallway with the woman.

Once they were alone, Trinity asked, "Are you really going to wait until he comes back?"

"You have a longer history with him so I can understand where your trust comes from," Carlion said, still watching the hallway. "I've been working for him less than a week and he's broken into a shop under cover of night, drugged two innocent men, and kidnapped the only physician from a frontier city." The Darkman turned and looked at Trinity with a furrowed brow and a frown. "He may be your friend, but his actions haven't done much to argue against the rumors whispered at the Sovereignty court."

"He also single-handedly defended Deccern from a B'nisct swarm that would have otherwise burned it to the foundation," Trinity said with his arms across his chest. "Julia and your boy would probably be dead if he hadn't been there."

"A good deed done when circumstances permit, even a large one, does not offset numerous bad ones," Carlion replied.

"I would have thought that working as a mercenary would have driven cavalier morality out of you," Trinity said. "And given how you got cashiered over a scandal, you're not in any position to lecture me about right and wrong."

"You son of a bitch," Carlion growled. His hands tightened into fists.

"You father of a bastard," Trinity countered.

"Gentlemen, if you please, take this unpleasant business outside," came a reprimand from behind Carlion.

Both Carlion and Trinity turned and saw that the woman who had escorted Thorne and Nion was back and looking at them with a disapproving scowl. She gracefully raised an arm and gestured towards the atrium's exit.

The Darkman looked back to Trinity and saw the mercenary's jaw unclench and his shoulders relax. "Stay here if you want, but I'm going to join Amos," Trinity said.

Carlion stared at Trinity's back as the mercenary left. His hot face started to cool only after the door had closed and he turned back to the woman. "Where's Thorne?" he asked shortly.

"Master Thorne is in a meeting that might last some time,"

the woman said. She had a composed manner and a practiced professional politeness that Carlion appreciated, but it also put a tangible distance between them. He would be tolerated in the Archive, but not truly welcome.

"I'll wait," the Darkman said definitively. He had promised Julia to return with a replacement for Nion, and wasn't going to leave empty handed.

"I see. Would you like a tour to pass the time?" she asked.

"You can do that?" Carlion asked genuinely surprised.

"It is one of my formal duties as major-domo," the woman said. "My name is Erma Kent. It is a pleasure to make your acquaintance."

Carlion knew the sentiment was a formality. He doubted Erma wanted a mercenary in the Archive, much less to give him a tour. However, now that the Darkman was here his curiosity was piqued, and he made a show to look around the atrium. He quickly introduced himself and gave a half-hearted smile in an attempt to be polite.

"Is there something here in the Archive that might interest you?" Erma asked.

"I'm not sure," Carlion admitted. "This is the first time I've been here." He paused and thought for a moment then said, "Where are your healers trained?"

"We have both classroom and laboratory curriculum for those with a medical interest," Erma said slightly confused. "Perhaps you'd like to see the infirmary? I'm sure there are a few initiates there who could comment on their training."

"Sounds fine," the Darkman agreed.

Erma led Carlion down a wide hall with windows along the exterior wall that looked out on the front plaza. The hall was bright and comfortably warm from the sunlight pouring in. Carlion noticed that the scent from the atrium had faded, but was now replaced by a more familiar alcohol smell.

Stopping in front of a set of open double doors Erma said, "We try to keep the volume of conversation low inside, but please feel free to look around. I'll inform the principal physician."

Erma disappeared behind a large white curtain leaving Carlion to study his surroundings. The room seemed large, but much of it was hidden behind curtains that divided the area into sections. A pair of skylights from the high ceiling also gave the room a feeling of openness, which was quite a contrast to the surgeon's quarters that Carlion remembered from his time in the Sovereignty military.

The short section of wall that he could see had shelves filled with containers and jars. Approaching one, the Darkman was unsurprised to find that the labels were in a script he couldn't read. A few of the jars had a peculiar odor wafting out of them, but otherwise things seemed clean and well organized.

Turning from the shelves and realizing he was still alone, the Darkman wandered down a short aisle looking for Erma. Near the end he found a small space where a woman was seated in front of a child of maybe ten years. The boy was grimacing slightly while the woman hovered an open palm over the boy's outstretched arm, which was resting in her lap.

"What do you want?" the woman asked, not looking up. Apparently she had seen Carlion approach out of the corner of her eye. Her brow was creased and was clearly irritated by the interruption.

"I'm getting a tour," Carlion mumbled, taken aback by the woman's aggressive manner. Regaining some composure he thrust his chin at the boy seated in front of her and asked, "What happened to him?"

The woman's frown deepened, though Carlion didn't know if it was because of the question or the answer. "Broken arm. Fell out of a tree," she said tersely.

"What are you doing?" Carlion asked.

"Applying mana to the fracture," the woman replied.

"Will that heal it?"

The physician stopped what she was doing and turned to Carlion with an annoyed expression. "No, I'm not a miracle worker," she said. Turning back to the boy she continued, "Don't the let Sovereignty propaganda or your grandmother's folk tales give you the wrong idea of what we do here. A precise dose of my mana will accelerate his body's ability to heal itself. It still takes time, though."

Carlion watched in silence as the physician appeared to finish what she was doing and carefully tied a splint around the boy's forearm. "What about diseases?" the Darkman asked.

"What about them?" the physician asked.

"Can you treat them here too?" Carlion asked.

"Depends on the disease," came the short reply from the woman. "Why, what have you got?"

"He's here with me," Erma said suddenly appearing at Carlion's side.

"Erma," the physician said exasperated. "I told you to keep the gawkers away from me. If I wanted to put on a show I would have joined a theater troupe."

Erma gently rested a hand on Carlion's forearm. "Come," she said and guided him out of the infirmary. After they had left and were walking back towards the atrium she said, "I'm sorry, normally our physicians have better bedside manner."

"It's alright," Carlion said. "You have impressive medical facilities," Carlion said with a level of earnestness he found surprising. He would never admit it to Thorne, but the mage was right. The healers here at the Archive outclassed Nion by a considerable amount based on what he had seen in Deccern.

"Any citizen is welcome to use them for a reasonable fee," Erma said. "Although I must admit, here we almost exclusively treat our own mages."

"Why do wizards need such a high level of care?" the Darkman asked.

"Being Aware is a chronic disease," Erma said. "It's the reason that mages are stereotyped as old or sickly. Here at the Archive we call it the Iron Bane because the arcane energy that enables our magic reacts negatively with the iron in our blood. Even if we never use our power, it is still slowly killing us all."

"Then why do it, be a wizard?" Carlion asked perplexed.

"Some of us don't have a choice," Erma said. "Some of us are born this way. For others, they want their minds opened to the arcane because they desire to push the boundaries of human understanding and to explore the fundamental building blocks of the world."

"You make it sound like those mages have noble intentions," Carlion said incredulous. "I have a hard time believing that all of them are so altruistic."

"Perhaps not," Erma admitted.

Carlion was struck by a thought and asked the major-domo, "Which type of wizard is Thorne? Born or made?"

Erma stopped walking and was clearly shocked by the question. Recovering quickly she said, "The background of any mage becomes unimportant after their traveling education and Transformation."

"Transformation into what?" Carlion asked. He recognized that Erma dodged his question, but decided to let it drop for the time being.

"Transformed into a fully Aware mage, having complete control of the arcane elements. A Master," Erma said.

"And how does that work? Some type of ceremony?" Carlion asked.

"No, in this case there is little metaphor with the term. I'll show you," the major-domo said. They had just reached the atrium, but Erma led them through another corridor and then down several flights of stairs.

Carlion felt a noticeable drop in temperature as they entered a hall that was lit by eerie glowing spheres hung on the walls. The place felt like a crypt but with more activity because the Darkman saw several people attending oblong structures that looked like sarcophagi. The material of the capsules was something Carlion didn't recognize and was a pearlescent orange color, which further reinforced the otherworldly feeling of the hall.

Erma escorted Carlion to a small alcove near the front of the hall only a short distance from the stairs they just descended. A thick braided robe was strung from the walls preventing access into the alcove, but Carlion saw that even if he got past the purely decorative barrier there wouldn't be much room to maneuver. Taking up nearly the entire space was what looked to Carlion like a giant chicken egg resting on a round stone platform. It was clear that the egg was empty as near the top of the shell there was a hole big enough for a man to pass through. The egg was a mottled green and brown color and looked dry and brittle.

"The first chrysalises were fashioned from dragon eggs, as dragons were the stewards of Awareness and taught the first mages," Erma explained. "As dragons faded from the world, there were accounts of dragons interacting with mages to continue the ancient pact of increasing our knowledge of magic's fundamental nature."

"I see," Carlion said, though he didn't understand. "So why do you have this egg here?"

Erma gave him a patient look and replied, "It's both a symbol and a relic. At the invitation of a dragon, the first mages entered into an egg. We know that dragons are born fully-grown so someone about human sized would fit inside, but much else of their lifecycle is a mystery. In any event, the dragon would initiate an astral projection of the mage into another place of existence we call the Void. By successfully transcending the physical plane and then returning from the Void, a mage would have shown their mastery of their mana and the arcane elements, and therefore could call themselves a Master."

"It sounds like their soul was pushed out of their body," Carlion said.

"There are some church ministers who believe that very idea," Erma said.

"This place, the Void? What is it? Hell?" Carlion asked, thinking that the priests were probably on to something.

"Nothing so ecclesiastical," Erma said. "The arcane elements originate from their respective planes of existence. I suppose the simplest explanation is that there are other dimensions, other worlds, which are the pure essence of the arcane elements. The Void is one of those worlds. It is the origin of mana, the energy that mages harness to power their magic."

"So you crawl into an old dragon egg, go on some sort of spirit journey, and then reemerge a wizard," Carlion said incredulously.

"The technology has advanced somewhat, but that is basically correct," Erma said. Pointing to one of the sarcophagi down the hall she said, "We've replaced dragon eggs with resin capsules we call chrysalises, but the use of astral projection has changed little."

At this point a young man that looked like a scribe descended the stairs and approached them. Erma turned and smiled at the newcomer, whom had light brown hair tied back in a ponytail and a well-trimmed goatee.

"Excuse me, major-domo Erma," the man said, "but I was told to inform Master Thorne's retinue that he will be indisposed for the remainder of the day." Looking at Carlion, he asked, "Is that you, sir?"

"At least part of it," Carlion replied. "What about Nion's replacement?"

"I'm sorry, I don't know about any of Master Thorne's affairs," the scribe said. "I was only sent to deliver this message."

"Perhaps I can inquire for you and send word over to your guild," Erma offered.

Carlion sighed as he rocked back on his heels. It appeared he wasn't going to get what he wanted today. He might as well go back to the guild, make peace with Trinity, and check in with Oskar to make sure the old man hadn't found someone else to feed the oxen. For the time being Carlion would just have to wait. At least when he came back to the Archive he now had a contact.

Carlion offered his hand to the major-domo. "I would appreciate it. Thank you for the tour," he said.

Shaking Carlion's hand Erma replied, "It was my pleasure."

CHAPTER FIFTEEN

THORNE

Thorne stared at the painting in his room, but wasn't truly looking at it. The mage had spent countless hours studying the delicate brushwork that detailed the bark on the willow tree. He had appreciated the deft hand of the artist that swayed the drooping branches of the tree and individual strands of the girl's hair, giving an impression of a breeze. However, today the artwork contained no movement and was simply a static picture in front of him as he wasted precious time waiting to be called on by the Archive council.

After leaving the mercenaries in the atrium, Erma Kent had led him and Nion directly to Tarbeck's study. Thorne had given a brief summary to the Sehenryu councilman, with Nion standing seemingly unconcerned beside him. Tarbeck said little, but wore a severe expression the entire time before calling for the Archive constable after Thorne finished his report. Nion was taken into custody and Tarbeck tersely told Thorne that the council would call upon him soon to resolve their end of the deal. That was the last he had heard from Tarbeck, or any member of the council, for the past two days.

There was no doubt in Thorne's mind that the council had interrogated Nion and bound his Awareness, making inaccessible what little command he had of the arcane elements.

What worried the mage was that it had taken so long for the council to contact him about removing his own binding mark and giving him access to his laboratory again. The irrational part of his mind was convinced that the council wasn't going to honor their deal, but Thorne knew there would be a revolt in the extremely democratic Archive if word got around that the council reneged on an agreement. Something else had commanded the council's attention and other matters, including his own, had been deemed less important and set aside.

A knock at his door broke the mage's reverie. "What is it?" Thorne said loudly, and then frowned as Olaf entered. When a councilor personally came to you unannounced, it was usually a bad sign.

Olaf casually entered the room and stood near Thorne's writing desk. He looked out the window as eleven high bells started to ring out. "You brought back a worrisome problem for us, Thorne," he said.

"That's not my concern," the mage answered. "I accomplished what I set out to do and now I want the binding mark removed so I can return to my laboratory."

Ignoring Thorne's demand, Olaf continued, "The council has interrogated Nion twice, and while you have determined the fate of Erza, you may have unwittingly stumbled upon a problem with a much larger scope."

"Your vagueness in conversation is not an endearing trait," Thorne said, irritated. "Be plain."

Olaf gave a practiced smile that had no warmth, and said, "Before he supposedly lost contact with his conspirators, Nion sent several rare alchemic components through an aperture."

"How?" Thorne asked. "Planar transport research is severely restricted, and I didn't see anything resembling an Engine in Nion's shops in Rell-Kyr or Deccern."

"That's the interesting part," Olaf said. "It appears that one of Nion's conspirators has found a way to make it work with only one Engine. Apparently, it is similar in theory to astral projection from a chrysalis, but is capable of transporting physical matter. Nion didn't understand the physics of it, only the results."

"This is too far-fetched," Thorne said with a dismissive wave of his hand. "I completed the bounty that was agreed upon and I would very much appreciate the council removing this binding mark." The mage pulled up his left sleeve to reveal the star tattoo on his wrist.

"I'm surprised, Thorne. I thought that the opportunity to investigate planar apertures generated outside the Archive would be of great interest to you," Olaf asked.

Thorne did his best to look disinterested and shrugged. "Why would I be interested in something like that?"

Rubbing his finger on the writing desk and not looking at Thorne, Olaf said, "Nion told the council he sent the reagents through the Void."

"Impossible," Thorne said in disbelief. "There are bookshelves here full of research demonstrating that the Void is too unstable to transport anything with mass."

Olaf made a surprised sound and turned to look Thorne in the eye. He lowered his head slightly and said, "You don't believe it's impossible, Thorne. Wasn't that the very research that destroyed your lab?"

"Why are you telling me all of this?" Thorne asked, suddenly very wary.

"Because I believe Nion," Olaf said with uncharacteristic intensity. "We absolutely cannot let technology like an Engine be constructed outside of Archive walls. If there is a group of rogue mages doing this, then they must be stopped immediately, regardless of their true purpose. Now, Nion seems to have been only a minor player, but his conspirators are likely to be much more dangerous."

"From his journal," Thorne said. "U and R."

"Nion made airs of stoicism and reticence, at least for his first day in isolation," Olaf said. "However, after Erica made it clear that his cooperation was the only route to freedom Nion reluctantly, but we believe honestly, shared the identify of U. He is Uksyo Serrant, a Master originally from the Savamont Archive. It seems that the identity of R was never shared with Nion. He only ever interacted with Uksyo, who in turn reported to R."

Thorne did not know anyone named Uksyo, but that was not what worried him now. Olaf was sharing information that the council would not want widely known, even within the Archive. The mage now wondered if not just Olaf, but the entire council feared Nion's story to be true. If that was the case, he might be able to use it to his advantage. "Where is Uksyo now?" Thorne asked.

"With the Engine, off the eastern coast on one of the Stormbreaker Isles," Olaf said. "Uksyo wouldn't tell Nion anything more."

"R might be with him there as well," the mage suggested.

"Perhaps, but that does lead to the reason I'm here," Olaf said, giving Thorne a probing look. "Have you received any recent communications from Reihana?"

Thorne started upon hearing the name and then frowned. "You put us on opposite sides of the continent," he said in an accusing tone. "And given that we weren't on the best of terms when you did, there's been little incentive to get in touch."

"I had to ask. My network has reported that she goes missing, sometimes for days at a time, despite being under surveillance. Granted, she can't do much harm with her Awareness completely bound, but using Nion's journal as a guide, I fear that she, Uksyo, and Nion are all puzzle pieces that fit together."

"What is it worth to the council if I go find out for you?" Thorne asked.

"Access to your laboratory again," Olaf said.

"I already have that secured with Nion's return," Thorne said. "I want some breathing room as well."

"What do you mean?" Olaf asked.

"No probationary period afterwards. No chaperones or surveillance of my laboratory," Thorne said. "I want to be able to work without interference or oppressive oversight."

"Done," Olaf replied without thought. "And to be clear, I am speaking for the council and I am here on their behalf."

Thorne then realized just how scared the council was of the prospect of an Engine being outside of Archive control. If they had anticipated and already approved Thorne's demands, then they were taking Nion's story very seriously and wanted a swift resolution to the matter.

"I'll leave tomorrow," Thorne said.

"There is one more thing," Olaf said. "The council wants you to have support during your investigation, and I'd like to introduce the two apprentices that will be accompanying you."

"What?" Thorne said in disbelief. "That's ridiculous. This trip could very well be dangerous, and there aren't any mages, let alone apprentices, that would be of help. I took your advice about the mercenary guild when I went out to find Nion, and I plan to continue taking that advice now. I need fighters, not scholars, for this investigation."

Olaf shook his head, "This situation has escalated and the council decided this has to now stay completely internal. We can't let the guilds or the Sovereignties know about this Engine or any rogue mages." The councilman raised his hands up in a placating gesture and said, "There's no stick here, only carrot. Work with us and when we get a satisfactory resolution, your laboratory will be rebuilt and returned to you without restrictions."

Thorne didn't like Olaf's vague phrasing, but the councilman had convinced him that the situation had become more serious. Not wanting to leave the investigation unfinished, coupled with the improved rewards, made Thorne decide in that moment that he would see things through.

"Understood," Thorne said. "Who has the council chosen to come with me?"

"I'll introduce you tomorrow, at four high bells in the atrium," Olaf said. "You can leave straight away for Port afterwards."

Thorne nodded agreement and Olaf quickly left the apartment. Once he was alone Thorne turned and faced his writing desk. He flipped his hourglass several times. Given what he did to his lab, there was no way the council trusted him to work alone or with hired swords. That had to be why Olaf insisted that he bring along two Archive mages. In all likelihood, they were there to watch him and signal for help if the situation deteriorated further.

Suddenly struck with an idea, Thorne opened a drawer and pulled out a sheet of paper and a pen. He scratched out a set of instructions and then tightly folded the note before shoving it into his trouser pocket. He was more than certain that Olaf's spies would be watching him tonight, but he should be able to meet with one of his agents in the Archive undetected long enough to pass along a message.

• • •

The next morning, Thorne was prepared to give his new handlers a cold reception, but his aloof pretense evaporated when Olaf walked into the atrium. At his side were a Sehenryu female and a Venhadar female, both carrying large packs that were typical for mages embarking on their traveling education.

The Sehenryu wore a sleeveless white tunic and fitted black pants that were the preferred garb of the feline race. The short grey fur of her exposed arms contrasted sharply against brilliant green eyes with vertical pupils.

The Venhadar looked every part an alchemist, in navy blue velvet robes and a black belt with numerous pouches cinched around her waist. A mane of wiry red hair framed a fair-skinned face. Typical of her race, she was thickly built and barely half as tall as Olaf.

"May I introduce Metauk," Olaf said as he gestured towards the Sehenryu, "and Shara," indicating the Venhadar.

Thorne frowned. A Sehenryu and a Venhadar were conspicuous traveling companions outside of the major cities. If Uksyo or R had any brains, they'd have spies watching the Archive.

"You're unhappy that we're accompanying you?" Metauk said with a probing expression on her face.

"There's nothing to learn by reading my feelings," Thorne said taking a step towards Metauk. "Sehenryu empathy is going to be more useful making sure we catch Uksyo by surprise."

"I thought we were supposed to be ready to leave now," Shara asked, looking at Thorne's satchel.

"I'm ready to go," The mage replied. "We're going to make one brief stop and then we'll be gone through the main gate."

Metauk and Shara both looked at Olaf who gave them a little nod and his well-known neutral smile. "I wish you safe travel," the councilman said before quickly leaving the atrium.

Exiting the Archive, Thorne led Metauk and Shara into the merchant district. As they walked, the mage acutely felt the tension that was often shared by people who didn't know each other, but were thrust together under stressful circumstances. It was uncomfortable and now, as in the past, Thorne didn't know how to break the ice with his new traveling companions.

Thankfully, Metauk must have felt the mage's uneasiness

and made an attempt at conversation. More loudly than she probably meant the Sehenryu said, "Are you really traveling with only a small satchel?" She hefted her full knapsack and added, "I have the Archive recommended gear for a traveling education here. What do you know that we don't?"

"That you'll lose half of that stuff within the first week and the other half isn't really that useful," Thorne replied. "You can lug that pack around if you want, but I'll procure what we really need when we need it."

"That seems a little reckless," Shara said with a tight expression on her face. "Until I'm convinced that you know what you're doing, I'll stick with the Archive guidelines. They've kept mages safe on their traveling education for a long time."

Thorne quirked an eyebrow, "Suit yourself."

Both Metauk and Shara gave the mage confused looks when he stopped in front of a distillery. Inside Thorne bought a small bottle of brandy.

"Rumor has it you don't drink," Shara said as the mage paid for the spirit.

"Rarely," the mage replied, placing the bottle gently into his satchel. "But this isn't for me."

"Who's it for then?" the Venhadar asked with a creased brow.

"It's a bribe," the mage replied.

"You didn't answer my question," Shara said, now angry.

Thorne ignored her while exiting the shop and walked towards the main city gate. For the first few miles on the road Shara and Metauk were able to maintain the pace that Thorne set. However, as the morning wore on the mage started to hear Shara breathing heavier. He looked back and saw both his companions were laboring under the weight of their heavy packs. He slowed his pace down and let them catch up. "Another reason to travel light," he commented.

That night Thorne set a small cooking fire on a low hill that overlooked the road as it bent away from the capital. Travel had been slow, and both Metauk and Shara had kept silent during most of the walk towards the coast. The mage had caught Metauk periodically looking over her shoulder back at Yaboon as if she had forgotten something. Her eyes had a pearlescent reflection in the firelight while she watched the road that wound back to the city.

Sitting next to the Sehenryu, Shara took large bites out of a sandwich. Thorne gave the stocky Venhadar credit. Despite not having much stamina for travel, she hadn't complained during the day and kept a stoic expression while rubbing blistered heels when they had rested in the afternoon.

As the sun slid below the horizon it was replaced with light from a quarter moon joined by an accompaniment of stars in the clear night sky. A slight breeze played with the smoke from the fire, twisting it into spirals and ribbons. Thorne was about to sit down next to his two handlers when a shrill whistle cut the air and shattered the pastoral scene. The mage saw both Metauk and Shara jump at the unexpected sound.

"Someone is looking for us," Metauk said in alarm. Her head swiveled back and forth as she stood up in an attempt to find the source of the sound.

"It's fine," Thorne said, taking a step away from the fire and towards the road. "I'm expecting them." He stuck a pair of fingers in his mouth and whistled loudly.

"Who?" Shara demanded as she stood up.

Thorne pointed towards the road. Slowly climbing the hill were two tall figures and a shorter one. At the edge of the firelight Thorne saw Trinity, Carlion, and Amos approach. Thorne was surprised to see the Darkman, but tried to keep his expression neutral. The note that Thorne had sent just asked for Trinity and Amos to rendezvous with him on the road.

Trinity clasped the mage's outstretched hand and said, "Did you really need the head start? Amos has short legs you know."

"It couldn't be helped," Thorne replied. "The Archive has spies throughout the city and the outskirts. I didn't want to risk the council getting suspicious."

"Why?" asked Amos squinting up at Thorne. "This is more cloak and dagger than I'm used to from you. Is this little adventure not approved by the Archive?"

"They're the ones sending me out here," Thorne said. "But they weren't too keen on having mercenaries come with me because they thought you'd be a security risk. I disagreed, so here you are." The mage went over to his satchel and retrieved the bottle of brandy. Handing it to Amos, he said, "And since I know you're not happy doing escort assignments dry, I thought I'd have this ready for you."

The corsair pulled the cork from the bottle and took a small sip. Smacking his lips, Amos said, "You went to Hamich's shop. There's a good mate. Cheers." He took a longer drink from the bottle.

Carlion finally found an opportunity to speak up and glaring at Thorne said, "I'm still waiting for what you promised in Deccern."

"I wasn't given much choice about leaving immediately," Thorne lied. "As much as it pains me, I am currently at the mercy of the Archive council. However, I am a man of my word. You will get your healer." Thorne added the qualifier of *eventually* silently in his mind.

"I'm here to make sure that I get what I'm owed," Carlion said, crossing his arms. "I could never go back to Deccern without the healer I promised Julia. You're stuck with me until you make good on your deal."

The mage appraised the Darkman with a critical eye, unsure if Carlion was going to be an asset or a burden. He had been of some use in Deccern, but the stakes were higher now that he had to contend with a Master mage. Deciding that at worst Carlion could be used as fodder, Thorne nodded and replied tersely, "As you will."

Thorne turned to Shara and Metauk, introduced the new arrivals, and saw the expected confusion from Metauk, but was taken aback by Shara's expression. The Venhadar's nostrils flared and hatred was in her eyes.

"Mercenaries!" she seethed. "You are disobeying a directive from the council, and I will not work with a band of cutthroats."

"I've learned over the years that the council wants results. If we come back with Uksyo, all will be forgiven," Thorne said.

"It's that attitude that got you banned from the alchemic labs," Shara shot back. Before Thorne could answer she jabbed a finger at the mercenaries and said, "You keep them away from me!"

As everyone settled in for the night, it was clear that the fire was meant to be the barrier that separated mages from the mercenaries. Thorne did not want to alienate either group, so he stood at the edge of the firelight, away from both groups. He watched Shara stare daggers at the mercenaries through the fire. Her body was tensed with an energy that ignored her exhaustion from the day's travel. Occasionally, Metauk would rest a hand on Shara's shoulder and whisper something.

Trinity rocked himself up to a standing position and sidled beside Thorne. The two of them stood in silence for a time and watched the flames writhe and eject the occasional spark skyward.

"Quite a night so far," Trinity said at last. "I know it's a bit much to ask, but I'd like your assurance that I'll wake up in the morning. Your very angry mage, what's her problem with us being here?"

"I don't know," Thorne admitted. "It wasn't something I

expected."

"Carlion has some contrarian tendencies, but at least I can depend on him in a fight," Trinity said. "Can the same be said for the new additions? From your message it sounds like we could be heading for trouble."

"Unclear," Thorne replied.

CELESTE'S MEMORY THAT

ONLY SOME SCARS FADE

The bungalow was built on stilts to keep it dry during high tide. A reed roof and rough-hewn siding gave it an earthy smell that contrasted sharply with the odors from the sea. Celeste leaned on the porch railing and took in the picturesque beach scene. The early morning sun was beginning to warm the black sand that blended into white surf before rolling back towards a vast blue ocean. Wispy clouds streaked the sky and were gently pushed along by a warm breeze.

Barefoot and wearing only a lightweight linen shirt that ran past her knees, Celeste felt a quiet moment of relaxation and peace. It had been some time since she had been to one of the volcanic islands far south of the continent. Before the dragon had left for the island she had allowed Barrow to return to her ancestral plane, something the pixie had been requesting for some time. Celeste was happy to accommodate her retainer, if only to be granted some degree of privacy now.

Over the sound of the breeze cutting thought the reeds hanging over the porch, Celeste suddenly heard a sharp cry from inside. She quickly entered the house and made her way to the bedroom where she found Thorne sitting on the edge of the bed. The mage was breathing hard, his face and bare chest were slick with sweat. His expression was the mixture of fear, confusion, and relief that one felt after awakening from a nightmare.

Celeste sat down next Thorne and wrapped her arm around his shoulders. "Are you alright?" she asked.

The mage gulped a deep breath and nodded. He rested his head on her shoulder and said, "I dreamt of fire again. I was standing in a barren field under a starless night sky, but I knew I was in Granick. Trinity and Claire were standing in front of me, but they were on fire. They were both just standing there burning, just standing there looking at me."

"You seemed pre-occupied before we went to bed last night. Were you thinking about the past?" Celeste asked as she looked down at the top of Thorne's head. She found a few strands of grey in his otherwise dark hair. The inevitability of old age was beginning to creep up on the mage.

"Claire always told Trinity she loved the ocean," Thorne said. "I was thinking what might have been if they had gotten the chance to settle down and start a family."

"A guilty conscience is a deep well from which to draw nightmares," Celeste said. "You couldn't save Trinity's wife, but at least you were able to avenge her."

Thorne leaned forward and slipped from Celeste's embrace. He then shifted on the bed to look at her squarely and said, "It was one of a very few times that I actually felt like I owned the title of Paragon. Now that the program is dissolved, it's unlikely I'll get that feeling again."

"It would not have been able to stay a secret forever," Celeste said, trying to be consoling. "Paragons were a risky venture to begin with. With the Archive proclaiming they don't make weapons or inventions for war, the creation of fighting mages was sure to be taken poorly by the princes. The guilds were only supportive so far as it furthered their own ambitions, but they surely would have betrayed the Archive given enough time."

"Perhaps, but I've no doubt that the council never intended for it to be revealed as it did," Thorne said. "Now it's easier to publicly disavow any knowledge of its existence. Not that it matters since only Reihana and myself are left."

"What about Ghent?" the dragon asked.

"What about him?" Thorne replied. "No one has seen him in over a decade. Not even Olaf's spies can find him, if they're even still looking. If Ghent's not dead, then he turned his back on the Archive a long time ago."

"In that case you should take comfort that you still have your Awareness and represent what was best about the program," Celeste said. "Reihana's is bound and a Paragon in name only."

"Only because I prostrated myself before the council," Thorne said bitterly. "And it's more her continued defiance against the council rather than her incredibly poor judgment that brought down their wrath. Despite what she did, the whispers in the Archive talk as if she's a resistance hero, whereas I'm a lapdog of the council. It's inflated her already unhealthy ego and emboldened her twisted ideas of arcane freedom. The council made a terrible mistake when they made her the principal agent."

"Do you still hate her that much?" Celeste asked, surprised.

"She's dangerous," Thorne said definitively. "My personal dislike of her aside, she had an agenda even before becoming a Paragon. If she ever got her Awareness back she would set fire to the continent and there wouldn't be anyone to stop her."

"You could stop her," Celeste said softly.

"And have another bloodbath?" Thorne said, not hiding the despair in his voice. "It would be Meren all over again. So many people were killed that I couldn't save."

The dragon didn't need Sehenryu empathy to know that

Thorne felt crushed under the weight of both the hurt he had inflicted and the tragedies he didn't prevent. It was a melancholy she had seen trouble the mage before, and this bout seemed like it would be particularly bad. As she had in the past, Celeste tried to ease his mind and said, "I have no doubt that those you did help are grateful, Trinity included. When you look back, why is it that all you see are the things you regret?"

Thorne did not meet her gaze and instead looked down at his lap. "I'm so tired of being shackled to the past," the mage said. "It would be such a relief to be able to forget it all."

"Do you really think you would be better if you forgot those painful memories?" Celeste asked.

"Not those of Trinity and Claire, or even my misdeeds as a Paragon," Thorne said, agitated. He stood up, rubbing his hands on the loose linen pants he wore. "What I'm really talking about is growing up an only child in Sunrock. I always felt weak and scared, and you know what? It's never gone away. The destruction and violence I caused as a Paragon came from a place where I was trying to lash out and kill whatever was haunting that timid little boy."

Celeste watched Thorne abruptly turn towards the door and leave the bedroom. She slowly got up and followed him though the open entrance of the bungalow and onto the porch. The mage was staring down the black sand beach, which ran far into the distance. The dragon reached out and placed a hand on his back and she felt him lean into it.

Still looking down the beach, Thorne said, "Despite searching countless volumes at the Archive, I found nothing that has hinted that memory could be influenced by alchemy, either altered or erased."

Celeste had helped Thorne weather these bouts of depression before, but his admission of trying to find a way to erase memories was something new. It broke her heart to see him in such torment, and the dragon decided to finally offer something she had been considering for a long time.

"It is," Celeste began slowly, "within my power to erase your memories."

Thorne's head swiveled around to look at her with an intense expression. "Dragons have such a power?" he asked astonished. "How can it be that no one knows of it?"

Celeste gave him a patient smile and replied, "You won't find any hint of it recorded because it is not something we wish to be known. It was decided long ago by the conclave that certain magic would remain hidden from mages. For memories, it was decided that they should fade naturally. Isn't that the point of the expression? That time heals all wounds?"

The mage shook his head and said bitterly, "Perhaps, but only some scars fade. And even when I was researching in the Archive, I knew that I wouldn't be able to rid myself of these crippling memories for many years. I must keep them until I am the only one left who remembers. When I am the last, then when I forget they will truly be gone."

Both Thorne and Celeste were quiet for a time and watched the waves roll across the dark sand before Thorne said, "If mages aren't supposed to know, then why did you tell me?"

"Because I love you and want you to be at peace," the dragon replied. "Despite these burdens you've achieved incredible things, but you appreciate none of them because you're stuck in the past. I want you to live in the present with me and find happiness."

"Then promise me," Thorne said, "Promise me that when the time comes you will erase my memories."

The desperation in the mage's voice made Celeste's heart ache. "I promise," she said.

Thorne exhaled deeply and then descended from the porch to the beach, his bare feet leaving depressions in the loose sand.

The mage reached down and picked up a handful and let it slip through his fingers and fall back to the ground. He looked up to the porch and said, "Maybe I'll take some of this back with me to Yaboon."

"What for?" the dragon asked.

"To make an hourglass," the mage answered. "I'll use it to keep track of the time and as a reminder of your promise."

CHAPTER SIXTEEN

CARLION

Carlion tasted salt in the light wind that blew in from the sea as he walked along the waterfront in the harbor city of Port. The journey to the coast had been uneventful, though the two new mages in the group kept to themselves and always maintained a careful watch on the mercenaries. He still didn't know why they were so distrustful of them, but Shara had been especially unpleasant and any attempt to engage her in conversation was met with only agitated, monosyllabic replies. Eventually, Carlion had given up trying to talk to her.

Everyone's spirits were raised when they saw the colorful banners flying in the breeze as they approached the city. Nearly as populous as Yaboon, and probably more prosperous, the city of Port was a hub of commerce that moved people and goods between the Sovereignty provinces. Nearly every major guild had a hall here, and all of them did their best to work within the confines of Sovereignty law, as there was also a sizable naval presence in the city. Carlion had only been to Port a few times during his military service, but had always been impressed with the cooperation between the Sovereignty naval fleet, the merchant ship captains, and the stevedore guild. The harbor was one of the busiest parts of the city and today the air was full of shouts from all parties as cargo was moved between ships and pallets on the docks.

Amos led the group along the waterfront towards the harbormaster's office to enquire about any ships passing by the Stormbreaker Isles that would be open to passengers. The former corsair had been exuberant when Trinity told him about Thorne's message and the prospect of traveling to the coast. However, Carlion was much less excited, and Trinity was surprised when he told the mercenary that he was going as well. There was no way that he was going to return to Deccern without a healer, partially because of the consequences with the governor, but more personally the Darkman didn't want to disappoint Julia.

"Thorne, you better come inside with me," Amos said as they approached a small building with heavily varnished siding and shutters. "We might need your deep pockets if we're to make any headway with Tommy, assuming he's still the harbormaster."

"I'm coming too," Shara said quickly. When Amos gave her a curious look she said, "I'm not standing around and looking like a lackey with a pair of mercenaries."

"Suit yourself," Amos said. Looking at Trinity, Carlion, and Metauk he asked, "Are you three alright on your own here for a while?"

"I can't imagine that we'll get into any trouble while you're gone," Metauk said.

Amos, Shara, and Thorne entered the harbormaster's office and left Carlion, Trinity, and Metauk outside. It didn't take long for Trinity's curiosity about the action on the docks to get the better of him. "Come on," the mercenary said. "Let's go see what they're unloading from that ship."

Heat radiated up from the stone walkway and the afternoon sun was intense in the clear sky. Carlion pulled the collar of his tabard to wipe away the sweat gathering on his upper lip. He didn't think that anyone would have seen his scarred cuirass with such a brief exposure, but he turned out to be wrong.

"Hey! Darkman! We don't need any pig fuckers from the Sovereignty gawking here on the docks," shouted a bare-chested man as he dropped a heavy crate near a pair of similar containers. "Go back to the capital where you belong."

Carlion gave the man a hard look but didn't slow his stride as he walked past the dock. People had called him far worse things, knowing that they could do so without reprisal.

"That's right keep walking, tough guy!" the dockworker shouted louder. "You probably got kicked out of the military for fucking that kata! Are you out here taking your pussy for a walk?"

Just as "dwarf" was a derogatory term for the Venhadar, so was "kata" for the feline Sehenryu. Carlion had no problem being maligned himself, but he wasn't going to tolerate such abuse aimed at someone else. The Darkman stopped and slowly turned around. Both his jaw and fists were clenched tight.

"We just got into town, we don't need any trouble now," Trinity cautioned as three more dockhands joined the bare-chested man on the dock. "These chaps have been on a ship too long and are itching for a fight. They have probably been insulting anyone who passes by the docks. Let's keep moving."

It was sound advice and some part of Carlion's mind agreed with it, just not the part that was leading him towards the sailor. A chorus of whoops from the flanking dockhands sounded out as Carlion approached and the man smiled wide, revealing several missing teeth. Before another word could be exchanged, the Darkman lunged out savagely. Carlion felt a satisfying crunch as his fist smashed into the man's jaw, which dropped him to one knee.

The dockhand looked up at him with a smile and Carlion

saw that blood had coated his remaining teeth. "Now, there's a good mate. Get him!" the bare-chested man called out.

Before the Darkman could back away he felt someone shove him from behind while the bare-chested man drove his shoulder into Carlion's knee. Knocked off balance the Darkman fell with a crash onto the ground. He felt someone kick his flank, but his cuirass deflected the blow.

"He's wearing armor!" someone shouted over him. "Smash his brains!"

Protecting his head with his arms, Carlion tried to roll away but a heavy foot stomped on his back and pinned him down. His face exploded in pain as it was violently pounded into the ground.

Through the grunts of the dockhands' assault, Carlion heard a familiar voice boom out, "What the fuck is going on here?"

With his face still pressed into the stone walkway, Carlion couldn't see what was happening above him, but heard one of the dockhands exclaim, "Oh shit! It's Captain Amos!"

"Back to work, you lazy fucks!" Amos barked. "If you're going to pick a fight, then do it on your own time."

Carlion rolled over and watched the dockhands scamper back to the cargo they were moving. Suddenly, filling his vision and backlit by the sun was Amos' scowling face. "Can't I leave you unsupervised for five minutes?" the corsair asked rhetorically.

"It couldn't be helped," the Darkman said, tasting blood and grit in his mouth.

Amos grunted and backed away, which gave Trinity an opportunity to pull Carlion off the ground. As he dusted himself off, the Darkman asked, "You were going to jump in eventually, right?"

"Nope," Trinity replied. "I had no interest getting a beating by following you into a trap. You did exactly what they wanted, you fool."

"Thank you all the same," Metauk said as she came to stand beside Trinity. "I know what you were trying to do, and I appreciate it." She gently rested her short-fingered hand on Carlion's shoulder. "If you had only waited a bit longer, I would have been able to tell you what he was trying to do."

"Sorry, I'm not used to waiting for an empath's advice before taking action," Carlion said.

"Let's go," Amos said, still angry and not interested in an explanation of what happened.

The Darkman fell in step with Trinity and the mages, and tried to clean himself up as best he could with his shirtsleeve. Everyone followed behind Amos as he walked down an avenue that led away from the harbor. Amos turned the corner and guided the group through a progressively narrower set of alleyways. They eventually had to walk single file and at one spot Carlion reached out and was able to touch the buildings on either side of the street. Locals populated this part of the city, and most gave the group suspicious glances as they squeezed past.

Finally, the street opened up into a wide cul-de-sac that was lined with tightly packed buildings. Amos walked up to a small shack that seemed to be built into the gap between two other buildings. The top of the entrance door stopped at Carlion's shoulder height and the sign above it read in bright yellow letters, *Shorty's*.

"This here's one of my favorite watering holes," Amos explained. "The harbormaster told me that one of my old mates was back in town, so I figured I'd find him here."

"I guess we'll wait out here then," Carlion said, looking at the small door.

Amos shook his head and pointed at the Darkman. "Oh no," the corsair replied. "You're coming in with me. You're on my shit list and I'm keeping you in sight until we leave the city."

"Since when do you get to make that call?" Carlion said irritated. "You're not paying me."

"But I am," Thorne retorted. "While we're in Port, we all follow Amos." Carlion had found the mage strangely deferential to the corsair since entering the city.

Metauk cut into the conversation and said warily, "We're being watched, and I'm feeling some territorial aggression."

The Darkman turned around and looked up. There were several people watching them from widows on the higher floors of the surrounding buildings. Some of their expressions were curious, but others were more critical.

"No more waiting around. We're burning daylight," Amos said forcefully. "Carlion, you're coming with me. Everyone else can either stay here or go back to the harbor."

"It's a bit claustrophobic here," Trinity said to Amos. "I'll meet you outside the harbormaster's office."

As Trinity and the others left, Carlion looked down at the small door. "Lead the way," he told Amos.

"Oh no," the corsair said. "You go in before me. I want to see the expressions on their faces when you come crawling in."

Carlion pursed his lips and groaned, but realized he had little choice now. Getting down on his knees he pulled open the door and shuffled inside the tavern. Expecting a cramped and dark space, he was surprised to see a large skylight letting the afternoon sunshine into the tavern and giving the room a more open feel. The thumping of clay mugs on tabletops and laughing conversations stopped as the patrons watched him move closer to the bar on the left side of the room. Scanning the tables, the Darkman saw that there were only Venhadar in the tavern.

"Hey! Look at the new lad I got to shine my boots!" Amos called out as he pushed past Carlion. The room erupted almost in unison, "Captain Amos!" What followed as a series of whoops and cheers, and Amos smiled widely as he soaked up the adulation.

As the corsair was swept away by several Venhadar and exchanged with them handshakes or hearty backslaps, Carlion realized that he actually knew very little about Amos. Trinity had told him that Amos was a mariner of some renown, and hinted at a life of piracy and smuggling but was always very vague on the details. The Darkman was instantly forgotten as Amos was ushered to a table by several patrons when the corsair suddenly stabbed a finger out at someone sitting at the end of the bar. "Dirty Dreebs!" Amos shouted enthusiastically.

A Venhadar at the bar swiveled on his stool and casually raised his mug in a salute before taking a drink. Carlion had met many Venhadar in his travels, but he had never seen one so thin. The Darkman thought Amos was going to fold Dirty Dreebs in half with an exuberant embrace as the two met.

Carlion waded through the crowd and knelt next to Amos just in time to hear him say, "The harbormaster said to come find you here." Amos looked over at Carlion with a blank expression as if he momentarily forgot that he was there, but then quickly made introductions.

"Dirty Dreebs," Carlion said with a crooked smile. "I'm guessing there's a story to that name?"

"Ha!" Amos barked a laugh. "When he was under my command he shit his pants every time we were about to raid a ship!"

"Lived to tell the tale afterwards though," Dirty Dreebs said in a gravelly voice. Changing the subject he said, "The harbormaster is right, though. The *Maddie* docked last night and offloaded her cargo early this morning. Captain Yves said we were at liberty for the remainder of the day."

"Where is he now?" Amos asked. "I've got a proposition for him. Easy money transporting half a dozen passengers out to

Stormbreaker Lighthouse."

Dirty Dreebs shrugged and then replied, "Don't know at the moment. He might be back on the *Maddie*. Want me to go check for you?"

"We'll all go," Amos said. "The rest of my people are milling around the docks anyway."

The setting sun turned the water a brilliant orange when they returned to the docks. The stevedores had completed their tasks, and neatly stacked towers of boxes were now on the walkway waiting to be logged and taxed by the harbormaster's agents. They picked up Trinity and the others along the way, and walked down a long pier where a small single mast sloop was docked. Dirty Dreebs ran up the narrow plank that bridged the ship and the dock and was gone for a few minutes while everyone else waited on the dock. Finally, he came back down and said, "Captain's at the glassmaker guild. I'll go fetch him for you. Just wait here a bit."

As Dirty Dreebs left, Carlion heard Shara say quietly to Metauk, "What have we gotten ourselves into? How are we going to scrub the stink of mercenaries and freebooters off of our reputations when we get back to the Archive?"

"It's the way of the outside world," Metauk said, seemingly unconcerned. "I would imagine all mages on their traveling education have to cross paths with their like at one time or another."

"Well at least he could have let us wait on the boat," Shara said to Metauk. Louder, so that everyone could hear her clearly, she continued, "Why can't we wait on the ship?"

"We don't have permission yet," Amos said like the answer was obvious.

Irritated, Shara replied, "That's ridiculous. Your malnourished friend said this was the ship that was going to take us to Stormbreaker Lighthouse."

"It hasn't been cleared with the captain," Amos said with crossed arms.

"Why wouldn't he take our money," Shara said exasperated. She turned toward the ship and continued, "You all can stand awkwardly there if you want, but I'm going up."

She was about to step on to the plank when Amos grabbed the hood of her robes and roughly jerked her back onto the dock. Shara whirled around and seethed, "You do that to me again and I'll burn your hand to a stump!"

Amos' expression was just as fierce, and through grit teeth he growled, "You try to go on this ship without permission again and I'll throw you off the dock." He looked out into the bay and then asked, "For all of your book learning, do you know how to swim?"

Shara answered with an angry grunt and stomped down to the end of the pier. Carlion watched the Venhadar mage retreat from the group, and then glanced at Amos. "You'd really do that?" he asked.

A booming voice made everyone turn, "I've seen Captain Amos throw plenty of deserving fucks overboard. Men, women, even dogs!"

Walking down the pier was a man that looked to Carlion the very definition of pirate. He wore black breeches tucked into tall leather boots and a white linen shirt only partially buttoned. Charms and medallions from at least a dozen necklaces jangled on his chest and a saber hung from his belt. The man's skin was tanned and leathery from a life on the open ocean and he had the shaved head of a mariner.

"It was just the one dog, Captain Yves" Amos said, smiling and reaching out to shake the man's hand. "And that fucker bit me first, so he had it coming."

Yves laughed heartily and slapped Dirty Dreebs on the back. "Go to my quarters and ready a drink for the captain," he said. "I want to toast his return to Port!"

Dirty Dreebs trotted up the plank and disappeared from view as Amos made introductions, including Shara, who had come back from the end of the dock when Yves had addressed the group. Stroking his chin thoughtfully, Yves scrutinized those assembled. "Your crew is an eclectic bunch, Captain," he said.

"Captain? He knows you're a mercenary, right?" Shara asked Amos disapprovingly.

"Doesn't matter what he is now," Yves said seriously. "He was, and always will be, the captain." Looking down at Amos, Yves gave him a deep nod of respect. "Since you've got three mages in tow, I'm assuming your trip has something to do with the impending blockade of Yaboon," he said to Amos.

"What?" Thorne exclaimed. "We just came from the capital."

Yves cocked his head and replied, "Rumor on the streets is that an Archive experiment went wrong and poisoned the Curven River. Farm guild started complaining of dead fish being spit out of the estuary that empties into the ocean. They then sent word about entire fields wilting. They're a powerful guild, and it seems that they finally convinced the prince to investigate, but you know that subtly isn't really his forte."

Looking at Thorne, Yves pointed back up the avenue where they had gone to meet Dirty Dreebs. "Guild hall is back that way. I doubt they'd be happy to see a mage pass through their doors, let alone a Paragon, but I'm sure they'd get over it to air their grievances with you. We won't be leaving the harbor until tomorrow's tide, so you've got the time if you wanted to confirm things for yourself."

Carlion saw Thorne tense and clench his jaw, but the mage then simply shook his head at Yves' suggestion. The Darkman leaned over to Metauk and whispered, "What does that mean? Paragon?"

166

Metauk gave Carlion a sidelong look and said quietly, "Thorne was part of a very small group of mages that were trained to use their Awareness for combat. It was an experiment by the Archive council, but it failed miserably." She looked over at Carlion and smiled reassuringly, no doubt having felt his unease. She told him, "Don't worry. There is only one other like him on the continent, and she is very closely monitored. Shara, myself, and every other Archive mage that has come after were never taught the advanced techniques and theories to wield our Awareness as a weapon."

"What about the desire to do so?" Carlion asked, concerned.

"I can't say there are many," Metauk answered. "Those seeking Awareness of the arcane usually do so without such bloodthirsty intentions, knowing the terrible cost to our bodies and minds."

"I find that hard to believe," Carlion said under his breath, not caring if Metauk heard him or felt his agitation. He turned his attention back to Yves, who was now talking to the group.

"You're welcome to sleep on the deck of the *Maddie*, but you ought to go find a tavern and eat first," Yves said. "The voyage to the lighthouse should only take three or four days with good weather, but the Stormbreaker Isles are the very definition of the frontier. Enjoy what Port has to offer tonight. When taking to the sea you never know when you'll get a hot meal served by a handsome face again."

CHAPTER SEVENTEEN

THORNE

It was the second day on the *Maddie* when the rain started. At first it was only a light mist, but when a proper shower started Thorne noticed that the main deck was now very sparsely populated. He had done his best to stay out of the crew's way, but the mage finally realized that he wasn't going to get an invitation to go below deck so he would have to take the initiative to avoid getting soaked.

Entering the forecastle, which was being used as both a storage area and the crew's sleeping quarters, the mage saw that Shara and Metauk were already there. There were also three members of the crew, two humans and a Venhadar, who were dozing on either the floor or the cargo. There was only a small lamp to provide light in the windowless room, which made it feel even more cramped.

"Where are Trinity and Carlion?" Thorne asked as he approached Metauk.

The Sehenryu shook her head and answered, "I don't know. Maybe they're with Amos? He's been spending a lot of time with Yves, so they might be in the captain's cabin."

"Why don't you go join them?" Shara said, making it clear that she wasn't in the mood for Thorne's company.

"I've no interest in getting any wetter than I already am,"

the mage said. "I'll just go find a seat over there." He nodded towards an area on the opposite end of the room. Shara didn't answer and turned her back on him. Metauk gave Thorne an apologetic look but also didn't say anything. He took the hint that he wasn't wanted and stepped away.

Leaving Shara and Metauk in the corner, Thorne crossed the room and found a small, open space between a number of barrels and crates that had been secured together and lashed to a bulkhead. Once he was seated, the mage noticed that one of the human crewmen had woken up and was intently watching Shara and Metauk. Thorne wasn't sure if it was because the mariner was unaccustomed to seeing a female or an Archive mage, as both were uncommon passengers on a corsair's ship.

A draft of cold, wet air swept into the room and caused everyone who was awake to look towards the door. Trinity quickly entered the forecastle and after shutting the door stood wiping rain from his face while waiting for his eyes to adjust to the dim interior.

"Trinity, over here," Thorne called out and gave a wave from his seat on the floor.

The mercenary banged his shins several times on cargo as he clumsily made his way over to Thorne. He sat down heavily on the floor next to the mage.

"Where have you been?" Thorne asked.

"Just taking in the scenery," Trinity said. "I hadn't realized until now that I missed the strange conflicting feelings of being confined to a ship but surrounded by the vastness of the ocean in every direction." The mercenary ran a hand gently along the wall and was quiet for a time before he said, "Amos tried to hide it, but I know he misses it, being on the water."

"It's only a manner of time before he gets the *Formica* back," Thorne said. "Vechas can't run forever."

"Perhaps," Trinity mused, his eyes distant for a moment.

With a slight shake of his head and a few hard blinks of his eyes, he said, "But speaking of biding your time, I found these laying around." The mercenary dug into his pocket and pulled out a pair of eight-sided dice. "You still remember how to play sevens?" he asked.

Thorne nodded and replied, "You go first. Beauty before wisdom, as they say."

Trinity shook the dice in his hand then tossed them against a crate. The small octahedrons tumbled to the deck and came to rest on a three and an eight. The mercenary grunted in discontent as he scooped up the dice and handed them to Thorne.

"Sitting in the belly of a corsair's ship waiting out a storm. This seems familiar," Trinity said as he watched Thorne lazily toss the dice.

"At least we're not smuggling ourselves this time," Thorne said. "And with Amos here we won't have to sleep with one eye open to make sure we don't get gutted in our sleep." The mage pushed the dice back in Trinity's direction.

Trinity was about to pick up the dice to make another roll when there was the loud bang of a fist hitting the top of a barrel on the other side of the room. Both Trinity and Thorne looked up to see that the two human crewmen had approached Shara and Metauk. From their posture it seemed like the Archive mages were not enjoying the conversation.

"No! I'm trying to tell you that's not something a mage can do. You're not listening!" Shara's said in a raised and angry voice.

"Bullshit! The Ishwos do it all the time," the bigger of the two mariners replied with matching volume.

"No, they don't," Shara shot back, banging the barrel again with her fist. "Climate can't be affected by Awareness. The amount of mana required would be astronomical." She put her hands on her hips and added, "And for the record, Ishwos don't do it all the time. The incidence of innately Aware Ishwos is the same for any other race, so we're talking one in several thousand. That could be ten to twenty familial pods, so it's extremely unlikely that you'd see wild magic in the open ocean."

"Maybe we should drag you outside anyway," the smaller sailor threatened. "If we dangle you from the railing then I bet you'll find whatever power you need to give us smooth sailing."

"Just try it and see what you get," Shara said. "I doubt your captain would even know you were thrown overboard before getting back to Port."

"She's busy making friends," Trinity muttered.

"Play nice over there," Thorne called over to the other side of the room.

"You're not the captain, so fuck off," the big sailor said to Thorne with an angry glare. It seemed like he was going to say something more when his smaller companion leaned in and whispered something. The big sailor's angry expression faded as he continued to study Thorne.

"Don't provoke a Paragon, you dumb fuck," said the Venhadar mariner who had been sleeping on a crate but now sat and watched the exchange. "I've heard they can kill an entire Sovereignty garrison by themselves."

"Fighting mages are a myth," the big sailor said, though his voice lacked the edge it did before. "So is the magic armor they supposedly wore. You take too much stock in old drinking stories."

"It's your funeral," the Venhadar mariner said and lay back down on the crate. "I'm taking your boots once I dump what's left of you out of them."

The small sailor used his elbow to jab his larger companion in the ribs and then shook his head. The big crewman scowled at Thorne and then Shara before stepping away. The pair went back to where they were resting before, but now both had their backs to the door and sullenly watched Shara or Thorne.

"Your reputation precedes you," Trinity said quietly, taking up the dice from the floor. "Though I haven't personally heard the story about wiping out a garrison, you did leave one hell of a body count when we left Deccern. I supposed it's a good thing that your martial abilities haven't atrophied, but I'm sure your little stunt will eventually make it back to the Archive."

"It couldn't be helped," Thorne said. "It's distressingly easy to act like I did in the bad old days when I'm let out of the house."

"How are they treating you now at the Archive?" Trinity asked, rolling the dice. He gave a disappointed grunt when he got a pair of low numbers.

"I'm like a guard dog that's snapped at its owner," Thorne said. "The council thinks I'm dangerous, but they keep me close for fear of me going off and aligning with one to the guilds or the Sovereignty. Either one would make their lives extremely inconvenient."

"What's to stop you from doing that now?" Trinity asked as he grabbed the dice from the floor and jostled them in his palm.

Thorne pulled back his left sleeve and showed the binding mark. "I need to behave myself so I can get this removed," the mage said.

"Why'd you let them do it in the first place?" Trinity wondered aloud.

"A gesture of submission after I made a pretty big mistake," the mage admitted. "My lab is melted beyond recognition and I have no doubt the council is worried that I'm trying to recreate some of my old research."

"Are you?" Trinity asked.

Thorne shook his head and replied, "All my work on weaponizing mana has been destroyed, as has that of all the other Paragons. There's nothing left in monograph, notebook, or letter, and with only two of us left alive, within a generation the Archive will have scrubbed a black mark off of their history."

"Then what were you doing? To wreck your lab?" the mercenary asked.

"You're unusually full of questions today," Thorne said. "I'll spare you the details, but I was trying to use alchemy to reach someone who's in the Void."

Before Trinity could ask anymore, the mage reached over and grabbed the dice from Trinity's hand. "That's enough of my troubles. In fact, if you had come to visit me sooner, I might not have been so lonely and tried to talk to someone on another plane."

"I told you before that I knew you weren't going anywhere," Trinity said. "I figured I'd get settled in Yaboon for a bit, maybe even see if any of the farms needed a foreman."

"Where have I heard that excuse before," Thorne said. "I told you a long time ago the fastest way to get provincial farmland is to get some farmer's daughter pregnant. Instant hereditary pastoral lifestyle, and then instead of spending your days fighting someone else's battles as a mercenary you can fight your own oxen to scratch lines in the dirt."

"Maybe I'll settle down when I get to be your age, old man," Trinity said with a grin.

Thorne chuckled and hefted the dice. "I know it's not our custom, but how about a wager? If I roll a seven here then you'll owe me a hot meal with food you harvested yourself. And maybe a kiss from your future wife."

Trinity gave a clipped laugh and replied, "If you're asking for such a valuable prize as a kiss, then you need to roll double sevens. With a single seven I'm only going to feed you."

Thorne closed his fist around the dice and could feel the edges dig into his palm. He pulsed a small amount of mana into his hand and pulled the density of the dice off center. The mage then flicked his fingers forward and the dice launched out of his hand and bounced off of the crate. When they both were still, each die rested showing a seven.

"Double sevens!" Trinity exclaimed. "That's uncanny luck. Wait, did you do something to those dice?"

Thorne tried to hide a smile behind an innocent expression. "Maybe," the mage said.

CHAPTER EIGHTTEEN

CARLION

The morning after the rainstorm, Carlion stood on the deck of the *Maddie* and scanned the horizon for any sign of land. The shower had lasted most of the night and the combination of wind and rain made the air smell less fishy. The sky was now free of clouds and the rising sun warmed the deck, both of which made Carlion hopeful that the fair weather would improve their chances of reaching Stormbreaker Lighthouse today. After three days of feeling trapped in the cramped confines of the ship, the Darkman was ready to be back on solid ground.

Taking a few steps back from the railing, the Darkman's foot hit a length of rope that had strayed loose from a coil next to the main mast. Carlion picked up the end and was about to drop it near the mast, but then he saw a thick metal ring attached to the mast near chest height. He knew it was used to secure cargo, but to the Darkman the first thing he thought of was a very similar looking ring used to tether horses at the Sovereignty stables. Almost automatically, he took the rope he held and tied a ring hitch to the hardware on the mast.

Just as he had finished and was about to leave the rope hanging from the ring, Carlion heard someone call down to him from the quarterdeck, "What type of knot was that?"

Looking up, the Darkman saw Dirty Dreebs watching him. "Come down here and I'll show you," Carlion replied.

The thin Venhadar slid under the quarterdeck railing and dropped to Carlion's level. Dirty Dreebs casually walked to the main mast and appraised the knot hanging on the metal ring. "Is that some type of horse knot?" he asked. "What's its purpose?"

Carlion pointed at the rope and answered, "It's a ring hitch. Cavaliers use it to secure their horses after they've dismounted, but it can be quickly undone." He tugged on the loose end of the rope and the knot unraveled and dropped to the deck.

"Securing horses, eh?" said Dirty Dreebs. "A quick release knot might be useful. Show me how to tie it."

Carlion picked up the rope and demonstrated the knot several times while the Venhadar watched closely. The Darkman then passed the rope to Dirty Dreebs to try.

"Your horse came from the southern continent on a ship?" Dirty Dreebs asked as he practiced attaching the rope to the metal ring on the mast. He was a quick study, handling the rope with skill.

Carlion nodded and answered, "She was traded to the Sovereignty as a foal and raised here."

"It must be a stressful voyage, to have such valuable cargo," Dirty Dreebs mused. "I'm sure the horse likes it none too much either."

"I've been told that building a stall for them makes the trip easier," Carlion said. "The mariners also have to make sure to secure the horse in a canvas sling so it doesn't break a leg when the ship rolls in a storm."

"Can horses get seasick?" Dirty Dreebs asked.

The Darkman shook his head and replied, "Not from the waves, but you have to keep fodder low on the deck so a horse's sinuses can drain. If a horse keeps its head high for too long it will get sick, so the stall and sling have to let it move some. Given how rare and expensive horses are on the continent, they're the best-treated passengers on a ship."

"Canvas sling and low food," Dirty Dreebs mused to himself. He untied the rope from the metal ring and handed it to Carlion. "Much appreciated," he said with a nod.

The deck creaked loudly behind Carlion and when he turned towards the sound he saw that Metauk was walking towards him. He raised his hand in greeting and asked her, "Finally came to get some fresh air?"

"And to stretch my legs," Metauk replied. "Being up top is nice, but I'm trying to stay out of the crew's way."

"They don't seem to mind the company," Carlion said. "In fact, I just taught him how to tie a new knot." Carlion turned around to gesture at Dirty Dreebs, but the Venhadar was back on the quarterdeck with his back to them.

"He's got quiet footfalls, that one," the Darkman said while he quickly tied another ring hitch to the mast.

"Metauk! I've been looking for you," came a call from behind.

Both Carlion and Metauk turned to see Amos crossing the deck towards them. There was sureness in the corsair's step and the Darkman had also noticed that Amos walked a little taller since he'd boarded the *Maddie*. When on the poop deck with Yves watching the crew during the voyage, Amos had projected a casual confidence that seemed to put the crew at ease. Likewise, Carlion got the impression that Amos was very much enjoying his time back on a ship.

The breeze pulled on the tails of Amos' blue and white striped bandana when he stopped in front of Metauk. "Can you scan the ship for me? I want to see how the crew are doing," the corsair asked.

The empath looked a bit surprised by the request but replied, "Sure. Hold on a minute." She closed her eyes and stood still for a short while. When Metauk opened her eyes and looked at Amos she said, "I felt a mixture of fatigue and boredom from the crew, but there weren't any especially strong emotions."

"That's good," Amos said, satisfied.

"You're not the captain of the ship, but are still looking out for the crew," Metauk said. "If this was how you ran your own ship, then I can see why everyone loves you in Port."

"It might also have something to do with making a lot of people rich with ill-gotten goods," Carlion said with a knowing grin.

"My operation was mostly smuggling, so not exactly ill-gotten," Amos corrected. "But I will give you that it made a lot of people rich." Gesturing towards Metauk he added, "How have you and Shara gotten on so far? I suppose that neither of you have traveled much by ship."

"We've both been fine," Metauk replied. "And aside from a minor disagreement we had with a couple crew members, we've gotten along with everyone. Which reminds me, I wanted to ask about how often ships like this run into a pod of Ishwos."

Amos shrugged and said, "If a ship has something an Ishwos wants, then they might make a deal. Otherwise, ships are ignored, and most mariners are fine with a live and let live mentality." The corsair looked at the knot tied to the metal ring on the mast and scoffed. "That's some sloppy rope work. Who did that?"

"I did," Carlion said defensively. "I was showing Dirty Dreebs how to tie a ring hitch."

"Any mariner that isn't green knows that one," Amos said.

"Then why would he pretend he didn't?" Carlion asked looking up to the quarterdeck. Dirty Dreebs was gone.

"What else did you two talk about?" Metauk asked.

"He wanted to know how horses get transported to the continent," Carlion replied.

"There it is," Amos said. "Yves has got some balls if he's going to start smuggling horses. It must have gotten to the point where it's lucrative enough to try. I bet some guild master in Port is looking for a way to further elevate their status."

"They'd never be able to keep it," Carlion said, shaking his head. "Unless you were a cavalier, or obviously with the military, you'd need an official set of documents to prove that you got the horse by the generosity of the prince."

"Forging credentials is far easier than smuggling horses across the ocean," Metauk said, absently looking out over the water.

"What would you know about that?" Amos asked. The corsair gave Metauk an incredulous look.

"Only what I've heard," Metauk said vaguely, glancing back at Amos. Turning to the center of the ship she inhaled sharply through her nose and then said, "Well, I should go check on Shara and make sure she's not picking another fight with the crew."

The Sehenryu turned away from the mercenaries and walked at a relaxed pace to the forecastle and went inside.

"There's much more to her than meets the eye," Amos said as the forecastle door snapped shut.

"What do you mean?" Carlion asked.

Before Amos could reply a shout from the bow cut across the deck, "Stormbreaker Isles on the horizon!"

CHAPTR NINETEEN

THORNE

At Stormbreaker Lighthouse the keeper met everyone on the small beach. A hearty man of middle age, he emerged from the heavily wooded island just as Dirty Dreebs was pulling the rowboat onto the sandy shore. Happy for the company, he talked at length about the weather around the archipelago and some of the interesting recent happenings. He told the group that his family had watched the same pod of Ishwos swim near the island closest to the lighthouse for several weeks. After getting a polite refusal for a tour of the island with his wife and children, and giving some notes about the surrounding islands, the keeper disappeared back into the woods where a steep path led up to the lighthouse.

Shortly thereafter, Thorne watched the rowboat retreat from the shore and back to the *Maddie*. The sloop wasn't able to navigate the archipelago and rock bars of the Stormbreaker Isles, so Yves had a rowboat take them to the lighthouse. Yves said that he'd come back for them at the end of the week, as that was all the time he could give them before his next shipping contract started.

When the rowboat disappeared against the backdrop of the *Maddie*, Thorne turned from the sea and looked at Shara. The Venhadar had continued to keep her distance from the mercenaries and only engaged Thorne when absolutely necessary. The mage had not made any headway in learning why she was being so hostile towards Trinity and the others, but thankfully she had not caused any major problems on the ship. However, they needed to start the search for Uksyo in earnest and Thorne needed to conserve his arcane energy. It was time to see if she was going to be useful.

"I heard you've gained a reputation for transmutation at the Archive," the mage said to Shara. "Let's see what you've got because I have no talent for that sort of thing. We should start the search with the island that the lighthouse keeper mentioned had all the Ishwos activity."

Shara looked at Thorne and the mercenaries who were standing behind him and scoffed. She turned and walked down the sandy shore a short distance to separate herself from the group. Then with a large sweeping gesture of her arms, a whorl of air suddenly erupted around her. The Venhadar's hair flew above her head and the sleeves of her robes flapped violently. From behind her, leaves were stripped from the trees and hurled upward in the spiral of air. As the leaves fell back to the ground they did so in an entirely unnatural manner. Guided by an unseen force, the leaves aligned themselves in offset layers into a pair of canoes and set of six paddles.

Lowering her arms, Shara approached one canoe and grabbed a paddle. With an easy motion she slid the hull into the water. Hitching up her robe the Venhadar climbed into the boat and knelt down at the bow. She looked back at Thorne and said, "You and Metauk are in this one with me."

The Sehenryu grabbed a paddle and bounced it a few times in her palm. Thorne followed suit and was impressed at how sturdy it felt despite being constructed only from leaves. Metauk nimbly stepped into the canoe, which left Thorne to push the vessel from the shore. The mage winced when icy water sloshed into his boots as he climbed into the back of the canoe. He pulled off his footwear and returned the water back into the sea.

While Thorne was wringing the water from the bottom of his trousers, he looked back to see the mercenaries still on the shore with apprehension on their faces. Finally, Trinity glanced up to the other canoe and called out, "Just how seaworthy are these boats? The walls are distressingly thin."

Shara gave the mercenary a sharp look and shouted back, "Just get in it. I'm not going to drown you. Yet."

Thorne watched Trinity and Carlion help Amos climb into the canoe. Despite the weight of the three mercenaries and their gear, the boat buoyed them with ease. A few powerful paddle strokes from Trinity drew the two canoes side by side. As everyone settled into more comfortable positions for paddling, Thorne saw that Carlion was rubbing his hands along the interior of his canoe.

"This is amazing," the Darkman said. "I don't feel any seams at all. How long will the leaves stay like this, as a canoe?"

"As long as I am near it," Shara said as she dug into the water, nudging the boat towards the island on the horizon.

"What happens if you get too far away?" Carlion asked.

"Without my mana to hold the leaves together what you're sitting in will cease to be a canoe," Shara said. "You'd be wise to keep me safe while we search that island or you'll be swimming back to the lighthouse."

The Venhadar made her last comment sound like a threat and they paddled over to the island in silence. Thankfully, there was a slight tailwind and it was not long before the canoes were within arrowshot of the island that was being frequented by a pod of Ishwos.

Thorne was now able to appraise more of the island's topography, and one entire side of the island was a sheer cliff of slate grey stone. As the pair of canoes began to follow the island's coast, Thorne could hear a rhythmic gurgle along with the slapping of water on rock. At first, he thought it was some strange echoing effect of the waves, but then saw the top edge of a submerged cavern. The sound of the water being sucked in and then pushed back out stayed with Thorne even after they paddled around the island and eventually found a small rocky shore that led up into the green and grey hued forest interior.

"What is this rogue mage going to accomplish on this island? If he's even out here," Amos asked once they had pulled both canoes up onto the rocks. Sliding his paddle underneath the overturned boat, the Venhadar then dried his hands on the front of his shirt.

Thorne looked at Amos and then up into where the struggling evergreens were casting grey shadows onto the shore. A cloudy sky had yielded only weak, intermittent sunshine during their paddle from the lighthouse. The mage shook his head and replied, "I don't know for certain, but I imagine being secluded was the whole point. No prying eyes here."

From his satchel, Thorne retrieved a rough sketch of the island that the lighthouse keeper had given him. The mage drew close to Trinity and asked quietly, "How long do you think it would take three of you to search the island?"

"Three of us?" the mercenary asked, drawing back in surprise. "Where's everyone else going?"

"The submerged cavern on our way here. It gave me a thought," Thorne said. "What if Uksyo's not working on this island, but under it?"

Without waiting for a response, Thorne turned to Metauk. Raising his voice loud enough for everyone to hear, the mage asked, "Any chance you've sensed strong emotions that aren't from the group?" Thorne gave a sidelong glance at Shara as he put the drawing back into his bag.

The Sehenryu took a few steps towards the water before turning around and slowly sweeping her gaze across what she could see of the island. She did this for a short while, sometimes with closed eyes and a furrowed brow. Finally, she looked at Thorne and shrugged her shoulders. Metauk sounded unsure when she said, "I think there's someone here, but the feelings I'm getting are vague and more like urges. Maybe there's more than one person here. What I'm picking up most strongly is an intense hunger, an impulse to feed."

"So, something on this island is hungry. That's no surprise, and standing here in the open makes us easy targets," Shara said loudly. She pointed an accusing finger at Thorne and added, "You had all that time on the *Maddie* to come up with a plan. What are we doing?"

"We're splitting up," Thorne said definitively. "There is likely a network of caverns under the island. If Uksyo wanted to work on something without being watched, that's where he'd hide."

"How can you be so sure?" Shara asked.

"That's what I'd do," Thorne replied.

"I wouldn't be so proud of thinking like a criminal," Shara muttered just loud enough for everyone to hear.

Metauk rested a comforting hand on Shara's shoulder and said, "We don't even know if he's here. This could all be a fabrication of Nion's. Let's search the island and get back to the lighthouse so Yves can pick us up." The Sehenryu looked at Thorne and asked, "Even if there are tunnels under the island, how will we investigate them?"

Thorne gave Shara a pointed look and replied, "Since I'm apparently thinking for everyone now, I do know what at least half of us are doing. I'm going to craft an Ishwos Bubble and we'll use it to search the submerged caverns."

"Half of us?" Carlion asked. "What does that mean?"

"Metauk, Amos, and I will go underwater. You, Trinity, and Shara will search on the island," Thorne said.

Shara violently kicked her foot into the ground and sent a spray of pebbles into the water. "I won't be alone with them!" she said angrily.

"What'd we ever do to you?" Trinity said angrily. He took an aggressive step towards Shara. "I'm getting tired of your attitude."

"Stay back!" Shara roared. Thorne heard instantly that the Venhadar's voice was amplified and manipulated by her Awareness. It had a volume and timbre meant to frighten any would-be assailants and was a defensive technique taught to all Archive mages before they went on their traveling education. Trinity recoiled and retreated a step, stunned by the outburst.

"Stop it, Shara!" Thorne's voice did not have the same power behind it, but was said with a commanding presence. In a severe but quieter tone he continued, "We don't have time for bickering. You supposedly chose to come out here with me of your own free will, knowing full well that I'm in charge. So do what I tell you and search the island with Trinity and Carlion."

"This is a mistake," Shara growled and stormed away down the beach.

"I'll go talk to her. Try to calm her down," Metauk said. The Sehenryu caught up to Shara in a few long strides. Thorne and the mercenaries watched the two mages for a short time. Metauk reached out and rested her hand on Shara's shoulder, seemingly trying to comfort her. The Venhadar shook her head violently and pointed back to the group. When she saw she was being watched, Shara turned her back so her face was hidden.

"Splitting up will make searching for your rogue mage faster for certain," Trinity said, "but what happens when one of us finds him?"

"Come back here," Thorne said. "We'll regroup and confront

him together." The mage looked grim when he said, "This isn't going to be like snatching Nion. If he's really out here, Uksyo is dangerous."

Carlion grunted, then slapped his hand hard against Amos' back. "Looks like you drew the short straw," the Darkman said. "Bet you didn't expect being an honorary Ishwos today."

Amos scowled and replied, "No, I try to keep my head above the water." Turning to Thorne, the corsair asked, "How'd I get to be your favorite today?"

"Given your size, I figure you'll suck up less air," Thorne said with a grin.

Amos' frown deepened for a second before relaxing as he laughed. "You can go fuck yourself," the corsair said with a chuckle.

It was then that Thorne saw Metauk return alone to the group. Shara was still down the beach and staring out across the sea. The Sehenryu looked at the mercenaries and said, "I think I calmed her down. She'll cooperate with you."

"What is her problem?" Trinity asked, exasperated.

"It's not my place to say," Metauk said, looking uncomfortable. "What I can tell you is that the sooner we search this island and get home, the happier we all will be. Thorne, if I'm going with you, I'm ready."

With the others looking on, Thorne waded into the sea up to his knees. As incoming waves splashed against his legs, the water around him began to churn. The mage found a single bubble and focused his Awareness on it. The bubble became unnaturally static and began slowly to enlarge as Thorne carefully added both film and air. When it was the size of an apple Thorne slowly moved the bubble to be positioned between him and the shore. Now with his legs blocking the incoming waves, the mage was able to grow the bubble slightly faster until it was the size of a large boulder. Floating on the surface of the dark water, the sphere had an iridescent sheen and appeared as glass, but it was only the strength of Thorne's mana that kept the bubble intact. He manipulated the bubble until it was resting just on the shore where it gently rocked back and forth with the movement of the waves coming ashore.

"Nothing fancy from you two," Thorne said to Trinity and Carlion. "If you find him, then you come back here and wait for us."

Trinity nodded and replied, "Likewise for you. Good luck."

Thorne turned to face the bubble and caught a glimpse of his own reflection. Behind his determined look was a face that openly wore its age and weariness. He closed his eyes as he walked into the bubble and felt the slimy film slick his exposed skin. The ground no longer felt uneven like the rocky shore, but instead smooth and slightly curved. Drawing a sleeve across his eyes and nose, Thorne then gestured for Metauk and Amos to join him inside the bubble.

Without ceremony, Metauk stepped inside the bubble to join Thorne, shielding her face with her hand as she passed through the film. Amos gave a casual wave to those remaining on the shore and entered the bubble. There was not much room to maneuver inside the suddenly claustrophobic vessel as Thorne focused his Awareness and moved the bubble away from the shore. He slowly rotated their underwater vessel so that it faced towards the submerged cavern and in a controlled manner piloted the bubble down into the water.

"How are you moving this thing?" Amos asked, looking up as the bubble became fully enveloped by the sea.

"By manipulating the water around it, both push and pull, I can change its course and speed," Thorne said.

"What happens if the bubble bursts?" Amos asked, still looking up at the surface.

The mage gave a small smile, "We get wet."

The bubble dropped straight down until the already pale sunlight barely filtered through the water. From inside the bubble, the sea looked a grey-green that darkened into blackness as they looked in any direction save up. They skimmed close to the bottom and made their way to the submerged cavern.

"We're going to need a light," Thorne said, looking at Metauk. In the cramped space he awkwardly reached into his satchel and pulled out a small glass sphere. Handing it to Metauk the mage asked, "Can you charge this so we can see where we're going?"

The Sehenryu engulfed the glass sphere in her fist and closed her eyes for a moment. Opening both her eyes and her hand simultaneously the sphere slowly illuminated with a warm yellow light that radiated out from the bubble.

Now able to see their surroundings, Thorne navigated the bubble into the cavern. The water in the cavern was moving past the bubble in a slow, rhythmic manner as water flowed into and out of the cavern's entrance. Despite all of the movement outside of the bubble, Thorne kept the vessel stable and moving smoothly deeper inside. They hugged one wall of the cavern as they ventured inward and Metauk's light shone on multicolored bands of rock.

"I'm surprised you still have such fine control of your Awareness," Metauk said, watching Thorne pilot the bubble. "I was told that binding marks dampen a mage's precision."

"It's only a ward to keep me from the alchemic labs," the mage replied. "Now that I'm nowhere near the Archive, it's just an ugly tattoo. When this is done, I was promised that it would be removed."

Metauk frowned slightly, "Even so, it will leave a scar. I don't think the infirmary will be able to do anything for it other than accelerate your healing."

"Only some scars fade," Thorne said with a distant

expression.

"What do you mean?" Metauk asked.

"It's not important," the mage said dismissively. "But it does remind me that Olaf never explained why you and Shara were recruited for this little adventure." Turning to look at Metauk, Thorne asked, "Could it be that I'm not the only pariah in the Archive?"

The empath gave a little smile, "Not so much." She adjusted the glow sphere in her hand and the shifting light briefly dilated her vertical pupils, which gave Metauk an acutely alert expression. "I've never kept it a secret that I'm tired of being confined to Archive walls. I want to go out and see the world," she emphasized the last word, "and I even had my mentor's blessing to start my traveling education early, but the council wouldn't approve it. They said I wasn't ready and needed to have more patience."

"What made them change their mind?" Thorne asked. "This is considerably more dangerous than the typical sabbatical from the Archive."

"Perhaps," Metauk said. "I don't think the council believes Nion's story, and they expect us to come back empty handed. In Tarbeck's view, this assignment keeps you out of the Archive on a wild goose chase, but now has the added benefit that I won't be bothering the council to leave on a premature traveling education."

"Fair enough," the mage said, who thought it seemed a reasonable justification and would explain her overall positive demeanor thus far. "But what about Shara?" he asked.

Metauk looked away from Thorne, but not before the mage saw a strange expression flash across her face. "She doesn't like being alone, and she worries," the empath said quietly.

Amos interrupted the conversation by interjecting excitedly, "Hey! Look there!" The corsair pointed at a shadow darting past the bubble. Metauk shoved her glow sphere up against the film just in time to see a humanoid with blue skin and long black hair swim away.

"It's an Ishwos!" Metauk said. "He's seen us!"

The Ishwos flipped around and darted away from the bubble. Thorne accelerated their vessel in pursuit.

"What's he doing here?" Metauk asked.

"Let's ask him," Thorne said, a predatory gleam in his eye.

"How are we going to do that?" Amos asked.

"I'm still working on that part," the mage said tensely.

The Ishwos skimmed close to the cavern floor, weaving around small protrusions of rock. He was corkscrewing and generating bubbles that made it difficult to track him.

"Don't lose him! Make this thing go faster!" Metauk urged.

"Brace yourself!" Thorne said.

"Against what?" Amos asked as the bubble lurched forward.

Thorne elongated the bubble into an ellipsoid. The three inside were now on their stomachs with heads arching back to look forward. The more streamlined shape gave the bubble additional speed, but the Ishwos was twisting wildly around outcroppings of rock, leaving pursuit difficult.

"Find him," Thorne commanded to Metauk when the Ishwos was lost from view. The Sehenryu gave the mage an irritated look and retorted, "My abilities aren't that precise. He's still in here, but I can't tell exactly where."

"What about that wide crack?" Amos said.

"Where?" Thorne asked.

The corsair pointed in the murky shadows near the base of a rock pillar. "Over there I can see something sparkling at the bottom."

Navigating the bubble to where the corsair had indicated, Thorne saw there was indeed a fissure. Surrounding the opening were shimmering flecks imbedded in cracks around the opening that seemed to flicker with their own light.

"That looks like pixie dust," Metauk said. "But why would it be here?"

"Maybe it's to mark an entrance," Thorne guessed. "It'll be a tight fit, but I think we can make it. We'll have to be very careful once we enter the tunnel. Maneuvering the bubble will get tricky."

The mage moved the bubble to the entrance of the narrow cave. He shrank the vessel even more, which pressed all three together to the point of it being uncomfortable, and slid through the narrow tunnel. As he got close to the bottom, he could see the sparkling sand that Amos mentioned. The iridescence reminded him of the pixie dust he found in Rell-Kyr. Thorne wondered if there was any connection, but didn't have time to dwell on it because the top of the bubble was suddenly bathed in an unnatural blue light.

CHAPTER TWENTY

CARLION

With Thorne now gone, Carlion trusted Shara only as far as he could see her. The Venhadar's outburst that pushed back the normally unflappable Trinity suggested that her hostile demeanor was not merely bluster. The Darkman was also skeptical of Metauk's assertion that the Archive didn't train mages for combat. While he had never seen one on a battlefield, Carlion had assumed before it was because of their fatal weakness to iron weapons. When Shara demanded that she walk behind the mercenaries as they searched the island interior, Carlion found that he looked over his shoulder often.

Upon leaving the rocky shore, they found the terrain was mostly sparse underbrush. The few trees that could take root in the rocky earth were stunted and provided no protection from the salty wind coming off of the sea. In fact, the entire island felt damp and cold, which did little to lessen Carlion's bleak mood. With the shore still in view, Carlion brushed his hand across the top of a pine tree that was struggling to grow straight. The constant wind pushing into the island's interior and the inability to take deep root left the tree in a sorry state.

A snapping noise at his side made Carlion quickly turn his head towards the unexpected sound. He saw that Trinity had twisted a thick branch from a bush and left it hanging by a strip of bark.

"What are you doing?" Shara asked irritated.

"Leaving a trail that we can follow back to the beach," the mercenary replied as if the answer was obvious.

"We're on an island. We can't get lost," Shara said.

"We won't because I'm doing this."

The Venhadar frowned and was about to reply when something caught her attention and she jerked her head back towards the shore. "Something's wrong," she said.

"What're you talking about?" Carlion said, but then sensed it also. It was a buzzing sound that he felt more than heard and left him slightly disoriented. Shaking his head to clear the sensation, the Darkman noticed that Shara's face showed a mixture of confusion and fear. She was looking down at her hands as if she didn't recognize them.

"What is it?" Carlion asked, taking a tentative step towards her.

Shara looked up at the Darkman with fear in her eyes and said, "I don't know. Something feels strange. What? No!" The Venhadar looked back to the shore and Carlion watched with her as the two canoes collapsed. The leaves then scattered in a gust of wind that carried an eerie whistle with it.

"What was that?" Trinity asked. The mercenary pulled his short sword free from his belt and began scanning the interior of the island.

Carlion drew his own sword and surveyed what little of the shore he could see from where they were standing. Something caught his eye and he pointed with the tip of his sword. "Look!" he exclaimed.

Lumbering slowly up to what remained of the canoes were two large, brutish creatures. As they came closer, Carlion saw they were minotaurs, their cloven hooves crushing the small stones that comprised the beach as they walked at an unhurried pace. They were clothed only in hide breechcloths with the rest of their dark, furred body and horned head exposed. The monstrous creatures held swords that were far too heavy for a man to wield, but could easily cleave one in half. Stopping to examine the piles of leaves that were once Shara's canoes, the wide nostrils of the creatures flared as they snorted and sniffed.

"What sorcery is this?" Carlion whispered to Shara. "They look like minotaurs, but such monsters are just stories told to children. They can't be real." He had initially felt an intense wave of fear wash over him, but his years of battle experience helped to quickly suppress the feeling.

"Minotaurs? What are you talking about? You don't see those two wyverns?" Shara said with a sidelong glance at Carlion. The Darkman gave a strange look in return, not understanding the Venhadar's statement. Shara saw his confused look and pointed to the shore where the minotaurs were poking at the leaves with their weapons. "Right there!"

"You've gone mad!" the Darkman said. "There aren't any dragonlings there! Trinity, tell her!" Looking to his fellow mercenary for confirmation, Carlion was shocked to see that Trinity's face had drained of all color.

Without thinking, Carlion grabbed Shara's shoulder and said, "We need to find cover."

"Don't touch me!" Shara shouted with a violent jerk of her shoulder.

Carlion jumped back a step. He was about to chastise Shara for giving away their position, but then realized it was too late. His eyes flicked to the shore and saw the minotaurs looking at them. With a pair of angry snorts, the two creatures slowly moved in their direction.

"They've seen us," Shara said, fear in her voice. "This is your fault!" she hissed at Carlion.

"Can you fight?" Carlion asked, looking at her. Trinity drew up beside the Darkman. Besides his short sword, the mercenary now also had a dagger in his off hand.

Shara quickly shook her head and continued staring wide eyed at the creatures on the shore. "I'm a laboratory alchemist," she said, almost apologetically. "I can move energy and transmute materials, but I– I don't know," she stammered at the end.

Trinity seemed to have regained his composure and stepped towards the shore. "We're at a disadvantage here," he said. "We need to meet them on the shore. Shara, you stay here and try to find a place to hide."

"Try to get around them," Carlion said, stepping ahead of Trinity and forgetting the Venhadar for the moment. "Let's see what we're up against," he said with more confidence than he felt. With his sword poised to attack, the Darkman slowly approached the creatures on the rocky shore.

Moving faster now that he was in plain sight, Carlion saw that the minotaurs walked with a strange gliding gait. Wasting no time, the lead creature swung its weapon with almost a casual gesture, which Carlion easily ducked under. From his crouch he leapt past the minotaur and sliced his sword across the creature's torso. The blade disappeared into the creature's body without resistance and the Darkman stumbled off balance.

As Carlion regained his footing, he heard swords clash and whirled around in time to see Trinity's short sword locked with the other minotaur's blade. The mercenary's teeth were gritted with effort as he tried to push his short sword forward. With a shout, he tried to stab forward with his dagger. Similar to Carlion's attack, Trinity's blade and part of his hand disappeared into the creature.

The minotaur shoved its sword forward and knocked Trinity to the ground. Carlion realized that he wouldn't be able to get to him in time with the other minotaur blocking the way. The Darkman dodged another slow swing and shouted in an attempted to draw both creatures' attention. The minotaur bearing down on Trinity wasn't going to be distracted and raised its sword high for the killing blow.

An unnaturally loud shout from where the shore met the underbrush made the minotaur look up. Shara had come down from the underbrush and was holding something over her head that emitted a bright, white light. With an impressively strong throw, she hurled the object at the minotaur looming over Trinity. The creature tried to swat away the projectile, but was too slow. The object hit the minotaur in the chest and an explosion of light erupted from the impact accompanied by the snapping boom of a thunderclap.

The creature howled and reeled backwards several steps. Carlion used the opening and ran to Trinity, then jerked the mercenary to his feet. Pushing Trinity towards Shara, Carlion shouted at both of them, "Run!"

Shara didn't need the prompt and was already sprinting back into the underbrush. Both mercenaries dashed to catch up to her, their boots sending pebbles scattering. With a final look over his shoulder, Carlion saw that the minotaurs were following them at an unhurried pace with that same peculiar gliding stride.

Shara's trail was easy to follow, as the Venhadar was haphazardly crashing through the underbrush in such a way that made Trinity's previous attempts to mark a trail seem subtle in comparison. The mercenaries eventually caught up to her because she had stopped in a small clearing to catch her breath. Bent over at the waist with her hands resting on her knees, Shara was taking big gulps of air when she looked up in alarm as the mercenaries approached.

"How far behind us are they?" Shara wheezed.

Trinity looked back the way they had come and replied,

"They didn't seem to be in any hurry, so maybe a quarter hour." After returning his weapons to his belt the mercenary untied the thread that held back his ponytail and shook out his hair trying to remove the twigs and brambles acquired during the flight from the shore. Giving Shara a questioning expression, Trinity asked, "What were those creatures? The way those bodies were stitched together was grotesque. What butcher could do that to a man?"

Shara stood straight and gave Trinity a confused look. "Have you gone mad?" she asked. "Those weren't men. Those were wyverns. Corrupted dragon spawn. But I don't understand where they came from. Wyverns haven't been seen on the continent for generations."

"Wait a minute," Carlion interrupted. "I didn't see a man or a dragon. I saw a minotaur."

Shara scoffed and said, "Minotaurs aren't real. Like you said before, stories told to frighten children."

Trinity was thoughtful when he said, "Perhaps. We all saw something different on the shore. How can that be?"

"Whatever they are, we don't have much time to come up with a plan to fight them," Carlion said. "They might not have been moving fast, but we can't run forever. We don't have the canoes any longer either."

"That's not my fault," Shara said defensively. Looking down at her hands she added, "My Awareness feels fragmented. I can't seem to focus."

"Fear will do that, especially for someone unaccustomed to fighting," Carlion said, trying to sound understanding. "Just try to calm down and help us come up with a plan. Your magic will probably return with some time."

The Venhadar gave him an angry look and spat, "I'm not afraid!" She reached down and snatched up a leaf from the ground and held it in the palm of her hand. Staring at the leaf, her nostrils flared as forced breaths threatened to flip the leaf out of her palm. Shara let out an audible sigh of relief when it finally levitated a few inches above her open palm and rotated slowly. Snatching the leaf with her other hand she exclaimed, "See! Not afraid."

"Fine," Carlion said, conceding the point. "Right now we need to either hide and wait for Thorne, or we figure out how to fight those things."

"There's really only one option since we don't know when they'll be back," Trinity said.

Carlion nodded in agreement and said, "Fight it is then. We'll set up an ambush, but to pull it off we need to work together." He said the last word with a pointed look to Shara. "You helped us escape. What did you throw?"

Shara reached into one of the pouches at her waist and pulled out a small glass sphere. "Mages use them to create light at night," Shara said. "I charged one with my mana, but I didn't expect it to explode like it did. It's not supposed to do that." Her expression fell when she added, "This is the only one I have left."

"What about our swords?" Trinity asked. "Could you magic those?"

The Venhadar shook her head and replied, "I could easily do it at the Archive, but I don't have the proper equipment or materials here. The only thing I can do here is energize objects with a direct transfer of my mana. I'd have to touch it." Shara's expression grew fierce and she jabbed a finger at Trinity, "But I won't burn my hand on mercenary iron. Never."

Trinity took a step towards Shara, who moved backwards the same distance. The mercenary's expression was grim when he said, "Whatever your grudge is against us, you need to put it aside for the next few minutes. If we don't work together, we're not going to last long on this island. I need your help now."

Carlion could see that Shara was struggling to reconcile pragmatism against principle. Finally, she thrust her chin behind Trinity and said, "Go cut some saplings to make spears. And get some rocks you could throw. I'll charge those. If we were fighting regular soldiers, it wouldn't do anything, but against these monsters it might work."

Satisfied, Trinity went to complete the task. The Darkman gave Shara an appraising look before joining the mercenary. As he sheared short branches off a tree, Carlion hoped that Thorne and the others were faring better. The Darkman was reluctant to admit it, but after seeing firsthand the rare power of combat magic, he wished Thorne was with them now.

CHAPTER TWENTYONE

THORNE

"I still don't believe it. The amount of mana needed to push this much water out of the caverns and keep it out is unreal," Metauk said, her fingers lightly running through the wall of water held back by an unseen power. When the bubble had buoyed to the surface, they found themselves in a small chamber devoid of seawater. The light they had seen on their ascent came from phosphorescent algae adhered to the moist floor. The blue glow cast indistinct shadows along a narrow tunnel that had opened into what, at first, seemed to be a large tunnel, but when Metauk went to inspect the subtly moving walls she found them to be made of water.

"We need to be careful," Thorne said. "We're lucky that no one was here when we emerged. If Uksyo catches us, he'll easily drown us all by flooding the tunnel." The mage looked at Amos, who was still trying to scrape remnants of film from the bubble out of his beard, and asked, "Can you make any sense of this? Where are we?"

The corsair pulled out a dagger and held it in a reverse grip loosely in his hand. "Once we get to a wall that's made of stone and not water, I'll let you know," he said.

"Be on your guard," the mage cautioned again. With a glance towards Metauk he asked, "Can you sense him?"

The Sehenryu stood still for a moment as if listening for something, but then furrowed her brow. "Maybe?" she answered tentatively. "I don't know if the displaced water or something else is interfering with my empathy, but what I'm feeling is more like an echo." She looked at Thorne with a tense face and said, "One thing I'm certain of is that whoever is down here has a powerful command of their mana." She reached into the pouch on her belt and pulled out a fist dagger.

Amos' eyebrows jerked up when he saw the weapon, "Well, aren't you full of surprises. Since when do mages carry an assassin's knife?"

Metauk gave a weak smile and adjusted her grip so the blade rested comfortably between her middle and ring fingers. "I wasn't always a mage," she said.

"Quiet!" Thorne hissed as he took the lead down the tunnel. Staying close to the walls, he quietly led the others deeper into the passageway. Despite the cool underground temperatures, the humidity clung to his skin and made his movements feel sluggish. The tunnel eventually opened into a huge cavern made of actual stone that had blue glowing algae on the walls and floor. Despite the extra luminescence, the ceiling and back of the cavern was still shadowed from where they entered.

"Spread out, but be careful," Thorne said. The mage heard Amos tapping his dagger against a wall in an attempt to use the echo to determine how deep they were underground.

Moving away from the others, Thorne realized that they had entered Uksyo's laboratory. Sculpted into a wall was a long workbench that had several alchemic retorts and alembics. There were also glass jars that contained solutions of various colors, metal filings, and dried powders, all neatly organized and labeled. Surprisingly, what weren't organized were Uksyo's writings. Scraps of paper were all along the table, written in small but precise handwriting. Some of the notes also contained drawings of archways or complex alchemical equations.

"Thorne, come look at this!" Metauk called from the back of room.

Joining the Sehenryu, Thorne stood in front of a raised area with a freestanding stone arch that was slightly taller than a man. Metauk suspiciously eyed the device while Thorne walked around the entire apparatus. Cascading down from the keystone and filing the entire space under the arch was a dark film. It appeared the same from either side, but completely blocked the view through the archway. Looking carefully at the film, Thorne realized he was staring at an entry point into the Void. The archway was an Engine, and the mage could feel a subtle pull coming from the aperture.

"I've never seen an Engine this big before," Thorne said in awe. "And stably open. This is incredible. Terrible, but incredible."

"What is the bastard doing here?" Amos asked, approaching Thorne. The corsair held up a fistful of notes from the table. "The engineering to construct a stone archway I understand, but this," he waved the paper scraps, "is gibberish to me."

"I don't know," Thorne said. "But he's made something that is heavily restricted by the Archive. Normally, these devices are only tabletop sized and used in planar transport experiments. The apertures generated by Engines are normally unstable and incredibly energy intensive to operate." The mage stepped back to take in the entire structure, "It looks like this one is big enough to send a person through. This took a high level of technical skill and extremely precise application of Awareness to construct. I don't know how he was able to do this all on his own."

"You could just ask me," an unfamiliar voice echoed in the cavern.

Thorne spun around and watched a silhouette backlit by

blue light slowly approach them. In the dim light it was difficult to determine the color, but the figure was wearing alchemist robes cinched by a wide belt. Dramatically pulling the hood back, he revealed himself as a man with a hard angular face. His long white hair was pulled back in a tight ponytail that exposed a high widow's peak. With narrow set eyes, the man stared at them with a predatory intensity.

Giving them an unpleasant smile, the man said, "This is a surprise. Of all of the dogs that the Archive could send, they loosed the one on the shortest leash. Welcome, Thorne."

"You know me," the mage said calmly. "I can't say the same for you, Uksyo Serrant."

"No matter," Uksyo said, stuffing his hands inside the sleeves of his robe. "As I think about it, you being sent here must have been Olaf's doing. A Paragon would be best suited for this business, no?"

"That's not who I am anymore," Thorne said tersely.

"Oh, I see," Uksyo said, clearly enjoying Thorne's reaction.

"You appear to know why we're here," Metauk said, though her voice was weak.

Uksyo gave the Sehenryu an appraising look and said, "I don't know you, but now I can guess how you were able to find me. Since you seem unharmed, I can only assume you never set foot on the island."

"Why?" Metauk asked with a stronger voice.

"I left a few surprises for anyone who would have explored the island," Uksyo said. He made a vague gesture upwards.

"What are you talking about?" Metauk asked anxiously. She took a step towards Uksyo only to have Thorne reach out and grab her shoulder and pull her back out of his line of sight.

"I was told they were called Terrors," Uksyo said with a feral grin. "They were a gift, but I doubt I would have been able to control entities from the Void very well, so I let them roam the island." Uksyo seemed to be struck by a thought and took a small step backwards and dramatically placed a hand over his heart. "Oh dear," he said with mock concern, "Did you leave some friends up there?"

"You're a piece of shit, mate," Amos growled. "It'll be my pleasure to kick your teeth in before we drag you back to Yaboon."

Uksyo peered at the corsair and made a wet clicking sound with his tongue. "I think Master Thorne will agree that is ill advised," he said. "If you would be so kind as to look up."

Amos did a double take when he examined the ceiling. "Fuck me," the corsair said quietly.

Not trusting Uksyo, Thorne only flicked his eyes upwards but it was enough for him to see that the cavern was much taller than it appeared because the ceiling that Uksyo constructed was made of water. The pale blue light from the floor shimmered on the surface, which masked that the ceiling was subtly moving. It appeared that Uksyo had only partially evacuated the cavern they were in now and could bring a deluge of water crashing down on them in an instant.

"You'd drown along with us," Metauk said, still staring up at the celling.

"I agree it would be a poor plan if I had not prepared something for myself," Uksyo said. He patted a pouch on his belt and continued, "But I have done so."

"Bullshit," Amos barked. He looked at Thorne, "Just say the word so we can bag this fucker and go home." The corsair tensed his body and just waited for the command to pounce.

"Wait! He's telling the truth," Metauk said quickly, her gaze now on Uksyo. "I'm not feeling any duplicity from him."

Uksyo bared his teeth in an imitation smile. "Isn't Sehenryu empathy delightful?" he said.

Tired of Uksyo's games, Thorne pushed a large amount of

mana into his right fist. A faint amber glow radiated outward and contrasted sharply with the otherwise blue tinted room.

Uksyo's smile vanished and his eyes narrowed. From the ceiling streams of water began to fall as if it was a leaking roof in a rainstorm. "Careful, Master Thorne," he warned. "I'm not a man to bluff. Are you prepared to fight and possibly die for the Archive once again? Didn't you just tell me you are no longer a Paragon?"

Metauk and Amos looked at Thorne, both trying to gauge the mage's reaction. Thorne was quiet for a moment, and the only sound in the cavern was the water dripping from the ceiling. Uksyo seemed to enjoy the rhythmic wet slapping sound and tapped one finger against his hip in time with it.

Finally, Amos blurted out, "Fuck!" The corsair was nearly vibrating with nervous energy.

Thorne glanced at Amos and smiled. He then looked at Uksyo and said, "A bit of a stalemate we have here." The mage slowly dissipated his mana charge and the amber glow faded from his fist.

Uksyo returned a toothy smile and replied, "Only if you don't want to drown. I'm not sure what sea water would do to the Engine, but I'd wager something would be salvageable." Water stopped falling from the ceiling and the cavern was once again silent.

"Indeed," Thorne said, striking a conversational tone. He needed to buy some time to figure out a way out this mess, before Amos tried to rush Uksyo. Despite Metauk carrying a dagger, the mage wasn't aware of any martial training the Sehenryu had obtained prior to her joining the Archive and wasn't going to take any chances with Uksyo clearly at an advantage. Trying to project casual interest he said, "How were you able to build an Engine of such size here? Transporting the required materials must have been challenge."

"I was able to buy cooperation from a pod of Ishwos easily enough. They brought me what I needed initially, but they could only deliver so much," Uksyo said with a relaxed expression. Seemingly without concern he walked past Thorne and Metauk. Approaching the Engine he added, "I had to make some improvisations."

Uksyo stared into the open aperture of the Engine, which periodically shimmered with an internal light in the otherwise cascading film of black nothingness. "I sometimes catch myself just staring into the Void," Uksyo said in meditative tone. "It reminds me of a simpler time, perhaps a happier time. Being fully Aware is a burden, don't you think? Tell me, Thorne, what do you see when you stare into the Void?" Uksyo looked back at the mage and gestured to his side, inviting Thorne to join him at the Engine's threshold.

Thorne moved to Uksyo's side and looked into the open portal of the Engine. The cascading ripple of darkness underneath the arch was both familiar and alien, comforting and threatening. Above all, it radiated a barely contained power that could only be described as entropy made manifest. "I see a black canvas on which I can paint all my past regrets," the mage said with an honesty that surprised him.

"Any insight worth having is paid for with such currency," Uksyo said contemplatively. "Give Reihana my regards if you see her." Then with a startling quickness, he shoved Thorne through the aperture of the Engine.

Thorne twisted as he passed through the black film and found that Uksyo still had a calm expression on the other side. The mage thought he heard Amos shout something, but the sound was muffled like the corsair was yelling under water. As his legs passed thorough the film and didn't hit a floor, Thorne realized that he was falling through empty space.

In the instant before he plummeted from the aperture,

Thorne acted instinctively and used a technique he had not called upon in years. Simultaneously charging and releasing his mana, the mage ejected a ribbon of magenta light from an outstretched hand. The tendril shot back up through the aperture and snaked around Uksyo's leg. Using the force of his uncontrolled decent for additional power, Thorne jerked his arm back and pulled the ribbon taut.

The mage heard Uksyo's surprised yell change in pitch as he was pulled from the cavern, through the black film of the aperture, and into the Void. Thorne released the ribbon from Uksyo's leg and the manifest mana snapped back into his hand. With the illumination from the ribbon gone, Uksyo was nearly swallowed up in the darkness of the Void save for the faint blue light filtering through the aperture.

Thorne's last glimpse of the aperture before he fell away completely was the water from the cavern ceiling crashing down.

CHAPTER TWENTYTWO

CARLION

"Do you think this is actually going to work?" Carlion asked Trinity quietly as they both stood behind the only large tree in the area. The mercenaries had stepped out of Shara's line of sight to relieve themselves. Both had learned a long time ago not to go into a fight with a full bladder. Trinity shrugged and looked at the pair of wooden spears leaning against a nearby tree. The tips had an unnatural pearlescent sheen where Shara had touched them with a glowing hand. Neither mercenary knew what the Venhadar had done to the makeshift weapons, but they hoped it would be effective against the otherworldly foes that were now hunting them. It had been a little less than a quarter of an hour since their flight from the beach, and there still was no sight of the monstrosities that pursued them. This brief respite gave Carlion little comfort, knowing it was only a matter of time before they would have to confront the slow-moving creatures again.

"You alright being bait?" Trinity asked, shaking off and pulling up his trousers. The mercenary grabbed a spear and rested it on his shoulder. "An ambush is the best tactic we have now, but I'm a bit concerned about her eagerness to put you in harm's way."

"She'll be on the ground with me," Carlion said, retrieving the other spear and walking around the tree back towards the clearing they had chosen for their attack. Dotting the rocky ground were clusters of knee-high ferns, but otherwise the area was free of the thicker underbrush they had passed through on their flight from the beach. Surrounding them were mostly thin pine trees, but a rare oak with low branches covered in broad yellow leaves broke up the canopy of blue-green.

As the mercenaries entered the clearing, Shara was dumping the contents of a flask into a clump of ferns. She pointed at Carlion's feet and said, "Don't walk through any of the ferns here or you'll get covered in lamp oil."

"What are you doing with lamp oil out here?" Carlion asked looking down to be more mindful of his steps.

"It's a recommended pack item for mages going on their traveling education," Shara said with a smug expression. "Thorne told me in Yaboon that the Archive recommendations were worthless, but I guess he doesn't know everything."

"Yeah, I'm sure he'd be impressed," Trinity said, doing little to hide his sarcasm.

Unperturbed, Shara carefully returned the empty flask to her rucksack. Pointing to the clusters of desiccated ferns in the clearing she said, "All of these are soaked so all it will take is a spark for them to go up in flames." Reaching back into her pack Shara pulled out a pair of leather gloves. Putting them on she returned to the bag one final time and retrieved two short rods. With a flick of her wrist, Shara sprayed a few sparks and Carlion realized she held flint and steel.

The Darkman nodded slowly when he understood what the Venhadar had done. Given the spacing and amount of foliage on the ground, anyone entering the clearing would have to move slowly and carefully to not come into contact with the oil-soaked ferns. Even though Shara didn't have an obvious weapon, she had created a highly flammable area and controlled the means of ignition.

"If what happened on the shore is any indication, you're only going to get one strike," Shara warned, pointing a rod at his spear. "Whatever those things are, it seems that the entire charge is going to be released on contact."

"Let's hope that's enough," Carlion said. He looked over at Trinity and then to the lowest overhanging branches of the lone oak tree in the area. "Enjoy the show," the Darkman said.

The mercenary gave a halfhearted smile and a little wave before nimbly scaling the oak. Trinity then crept out onto a thick branch that overhung the clearing. It was not a dangerously high drop to the ground, but he would need to take care not break an ankle when crashing down. The goal was to land on one of the creatures, preferably spear point first.

Carlion turned to Shara and appraised the Venhadar. She was watching Trinity up in the tree with narrowed eyes and her gloved hands akimbo. Even now that they were forced to work towards a common goal, there was still hatred in Shara's eyes. The Darkman adjusted his grip on the crude spear, trying to rub the nervous sweat off of his palm. "You ready?" Carlion asked in a low voice as he stepped close to her.

The Venhadar's eyes flicked towards him and she gave a barely perceptible nod. "Where is the other one?" Shara said, trying to project her voice into the forest.

"I thought he was with you." Carlion said at equal volume. They had decided on the general tone and topic of conversation to try to draw their adversaries to them while Shara was charging the spears. With Trinity hiding above them, they thought an argument about him being lost would be a good place to start. The goal was to make as much noise as possible and lure the creatures into the clearing and underneath Trinity.

"You idiot! He's gone missing!" Shara said angrily. She

waved her arms in a gesture of frustration. "It's getting dark and those things are still out there."

"Well, your shouting isn't helping things," Carlion said and reached out to touch her shoulder. "You need to calm down."

"Don't touch me!" Shara shouted and took a step back.

"Or what?" the Darkman said, bending over so his face was a few inches from hers.

Shara's fist connected with Carlion's jaw with a crunch that sent violent vibrations through his skull and down his spine. Unprepared for a genuine blow, the Darkman's vision swam and he dropped to one knee. Looking through tearing eyes, Carlion tasted blood from a split lip. "You bitch!" he shouted with genuine feeling.

Shara held the flint and steel rods like daggers and was about to take another swing at Carlion when an ear-piercing shriek made her stop. Looking past the Venhadar, Carlion saw the two creatures, which to him still appeared as a pair of minotaurs, push through the undergrowth to stand at the edge of the clearing. They appeared to be probing the air with flaring nostrils and deep snorts. With rumbling growls and raised cleavers, the minotaurs looked ready to attack, but continued to stay at the edge of the clearing.

Standing up and wiping the tears from his eyes and blood from his lip, Carlion asked quietly, "What are they waiting for?"

"I don't know," Shara said, but then her eyebrows shot up. "They smell the lamp oil! We've been in this clearing long enough that we're desensitized to the odor."

The Darkman reached down and picked up one of the rocks that Shara had charged. "Come get us, you cowards!" he shouted and heaved the projectile at a minotaur. The opalescent stone impacted on the creature's chest with a burst of white light and an electric snapping sound. The minotaur staggered back a step and the Darkman saw a dark blistered patch of hide at the point of impact.

The creature threw its chest forward in a savage roar and then stormed towards Carlion and Shara. With startling speed, the minotaur rushed at the pair and the creature completely filled Carlion's field of view before he could raise his spear. As the beast crashed bodily into him, a flash of brilliant light momentarily blinded Carlion when his spear pierced the creature. The minotaur's momentum impaled the spear into its torso up to the Darkman's hands, and the pair toppled to the ground. Carlion had braced for the crushing weight of his foe on top of him, but was surprised to find that the minotaur was unnaturally light.

As the Darkman struggled to get out from under the prone minotaur, he heard Trinity shout from the oak branch. Carlion felt a hard impact and heard a muted crackling sound and realized that the mercenary had leapt down onto the minotaur and slammed his spear into its unprotected back. The creature reared back and shrieked, which gave Carlion enough time to roll out from underneath it.

Quickly pushing himself up to his feet, Carlion scanned the clearing to get his bearings. To his right, Trinity was pulling his short sword free from his belt. Off to his left, the dying minotaur was trying to regain stable footing by leaning on its cleaver, but ended up pitching over it and collapsed on the ground. The minotaur folded in on itself as it died and seemed to morph into a horrific hybrid of minotaur, wyvern, and decomposing human before dissolving into a glistening mass of black gel.

The Darkman swiveled his head around, searching the clearing. He saw the second minotaur chopping his cleaver through the ferns and grunting angrily. "Where's Shara?" Carlion panted as he drew close to Trinity. The mercenary shook his head with a panicked expression. The Venhadar had disappeared.

"Shara!" Trinity shouted as he looked over both shoulders. The call did not elicit a response from the Venhadar, but drew the attention of the minotaur. The creature stopped thrashing the ferns and focused its attention on the mercenaries.

Carlion drew back when he saw Trinity reach into his pocket and pull out the small stone that Shara had charged for him. The mercenary threw it at the minotaur with a shout. The missile glanced off the creature's shoulder, and the resulting spark of light was weak in comparison to what Shara had done back on the beach, but it was enough to provoke the creature to action. Raising its cleaver to strike, the minotaur stomped across the clearing towards the mercenaries.

In a fluid motion, Carlion drew his sword and advanced on the minotaur with a measured step. Out of the corner of his eye, he could see Trinity moving to flank the creature. The minotaur swung its cleaver in a horizontal arc that pushed both mercenaries back on their heels and followed with an overhead strike at Carlion. He was able to block the blow with his sword, but the strength of the minotaur forced Carlion to his knees as their blades locked. The minotaur shoved its cleaver downward with both hands and brought it dangerously close to the Darkman's face. Behind the cleaver, Carlion could see bloodlust in the feral eyes of the creature.

A shout from the left caused the minotaur to break eye contact with Carlion an instant before Trinity stabbed his short sword into its flank. The blade effortlessly sunk into the creature just above its hip and brought the mercenary too close to the minotaur. Seemingly unaffected by the wound, the minotaur shoved Carlion to the side and smashed a fist into Trinity with a backhanded blow. The force of the strike blasted Trinity off of his feet and knocked him out of the clearing and against the trunk of a slim pine tree. The mercenary slid down the trunk and crumpled underneath it.

Carlion scrambled to stand, but was not quick enough before the minotaur lashed out with a vicious kick that hit the Darkman in the chest. His armor protected him from a caved in ribcage, but the rapid impacts from the kick and then hitting the ground knocked the breath from his lungs. Still stunned, he tried to prop himself on one hand and brought his sword in a parrying position, but Carlion knew he would be unable to defend against another crushing attack.

Seated on the ground, Carlion watched the creature snort and draw in a deep breath as it raised the cleaver high over its head. The Darkman steeled himself for his end and kept his eyes open to watch the cleaver fall, so it was with great surprise when he saw the minotaur burst into flames. As the fire rushed up the screeching minotaur, Carlion caught the scent of lamp oil as he pushed himself backwards.

Quickly getting to his feet a safe distance away, Carlion watched the minotaur combust. The creature seemed to be melting instead of burning as it dropped to the ground. After the flames flickered out from the now molten black mass, Carlion saw Shara standing behind it with a set jaw. The Venhadar was tightly holding the flint and steel rods and breathing heavily. She looked up at him suddenly and then purposefully walked forward with hard eyes. For a moment, the Darkman thought she was going to set him ablaze next and his body instinctively tensed.

"Don't think I'm happy that I had to save your worthless life," Shara said, pointing a rod at him threateningly. She then clapped the rods together and shoved them into a pouch at her waist. The Venhadar then pulled the leather gloves off her hands, tucked them into her belt, and then rubbed her palms on her pants.

"You could have waited until that thing cleaved me half before lighting it on fire," Carlion said warily. He still wanted to keep his distance from Shara and took a slow step backwards.

"Oh, I thought about it," Shara said, "but Metauk made me promise not to actively try to get you killed."

Not knowing how to respond, Carlion looked down at the slimy black pile where the minotaur had died and asked, "What were those things?"

"Something not from this world, that's for certain," Shara replied. Looking across the clearing, she callously said, "Go check if your friend is dead."

Carlion crossed the clearing and knelt down in front of Trinity and was relieved to see that he was still breathing. The mercenary's eyes partially opened when Carlion spoke his name. "Easy there, mate. The danger has passed," Carlion said. "You took quite a knock. Anything broken?"

Trinity slowly rolled his shoulders and took a deep breath, which caused him to wince. The mercenary's eyes focused and the vacant expression faded from his face when he replied, "Nothing broken, but probably a bunch of bruised ribs. And I'll have a knot on the back of my head for a long time after this splitting headache goes away." Trinity peered over the Darkman's shoulder and said slowly, "She came back. Where'd she go?"

Carlion looked back at Shara who was glaring at them impatiently. "I'll tell you on the way back to the beach," the Darkman said. "I think we've had enough excitement for today and I want to rest somewhere with clear lines of sight."

He didn't say it out loud, but Carlion also wanted to be on the beach because it would be harder for Shara to hide from them. The Venhadar had saved his life, but he was still a long way from trusting her.

CHAPTER TWENTYTHREE

THORNE

L ooking down into the absolute nothingness below him, Thorne vividly remembered his Transformation. Though his body had remained in a chrysalis at the Yaboon Archive, his astral projection had been flung into the Void. Then, as now, it was the same terrifying descent into complete darkness with a frantic attempt to stop the free-fall.

Still holding his breath, Thorne created an image in his mind of a cobblestone street. Focusing his Awareness, he willed the street into existence underneath his boots. His landing was more abrupt than he anticipated and he dropped to one knee, letting out a sharp grunt with the force of the impact. Slowly standing and breathing normally again, the mage saw cobble-stones stretch a short distance around him before suddenly ending in black vacuum.

Craning his head up, Thorne saw that Uksyo had already recovered from the shock of being pulled into the Void and had slowed his decent significantly. Uksyo was radiating a weak light, which Thorne knew was an aura of his Awareness. Since Uksyo seemed to be steering his descent towards Thorne's small patch of ground, the mage surmised he must be similarly illuminated. Uksyo landed lightly a few steps from Thorne and greeted him with a smug look.

"Always full of nasty surprises, you Paragons," Uksyo said. "Though I suppose even more so for your friends." He gestured upwards and said, "The aperture collapsed not long after you pulled me through, so the cavern is completely flooded by now. I imagine that drowning in murky darkness is a terrible way to die."

"I'm sure," Thorne said evenly, trying not to think about Amos' and Metauk's fate. "And now you're trapped here with me."

"Not at all," Uksyo replied lightly. He took a step towards the edge of the cobblestone island and peered down. "Physical transport through the Void was the whole point. Even if my Engine was destroyed, I have the coordinates for another. Once built it will be easy enough for—" Uksyo stopped mid-sentence and his whole body lurched as if a pair of invisible hands had shaken him.

Slowly, Uksyo looked at Thorne with a more pleasant expression, "It doesn't have to be this way, Thorne. Despite our past differences of opinion, you would be a welcome addition."

"What are you talking about?" Thorne asked with a creased brow, unsure what to think about the sudden change in Uksyo's demeanor.

"I have appropriated Uksyo's physicality for a moment to converse with you," Uksyo said. "He is a willing agent of mine and now I speak through him."

"Who are you?" Thorne asked warily.

"Perhaps not quite an old friend, but someone who understands you," Uksyo said. With a sweeping overhead gesture Uksyo somehow filled the black space above them with stars and an unnaturally bright full moon. A lush carpet of green grass sprung through the mortar between the cobblestones and quickly covered the surrounding area. Behind Uksyo, a tall willow erupted up from the ground beside a small section of river, ending on either side in cascading waterfalls into the abyss below.

"How is the likeness to the painting in your chambers?" Uksyo asked in a self-satisfied manner as he took in the new scene around him. A slight breeze shifted the deeply bent willow branches, some of which were hung low enough to brush the surface of the slowly moving river.

"Imperfect," Thorne said, trying to maintain a façade of composure. "It's not dark in the painting."

Uksyo casually shrugged and said, "Close enough to make my point. I know it's a painful memory of yours." Uksyo's face saddened and he shook his head and continued, "It must have been hard to lose a beloved sister at such a young age, and I'm sure you've given considerable thought as to what you'd give in exchange to have her back. That is what I am offering."

Thorne was unprepared for this sudden turn of events, and his mind raced to assemble the pieces of seemingly unrelated information together. With Uksyo possessed by a dominating will, Thorne guessed that he was now conversing with the one Nion called R. More concerning was Uksyo's mention of Reihana before pushing him into the aperture, and the mage now wondered if the only other known surviving Paragon had learned some terrible new abilities despite having her Awareness bound. Whoever was in control of Uksyo was powerful, of that there was no doubt, and given the obvious danger Thorne needed to stall for time so he could think of an escape plan.

"How?" Thorne asked after a long pause.

Uksyo took a step closer to Thorne and said, "The Void is a plane of possibility. I have learned that the limitations of the body and mind no longer apply when your physicality is here." He pointed at Thorne's arm and said, "Perhaps you have not noticed it yet, but your fetters are gone. Tell me, do you enjoy being a pawn of the Archive?"

"Not so much," Thorne admitted. He pulled on the cuff of his left sleeve and found that the binding mark on his wrist was indeed gone. "But pawns often move first and can be promoted," the mage said.

"Would you like that promotion now?" Uksyo asked, taking another step closer to be less than an arm's length away from the mage.

"What did you offer Uksyo?" Thorne asked.

"An alchemic formula to convert mana to fire. I have learned how to make it," Uksyo said. "It is a trivial thing to exchange comparatively, but I am willing to offer you something of much greater value because you would not be a simple soldier to me. You would be a commander, and for your service I would bring your sister back to you."

"A rather bold promise," Thorne said thoughtfully. "You clearly have the power to speak through Uksyo, though I wonder if you can actually do as you say."

Uksyo held both his open palms up to show Thorne they were empty and then he rubbed his hands together like he was washing them. As his palms passed over the back of his hands they were coated in flame. Uksyo held up his hands and the fire flared brightly. Thorne could feel the heat against his face. Uksyo collapsed his hands into fists and extinguished the flames. He had a self-satisfied look on his face when he said, "Though I may be controlling his body, it was his mana that ignited and fueled that fire."

Thorne was dumbfounded with what he had just witnessed. Hundreds of years of experimentation and research into understanding the arcane elements had never yielded any progress on how to manifest fire solely from mana. At this point it was thought to simply be impossible. The mage licked his dry lips and said, "I must admit that moving beyond manipulation of the arcane elements to creating them is the desire of many alchemists. However, your offer of resurrection is beyond fantastical and encroaches on the territory of religion."

"Resurrection?" Uksyo laughed. "Thorne, you misunderstand. I'm not talking about some crude necromancy. I can stop your sister from ever drowning in that river. I am talking about reversing the flow of time."

"What?" Thorne blurted out in disbelief.

Uksyo was about to reply when a painfully loud howl reverberated around them. Both men looked up towards the simulated night sky just in time to see a silhouette glide across the moon. A streamlined body and translucent membranous wings were instantly recognizable features of a dragon.

"That damn beast harries my every move!" Uksyo snarled, trying to track the airborne creature's movements.

Momentarily forgotten, Thorne took the opportunity to attack. With Uksyo distracted, the mage lunged forward and crushed Uksyo's chin with an uppercut. The blow snapped Uksyo's head back and Thorne saw Uksyo's eyes roll back into his head. With a look of disdain, the mage watched Uksyo fold together as he collapsed to the ground. Only after he was sure that Uksyo wasn't going to get up back up did Thorne shake his hand and curse in pain. He hadn't punched someone in a long time and had forgotten how much it hurt.

The willow tree suddenly vanished in front of Thorne, then the river, and finally the grassy plain. The simulated night sky winked out and left the mage once again on his small barren patch of cobblestones floating in a black expanse. Thorne surmised that whoever had been controlling Uksyo had lost connection when he was knocked out.

A second howl echoed around Thorne and the mage swiveled his head trying to find the dragon. With Uksyo unconscious, Thorne didn't hide that he recognized the howl. In fact, the dragon was the reason he had destroyed his Archive lab. Overcome with emotion, Thorne's face tightened until he could bear it no longer and cried out, "Celeste!" Staring upwards, the mage screamed the name over and over until his throat was raw.

With a heaving chest, Thorne stopped shouting and strained to hear a reply. At first all he could hear was his own heartbeat in his ears, but then he did hear another sound. It was not the dragon's howl that he wanted, but he recognized it as a pair of familiar voices. Scanning the area above him, Thorne finally saw a faint aura around a flailing shape and realized that only Metauk would be visible against the black emptiness. The empath didn't seem to be moving but instead was kicking her legs and wheeling her arms in an attempt to generate momentum.

Although it seared his throat, Thorne channeled some mana to his larynx to amplify his voice and boomed, "Stop struggling! I will create a path to you."

Thorne concentrated on a mental image of a desolate street. Pushing more of his mana into the ground the mage extended the cobblestone path in front of him. With no other points of reference other than the strip of ground in ahead of him, it was difficult for Thorne to shift his perspective of space and gravity to be in line with Metauk. The mage felt his stomach lurch as his sense of balance struggled to keep pace as his anchor points of up and down shifted with the ground. Thorne felt a wave of vertigo wash over him and he shut his eyes tight. After a moment his head stopped spinning and Thorne was relived to open his eyes and see Metauk and Amos running towards him.

"How did you move the path up to us?" Metauk asked with an expression of wonder after stopping in front of the mage. The empath's aura was much brighter now that she was closer to Thorne, which contrasted sharply with Amos. The corsair was only illuminated by the auras from Metauk and Thorne, which gave Amos a dark and indistinct appearance.

"What were you shouting?" Amos asked between labored breaths. He pulled the bandana off of his head and wrung it out in his hands. The cobblestones underneath both Amos and Metauk darkened when the water from the corsair's wet headgear dripped onto them.

Thorne waved both questions away and asked, "How did you two get here?"

Amos grunted and replied, "It was either drown in the cave or follow you." He tied the bandana back on his head and pulled a hand down his face. "Still got soaked."

"Is this really the Void?" Metauk asked, looking around.

"He seems to think so," Thorne said gesturing down to Uksyo.

"Is that sack of shit still alive?" Amos asked with an angry expression.

"For now," Thorne said. "But I don't want him making things worse when he wakes up. Use your bootlaces and tie him up."

"What'd you do to him? I doubt you got him to drink Papaver extract," Amos said as he bent over and pulled off his boots.

Thorne flexed his still aching hand and said, "Trinity taught me how to throw a decent punch, but I think I did something wrong because my hand still hurts like hell."

"Probably broke a knuckle," Amos said absentmindedly as he yanked the laces out of his boots. "Why didn't you just zap him instead?"

"Uksyo would have been expecting that from Thorne," Metauk said. "A physical blow probably caught him by surprise."

While Amos was binding Uksyo's hands behind his back,

Thorne turned to Metauk, "We need to let Trinity and the others know what happened."

"How?" Metauk asked. "The Engine was destroyed while we were passing through it. We can't get back that way." The empath made a show of looking around her and continued, "And if the Archives' research is to be believed, we shouldn't even be alive in here. Physical matter, let alone something with a pulse, isn't supposed to be viable in the Void."

"It's not that it can't exist here," Thorne said, "but it has to survive passing between planes. That's always been the bottleneck and why Uksyo's Engine is so remarkable. He's discovered the formula for a stable transition, and with it we could theoretically emerge anywhere that has been charged with enough mana."

"You seem to know a lot about this," Metauk said suspiciously. "Did Uksyo explain all this to you before we got here?"

The mage knew it was pointless trying to lie to a Sehenryu. "No. It's the research I was doing when I slagged my lab," he admitted. Thorne held up a hand to stop any more questions from Metauk and said, "Right now we need to tell the others they need to get back to Yaboon. I need you do something that will sound crazy."

"Today seems to be the day for it," Amos said, stepping close to Thorne. Nodding towards Uksyo, the corsair added, "He's all trussed up."

Thorne gave a little smile as a manner of thanks. The mage was appreciative of the Venhadar's even keel, especially in the current situation. Turning to Metauk he said, "You need to send an astral projection to the island."

Metauk laughed in disbelief and said sarcastically, "Is that all? There's no way that could possibly work."

"Why not?" Thorne asked, irritated by Metauk's instant dismissal.

The empath scoffed as if the answer were obvious. Then counting on her fingers, she said, "Without a chrysalis to focus my mana, any astral projection I make would just dissipate. Never mind the fact that I have no sense of direction for how far an astral projection would need to travel. Finally, the chance of an astral projection being seen by the others is impossibly small. The timing would have to be perfect."

"We are physically in the Void," Thorne said slowly for emphasis. Spreading his hands out he added, "There isn't a more powerful amplifier than the Void to push an astral projection. That takes care of your first concern. You can use Uksyo's lab as the focal point for directionality and then project upward. Your memory of the beach should be recent enough to give a decent approximation of direction without specific coordinates. It's a bit brute force, but the best we can do given the circumstances. As for the timing issue, that's a bit trickier to solve, but if you echoed your astral projection with enough mana it might remain on the shore long enough for the others to see it."

"An astral echo? That's a sophomoric stunt pulled by apprentices pretending to haunt their family," Metauk said with disdain. "If this idea is so great, then why don't you do it?"

Thorne sighed and crossed his arms across his chest. "My skills with astral projection are barely adequate. You'll have a better chance of success because Sehenryu empathy gives you an innate talent for astral projection."

Metauk seemed to consider Thorne's argument for a moment. "Perhaps," she said. "What kind of message do you want sent, assuming any of this works?"

"Keep it simple and visual," Thorne said. "An astral echo won't be able to move or speak. You'll need to use your mana to make sure the echo will persist even after we've left the Void. The amount of energy you'll be using won't be trivial."

"For what it's worth, Trinity and Carlion would want to

stick close to the boats on the shore after searching the island," Amos said. "You probably want your ghost to stand there."

"Right," Metauk said absently. She took a step away from Thorne and Amos and turned her back to them.

Thorne stared at the empath and watched her relax her shoulders and bow her head. The aura around her brightened and expanded slightly. From the light radiating around Metauk, Thorne saw a ghost-like image of the empath superimpose itself on her. The astral projection then took a single step forward and separated itself from Metauk and pulled an object out from a pouch at its waist. From where he was standing, Thorne could not see what the astral projection held out in the palm of its hand. With a rapid flare and then contraction of light, the astral projection blinked out of existence.

The mage could hear Metauk gasp as she threw her shoulders back. She turned around and looked at Thorne with wide eyes. "It felt so real. It was like I was really at the beach," she said breathlessly.

Thorne was impressed with Metauk's stamina after such an exertion of her Awareness. Mages trained both their mind and body to resist the extreme fatigue of using their own internal energies to power arcane manipulations, and this, along with whether a mage was innately Aware or not, were the major factors in determining a mage's overall power. Because Metauk looked so alert at the moment, Thorne guessed she was probably buoyed by the adrenaline rush that came with successfully completing such a complex astral projection. However, the empath would still need time to recover before doing something even remotely taxing again.

Thorne was about to suggest that Metauk sit down and rest when a groan from the ground drew the mage's attention back to Uksyo. As Amos roughly pulled him up to a sitting position Uksyo groaned, "Oh? You two both survived. That's a surprise." He opened his mouth wide and shifted his lower jaw from side to side. "I never expected you to resort to physical violence, Thorne."

Thorne knelt down with an unamused expression. It seemed that Uksyo had command of his own body once more. "What are the coordinates for the other Engine?" the mage demanded.

"There's another one?" Metauk said.

Ignoring the empath, Uksyo said to Thorne, "Why would I tell you?"

Amos reached down and jerked the collar of Uksyo's robe. "Because I'll take great joy in stomping your face in if you don't do what he wants, you cocky fuck," the Venhadar growled.

Uksyo's expression became annoyed as he matched Amos' stare, "Save your threats for someone else. You're not going to kill me here. I'm the best chance you have of leaving this place. Besides, if Thorne's going to collect my bounty, I need to be returned to the Archive alive and intact." Uksyo tilted his head to look past Amos. "That is," he said, "unless Thorne is weighing an alternative offer."

Amos looked over at Thorne and asked, "What's he talking about?"

"We've stumbled into a much larger problem than just one rogue mage," Thorne said as he stood up. "I've changed my mind. I want the coordinates for the Yaboon Archive."

"Untie me first," Uksyo said.

"Not a chance," Amos replied angrily. The corsair looked up at Thorne and said, "Let me throw this asshole off the edge. I'm sick of looking at his smug face."

Metauk gently rested a hand on Amos's shoulder. "Let me try," she said, quietly giving him a weak smile.

With a shrug, Amos backed away and gave Metauk room to approach Uksyo. Thorne furrowed his brow as he watched the empath kneel behind Uksyo and put her face close to his ear. "You said alive and intact before," the empath said. "But I imagine that the council really only cares about the former."

"It matters not where the idle threats come from," Uksyo said, turning his head to try to look at Metauk. "You're going to have to do more than—"

Uksyo screamed in pain and tried thrash away, but only succeeded in falling on his side. Metauk slowly got up and stood over Uksyo and made a show of the push dagger in her hand.

"There's an incredible number of nerve endings in your hand," the empath said with matter-of-fact tone. "Even shallow cuts that don't draw much blood can be cripplingly painful, and when a finger is damaged it reflexively bends. That's a problem when there's a blade in your palm. Severed tendons rarely heal cleanly, assuming you can even stretch them back into place." The empath started to reach down to grab Uksyo's arm.

Stop!" Uksyo cried with a mixture of pain and fear. "Inside my chest pocket there's a black pouch."

Amos reached into Uksyo's robes and pulled out a small bag. Yanking it open, the Venhadar retrieved a small piece of pinkish-orange resin. It was irregularly shaped and looked like something that was broken off of a sculpture. Handing it to Metauk, Amos asked, "What did you say you did before you starting studying at the Archive?"

The empath gave a cryptic smile and replied, "I didn't." She brought the resin piece up to her eye and examined the translucent material before giving it to Thorne. Metauk then reached down and pulled Uksyo to his feet.

"There is no formula per se to derive coordinates once in the Void," Uksyo said with a fearful sideways glance at Metauk. When the empath took a step back, he continued, "However, by pushing mana through something with an arcane memory of a place, you can use the resonance here in the Void to generate a beacon. You can then open an aperture that will take you to that place. What you're holding is a piece of my chrysalis that I broke off before I left the Archive."

"A chrysalis isn't an Engine," Metauk said. "How do you generate an exit aperture to the material plane?

Uksyo's eyes flicked back and forth between Thorne and the empath before answering. "From the Void you don't need an Engine to enter the material plane, but having one makes the aperture considerably more stable. That's why I chose a chrysalis for my escape plan. It's designed for astral projection to the Void and, theoretically, can be reverse engineered to become an Engine."

"How?" Thorne demanded with an eagerness he instantly regretted. In a more measured tone he said, "It doesn't matter now, but I'm sure the council will be interested in hearing how you generated a stable aperture to the Void with your Engine in the cavern."

The mage closed his fist around the resin and charged it with his mana. The resin absorbed the arcane energy greedily, which was its purpose. At the Archive, a chrysalis modulated a mage's mana to facilitate astral projection. Slowly opening his hand, Thorne was surprised to find that the resin did not emit a uniform radiance as he was expecting. Instead, a single line of yellow light sprang from the resin and ran seemingly into infinity at an angle above Thorne and to his left.

"Tether an aperture to the beacon line," Uksyo said. "Use the same principles you developed during your Transformation. We'll emerge in my chrysalis." He sneered and added, "Hope there aren't any skittish Vigil Keepers around when a supposedly empty chrysalis opens up and four people stumble out."

Thorne frowned. Trying to form a stable aperture using an Archive chrysalis was what destroyed his lab. He had lost his temper when a technique he didn't fully understand overloaded and backfired. However, as they were now in the Void, they shouldn't be in danger because there was nothing to over-load. There was no guarantee that it would work either, but the options available now were very few.

The mage decided that his internal debate was pointlessly academic and shoved the resin piece in a pocket. He put his arms out in front of him and spread his fingers. Thorne then charged just his fingertips with mana so he could actually feel the ether of the Void. He could detect ephemeral wisps passing between his fingers, but any attempt to grasp them was like trying to catch smoke.

Clenching his jaw, the mage brought his fingers together and then splayed them out again, filling the gaps with a layer of his mana and giving his hands the illusion of being webbed. He felt a tendril of ether try to snake around his hand, but he was able to catch the loose thread from the Void. Jerking his hand down hard, the sensation felt like pulling the stitching from a seam. As Thorne pulled down, a jagged line of white light elon-gated in front of him and made contact with the light from the beacon and fixed it in place. With both hands Thorne reached into the tear and pulled it open, exposing a large, rough circle of gauzy white light.

The mage could not see into the aperture he had just created because the white film was merely translucent, but something felt familiar about it. Dissipating the charge from his hands, Thorne stepped back and realized he was holding his breath. Slowly blowing it out he watched the ragged aperture edges flicker and contract slightly.

"This aperture is very unstable," Uksyo said with a mixture of amazement and concern. "Did you really just tear a hole in the Void to return during your Transformation? Brute applica-tion of your mana like that should have dissolved your astral projection and killed you."

"I'm lucky that way," Thorne said tersely, not taking his

eyes of the aperture. "I'll stay here and buffer the aperture if needed. I want to make sure it doesn't deteriorate."

"I'll go first," Metauk volunteered quickly. Looking at Uksyo she said calmly, "Amos, you guide him through. If he does anything that annoys you, break a couple fingers." She turned decisively, boldly strode through the white film of the aperture, and disappeared.

The Venhadar grunted and gripped Uksyo's forearm. "Let's go, mate." With less enthusiasm than Metauk, Uksyo and Amos entered the aperture and vanished from the cobblestone platform.

Standing alone on a seemingly tiny patch of ground engulfed by an oppressive nothingness gave Thorne an eerie feeling. He glanced down at his bare wrist where the binding mark should have been. Looking up, the mage hoped that by some miracle of perfect timing he would see the dragon overhead.

"Celeste!" Thorne called out again. It might not have been intentional, but Thorne had finally achieved what he had wanted for so long, what he had destroyed an Archive lab to do. Now that he was physically in the Void, he just had to find the dragon so she could erase his memories.

Looking at the aperture Thorne wondered what the others would think if he didn't return. Metauk would be able to relay to the council Uksyo's unsanctioned activities underneath the island. The mage was less sure if the council would get Uksyo to reveal what he had hoped to achieve by constructing a pair of Engines.

Then there was the matter of Uksyo's possession. He had no proof, but Thorne suspected that another ghost from his past had come back to haunt him. If Reihana had also found a way to physically enter the Void, then all of the Archives across the entire continent were in danger. Her hatred of the council was well documented after the dissolution of the Paragon program.

What she had been doing in the intervening years, Thorne had only a vague understanding, but clearly she had not been sitting idle after the council bound her Awareness.

Thorne clenched his fists and blew an angry breath out of his nostrils. If he went back, he might never get another chance to physically return to the Void. If he stayed to search for the dragon, then he might be putting the Archive at risk because he didn't know how many other conspirators Reihana was leading, or their objective. Thorne wondered which decision he would regret more as he looked down at the cobblestone pathway that stretched out a short distance before being swallowed by blackness.

CHAPTER TWENTYFOUR

CARLION

Carlion woke up with the taste of the sea in his mouth and a stiff back from sleeping on the rocky beach. He and Trinity had fallen asleep quickly after their meager dinner and well before their campfire had turned to embers. Shara had made a show of keeping her distance from the mercenaries after it had gotten dark, and was still awake when Carlion had turned over to put his back to the fire. Now, as the Darkman rolled to a sitting position, he saw the Venhadar was standing near the gently lapping waves periodically throwing a pebble out to sea. Trinity was nowhere in sight.

The Darkman got up and stretched his back before slowly walking to Shara. He watched her bend down and pick up a fist-sized rock and hold it at her side. Carlion tried to keep the stone in his peripheral vision as he looked out at the ocean. With no tower bell to ring the hour he had no idea what time it was, but the morning mists had not been burned away yet, so it was early. Now that he was away from the fire, Carlion shivered as the breeze that came off the water chilled his damp clothes.

"Where's Trinity?" he asked, resting a hand on the hilt of his sword.

"On patrol," Shara replied, pointing down the rocky shore.

Carlion followed her gesture and could see a distant figure far down the beach walking just out of the wave's reach.

"What's he doing?" the Darkman asked.

Shara reached back and flung the stone, which made a sonorous plopping sound when it hit the water. "He's far away from me is all that matters," she said irritably. "Let him stay down there until the others come back for all I care. In fact, why don't you go join him?"

Carlion sighed. He was getting tired of Shara's adversarial attitude. He thought she would have relaxed some after their encounter with the pair of nightmarish creatures yesterday, but that did not appear to be the case. He didn't have the energy to try engaging her anymore and turned back to the canoes that Shara had reconstructed when they returned to the beach.

Unexpectedly, he saw a person standing near the boats and cried out in surprise. It took him a moment to realize it was Metauk facing towards the island interior. The Sehenryu was standing right in the middle of the camp, so it was strange that she wasn't facing towards them.

"What's your problem?" Shara asked, looking at Carlion before following his gaze to the canoes. "Metauk!" she cried and took off running towards the empath.

Carlion watched her short legs pump away from him before he searched for Trinity down the beach. After spotting him again, the Darkman shoved two fingers into his mouth and whistled loudly. He saw Trinity raise his hand and wave. After making sure that the mercenary was returning, Carlion trotted back to the campsite.

The Darkman noticed Shara's face had a strange expression before he even finished approaching Metauk. Circling around the empath he realized that she was slightly transparent. Under more scrutiny, Carlion saw that the spectral Metauk wasn't breathing and her unblinking gaze was fixed straight ahead and not looking at anyone. Her right hand was extended with a small object in her open palm. "What the hell is this?" he asked Shara.

"An astral echo," the Venhadar said absently. Her attention was focused on what Metauk was holding.

Trinity came running up to meet them, but then pulled up short when Carlion passed his hand through the ghost-like image of Metauk. "What's this? Where are the others?" the mercenary asked out of breath.

"We need to get back to the Archive right now," Shara said forcefully.

"Whoa, wait a minute!" Trinity exclaimed. "Is this an astral projection? Are they in trouble? Why does she have a key in her hand?"

Carlion could hear the worry in the mercenary's voice and rested a reassuring hand on his shoulder. "This has got to be a message of some sort," he said. Looking at Shara, the Darkman asked, "Do you have any answers?"

Shara fidgeted with her hands as she replied, "Astral projections are a merging of a mage's consciousness with their mana that allows them to transcend the physical plane. This is more like an afterimage when you stare at a candle too long." She pointed at the object in Metauk's stiff hand and continued, "That key is to her alchemic lab at the Archive. I have one that looks just like it for my own. She wants us to go back."

"Why?" Trinity pressed.

"I don't know!" Shara snapped. Throwing her hands to her sides she exhaled hard and then said, "What I do know is that it takes a huge amount of mana to generate an astral echo without a chrysalis. If she is willing to expend that much energy, knowing how long it will take to recover, then it must be something important."

"What do we do when we get back?" Trinity asked.

Shara pointed to Metauk's open hand and replied, "I'm going to find her."

"Yves might have something to say about us leaving without Amos," the mercenary said. Gesturing to the apparition he added, "I'm not sure he's likely to believe that Metauk sent a message to us from the beyond to abandon the others and go back to Port."

"As long as he gets paid, I doubt he'll care," Shara said dismissively. "Besides, the only reason he'll be out this way is to pick us up. He'd have to return to Port anyway. Once we're on the ship it won't matter."

Shara took a few steps to her pack and then hoisted it into a canoe. As she continued preparing to leave Carlion sidled close to Trinity and said, "I wish I shared her confidence. Any bets that Yves will throw us overboard halfway to Port?"

The mercenary's face soured, "I'd give it even odds."

It did not take them long to break camp and begin their paddle back to the lighthouse to await the *Maddie*. Carlion looked back only once and saw the astral echo of Metauk was still there standing motionless on the beach. While the Darkman knew that he wasn't really leaving her behind, he still had an odd feeling of abandonment.

• • •

"I reckon Captain Yves won't like your tall tale," Dirty Dreebs said as he pulled on the dinghy's oars. The Venhadar mariner has repeated the sentiment nearly every third or fourth stroke as the small boat made its way back to the sloop.

With Trinity's help, Carlion had been able to intimidate the much smaller Dirty Dreebs into ferrying them out to Yves' ship, but as they drew alongside the *Maddie*, he was feeling less bold. When the rope ladder was lowered down to the dinghy, the Darkman could almost feel the mood on the deck of the sloop change. "I've changed my mind," he said to Trinity. "I'm fairly certain we're going to be swimming here very shortly unless we're careful."

While Dirty Dreebs prepared the blocking to raise the dinghy, Carlion watched Trinity and Shara climb the rope ladder to the deck of the ship for a minute before starting his own ascent. He was halfway up before he could hear the angry chatter on the deck, but it was only after he had pulled himself over the railing to stand next to Trinity and Shara did Carlion appreciate the situation he was in now. No fewer than six deckhands had gathered around them, some holding belaying pins or mallets, with expressions that were equal mixes of confusion and anger.

"I told you," Shara was saying to one of them, "We need to get back to Port immediately. Amos isn't on the island anymore."

"Then where the fuck is he?" erupted Yves' voice as the captain emerged from his cabin. Shoving a crewman aside, he loomed over Shara with a hand resting on his saber. "Why'd you let them get in the boat?" Yves asked as Dirty Dreebs landed on the deck behind the mercenaries with a thump of wet boots on wood.

"They didn't give me a choice, Captain," Dirty Dreebs said, shrinking back from the captain's anger.

"You cowardly shit," Yves cursed as he rocked back on his heels. Looking at the mercenaries he said, "Did you think you'd be able to just board my ship and I'd gladly sail you back to Port when the one person whose life I actually care about isn't with you?" Yves' rage boiled over and he pulled his saber free from his belt. "Give me a reason not to cut you down where you're standing. Be quick."

Carlion felt his body tense as he saw the crewmen tighten the circle around them. Reaching for his sword was pointless, as he'd be knocked down before he could pull it free. Instead, he held up both hands slowly and said as calmly as he could, "I understand that our story seems far-fetched, but given that we had three wizards in our group, you must have known something like this could happen."

"We're still going to pay for our transport back to Port," Trinity said.

Yves shook his head and replied, "I'm not going to Port. I'm going to kill you two and take this small one back to the lighthouse and start breaking bones until she tells me where to find the captain."

"Stop!" Shara cried, not trying to hide the fear in her voice. "If you get us to Port, then I will owe you a favor."

Carlion had heard tales of Venhadar favors always being returned, even for the direst of requests. He had always thought them children's stories, but when Yves' expression became one of surprise, the Darkman wondered if there was an amount of truth to them. More than one crewman murmured under their breath and closely watched their captain for his reaction.

Yves lowered his saber and looked at Shara with a critical eye. "What do you think, Dirty Dreebs?"

"A favor from a Venhadar isn't something you get every day," Dirty Dreebs replied. "One from an Archive mage is even rarer. I don't think she'd offer one up to you unless they were telling the truth. They must really and truly need to get back to Port."

The captain took a deep breath, slowly exhaled, and appeared to consider Shara's offer. He then returned his weapon to his belt and crossed his arms over his chest. "If you're going to do this, then do it proper," he said to Shara. Scanning the faces of his crew he commanded, "Step back, mates. A Venhadar favor can't be offered under duress."

Shara retrieved a small resin knife from her belt and inspected the blade. She closed her eyes and stood still for what seemed like a long time before opening them and said loudly, "In exchange for safe passage of myself, Trinity, and Carlion back to Port on the vessel *Maddie*, I, Shara, grant the captain of this vessel, Yves, a favor." She then reached up and grabbed a thick handful of her long red hair and sheared it off with the knife. Shara put the knife away and tied a single knot to keep the lock together. Holding her cut hair in both hands, she offered it to Yves.

Carlion expected the pirate to gleefully snatch the token, but instead Yves used two hands to gently collect the knotted hair. "Shara and her companions are to be treated kindly on the voyage back to Port," Yves called out to his men. With a small bow to Shara, the captain left the deck and returned to his cabin.

The crew slowly dispersed and resumed preparations to set sail for the mainland while Carlion, Trinity, and Shara stowed their gear. A few hours later, fair winds from a clear sky pushed the sloop through red tinted waves as the crimson sun dipped into the horizon. Nothing more was said from the crew about what Shara did, but Carlion caught Dirty Dreebs watching her from time to time with a contemplative expression on his face. The Darkman and Trinity were standing at the rail and watching the sunset when Shara approached them.

"I don't care what the hour is when we land at Port, I want to leave immediately for Yaboon," the Venhadar said.

"Yves acted like you gave him a king's ransom," Carlion said, in way of response. The ritual he had witnessed before seemed important, but the Darkman didn't know enough of Venhadar culture to know for sure.

Shara grunted and then said, "I'm sure I'll regret it someday. No amount of rubium was going to save us. That much was clear by the way he reacted to Amos not being here. It's not like Thorne buying your loyalty."

"Now wait a minute," Trinity said with an edge in his voice.

"Let me be very clear. Thorne's my friend so I think I under-stand Yves more than you think."

"Friend?" Shara barked a laugh. Looking at them both she said, "Mercenaries understand only two things, money and killing."

Trinity pushed off from the rail and glared at Shara. "What the hell is your problem?" the mercenary demanded. "Did we wrong you in some past life? You've been spitting nails at us since we met. In fact, I'm more than a little surprised you included us in your negotiation with Yves."

"I'm not a murderer, and that's what I would have been if I had saved only myself," Shara said. "I doubt you would under-stand, being little better than a cutthroat with guild distinction. At least with someone like Yves, you know where you stand. Corsairs still live by the laws of the sea."

"You're not making any sense," Carlion said, in an attempt to reason with her. "The mercenary guild has an apprentice-ship system just like everyone else, and lots of people get their guilders stripped from them for misconduct. If you're part of the guild, being a mercenary is a legitimate profession and we count retired Sovereignty soldiers and City Watchmen as members. Yes, we sell our swords, but there are contracts and taxes and guild charters involved as well. That's the difference between us and just being a brigand in a gang."

"So you say," Shara replied and turned to look out across the ocean. She was silent for a long time while the water's surface darkened to purple as the sun continued its decent. The first few stars were visible in the sky when, with a distant expres-sion, Shara said, "I was in a relationship with someone, another mage from the Archive, a long time ago. Mercenaries killed her just after she started her traveling education."

"What happened?" Trinity asked softly.

Shara swallowed hard and said, "She was supposed to help

bolster the fences around a frontier farmstead that was being harassed by a B'nisct swarm. I made her promise to be careful and stay safe. She thought she was doing that when she hired two local mercenaries. But when those bastards found out that she was from the Archive, they thought she was wealthy and tried to rob her after the fences were rebuilt. She tried to fight back and got a dagger in her gut as a result. She died alone in one of the farmer's fields."

Despite an obvious effort to keep her emotions under control, Shara couldn't stop a few tears from sliding down her checks. Quickly wiping them away, she looked up at the mercenaries with a pained expression. "Tell me you're different from them," she said weakly.

Carlion had not been prepared for the Venhadar's confession and was stunned into silence. In fact, he very much doubted he could give an adequate response. The Darkman glanced over at Trinity and saw that the mercenary was staring at his boots and was close to tears. The muscles in his cheeks and around his mouth were tight as Trinity tried to keep his composure.

Not looking up, Trinity asked, "Were you able to lay her to rest? To say goodbye?"

Shara seemed momentarily taken aback by the question, but then answered, "Yes, I was. Why?"

Trinity took a deep breath and looked at Shara. Not being able to hold her gaze, he turned his face up to the darkening sky and answered, "I was married once. It seems like a lifetime ago. She was beautiful and I loved her. So did another, but he loved her as a possession. He was scheming, and rich, and not used to being denied. He had her kidnapped her not long after we had just settled onto our new farmstead. I tried to find him myself, but I didn't know where to even start. I was desperate and eventually found myself at an Archive. It was mere chance, but Thorne was there too and he helped me. We were able to track her kidnappers down, but by the time I got my revenge, my wife was gone forever. There was a fire and I never got to say goodbye. Not properly."

"At least you got revenge," Shara said bitterly. "The mercenaries were never seen again in that area and the murder was forgotten in a few short years. They're both dead now, if from nothing else than old age. What I'm talking about happened before you were even born. Still, even just a few days ago, I got so angry walking past the mercenary guildhall when Metauk and I followed Thorne out of town. I guess the decades still haven't blunted the edge of my anger."

"They never will," Trinity said. "It's been nearly twenty years since I lost Claire, and my heart breaks anew every time I travel past a farmstead. All I think about is the life that was taken from me, and at those times I feel most alone."

"In twenty years you could have remarried, started a new life. Why didn't you?" Shara said, but it sounded like she was more talking to herself than Trinity.

The mercenary put his hand over his heart and replied, "Claire and I were followers of The Small Family, and that's a religion where marriage lasts for the lives of both people."

In the silence that followed Shara and Trinity's confessions, Carlion felt empty. The justifications he had used to convince himself that he needed to return to Julia as some sort of savior seemed juvenile now. He realized that just being there for her and Natty would be enough. Carlion decided right there, on the deck of the *Maddie*, that with or without a healer he would return to Deccern immediately. He still had a duty to perform, but as soon as Shara was safe at the Archive, he would return to Deccern and be reunited with his family.

• • •

"I wish Metauk was here," Shara told the mercenaries as

they walked up the main road towards the Archive. "She'd be able to make sense of this nervous energy in the air."

The voyage back to Port was thankfully swift and uneventful. The *Maddie's* crew left them alone per Yves' instructions, though Shara did have one whispered conversation with the caption just before leaving the ship. With only the briefest stops to get enough food and drink for one overnight camp, Trinity led them quickly out of the harbor city and onto the road back to the provincial capital. Both the weather and road were in good condition and they entered the city just before the tolling of nine high bells.

"We don't need an empath for that," Carlion said, pulling his tabard straight. "Look," he pointed at the City Watch quarters where two Sovereignty soldiers were leaving.

"Why are they coming out of the City Watch barracks?" the Venhadar asked.

"They've commandeered it," Carlion said, as if it were obvious. The Darkman knew that Yaboon was a powerful guild city and didn't often see a large Sovereignty military presence unless the prince had business here with the guild masters. Otherwise, the prince spent most of his time on his ancestral lands closer to the coast. "A garrison must have arrived after we left," Carlion added. "The question is, why are they here?"

"Maybe the rumor Yves heard about the Archive being blockaded had merit," Trinity said, apprehensively.

As the Archive came into view, the trio saw the truth in Yves' warning. Small groups of archers wearing the Yaboon Sovereignty colors of green and silver loitered on the garden lawn at the front of the building. Carlion was able to see at least three active patrols of pikemen walking a wide perimeter, with another half dozen standing guard near the large entrance doors.

When it became apparent that they were intent on entering

the Archive, a pair of pikemen stepped forward to block their advance, while another pair flanked them. The pikeman standing in front of Shara asked, "Are you mages? What is your business here?"

With an unforgiving expression, Shara jerked out her Archive guilder and showed it to the lead pikeman. "I am an Archive mage. What is the meaning of this?" she demanded.

"You need to return to the Archive at once," said the pikeman, ignoring the Venhadar's question. Looking at Carlion and Trinity he continued, "Are you mages?"

Trinity shook his head and retrieved his mercenary guilder. Carlion followed suit and said, "We were hired as an escort to Port. We're just returning."

Examining the guilders, the soldier said, "If you two aren't mages, then you need to leave immediately. Only mages are to be housed in the Archive during the injunction."

"What injunction?" Shara demanded loudly.

"Hold!" a forceful command boomed behind Carlion. The Darkman turned and felt panic grip his throat as a Sovereignty cavalier atop a huge warhorse trotted slowly towards them. The woman had a hawkish nose and a short grey ponytail. Rough looking hands gripped the reigns of the warhorse with an easy strength. She looked down at the entire gathering with a glare of disapproval as she pulled her mount to a stop.

"Escort these two to the entrance," the cavalier said, pointing to Trinity and Shara. Looking Carlion square in the eye the cavalier said, "I would have a word with Sir Cantra before he joins them."

The pikemen that were in the flanking position shifted to isolate Carlion, while the two blocking the path forward took a step aside to allow Shara and Trinity access to the Archive main door. As they neared the arched overhang that covered the entrance, Shara pointed at Trinity's sword and said something that Carlion could not hear, but he could tell from Trinity's reaction that it wasn't welcome. The mercenary gestured angrily then pulled his weapons from his belt. When he took a step into the archway, he slapped his short sword and dagger against the wall where they stuck and were held fast. Carlion heard the pikemen laugh at the mercenary as Trinity entered the Archive.

The snort of the warhorse made Carlion turn back to the mounted cavalier. "You know me," Carlion said, making it sound like an accusation.

The cavalier gave a single slow nod and replied, "To become a Darkman is a rare thing these days. Training and equipping a cavalier is a significant investment for a Sovereignty." She pointed at Carlion's tabard and said, "It doesn't help that the rumor about you still wearing your ruined cuirass is actually true."

"What do you want?" the Darkman said bluntly.

"As you can no doubt tell, we have been dispatched for a civil siege of the Archive," the cavalier said. "Relations between the military and the mages is rather poor and we don't know how well prepared they are for such an event. This is a rather unique situation, given that we are not blockading an entire city, but rather a fortification within one."

"The quality of spies you employ must be lacking," Carlion said, trying to goad the cavalier into losing her composure. He knew it was petty, but given the circumstances it was the most defiant thing the Darkman could do.

The cavalier pursed her lips and seemed to weigh her words carefully before she replied, "They have been unreliable, which brings me to my request. I want you to determine their capability to circumvent the blockade. We need to know if they have any secret supply lines that connect to their catacombs."

"Why would I do that?" Carlion asked.

"How about to protect Julia and Nathaniel," the cavalier

said, leaning forward in her saddle.

"How do you know about them?" Carlion asked, trying to hide his shock.

"It's common knowledge now, not that you would know," the cavalier said with a predatory smile. "The commander thought admitting everything to the prince would lessen the scandal. He's publicly disowned his daughter and bastard grandson. For all he cares, they can live a wretched existence and die isolated in Deccern." The cavalier dramatically raised her eyebrows in mock surprise and said, "She never told you?"

Ignoring the question, Carlion growled, "If threatening a man's family is what the Sovereignty military has reduced itself to, then I consider my cashiering a promotion."

The cavalier shrugged and replied, "Perhaps, but it's a weakness that is easy to exploit." Opening her arms in an offering gesture she said, "You're a mercenary, so consider your family's safety in Deccern my payment to you while you are confined in the Archive. You're going to be trapped there, perhaps for some time, so why not make yourself useful?"

Carlion clenched his jaw so tight it started to hurt. He was trapped and the cavalier knew it. "What assurances do I have that you'll do as you say?" the Darkman asked sourly.

The cavalier leaned back in the saddle, this time giving Carlion a smug grin. "You have my word," she said.

The Darkman crossed his arms across his chest and growled, "Not good enough. I want an oath."

With eyes flashing genuine anger, the cavalier barked, "Oaths are given, not demanded. Let's make one thing clear, Darkman. I am here to establish this civil siege with the garrison and wait for the prince's order to relent, or for the mages inside the Archive to starve."

She ran a hand lovingly along the warhorse's neck and looked down upon it with affection. The cavalier looked back at Carlion with the hard eyes of a trained killer and said, "But long sieges, especially civil ones, are so dull. I could travel to Deccern and back in a day, just as an excuse to stretch his legs. The fate of your dearest and her son is yours to decide."

The pikemen flanking Carlion prodded him towards the Archive main door. As he turned away, the cavalier said, "I'm not known for my patience, so I would get the information soon. I suppose it goes without saying that you won't make much progress if the mages inside knew about our little arrangement."

Carlion squared his shoulders and did not look back as he walked stiffly towards the Archive main door. A few steps from the archway entrance, one of the pikeman grunted a laugh and asked, "What are you going to do with your armor now, Darkman?"

Carlion looked at Trinity's weapons adhered to the archway wall and frowned. He quickly stripped off his tabard and unbuckled his cuirass. Pulling the armor over his head he attempted to gently push it towards the wall. A powerful force gripped the cuirass, ripped it from his hand, and slammed the armor against the wall with a metallic crunch. Pulling his sword free, Carlion slapped it next to Trinity's weapons on the wall. With more care he removed his ring and placed it next to the hilt of his sword where it held fast to the lodestone wall.

"It's yours if you can pull it down," Carlion growled to the pikeman before yanking open the heavy entrance door.

When his eyes adjusted to the interior lighting of the atrium, the Darkman saw that Trinity was talking to the major-domo, Erma Kent. The area was otherwise empty and Shara was gone.

"What was that all about?" Trinity asked as Carlion approached them.

"She saw my armor," Carlion lied. "Dressed me down in front of her men and enjoyed doing it too. She told me I belonged in here with the rest of the heretics."

"That doesn't make any sense," Erma said. "The Archive holds no religious affiliation."

Carlion shrugged and replied, "I'm sure that point is lost on the military. Where's Shara?"

Trinity pointed down a hall and said, "She went straight to find Metauk."

"Is she here?" Carlion asked hopefully. "What about Thorne and Amos?"

Erma raised her hands in a calming gesture before saying, "Yes, all three are here. Master Thorne has been meeting with the council frequently, so he might not be available now. Your compatriot from the mercenary guild, however, has the same access to Archive facilities as any other guest." With a small smile she continued, "I believe he has spent most of his time in our cafeteria trying to negotiate for a personal supply of wine from our vintner."

"Let's go find Amos," Carlion suggested. "I could use a drink, and I, for one, want to know how the hell he got back here." Looking at the major-domo he added, "I might take you up on your previous offer for another tour of the Archive. It sounds like we'll have the time, so maybe you can take me off the beaten path."

Erma gave a weak smile and replied, "Of course." As she ushered the mercenaries out of the atrium, the Darkman took a quick look towards the main door. Turning back, Carlion caught Trinity watching him with a grim expression that the mercenary quickly tried to hide as they went to reunite with Amos.

CHAPTER TWENTYFIVE

THORNE

The skin around Thorne's eyes felt tight as the mage futilely tried to rub the weariness from his face. It had been some time since he heard eleven low bells echo quietly from outside his apartment window, and the mage was finally ready to give up for the night. In frustration he snatched the collection of notes that lay on his writing table and crumpled them in his fist. He had exhausted his spy network within the Archive and had learned nothing useful about Uksyo's fate, save that his Awareness had been completely bound.

As Thorne predicted, the emergence of four people from a chrysalis caused a stir in the Archive. However, it was quickly superseded by debate about how to manage the crisis brought on by the Sovereignty military blockade. Relinquishing Uksyo to the Archive constable, the mage found that when the Sovereignty garrison cut off the Archive's access to the city only council members Tarbeck, Olaf, and Erica were present.

Unfortunately, it turned out that Olaf was the only one who listened to Thorne's report with any interest. Erica and Tarbeck wanted to hear nothing about Thorne's warning of a second Engine or Reihana being part of a conspiracy with nebulous intentions. To them, the only thing that mattered at the moment was establishing a dialog with the prince and ending the civil siege on the Archive. They promised Thorne that they would remove the binding mark on him once the current crisis was managed, but then the council appeared to immediately forget about the mage.

Tossing the small wad of paper into the unlit hearth, Thorne sat heavily on the edge of his bed. His reunion with Trinity, Carlion, and Shara had been a brief moment of happiness, but now that the adrenaline rush of the past few days had left his system the mage acutely felt the walls of his room pressing in on him. With Uksyo inaccessible and the council fixated on the military blockade, Thorne was left to brood over what had happened to him in the Void and second-guess his decision to return to the Archive.

Sitting still made his restlessness worse, so Thorne stood up and began pacing the length of his room. His thoughts kept returning to something Reihana said through Uksyo about being able to rewind time and change the past. The mage knew to never discount the impossible, but the concept seemed too far-fetched. The rigidity of time was absolute, even more so than the laws that governed Awareness. The arcane elements could be manipulated, but adhered to the principle that mass and energy were conserved. In fact, many mages thought of themselves as accelerators or decelerators of chemical reactions and physical forces rather than the wielders of unknowable powers. However, for something as fundamental as time, no mage had yet discovered a way to alter its seemingly singular speed and direction.

Thorne stopped pacing in front of the painting of Rose. He sighed heavily as he looked at the small figure positioned next to the willow tree. The artist had given her a melancholy smile, and Thorne felt a familiar mixture of sadness and guilt press down on him. What would she have thought about the path his life had taken?

"Acceptable framing of the scene, but careless brushwork," said a voice from behind Thorne.

The mage spun around, startled by the unexpected intrusion. On the table next to his hourglass stood Barrow. The pixie was dressed in dark grey alchemist robes cut in the traditional style. Her violet hair was now short and her vividly bright eyes looked up at Thorne with a contemptuous expression.

"How did you get in here?" Thorne asked, agitated.

"Your door was unlocked," Barrow replied as she rested a hand on one of the hourglass's supports.

"That's not what I meant," the mage said with a lowered brow.

"But it was what you asked."

"What are you doing here, Barrow?" demanded the mage, already tired of being toyed with by the pixie.

Barrow nimbly climbed up on top of the hourglass and sat with her legs dangling off the edge. "I bring a message from Celeste," she said, "She expected you would eventually find a way to physically enter the Void, though how you actually did was surprising. You called out, and she heard you."

"But didn't answer," Thorne said sourly. "She sent you instead."

"You sound disappointed," Barrow replied.

Thorne crossed his arms across his chest. His voice had an edge when he answered, "I am."

Barrow gently slapped the top of the hourglass and said, "You still have the broken hourglass. Celeste told me about this peculiar personality quirk of yours, to display mementos of your failures. Under different circumstances, I think she would be pleased to see you still keep this close at hand."

Barrow was doing her best to provoke him, but Thorne checked any reckless impulses. Despite the pixie's total height being less than the length of Thorne's forearm, she commanded an incredible amount of mana and had shown herself to be a fierce adversary in the past. Trying hard to not lose his composure, Thorne said, "Stop antagonizing me and relay your message."

Barrow scoffed and narrowed her eyes at the mage before she said, "Celeste wasn't ignoring you deliberately. She can't leave the Void right now and sent me in her stead. She wanted me to tell you she still intends to fulfill her promise to you. If you can physically enter the Void again, she will erase the memories you want gone." The pixie looked from Thorne to the painting and said, "If you figured out a way to physically enter the Void, why did you leave?"

Thorne cocked his head quizzically, "Celeste didn't tell you?"

Barrow shook her head and answered, "It is not my place to intrude into my master's affairs. I serve her without question, though I ask myself often why she still loves you."

The mage turned around to face the painting so Barrow would not see his pained expression. His past relationship with both the dragon and pixie had been complicated. "You've delivered your message. Now get out of my room," Thorne said stiffly.

The ringing of twelve low bells filtered through the shuttered window. Thorne turned back to face Barrow, but the pixie was gone. While looking at the top of the hourglass where she had been sitting something caught his eye. As Thorne picked up the hourglass, a shower of fine iridescent sand slid off of the top and spilled onto the table. Thorne pinched some of the sand and rubbed it between his fingers. Inspecting the sand closely, the mage saw that it shimmered with an unnatural light and he realized it was pixie dust.

Struck by a thought, Thorne went to his satchel and pulled out the map stolen from Nion's shop in Rell-Kyr. Taking it to the table he carefully unfolded and shook it. A few grains of sand that had been stuck to the paper were knocked loose and bounced to the table. The sand from the map did not shimmer any longer, but Thorne's suspicions were all but confirmed.

"What have you been doing, Barrow?" he said aloud.

Impulsively, Thorne strode out of his room in pursuit of the pixie. Due to the various wards erected around the building Barrow would have to physically leave the Archive before being able to phase to Celeste. Greeted by an empty corridor, the mage could only guess which way Barrow had gone. Thorne quickly descended the stairwell and entered the atrium to find it empty save for a pair of sentries that were standing near the main door. Wearing the white sashes of the Archive constabulary, the two men stopped their quiet conversation and looked pointedly at Thorne in unison.

"Have you seen anything unusual tonight?" Thorne said from across the atrium, his voice unintentionally booming in the quiet empty space.

The constables looked at each other and one mumbled something that Thorne could not hear. The man looked at Thorne and shook his head. Without acknowledging either one again, Thorne quickly walked out of the atrium and down the hall that led to the infirmary and Masters Hall. Both had auxiliary exits to the outside and Thorne hoped this was the route that Barrow took because the pixie would be long gone before the mage could search elsewhere.

His instincts were to go underground and the mage nearly lost his footing in his haste down the stairwell to Masters Hall. Ignoring the disapproving looks from the Vigil Keepers, Thorne went to the exit at the back of the hall that was again guarded by two more constables.

"Has anyone left through here tonight?" Thorne asked without preamble.

"With the blockade, there's nowhere for them to go," one said shaking her head. "You're the most action we've seen all night."

Thorne turned and stomped back to the middle of the hall before he regained his composure. Barrow was likely out the Archive now and once outside would likely revert to her elemental form and enter her home plane before returning to Celeste in the Void.

As the mage calmed down, he found that he was unconsciously walking toward his chrysalis. It was still unoccupied and sealed, the weak blue light from the wall mounted glow globes contrasting sharply with the orange-pink resin. Slowly running a hand over the textured curves of the chrysalis lid, Thorne's shoulders felt tight. With his face squeezed in a frustrated expression, the mage bowed his head and tried to make sense of the unexpected meeting with Barrow.

Everything about the pixie's appearance and message was suspect. Why was there pixie dust at both Nion's shop and the underwater entrance to Uksyo's secret laboratory? What was Celeste doing in the Void that prevented her from answering his calls? Was Barrow secretly serving two masters, Celeste and Reihana, and playing them at odds for reasons Thorne could not fathom? Without returning to the Void Thorne had no way of learning any of the answers, but as he was still denied access to any Archive laboratory there was nothing he could do. The feeling of powerlessness was agonizing.

"The look of someone wrestling with an intractable problem doesn't suit you, Thorne," a familiar voice said softly. The mage looked up and saw Olaf approaching him. The councilman gave a tight-lipped smile when he reached the chrysalis and rested a hand on the lid. "I won't waste your time with idle pleasantries," Olaf began. "Do you truly believe that Reihana is behind Uksyo's actions and the creation of a second Engine?

He said it was hidden near the ruined Archive in Momontre."

Before answering, Thorne watched several Vigil Keepers quickly, but discretely, leaving the area. Where they stood was now conspicuously empty. It appeared that Olaf wanted to keep the conversation private. The mage carefully tried to detect any change in Olaf's practiced neutral expression when he replied, "Had I known it was there, I would have already left if it wasn't for the Sovereignty military at our doorstep. We can't let something like an Engine be outside of Archive control. However, what worries me more is why one was secretly built at all. While Tarbeck enjoyed mocking me about it when I delivered Uksyo, I am telling you that if Reihana is in the Void or found some way to circumvent her binding, then all of the Archives, and the council, are in very real danger."

"I agree," Olaf said flatly. "That's why I'm here to help you."

"You could have done that in the council chamber, but I remember your comments were rather noncommittal," Thorne said bitterly.

"There's what I say, and there's what I do," Olaf replied. "There can be no official council action because the other council members are in other regions and travel here is tantamount to imprisonment. However, I'm not here as a member of the council, but as a regular Archive mage."

"What are you offering?" Thorne asked.

The councilman reached into his vest and retrieved what looked like a fragment from a giant egg. The chalky hue of the thin shell appeared brittle, but Olaf did not seem concerned about its apparent fragility. He extended his hand over the chrysalis to Thorne and said, "This is a shard of dragon shell recovered from the Momontre Masters Hall shortly after that Archive was destroyed. It is a personal memento of Erica's that she obtained some time ago."

Taking the shell piece, Thorne found it to be surprisingly

durable. Holding it between his fingers, the mage could feel a faint charge of mana from the shell piece. "I won't ask how you got this," Thorne said. "But it's not enough. We also need an Engine of our own to physically enter the Void."

"Given his current circumstances, Uksyo fears the council more than Reihana," Olaf said. "Despite being considerably more powerful than Nion, he turned out to be a coward. As such, Uksyo is cooperating with us fully. He has given me the equations that will change the resonance state of a chrysalis. With some modest recalibration any chrysalis here could move you into the Void."

Thorne continued to rotate the dragon egg fragment in his hand and considered the councilman's words. Olaf was many things, but altruistic was not one of them. A flush of anger followed a bolt of insight as Thorne realized what Olaf was doing. If Thorne found proof of an Engine, then the council could show the Sovereignty that the Archive had its house back in order. However, as this was an unofficial action, Olaf could deny all knowledge and serve Thorne up as a scapegoat if things went awry.

"Given the rather rigid schedule of Masters Hall, I can give you only a small window of time," Olaf said, taking his hands off the chrysalis and leaning back on his heels. "The night after next at seven low bells, you need to be ready. Now, I must ask a favor in return, albeit a small one. Please take your mercenary companions with you. The journey will likely be treacherous, even for a former Paragon. I'm sure your companions would welcome leaving here, and the expelled cavalier is making some people especially uncomfortable given our current circumstances, so it seems to benefit all involved if they go."

Thorne's lip screwed up in dissatisfaction. The mage wanted to be rid of the Darkman, but it looked like Olaf was trying to use this situation to simultaneously solve two Archive problems.

"What about Shara and Metauk?" Thorne asked. "They turned out to be surprisingly useful in apprehending Uksyo."

Olaf shrugged and answered, "The task given to them by the council is complete, and so they are not obligated to go with you. That being said, if you tell Metauk what you plan to do, then I am certain she will want to join you. And where Metauk goes, Shara is not far behind. I have no complaint against them going as well."

From behind Olaf, the Vigil Keeper Inge came around the corner. She paused at the sight of Thorne and Olaf, but when the councilman turned and raised his hand in greeting, Inge inclined her head and slightly bowed before continuing down the hall. Whatever privacy Olaf had arranged was now over.

"Now, if you'll excuse me, Master Thorne, I am going to secure you the healer requested for dispatch to Deccern when all of this is over," Olaf said with a slight bow. The councilman turned and took a few steps away from the chrysalis, then stopped. With his back still to Thorne Olaf said quietly, "You're doing the Archive a service, Thorne. It will not be forgotten." The councilman then continued on his way out of the hall.

Thorne didn't like the double meaning and waited until Olaf was out of sight before he walked back to his room. The mage was finally tired, and he needed to rest and think about how he would approach the mercenaries, Metauk, and Shara to discuss what was certain to be a dangerous journey. Thorne crawled into bed fully clothed and his head barely made a dent in the pillow before he was asleep.

CELESTE'S MEMORY OF AN

INTRODUCTION TO THE BEAST

"**W**hy are we doing this again?" Barrow asked, annoyed. Even when standing at full height, only the pixie's head protruded from the breast pocket of Celeste's jacket.

They stood at the threshold of the silk merchant guild in the coastal city of Port. The late morning sun from a clear sky hit the glossy green paint of the guildhall door and made it shimmer like an emerald. Celeste had insisted on traveling as a human and negotiated passage on a ship from the southern islands to the continent. The dragon relished the mundane sensations of traveling, but Barrow had grown increasingly surly as the journey wore on. A few discreet inquires later, they had found out that the person they were searching for was here.

"Given all the secrecy, the conclave wants to learn what this Paragon business is all about," the dragon replied to her retainer. "Normally the Archives are very transparent in all their dealings, so it's strange that they now have something that plays right into the militaries' propaganda of a secret society bent on undermining the Sovereignties' rule."

"From what I gather, the Sovereignties are more concerned about taxes lost from the rampant smuggling taking place on the open seas," Barrow countered. "The princes seem to have stumbled upon the rumors of Archive mages suddenly being able to use magic as a weapon by happenstance. But now it gives them the pretense to be more aggressive with both the Archives and the guilds."

"It's a circular argument," Celeste said. "The guilds are overburdened by steep taxes, which leads them to smuggle their goods between provinces. The smuggling results in rampant piracy and consequently, loss of profit. With less tax revenue returning to the capital, the prince raises taxes again to make up the deficit. Round and round it goes."

"So of course when the Archive provides a hush-hush solution to protect the smugglers, the guilds would jump to accept," Barrow said. "Especially when they don't want money, but instead favors, allies, and influence in guild proceedings. Even without a seat at the guild masters' table, the Archive now has a hand in shaping commerce and communication across the continent."

"The politics of it are of little interest to me," Celeste said. "However, I very much want to meet one of these fighting mages. Using Awareness for combat isn't something I've thought seriously about in centuries. I'm curious if they've come up any innovative techniques, but more interested in who would want such power."

"Oh, I can venture a guess," Barrow said sourly. "Let's get this over with."

Celeste pulled the door open and as she walked inside was struck by the beauty and elegance of the receiving room décor. Behind a richly stained desk sat a man with a rotund body and double chin. His black hair was slicked back, revealing a high forehead and the skin tone of someone who had origins from the northern coast. Not surprisingly, he was expensively dressed.

"Good afternoon, madam," the man said looking up from the document he was reading. "My name is Tram, I am the guild secretary. Do you have business with us today?"

"A pleasure to meet you Tram," Celeste said with a warm smile. "I believe that the guild master is currently hosting an agent from the Yaboon Archive. I would very much like to speak with him."

"I'm sorry, but the guild master's schedule is quite full today," Tram said. "I might be able to fit you in next week. Whom do you represent?"

The dragon maintained her smile when she replied, "I'm sorry, but you misunderstand. I wish to speak to the guild master's guest, the Paragon."

Tram's face rapidly shifted from surprised to trying too hard to be perplexed. "What is a Paragon? I'm sorry, madam, I believe you have made a mistake."

Celeste raised her hand, which pulsed a soft white for an instant as she influenced the man's mood, and then said, "It's been a busy day for you, Tram. Why don't you go home and rest? I can find my way upstairs to the guild master's office."

The secretary's eyes unfocused for a moment and the muscles of his neck and shoulders relaxed before Tram jerked back to alertness. "Goodness, I'm sorry, madam! I don't mean to be so rude, but today has been incredibly fatiguing. The guild master is upstairs in his office with the Archive representative. Please take the stairs to my right to reach them. If you'll excuse me."

Tram stood up from behind his desk, sidled past Celeste, and exited the guildhall.

"It always amazes me how easily you can alter the brain chemistry of humans," Barrow said once they were alone. "If the Archive knew how precisely dragons can manipulate the arcane elements it would drive them mad with envy."

Celeste replied, "You make it sound so crass. I dislike using such an aggressive method, but I doubt we would have made much headway with Tram."

The dragon ascended the stairs that the guild secretary had indicated and then looked down the hall when she reached the top. There were doors opposite each other all the way down and one at the end. The hallway doors were open and looked to be small, unoccupied meeting rooms or offices. The door at the end of the hall was closed and Celeste paused in front of it to listen. When she heard conversation inside, the dragon grasped the handle and without announcing herself opened the door.

As she stepped into the room, Celeste watched the two men inside have very different reactions to her intrusion. The elderly man behind a large darkly stained desk seemed to quiver in agitation at the interruption. While well dressed, he was thin to point of gauntness with a crown of unruly white hair. His sunken eyes nearly disappeared when he squinted disapprovingly, which crushed his lips into thin line.

In contrast, the young man that reclined on the couch before the desk looked amused at the interruption. He was sitting with his feet propped up on the low table. His arms were outstretched and resting on the back of the couch and the dragon could clearly see a set of peculiar armor that the man wore casually. Not made of the typical steel mail or plate, this armor was constructed from an amber resin and looked more like the transparent shell of a tortoise than anything else. Celeste knew this was the man she was searching for despite that fact that he looked more like a mercenary than an Archive mage.

"What is the meaning of this?" the guild master croaked. He held his stylus in front of him with an unsteady hand and pointed at Celeste and added, "Who are you?"

"Your secretary Tram had to leave unexpectedly," Celeste said calmly. "Would you be so kind as to take his place for a few minutes? I would like to speak with your guest here."

The guild master stood up and barked, "I will do no such

thing, madam!"

Before the old man could finish his tirade, Celeste raised a hand and relaxed his mood as she had done with the guild secretary.

"Oh, excuse me," the old man said with a sudden change in tone. "I mustn't leave the receiving room unattended." Addressing the man on the couch he said, "I promise to complete the letters of support that the Archive requested later today. My apologies."

As the guild master shuffled out of the room, the man on the couch still had an amused expression on his face, but now he was much more focused on Celeste as she walked around to face him. Leaning back and balancing her backside on the edge of the desk the dragon said, "You seem to be taking this all in stride, Thorne, though I suppose nothing much unnerves a Paragon."

"It seems that I'm at a disadvantage, as you know who I am," Thorne said surprised. "That was a curious trick you pulled with the guild master. Which Archive are you from?"

"Not an Archive," Celeste replied. "I represent another interested party. I was sent to evaluate you as the Paragon with the reputation for being the most destructive."

"I would imagine that there are several interested parties, as you say, that would want to ally themselves with the most powerful fighting mage," Thorne boasted. "What is the business of your particular organization?"

"We wish to determine your potential," Celeste answered.

"Potential for what?" Thorne asked, his face now darkening. He slid his feet off the table and leaned forward.

"For being a threat to the people of the continent," Barrow said from Celeste's jacket. As her head crested the top of Celeste's pocket she added, "And let's be clear, we know you're not the most powerful Paragon, just the most bloodthirsty. The most powerful Paragon was born Aware, and as a made mage you still have a lot of catching up to do. True power is derived from controlled force, not reckless violence. The way you wield your Awareness like a cudgel makes you nothing more than a beast."

"A pixie!" Thorne exclaimed, standing up. "I'm beginning to understand who you represent."

"Then you'd be wise to stop with the bravado and speak with us plainly," Barrow threatened.

"Is that so?" Thorne said with a self-satisfied smile. "That's all fine, but I must admit that you've shared a captivating idea. I think it might make some of my future assignments easier if the opposition knew they were dealing with The Beast."

"It's wasn't supposed to be a compliment, you lout," Barrow fumed.

"Easy there, pipsqueak," Thorne warned and held up a finger at the pixie. "There's no reason we can't all be friends here. We just met after all."

"Sit down!" Barrow commanded. She raised her fist up and rapidly jerked it down to her shoulder.

The mage was pulled back down to the couch by a powerful force. Thorne's startled expression was quickly replaced with narrowed eyes and hardened features when he looked at Barrow. Both of the mage's hands were clenched tightly and his body tensed, never taking his eyes off of the pixie. Celeste was unsure if the mage truly wanted to attack Barrow, but any more provocation from the pixie would likely result in the guildhall being reduced to splinters.

"Barrow, that's enough," Celeste said severely, as she looked down at the pixie. "You're making my job harder than it needs to be right now."

"He started it," Barrow said sullenly. When Celeste gave her a disapproving look, the pixie slid down into the pocket and the dragon could almost feel her retainer sulk.

"I apologize for Barrow," Celeste said to Thorne. "Overstepping boundaries is a bad habit of hers."

Thorne tried to look gracious, but his face was taut and it left him looking pained. "Think nothing of it," he said. "Your familiar has given me something very interesting to think about. It appears the tales about a pixie's disproportionate power are true. Her manipulation of the arcane elements is something that I would be eager to learn."

Celeste could feel Barrow bristle with rage at being called a familiar, and the dragon suspected that Thorne had made the insult on purpose. Trying to ignore the wriggling pixie, Celeste said formally, "Despite our rocky start, I am very happy to meet you Thorne. My name is Celeste, and I am a member of the dragon conclave."

Thorne stood again and bowed as far as his armor allowed. "It is incredibly rare to be sought out by a dragon," he said. "I am honored and will assist you in any way possible."

"Excellent," Celeste replied as she moved beside him and sat down on the couch. "Let's begin with the origins of the Paragon program."

CHAPTER TWENTYSIX

CARLION

A few days after their return to the Archive, Carlion and the mercenaries were in their guest quarters getting ready to make their way to the cafeteria for breakfast when there was a sharp double knock on the door. Without waiting for a reply, Thorne entered and quickly closed the door.

"To what do we owe the honor?" Trinity asked in a friendly but mocking tone. However, the smile on the mercenary's face vanished when he saw Thorne's grim expression.

"I can get you three out of here," the mage said without preamble. He gave each of the mercenaries a pointed look as he spoke.

"What happened to the blockade?" Carlion asked, surprised. Scrutinizing the mage, he thought Thorne looked tense, on edge. Something had happened, but the Darkman could not tell if it was for good or ill.

"It's still there," the mage answered. "And it will be until the prince recalls the garrison."

"Then you're sneaking out," Amos said.

The mage's impassive pretense cracked as he gave a small grin at the Venhadar and replied, "Something like that, yes. I want you to come with me on one more errand."

"And?" Amos prompted, clearly waiting for the other shoe to drop.

"We'll need to go back into the Void to get there," Thorne finished.

"There it is," Amos said in a not quite patronizing tone.

"Forget it," Carlion said with glance at Amos. "From what I hear you almost didn't escape that place."

"I know what I'm doing now," Thorne said. "Besides, Metauk and Shara are coming, too. I just came from talking with both of them."

"That's hardly an incentive," the Darkman said sourly.

"What's the errand?" Trinity asked, louder than needed, clearly trying to bring the conversation back on topic.

"Find Uksyo's other Engine and destroy it," Thorne said.

"Where is it?" Trinity asked.

"The ruined Archive in Momontre," Thorne answered.

"But it's at least a two-week journey to get there over the mountains," the Darkman said. He shook his head, silently thinking about how Julia and Natty would be in very real danger if he couldn't find a way to them in that time.

"Not if we go through the Void," Amos said. "We were a lot further away on the Stormbreaker Isles, and we just popped back here like it was nothing."

"Maybe that type of instant travel is the whole point of the Engines," Trinity said. "I shudder to think what would happen if one of the Sovereignties gets ahold of it."

"You're on the right track," Thorne said, "but I'm more concerned about the mages who made it in the first place. What do they really want to do with it? What's their end goal?"

Carlion looked to his fellow mercenaries, but they too remained silent, as no one seemed to have a reasonable answer to Thorne's questions. The Darkman then realized that the mage might be his next best chance to escape the Archive if he was unable to pass any useful information to the cavalier in charge of the blockade. The ruined Archive in Momontre was considerably closer to Deccern than Yaboon and once there, it was likely he could part ways with the others with little difficulty. While a small pang of guilt cut through him with that last thought, Carlion reminded himself that he had to think of Julia's and Natty's safety first, and the best way to protect them was to get to Deccern as fast as possible.

"I imagine that this device will be protected somehow," Carlion said, finally breaking the silence. "We're going to need our weapons and gear back. How do we get them unstuck from the wall?"

Thorne shook his head and replied, "You can't bring iron where we're going, but don't worry. I can get you something that I think you'll find suitable. Can I count on you three?"

Trinity gave a crooked grin and answered, "As if you had to ask."

"Likewise," Amos said. "I rather fancied that little tingle I got passing through those magic doors."

"I'll go," Carlion said with much less enthusiasm than the other mercenaries. He still intended to follow through with the plan he had come up with the day prior, but it didn't hurt to have something in his back pocket if that didn't pan out.

● ● ●

"What's on the agenda for this afternoon?" Carlion asked, trying to sound casual. The Darkman was opposite Erma Kent in the atrium of the Archive. The angle of the sun from the domed skylight above them had darkened the back of the large hall, and the air was heavy and warm. All of the windows on the first level had been shuttered to keep prying eyes and shouted curses from penetrating inside, but the reduced ventilation left the corridors and communal areas feeling stagnant.

"Perhaps something on the second floor where there are still a few open windows," Erma offered as she led him out of the atrium and down a wide hallway.

Due to the poor ventilation on the first floor, most of the rooms they walked past had their doors open. In one open studio on their way to the stairs Carlion saw several people sitting on the floor. In front of them were tables with holes cut in the center and long strips of gauze affixed along the edges. The seated mages had their hands under the tables with their palms upward. Some of the gauze strips were being blown up through the holes while others were hanging still. Most of those seated were sweating heavily and a few were quietly grunting.

"How are they doing that with the wind?" Carlion asked after they had passed and started ascending the adjacent stairwell.

"They feel the weight of the air and use their mana to heat it and create an upward draft," Erma said looking back at him. "They will have mastered that technique and many others by the time they leave on their traveling education."

"That's something I still don't understand," Carlion said. "It doesn't make any sense to send a partially trained wizard out into the world. It seems rather irresponsible on your part. You'd never send a soldier into battle with only a rudimentary understanding of the weapon they're holding."

"A good thing we're not in the business of war, then," Erma replied, drawing alongside the Darkman. "It's true that apprentices on their traveling education are only partially Aware, but that means they are much less likely to cause any substantial damage should something go wrong with an elemental manipulation."

Reaching the top of the stairs, Erma stopped and turned to Carlion. "The purpose of an Archive traveling education is twofold. First, it's an attempt for mages-in-training to experience the world outside the comfort of a big city. The frontier can be an unforgiving place and it's a real eye-opener for most of them on how hard it is to eke out an existence without Sovereignty accommodations."

"What's the second reason?" Carlion asked.

"To show the Sovereignties that Archive mages provide significant benefit," Erma said before leading Carlion down another hallway. "We have to work very hard to counteract propaganda that mages are dangerous."

"There will always be rumors," Carlion said dismissively. "However, the Sovereignties and the Archives have a mutually beneficial relationship to develop science and commerce. The prince's coffers stay full from your alchemy, and the Archive enjoys autonomy from the guild system."

"It shouldn't surprise you that our unique relationship with the Sovereignties is the root of considerable jealously and dissatisfaction," Erma said. "There are court advisors and certain guilds who want to destabilize that relationship. For example, the military wants the Archives to weaponize our research, something that we have resisted for generations. This refusal has made us suspect to them, despite the perceived financial gain," Erma said.

Carlion nodded in agreement. Back when he was still a cavalier it was a constant undertone when discussing war. "What about Thorne?" the Darkman asked. "Wasn't he part of some special group of fighting wizards?"

"The Paragon program was a mistake," Erma said disdainfully. "I'm very thankful that there are only two left."

The major-domo stopped in front of a door blocked by two young men who were wearing gaudy white cloth belts. "We'd like to take a bit of fresh air, if you don't mind," Erma said to them.

"Be careful, Master Kent," one of the sentries said as he

stepped aside. "There have been reports the archers down below are taking shots at the upper windows when their captains are not watching them."

"We'll be careful," Erma assured him as she opened the door slowly and walked out onto a wide balcony with Carlion close behind.

The Darkman gripped the top of the short wall as he looked down over the balcony edge. He had never participated in what the military termed a civil siege, but understood the theory behind it. By preventing access to a section of the city the military could quarantine a sick population or quiet a disruptive guild without generating too much ill will from the city's residents. The threat of a civil siege was taken seriously, as they were quick to establish but very slow to end, as it usually took an order from the Sovereignty prince to recall the garrison.

In the plaza below, Carlion could see several patrols of pikemen walking the grounds around the Archive and trios of archers within range of every window. He did not see the cavalier who had spoken to him the day before, which made the Darkman anxious. She had not come across as a person with a reserve of patience.

Erma mistook the reason for his worried expression when she said, "This is meant to look intimidating, but I can assure you we are much more secure than you think. We had a little time before the garrison could seal us off completely and we were able to dispatch several messages to the other Archives and the prince directly. Aid will be coming soon. In the meantime, this building has many safeguards against intrusion. Anyone with so much as iron shod boots will find themselves trapped in a magnetized doorframe."

"If they really wanted to breach these walls then they'll come with leather armor and oak cudgels," Carlion said.

"Both of which are very flammable," Erma replied with sly

grin. "There's a reason why this building is floor to ceiling stone with no tapestries or drapes on the walls. It's a safety precaution against accidents in the alchemic labs and has the added bonus of making ignited arrows pointless. All of our records, documents, and books are in interior rooms, so there's nothing to catch fire near a window."

A long thin cloud drifted in front of the sun and erased the shadows from the plaza. Carlion reveled in the immediate temperature change as the air quickly cooled. The Darkman sensed now was the time to find out just how prepared the Archive was for the civil siege. He gave Erma a quick glance before looking back down on the plaza and said, "It sounds like the odds are in your favor against a direct assault, but what happens when the garrison decides to just wait and starve you out?"

"We've been threatened with a blockade before," Erma said confidently. "While we've never kept it a secret, it doesn't seem to be widely known that there is an underground spring that we've tapped into so we aren't dependent on the city water system. Food won't be a problem either. I was in a meeting yesterday to take stock of our provisions, and with the current number of people trapped inside we can eat comfortably for three weeks, maybe a month with a little rationing. They won't be the tastiest meals, but nourishing enough until help arrives."

The Darkman tried to keep a neutral expression while he inwardly exulted. He had just gotten the information that would save his family. He only had to find a way to discreetly get outside and find the cavalier. Trying to explain what he was doing to the Archive sentries might be a problem, but he would make up a pretense after he was alone. Pushing back from the balcony wall he said, "I hope you're right, thought I doubt anyone wants to be confined here that long." He looked back at the door and asked, "Shall we move on?"

"Of course," Erma said, turning towards the door. The

major-domo pulled on the handle and led the way back inside. As they walked back towards the atrium she said, "I thought I might take you to one of our libraries next. There are a number of histories that discuss the mercenary guild that might interest you."

"Sure," Carlion said, trying to sound agreeable.

As they entered the atrium, Carlion saw Trinity, Amos, and Metauk standing near the reception podium. It seemed that they had been waiting for him, as all three looked in their direction eagerly. Amos drained the cup he was holding and slapped it on the podium before following Trinity and Metauk to the middle of the hall where everyone met in a small cluster.

Looking at Amos, Carlion said with a hint of sarcasm, "One for the road?" He pointed back at the cup on the podium.

Amos grunted and replied, "Got a fair share of dirty looks for taking that mug out of the cafeteria, those miserable fucks. Did you know she doesn't drink either?" The corsair jutted his chin at Metauk and continued, "This has got to be some perverse cosmic punishment to be stuck here with a couple of abstainers."

Metauk gave Amos a patient smile, and then looked at Carlion, "I hate to cut the tour short, but can I borrow you for a short while?"

"Alright," Carlion said, slightly confused. "Where are we going?"

"My alchemic lab. I have something for you," the empath replied.

Leaving Erma in the atrium, Carlion and the mercenaries followed Metauk up to the second floor of the Archive and down the corridor where the alchemic laboratories were housed. When the Sehenryu stopped at a door in the middle of the hallway and gently pulled it open, the Darkman commented, "You don't keep your workshop locked?"

"For safety and research transparency, alchemic labs are never locked," Metauk said, looking over her shoulder. She wrinkled her nose and added, "Sorry about the chlorine smell."

Unsatisfied with her answer Carlion asked, "Then what was the key in your ghost message all about?"

Taking a step into the lab, Metauk replied quickly, "It's for an apartment here in the Archive. That's not important anymore. I want you to look at what I have in here."

"But why did Shara say it was for a lab, back on the island?" Carlion mumbled to himself as he followed Metauk into the lab. The question was instantly forgotten once the Darkman was inside and surveyed the room.

Floor to ceiling shelves and cabinets lined the walls on three sides of the room, with a large bank of windows filling the fourth. Two long workbenches were arranged parallel to one another in the center of the room. Topped with a dark grey stone, the benches showed signs of severe wear that included splotches of discoloration and deep pitting in a few areas. Hung over each bench was an enormous inverted funnel that disappeared into the ceiling. An assortment of glassware was bunched together on one workbench, while on the other rested a curious set of armor and weapons.

Metauk scooped up a sheathed short sword from the table and pulled the blade free. The harsh white light from the numerous glow globes affixed to the ceiling showed a weapon not forged from metal, but some type of translucent amber material.

"That looks like Thorne's knife," Trinity commented as he watched the empath inspect the edge of the short sword.

"Polymerized oak sap with an epoxy fixer," Metauk said with a hint of pride. "Twice the durability of steel and holds an edge indefinitely. At least that's what we've found with limited experimentation."

"I thought enchanted weapons were a myth," Carlion said incredulously.

Metauk slid the blade back into its scabbard and returned it to the workbench. "They are a myth. These weapons don't hold any mana in them. They were made with alchemy."

"What's the difference?" the Darkman asked.

"For you, perhaps there is none," the empath replied. "What I can tell you is that these are incredibly hard to craft, and these weapons are generations old. The only thing that has been made in recent memory is this." She picked up a cuirass that looked to be made from the same amber resin as the short sword. Holding it out to Carlion she said, "If it fits, it's yours. On loan, of course."

As Trinity and Amos went over to the workbench to inspect the small collection of swords and daggers, Carlion pulled the cuirass over his head. After adjusting the leather straps at the shoulders, he tested the flex of the material at the edges and rapped the center of his chest a few times. Giving a nod of approval at Metauk, he said, "It feels like it was forged for a smaller frame, but I'll make it work. It feels rather flimsy, but I suppose some protection is better than none."

"If this stuff is so rare, how did you get ahold of it?" Amos asked. A matching pair of resin daggers was now sheathed on his belt.

"Thorne wanted you to have some decent equipment before we get dropped in Momontre, so he collected some support he was owed," Metauk said. "Anyway, that's all I wanted from you three. You've got at least a day to get used to the weight and balance of those. You can take them now or leave them here until we are about to leave, but I've got a few other things to take care of before tomorrow night, so let's go back to the atrium."

Metauk left the mercenaries next to Erma's podium, but the

major-domo was absent. Amos reached up and retrieved the mug that was still there. "You know where to find me," the corsair said as he made his way back to the cafeteria.

Watching Amos' back, Trinity said to Carlion, "Let's go get something to eat and make sure he stays out of trouble."

"I'll catch up," Carlion said. Pulling on the leather strap of the resin cuirass, he added, "I don't want to be wearing this inside. I think it would send the wrong message."

Before Trinity could protest Carlion quickly left the atrium and returned to the small guest apartment that he had been given to share with the other mercenaries. Like the alchemic labs, there was no lock on the door, which still upset the Darkman's sense of privacy and security, even after several days of residing in the Archive. He doffed the resin armor and set it at the foot of his cot.

Standing over the cuirass, Carlion took a deep breath and tried to mentally prepare for his next course of action. He had no affiliation with the Archive and no mages here that he would count as friends, so why did it feel like he was contemplating a terrible betrayal? Reporting on the readiness of the Archive for a civil siege was going to keep his family safe, and that was the most important thing right now. Trying to keep that thought fixed in his mind, Carlion turned his back to the armor crafted by a mage's hands.

Leaving the apartment, the Darkman slowly walked back to the atrium and paused where the hallway opened into the cavernous room. Trinity was gone and Erma's podium remained vacant. At the moment the only occupants of the atrium were a pair of white sashed constables standing in front of the main door. They looked bored but instantly grew alert when the Darkman approached them.

"Is there something we can help you with, sir?" one of the sentries asked with forced politeness.

"Let me outside," Carlion demanded.

"We've orders to keep everyone inside," replied the other sentry. "We don't want to antagonize the garrison and are trying to ensure the safety of everyone here, mages and guests alike."

Carlion tried to strike a friendly but exasperated tone and said, "Look, I know you're just doing your job, but I'm going stir crazy in here. I need to breathe some open air and walk on grass, if only a few feet from these walls. I won't cause any trouble for you, I promise." When it looked like the first sentry was about to protest, Carlion quickly added, "Five minutes is all I'm asking."

The first sentry gave Carlion a hard look before stepping aside. "It's not on us if you get killed," he said.

"Thank you," the Darkman said with genuine relief as he pushed past the guards and opened the heavy door. After breathing the unmoving air from Metauk's laboratory, the slight breeze that hit his face felt incredibly refreshing.

He had only cleared the stone archway a few steps before a hoarse voice called out to him, "Get back inside chum. No gawking here." Two archers sauntered up to him with a third trailing behind. The uniforms of all three were wrinkled and unwashed, which hinted at them being the only clothes these soldiers had available despite being garrisoned in the town. The two lead archers blocked the road while the third took a flanking position to Carlion's left.

Giving only a brief glance to the archer at his side, the Darkman addressed the men in front of him, "Go get the cavalier. I have a message for her."

"Sir Baton is on patrol, you pissant," replied one the archers, emphasizing the cavalier's title. "Whatever the message is, you can give it to me and I'll relay it to her."

"Go get the cavalier," Carlion slowed his cadence for

emphasis. "Tell her that Carlion Cantra has her information."

"Wait, Cantra? The Darkman?" asked the archer at Carlion's flank.

Carlion turned around and pointed at the scarred cuirass that was still stuck to the archway. "My armor is right there if you think I'm lying," he said with all the contempt he could muster.

Carlion's demeanor, if not his words, seemed to have an effect on the soldiers. The pair of archers in front of him looked at each other before one said to the other, "Go get Sir Baton. I believe she's currently at the barracks."

While the archer jogged away to find the cavalier, Carlion glared at his companion in silence. It was not long before he saw the garrison commander storming up the path with two pikemen in her wake. The archers that were blocking the way quickly moved to the side when it became apparent the cavalier intended on plowing through them to get to Carlion.

"They have provisions for a month," Carlion asserted without preamble as Baton stopped before him.

"That long?" she mused with a raised eyebrow.

"And an underground spring that runs under their cellars," the Darkman said.

"That's no secret," Baton said. "You've told me nothing of use, Cantra. Are you done wasting my time?"

Panic gripped the Darkman as he felt his chance slipping away. Without thinking he blurted out the only other secret he had, "And the mages have some sort of transport device at the ruined Archive in Momontre."

"What?" the cavalier asked with a skeptical eye on Carlion.

The words tumbled out of Carlion in a rush, "I don't understand how it works, but the mages have something called an Engine that lets them travel great distances instantly. It's something that's being worked on in secret, but doesn't seem to be functional yet."

As soon as Carlion finished he realized how outlandish the claim was, but it was the truth. At the very least, the information might buy him precious time while it was verified, since the military was ever vigilant for Archive technology to appropriate.

"So, the rumors were true," Baton replied as she nodded to herself.

"Are you satisfied? Let me pass," Carlion said breathlessly. After getting no reply he took a step off the path to go around the cavalier.

Baton flung a mailed hand in front of Carlion to block his way, and said, "You didn't think I'd just let you go, did you?"

Carlion noticed that the pikemen behind the cavalier tensed and readied their weapons, each with a wolfish expression. At his side, he saw that the archers now had arrows nocked but not yet drawn. It appeared that the soldiers were hoping for a fight.

Baton tilted her head back and looked down her nose at Carlion before she said, "If there's truth to what you say, then in a month the wizards will agree to any Sovereignty terms to save their skins, even more so if we control whatever devilry they've been hiding in Momontre. However, if you've just lied to me, then I wouldn't bother making the trip to Deccern when you're allowed to leave. There won't be anyone left there for you."

"The mercenary guild might have something to say about my confinement," Carlion bluffed. "The Sovereignty can't collect taxes on unearned wages. I don't get paid if I'm stuck here. The guild master's records will show my unfulfilled contract." He hoped the lie didn't sound as desperate a gambit as it felt.

The cavalier barked a single mirthless laugh and replied, "I doubt the prince will miss a scant few coins." With a dismissive gesture at Carlion she said, "You've had your chance to give me information. For your sake, I hope what you've told me is true."

As Baton turned and left, the pikemen took her place and with a rough shove, spun Carlion around, and marched him back to the Archive entrance. Without acknowledging the soldiers Carlion pulled open the door, which seemed to startle the sentries inside.

"That was longer than five minutes," said one of the sentries as Carlion entered and then closed the door.

"Sorry," Carlion replied without thought as he walked past them and turned down the hallway to the guest apartments. The Darkman wasn't interested in joining Trinity and Amos any longer. He had lost his appetite.

CHAPTER TWENTYSEVEN

THORNE

Thorne walked with a carefully measured gait down the guest wing of the Archive in an attempt to keep his nerves calm. It was nearing the middle of the night and the window of opportunity to escape the Archive was about to open via a modified chrysalis in Masters Hall. The mage thought it would look less suspicious if he led the mercenaries into the depth of the Archive, rather than have them meet him there. When he stood in front of their apartment door, Thorne took a long moment to compose himself before giving a quiet double knock.

"Come," came a command from inside. The mage recognized Trinity's voice and quickly entered, being careful to close the door quietly behind him. The mercenaries were dressed for travel and appeared to have been ready for some time. The carpet had dark tread marks at an oblique angle that betrayed the mercenary's pacing the length of the room. Carlion was staring out the window down at the Archive grounds with a brooding expression. The Darkman either didn't notice Thorne enter the room or refused to acknowledge him. Only Amos seemed to be at ease sitting in the apartment's sole chair with his feet propped up on the small writing desk that was situated against the wall opposite the fireplace. The Venhadar held an unlit pipe and used it to point at Thorne.

"Rather simple dress for you," the corsair commented before sliding the pipe between his teeth.

The mage looked down at his clothes. He wore grey canvas pants that were tucked into black leather boots. A wide belt with an array of pouches cinched his waist, and a dark green shirt with long sleeves covered his torso. A matching cloak was wrapped over Thorne's arm and his satchel hung off of one shoulder.

"If we're caught skulking around the Momontre Archive it's better to not telegraph I'm a mage," Thorne said. "Shara and Metauk will be dressed similarly. I doubt we'll run into a Sovereignty patrol, but if we do then the three of us will just claim we're prospectors on an exploratory expedition from the mining guild and have hired you as protection from the dangers of the road."

"If a Sovereignty patrol stops us, that story won't hold if they ask for a miner guild medallion," Amos said as he slid his feet off the table and stood up.

Thorne reached into his satchel and pulled out a plump leather pouch. When he jiggled the bag, the coins inside clinked loudly. "I have my medallion right here," the mage said before stuffing the pouch into his satchel. "If you're ready, then we should go to Masters Hall and meet Metauk and Shara."

"Are you sure this is going to be a one-way trip?" Trinity asked, clearly hoping for a different answer than he had gotten before. "The Momontre Archive is over the mountains and it'll take weeks to walk back here, and that's assuming we don't stop to resupply and rest at Nanock along the way."

"Is there someplace you need to be?" Thorne asked with a chuckle. With a shake of his head the mage continued, "It's extremely unlikely that there's a functioning chrysalis in the Momontre Archive. It's been stripped bare of anything useful for a long time, and what couldn't be stolen was smashed out of spite. Besides, Olaf didn't share how to convert a chrysalis into an Engine. There's just going to be something ready for us down in Masters Hall. For better or worse it will be easy travel there, but slow on the way home."

"No need to hurry back, in my opinion," Amos said. "If the Sovereignty still has this place under blockade, then we'd be crazy to march up to the door again."

Carlion must have been listening, even if he did not appear to be, as he abruptly turned from the window and grabbed his small travel pack at his feet. "Some of us have no intention of coming back. I'm ready to be done with this whole damn city. Let's get this over with."

Spurred to action by the Darkman's words, Trinity and Amos retrieved their weapons and belongings. Thorne led the group quietly down to the lower level of the Archive and into Masters Hall. The corridors were illuminated a pale blue from the wall mounted glow globes, which gave everyone a ghostly pallor. They passed only a few individuals, but were never given a second glance. The psychological effects of the blockade were starting to manifest amongst those trapped inside and many of the Archive's occupants were becoming preoccupied with personal pursuits in an attempt to keep their worries at bay.

As Olaf had promised, Masters Hall was empty. The serene environment that the Vigil Keepers tried to create was now made eerie by the complete absence of people. Rows of unattended chrysalises made the hall truly feel like a tomb and Thorne caught Carlion looking over his shoulders more than once. He led the mercenaries to the vestibule that housed his chrysalis and found Metauk and Shara waiting for them.

Both the Sehenryu and Venhadar were dressed similarly for travel. In addition to her sturdy pants and tunic, Metauk also wore a pair of black fingerless gloves. Shara had on a vest over long sleeves and a maroon muffin cap pulled low on her brow. At their feet were familiar looking backpacks.

Shara took off her cap and vigorously scratched a completely shaved head. She groaned and said as a way of greeting, "I hate this damn hat. Whoever made it used the cheapest felt they could find and it itches like mad."

"What happened to your hair?" Carlion asked, jerking his head and shoulders back surprised.

"Venhadar tradition is to give a lock of hair as a symbol of the favor we owe," Shara said. "You saw me do this on Yves' ship. We then keep our head bare until the debt is repaid." She gestured at Amos, "Did you think the rag on his head was just to keep from getting sunburned?"

Amos adjusted the edge of his bandana and said roughly, "Enough of the fucking cultural exchange. Get us out of here Thorne."

The mage was not entirely sure if Olaf was as good as his word. "Are we alone?" he asked Metauk. "The walls might still have ears."

Metauk closed her eyes and stood very still a moment. "It's just us," she said after a pause. "Even the sentries that were posted at the rear gate are gone."

"So far so good," Thorne said. "Let's see what the good councilman has left us."

He peeled open his chrysalis lid and leaned inside. The molded seat was set in a deeply reclined position. It would be a tight fit, especially with the gear coming along, but the mage thought the cavity could fit two people at a time. Situated in the bottom interior corners of the chrysalis were small pyramids made of a dull metallic substance and connected by grey translucent resin. Thorne surmised that he was looking at Uksyo's modification to convert a chrysalis into an Engine.

Pulling his head out from the chrysalis interior, Thorne saw that Metauk was at the head of the capsule and had her hands on the two bulbous protrusions that were the charging pads to the device. He saw her arms go rigid as she pumped mana into the chrysalis. There was a barely perceptible vibration that ran up his legs as the chrysalis activated and radiated a faint coral light.

"I guess you're going first," Thorne said to the empath. "Down in Uksyo's lab the Engine was already open, but this time you'll have to do it yourself. Given what you did with your astral echo in the Void, I doubt you'll have any trouble." With an exaggerated sweeping gesture towards the mercenaries he added, "Which of these charming lads are you taking with you?"

Before Metauk could answer, Amos slapped Carlion on the back and said, "Now you'll see why I didn't eat a big supper." The corsair stepped forward and climbed into the capsule after Metauk.

Thorne looked down at Metauk and saw that empath had her eyes closed and was breathing in a slow and controlled manner. The mage folded the chrysalis lid over the occupants and sealed it. He took a step back from the device, which the others did as well, and then waited. Suddenly, the coral glow from the chrysalis winked out and the vibration from the device ceased, which under normal circumstances would have indicated a successful astral projection. The mage hoped that now it meant that Metauk and Amos had physically transitioned to the Void. Trying to hide his trepidation, Thorne approached the chrysalis and peeled back the lid. He exhaled a held breath in relief when he saw that the interior was empty. The four small pyramids were radiating heat and colored like embers.

"It smells burnt in there," Carlion said as he scrunched up his nose.

"Don't worry about it," Thorne said. "It's just a consequence of the chrysalis being used under non-standard conditions." The mage hoped what he said was true and it wasn't something more serious.

Shara moved to the head of the chrysalis and energized it as Metauk had done before. She reached down and tossed her backpack into the chrysalis before climbing inside. She stood up and glared at the mercenaries as neither had made a move to join her. "I'm not excited about this either," she said with a scowl. Pointing at her feet she commanded, "One of you get in here."

Thorne watched Trinity and Carlion look at each other, but neither said anything. After an awkward moment the mage said decisively, "We're short on time. Trinity, go with her."

"Alright," the mercenary said quietly. Grabbing his small leather bag from the floor Trinity held it close to his chest and with one hand hoisted himself up onto the lip of the chrysalis. Carefully swinging his legs over the edge, he wedged himself against the wall of the capsule, being careful with the placement of his short sword before Shara closed the lid.

As before, after a brief delay the light and hum from the chrysalis ceased, and when Thorne opened the capsule again it was vacant. Looking back at Carlion, he said, "And then there were two. Get in and I will charge it." While the Darkman was not quick to follow the order, he did as he was told.

As Carlion struggled with his cuirass to find a comfortable position inside the chrysalis Thorne went to the front and placed his hands on the still warm charging pads. Channeling mana into his palms, he felt the resin absorb the energy like a sponge. Charging a chrysalis for astral projection was actually the first challenge for a mage undergoing the Transformation. If they hadn't built up enough mana over the course of their study and training, they wouldn't even be able to activate the chrysalis.

Thorne climbed into the chrysalis and suddenly realized it would be the most cramped of any pairing thus far. Carlion's hot breath coated the mage's face as he pulled the lid closed and extinguished all outside light. They were now immersed in an absolute and claustrophobic darkness. "Did you ever think you'd be stuck in a small magic box about to tear through the fabric of space and time to enter a plane of existence that the religious think is hell?" Thorne asked with an impish grin that he knew Carlion couldn't see.

"No. I must live a charmed life," the Darkman replied flatly.

Although it was unnecessary, Thorne closed his eyes. The mage then focused on a single point below him. He visualized that single point being distant on the horizon, but that point was the aperture to the Void. In his mind, he pulled the point towards himself and visualized it growing in size. Again and again, Thorne pulled the aperture towards him until he visualized it was right below him. There were white swirling mists that circled around the aperture, but it was opaque and Thorne could not see inside. He visualized his body was floating right over the aperture, which was now slightly larger than a normal doorway. At this point the mage discharged the mana that was stored in the chrysalis.

An aperture iris opened and Thorne physically felt an incredible gravity suck him through. He heard Carlion cry out as they both tumbled downward. The mage opened his eyes and saw Carlion flailing a few feet below him with eyes wild in fear. Rapidly focusing his Awareness, Thorne jerked his hand over his head. Like pulling a marionette's strings, Carlion shot up to be on the same plane as the mage. Reaching out and grabbing the Darkman's flapping cloak Thorne then slowed their decent for a few seconds before he conjured a floor for the two of them to settle upon.

While Thorne was able to land on his feet, Carlion crashed

down on his knees and violently vomited across the dark gray stones. Thorne laid a hand on Carlion's shoulder and tried to be reassuring, "Slow breaths now. The dizziness will pass and gravity should be stable until we make the next transition."

The Darkman wobbled as he rose to his feet before running the back of his hand over his mouth. "We have to do that again?" he asked hoarsely.

The mage nodded and replied, "The next one will be easier because I can dictate directionality now. We just need to find the others first."

Carlion swiveled his head around and asked, "How can we see anything here? Wait, why are you and the floor glowing?"

Thorne ignored the Darkman's questions as he surveyed his surroundings. Other than the ground beneath them, there was nothing but an oppressive blackness. The mage knew that in the Void up and down could be the same direction, as directionality was fluid and dependent on an individual's ability to manipulate their Awareness. After a moment of searching Thorne saw a mote of light above him. Pointing overhead he said to Carlion, "There's somebody."

"How do we get there?" the Darkman asked with his face turned upwards.

"We walk," the mage replied. "But first we need to be on the same plane as them. Lay down so you're looking up at the light. I need to shift our gravity."

Thorne was prepared for Carlion to refuse or ask a series of tedious questions, but the mage was surprised when the Darkman did as he was told without protest. Thorne lay down on his back next to Carlion and looked up at the point of light, which seemed slightly larger now. "Try to relax," Thorne said. "This might feel strange."

Perpendicular to the ground they were laying upon Thorne conjured what appeared as a wall nearly identical to the ground they were resting on. He placed the wall very near their feet and he focused his Awareness to slowly rotate the pull of gravity such that the new wall became the floor. Both he and Carlion slid downward a short distance before they gently landed on the new surface.

Carlion groaned and held out his arms to steady himself. "How are you not getting sick by doing this?" he asked with a grimace.

"I've done this many times before as an astral projection for various research projects over the years," Thorne said before slowly taking a step towards the growing sphere of light ahead of them.

"I'm almost afraid to ask about your interests," Carlion said as he quickly caught up to the mage and walked at his side. "What did you expect to find here?"

The quiet sound of their footfalls was the only perceptible sound for a time as Thorne remained silent. Many people before had asked the same question, but he had never answered in complete truth. The mage glanced at Carlion and wondered if a Darkman would understand. Deciding he was willing to try his luck, Thorne replied, "Do you have any painful memories?"

Carlion gave Thorne a confused look at what must have seemed an odd question. "More than a few," he said eventually.

"If you could erase them, would you?" the mage asked.

"No, they've made me who I am now," Carlion said with a shake of his head. "I'd want to remember the lessons that were hard learned."

It was a typical answer he'd heard in philosophical debates at the Archive on the nature of memory. "But what if those painful memories had outlived their usefulness?" Thorne argued. "What if they were actually impeding you from moving on with your life? What if they were now an anchor, dragging down and keeping you from becoming something different, perhaps better?"

The question seemed to give Carlion pause and the Darkman remained silent. While Thorne was wondering if he was going to get an answer, he watched the point of light ahead of them steadily elongate and then split. The mage was finally able to discern forms within the light and he realized that it was Shara and Metauk. The pair trod on a small patch of grass and trailing behind them were Amos and Trinity, although they commanded no Awareness so their bodies were not glowing. The ground from the two parties merged as they approached each other and now looked like a stone path that abruptly transitioned into pasture.

"The difficult part of this trip should be over now," Thorne said once everyone had gathered close. He reached into his satchel and retrieved the shard of dragon shell that Olaf had given him. Handing it to Metauk he said, "You have to take the lead from now on, but Shara and I can support if needed."

The empath held the shell fragment carefully in her open palm. "Now let's see if we can find your home," she said quietly. Holding the shell out in front of her, Metauk closed her eyes. A single chime rang out unnaturally loud in the absolute silence of the Void. A few seconds later, they heard an echo in the distance. Metauk opened her eyes and turned towards the sound. "Found you," she said with a satisfied smile.

In the distance a point of light appeared as an aperture opened. Metauk closed her eyes again and another chime sounded out. Seeming to travel along with the accompanying echo was a thread of light that came from the distant aperture. The Sehenryu flinched as the thread of light connected the distant aperture and the shell fragment in Metauk's hand. "This line has physical mass," she said in surprise.

"Incredible," Thorne said, breathlessly. The mage reached out and grasped the thread, which was indeed corporeal despite its appearance. The line connecting the dragon shell fragment and the distant aperture felt coarse in his hands and hummed with mana similar to the charging pads of a chrysalis. With slow deliberate movement, Thorne pulled the thread and saw the distant light of the aperture grow slightly larger. The mage didn't know if he was pulling the aperture towards their platform or they were moving to the aperture as he kept drawing the thread, which collected in messy glowing coils at his feet.

It did not take long before their platform drew next to the oval of light and swirling mists of the aperture. When the bottom arc of the aperture touched the stone of Thorne's conjured platform the thread of light winked out with a sound similar to delicate glass shattering. Metauk made an attempt to give the shell fragment back to Thorne, but the mage shook his head, "I could never use it as well as you did just now. Keep it."

Despite standing right in front of the aperture, Thorne caught himself glancing upward. If Barrow was to be believed, Thorne could still find Celeste here. The mage was not sure how many second chances he was going to get to find the dragon. Back at the Archive, he had felt compelled to do something about the Engine being built in Momontre and stopping Uksyo's conspirators. Now he had another opportunity to find Celeste, but would have to leave everyone to fend for themselves. Trinity, and maybe Amos, might eventually forgive him if they learned the truth, but Thorne doubted the others would be as understanding.

"Is something wrong?" Metauk asked. "You're anxious."

"What? Oh," Thorne said when he realized that the empath had sensed his internal struggle. "I'm concerned about the state of the Masters Hall on the other side. Hopefully, it isn't sealed off and we're not trapped there." Thorne tried to make the lie sound convincing as Metauk could only feel his emotional state and not any actual thoughts.

"Well, we're never going to find out just standing here,"

Amos grunted. Gesturing at Thorne he said, "Get in there."

Trinity placed a hand on the mage's shoulder to hold him back. "Let me go first," he told the mage with a crooked smile. "Like back in the old days."

"Be more careful than back in the old days," Thorne said, genuinely concerned.

The mercenary squared up to the aperture and without looking back took a decisive step into the light. His body seemed to fall forward as he was swallowed up by the aperture and was then gone. Where he had passed, the mists twisted upwards in violent eddies before dissipating.

Watching Trinity confidently enter into the unknown tugged strongly on the mage's emotions. That level of trust was hard to earn and to betray it now would just replace one regret with another. Thorne knew that he'd have one final chance to physically enter the Void if they found the Engine that Uksyo had alluded to in his clandestine laboratory, but was unsure if circumstances would permit it.

"Go stand over in the grass," the mage instructed Carlion. "My platform will dissolve after I pass through."

Without waiting to see if the Darkman was doing as he was told, Thorne turned and passed through the aperture. The mage felt gravity jerk him forward and he crashed to one knee, which sent a painful jolt up his leg. Thorne had made the assumption that the aperture exit would be perpendicular with the floor, but that was not the case. Hovering at an angle above ground, the aperture had instead dumped him into a room that was thick with dust.

Thorne crawled on his hands and knees until he was out from under the aperture. He started to rise when he heard a shout from behind, but before he could turn was hit by a blindside tackle.

"Ambush!" Trinity shouted in his ear.

CHAPTER TWENTYEIGHT

CARLION

Carlion stepped up to the aperture and drew the resin sword he had taken from Metauk's lab. He was still getting used to the balance of the new weapon and hoped that the unconventional blade would be a match against steel.

"What are you doing?" Shara asked with a creased brow.

"I'm not jumping blindly into that thing," the Darkman said. "We don't know what's on the other side."

The Venhadar replied irritably, "Yes, we do. Masters Hall of the Momontre Archive, which has been abandoned for some time."

Carlion shook his head unconvinced. "It's been abandoned by mages for some time," he corrected. "Do you know who occupies it now?"

Shara scoffed, but didn't answer.

"So, you don't know either, but in the amount of time it took for us to reach this gate, anyone on the other side could have set up a trap," the Darkman said, holding the sword in a relaxed grip at his side.

"Or they could have gotten scared and run away," Metauk offered. The Sehenryu had drawn close to Shara and rested a reassuring hand on her shoulder.

Amos pulled a pair of resin daggers free from his belt. "I'd rather look foolish holding my knives in a vacant room then show up to a fight empty handed," he said. Looking at Carlion, he added, "But I still want you to go next."

Carlion raised the tip of his sword in a mock salute to the corsair before stepping into the aperture. He felt his stomach churn as his sense of up and down violently shifted and he thrust his arms outward. His free hand hit the stone floor first and took the brunt of his weight before the knuckles of his other hand hit the ground. The Darkman rolled onto his back and away from the aperture so whoever came next wouldn't drop on top of him.

Carlion quickly repositioned himself into a low crouch next to what looked like a gigantic chicken egg, yellowed with age. The only light came from the aperture, but he was still able to survey his surroundings with little difficulty. While it had the same general layout as the Masters Hall in the Yaboon Archive, this room was considerably smaller and littered with rubble. Several chrysalises were open or partially destroyed, and a layer of dust covered every surface. A wide stairwell to the floor above was off to his left and a dry breeze came from a large hole in the wall at the opposite end of the room.

From behind the giant eggshell, Carlion heard the sound of a struggle. The Darkman peered around the corner of the shell and saw that Trinity and a much larger attacker had their blades locked. The mercenary was on the defensive and leaning back as the other man pushed his full weight down on his sword. A few steps away, Carlion watched Thorne backpedal from a second assailant, who was currently on the ground but scrambling to his feet.

Rapid scuffling from the stairwell made Carlion look back over his shoulder. From his position he saw three more men descend into the room. One was holding a lantern in one hand

and a sword in the other. Two archers holding bows with arrows nocked flanked him. All three were wearing the maroon and gold uniforms of the Momontre provincial military.

"Watch out! This one's a wizard!" called the assailant next to Thorne, now on his feet. The soldier held his sword in a defensive position and pulled out a thin tube from inside his vest.

Carlion's head swiveled back to the stairs just in time to see the archers draw back their arrows. Before a shot could be fired, Amos burst through the aperture with a flash of light like a lightning strike accompanied by a loud unintelligible curse from the corsair. One of the archers swung his bow towards the aperture and fired at Amos, but the shot went over the Venhadar's shoulder and ricocheted off of an open chrysalis.

"Get down!" the Darkman yelled. The archer had missed before due to the erratic lighting in the room and Amos' small size, but Carlion was worried Metauk or Shara wouldn't be as lucky. Grabbing a fragment of stone from the floor, the Darkman stood and flung it at the archer who still had an arrow nocked.

The makeshift projectile missed the mark but it was enough to draw the attention of the archer, who turned and fired at Carlion. The impact of the steel arrowhead on the resin cuirass staggered him, but the missile didn't penetrate the armor and was deflected away.

"More wizards from the light!" shouted the lantern-carrying soldier.

Nearly in unison the archers dropped their bows and pulled short swords from their belts and withdrew thin tubes from pouches at their waists. The solider with the lantern set it on the last step of the stairwell and produced another thin tube. The low light from the lantern threw long gaunt shadows of the soldiers on the walls as all three spread out amongst the rubble and stalked towards the aperture.

Carlion dashed along the wall to engage the rightmost

soldier. The Darkman hoped that the rubble littering the floor would make a flanking maneuver difficult and no one would get behind him because the tight spaces between chrysalises and broken pillars would make it hard to retreat. The soldier saw him and got his sword up to easily block Carlion's overhead strike. As they traded blows, Carlion saw in his peripheral vision a pair of lightning flashes that heralded the entry of Metauk and Shara into the room.

The Darkman parried a low stab that was an obvious feint, but before Carlion could retaliate the soldier shoved the tube he carried into his mouth and blew out a cloud of dark powder. Carlion jerked backward as a metallic taste filled his mouth and he choked down a cough to keep his eyes on the soldier. When the soldier tried to stab him in earnest, Carlion was ready and twisted out of the way. The Darkman countered with an upward slash that cut deep into the soldier's inner thigh. With a shrill cry, the soldier fell to the ground and curled into a fetal position. Carlion had learned long ago to never turn your back to a wounded adversary, and with a downward stab made sure the soldier was dead.

Looking over his shoulder, the Darkman was relieved that he could not see any other soldiers standing. He saw Metauk crouching near the body of a soldier. The Sehenryu was holding a fist dagger and the Darkman wondered how she could have killed the soldier so quickly with such a small weapon. The soldiers who had attacked Thorne and Trinity were also motionless on the ground. The one next to Trinity was laying in a pool of blood, but more unnerving to the Darkman was the dead man at Thorne's feet. The soldier's bloodless body was laying face down and was completely rigid, as if he had been dead for days. Carlion was unsure how Thorne had killed the man, but he wondered if being cut down by a sword would have been preferable.

The Darkman walked back to the aperture, where he found Amos and Shara standing close to what remained of the dragon's egg. "There is still one more in here," Carlion said loudly after counting the number of dead soldiers. "He's hiding somewhere."

"Find him," Thorne commanded. "We can't have anyone know that we're here."

Carlion cautiously walked toward the back of the room when his foot brushed against something that produced a metallic rasp against the stone floor. Keeping aware of his surroundings Carlion knelt down and picked up a steel short sword. The hiding soldier must have abandoned his weapon to keep it from hitting something and giving away his position. Carlion slid the short sword into his empty scabbard and continued to search along the destroyed back wall.

The hole punched into the wall was easily large enough to accommodate two people at a time. Carlion saw that the hole was the end of a tunnel, and he could detect the faint smell of wet earth from inside.

"He's not here," Trinity called from near the center of the room. "Did he escape through that hole, Carlion?"

The Darkman turned back and motioned for the others to join him at the back of the room. Once gathered, he pointed with his sword into the tunnel and said, "If he ran out that way, it must mean the tunnel exits to the outside. That might explain how they got here in the first place."

"Quiet!" Shara said in a harsh whisper. She pointed back towards the stairwell as lantern light started to roll down the steps.

Everyone stood still to watch the stairwell, so they were all distracted when the soldier that was hiding sprang out from behind a pillar and blew the contents of a tube into Thorne and Trinity's faces. The mage cried out and grasped at his throat while the mercenary staggered a few steps into the tunnel before he doubled over in a coughing fit. Thorne dropped to his knees and choked for a moment before he collapsed.

With his position now exposed, the soldier sprinted back towards the steps and shouted, "Help me! There are intruders in the crypt!"

A chorus of shouts echoed in the room as six soldiers came running down the stairs. Two were holding lanterns and swords and the remaining four were archers with bows at the ready. Before they had even finished descending the stairs, the archers had already loosed a series of arrows at the back wall.

Metauk tried to approach Thorne, but started to cough and drew away from the haze that still hung in the air. Whatever had caused Thorne to fall was affecting the empath as well. Carlion reached down and hooked his arms underneath Thorne's and began to drag the mage into the tunnel. As he passed through the hole, he stumbled a step and lost his grip on his sword.

After he had pulled Thorne into the tunnel, Carlion turned back and saw that Shara was standing in front of the hole. She glanced back at him, oblivious to the arrows whistling past her and called out, "Stay back!"

The Darkman watched from inside the tunnel as Shara reached up with both hands and seemed to grab an invisible handle above her head. Straining with effort Shara pulled her arms down with a wordless scream. The ceiling in front of her came crashing down and filled the hole with shattered stone blocks and earth.

For a tense minute, the only thing Carlion could hear was his heart pounding in his ears and the heavy breathing of the group. They were in complete darkness, even more so than in the Void, as here the mages' bodies did not generate any ambient light. The Darkman heard someone shuffle a few steps to his right, and then a weak blue light illuminated the immediate surroundings. He saw that Shara held a small glow sphere in her hand.

Surveying his surroundings, Carlion found that everyone had made it into the tunnel, but not everyone was standing. Thorne was lying on his back and looked to be unconscious, while Metauk was sitting on her haunches near the cave-in. Trinity and Amos were further back in the tunnel, with the mercenary leaning on his shorter companion for support.

When Shara saw Metauk, she immediately knelt down next to the empath and whispered something that Carlion could not hear. Metauk uttered something and waved Shara away. With her concern intensifying, Shara stepped over to Thorne and bent over to examine him.

The Darkman approached Shara, which she did not acknowledge, and looked down at Thorne's face. The mage's forehead was covered in grimy sweat, but underneath his skin black veins protruded across his face. His breathing was shallow, and the occasional twitch or gasp was the only indication that he was still alive.

"What the hell was that powder?" Carlion said, astonished. Having seen the power that Thorne could wield, to see him incapacitated in such a manner was distressing.

"Iron filings," Shara answered seriously. "If a mage breathes in any it would cause terrible damage to their entire body. You should be fine, but it's toxic to anyone who has Awareness. Those soldiers were trained to be mage killers."

Amos approached Shara and said, "I want to go see if this tunnel leads outside." The corsair pointed to the glow globe in Shara's hand. "You got another one of those?"

Shara nodded and reached into a pouch on her belt. She retrieved a small glass sphere and after a moment of concentration the globe produced a soft blue radiance. "The farther you get away from me the dimmer the light will get," she told

Amos.

"I'll turn back before it goes out, don't worry," the corsair replied and took the offered light. He walked down the tunnel and it did not take long for the light to be swallowed by darkness.

Trinity walked to the pile of rubble that sealed off the tunnel and rested a hand on a thick tree root that had been exposed. "I appreciate Amos scouting ahead while we catch our breath, because we'll all have to move soon. I can't begin to guess Thorne's injuries, but we need to return to the Archive. Metauk, how are you feeling?"

The empath rose on shaky legs and tried to answer, but a fit of coughing choked off her words. "I've been better, but I'll live," the Sehenryu said hoarsely once she could speak again. Sliding her hand along the tunnel for support, she slowly walked to Thorne and frowned when she looked down. "I think he's dreaming," she said. "His emotions keep shifting, but it feels like he's struggling against something."

"A nightmare," Shara said quietly. Her expression darkened and she looked at Carlion, "You had your sword ready in the Void. It was like you knew they were going to be here. And you didn't warn Trinity or Thorne before they went through the aperture."

"Now wait a minute," Carlion said with his voice taking an edge. "If you are accusing me of something, then be plain about it."

Shara stabbed a finger at the Darkman and accused, "Did you think that betraying us would get you reinstated? What deal did you make with your old Sovereignty contacts?"

A jolt of shame pierced Carlion as he remembered the deal he had made to save his family. Trying to match Shara's angry tone he said, "Once you're cashiered, that's it. There's no going back, so I have no reason to associate with any Sovereignty military any longer."

"That's a lie," Metauk said, looking at the Darkman. "I can feel your guilt. You're hiding something." The empath took a step towards Carlion and looked him up and down before she stopped at his belt. "Where's the weapon I gave you?" she asked.

Carlion followed her gaze down to the steel sword at his hip. Metauk must have thought he had intentionally dropped the resin sword on the other side of the cave-in. Carlion realized now that he hadn't had time to explain why he took the sword he found or how he lost the resin one dragging Thorne into the tunnel, but before he could explain Trinity grabbed his collar with both hands and shoved him against the tunnel wall.

"What have you done?" the mercenary seethed between clenched teeth. "I remember now that you had a nice little chat with the cavalier in charge of the blockade before being let into the Archive. What did you talk about? No lies. Metauk will know."

"I was trying to save my family," Carlion began.

"What did you do?" Trinity screamed. The sound echoed down the tunnel.

Even in the dim light Carlion could see the pained expression on Trinity's face. Despite the reputation of a mercenary's only bond being the contract to be paid, there was still a certain level of camaraderie amongst the guild members, and having a few close friends was not uncommon. The Darkman was not sure what hurt Trinity more, his perceived treachery, or that the life of one of the mercenary's oldest friends was now in the balance because of it.

There was no sense trying to hide anything with Metauk watching him closely, so he decided to tell them the truth. "The cavalier in charge of the civil siege wanted to know how long the Archive could hold out before its supplies were exhausted,"

Carlion said. "I got the major-domo to tell me and I convinced the sentries to let me out last night." When he saw the stunned expression from Trinity, Carlion's voice took on a pleading tone when he said, "The commander knew about Julia and Natty. She threatened to go kill them while I was trapped inside if I didn't get her that information."

"None of that information is special," Metauk said. "What else did you tell the commander? Don't think you can hide anything from me."

The pit of Carlion's stomach felt hollow and seemed to pull his insides down to his feet. "I told them about the Engine here," he admitted. "I thought if I gave them some Archive technology, even if you destroyed it, then they would let me go."

"You fiend," Shara said, after a stunned moment of silence. "You didn't just betray us, but the entire Archive. The military now has the proof they've always wanted to show we're working outside of Sovereignty law. With one thoughtless and selfish act you've destroyed a truce that has been precarious for decades."

Trinity let go of the Darkman's cloak with a rough shove and stepped back. "There is no way word would have come here so quickly from Yaboon," the mercenary said. "Momontre is a different Sovereignty province, so what's going on in Yaboon doesn't explain why there were soldiers here."

Carlion's eyes widened at Trinity's deduction. Maybe Thorne's injuries were not his fault after all. "They must have already been here for another reason," the Darkman said.

"It doesn't matter," Shara said, glaring at the Darkman with an open hatred. "You sold us out and came along because it was your best chance to get back to your family before the blockade ended. I should have burned you to the ground when I had the chance back at the Stormbreaker Isles."

Metauk turned to look down the tunnel and said, "Amos is

coming back." A distant wobbling pinpoint of light did not take long to grow and reveal Amos running back to them. When the corsair stopped, Carlion couldn't tell if it was the feeble light from the glow sphere or something else, but the corsair's normally dark skin had taken an ashen hue.

"I found the Engine," Amos said between gasping breaths. "And that's not all."

CHAPTER TWENTYNINE

THORNE

As his blurred vision cleared, the first thing that Thorne recognized was the willow tree. Blinking several times to remove the film from his eyes, the mage saw that he was standing a short distance from a river that had the lone tree near a bank otherwise hidden by tall grass. With a cloudless blue sky overhead, Thorne felt a breeze on his face that also rhythmically swayed the branches and grass. His bare hands were warmed by the sunshine and he stretched out his arms in an attempt to absorb more. It was then that Thorne saw that not only the binding mark on his wrist was gone, but also that he was wearing an expensively dyed linen shirt and tailored trousers with matching shoes.

The mage took a deep breath and held it when he realized that his lungs were not in agony from breathing something caustic. The iron powder that the Momontre soldier blew at him had been used in previous generations as a sham test to determine if an alchemist was a warlock and bound to a demon. While the dark times of burning mages as devil worshipers had thankfully passed into distant memory, Momontre was still a Sovereignty that openly despised the Archives and had trained their soldiers in particularly brutal methods to incapacitate and kill mages.

Trying to piece together why he wasn't still in Masters Hall, but instead a familiar field not far from his childhood home in Sunrock, led Thorne to only one conclusion.

"I'm dreaming," the mage said quietly, looking down again at what had been his favorite outfit as a youth.

"Come on, big brother! Let's see if there are any tadpoles near the shore," a joyful voice rang out.

Thorne turned just in time to see a small girl dash past him. She ran up to the riverbank and parted the tall grass as if it were a curtain. Kneeling down, the girl then leaned over to look into the water with a delighted squeal.

"Be careful, Rose!" Thorne called out, instinctively reaching for her though she was now distant from him. He walked quickly to her and hooked one arm around her waist and pulled her back from the river. She laughed when hoisted into the air and had a big smile when the mage set her down.

"My hero! My cavalier!" Rose called out playfully. "But you're following mother's directions too strictly. Relax and let's enjoy the bit of freedom we've been given!"

"Just stay where I can see you," Thorne said seriously. "And don't get too close to the water."

Rose danced over to the willow and reached up to brush her hands through the thin stooping branches. She pulled hard on a branch before snapping off a length about as long as a sword. The girl slowly walked back to Thorne, who watched her with disapproval.

"Kneel, my over-protective brother, so that I might dub thee, Sir Killjoy!" Rose said with an impish grin. She held out the branch expectantly.

Thorne snatched the branch from Rose's grasp. "Stop that," he commanded, which elicited an angry pout from her.

"If you're not going to play with me, then just go back to the guildhall and write notes in ledgers all day like father wants you to do," Rose said with the stamp of her foot. "You're being a thorn in my side again!"

As he watched the girl storm off towards the willow with a rigid posture, Thorne slowly blew out the breath he didn't know he was holding. He had always hated it when Rose lost her temper when he didn't go along with her little fantasies. Looking down at the willow branch in his hand Thorne made a few awkward stabbing motions as he pretended it was a sword. Like all boys, he had dreamt of being a solider in the Sovereignty military, a cavalier that rode atop a rare, imported horse.

Thorne turned his back to the tree, and as he walked near the riverbank he began flicking the willow branch in front of him so it made a snapping whistle through the air. As was true for many adolescent boys, Thorne was angry with his father for wanting him to continue the family business, in his case, as a cloth merchant. His father had not approved of his only son wanting to be trained to kill other men so a prince could become wealthier. This repeated argument between father and son was what prompted Thorne to retreat to his favorite spot on the family estate, and Rose had come along to cheer up her brother on that day so many years ago.

The splash and scream were almost simultaneous and shook Thorne out of his daydream. Rushing back to the willow, Thorne was horrified to see that Rose had fallen into the river and that the current had already pulled her downstream. Rose was a weak swimmer and in her panic was flailing her arms wildly. Her shrieks became wet gasps as her head repeatedly went under the water.

Racing down the bank to get ahead of his sister, Thorne leaped over the tall grass and into the river. The current jerked his entire body and he had to quickly widen his stance and dig his feet into the sand so he wasn't also swept away. "Rose!" he screamed when her head broke the surface and he reached out with the willow branch.

The slender lifeline slid from her grip and Rose went under the water and did not come up again. Thorne felt a buzzing feeling along the back of his skull and down his neck, and he was sickened with a feeling of extreme disorientation. Hearing the sound of the river and the breeze whistle through the grass, he understood that the feeling was the realization that something terrible had just happened, but the world didn't care. Worse, it didn't even notice.

"Rose, I'm sorry," Thorne whispered. It was something he had not uttered when the event had happened all those years ago, but whenever he had the nightmare as an adult it was something he remembered saying before he woke up in a cold sweat.

"What a terrible way to lose a sibling," came a voice from the shore.

Thorne turned around and saw Celeste. She wore a long gossamer dress with silver threads running through it that caught the sunshine and sparkled. Straight silver hair hung past her shoulders and framed a graceful face that exuded vitality despite an advanced age. The dragon's eyes showed a sad compassion as she watched Thorne slowly walk out of the river.

"Is there a pleasant one?" the mage replied when he stood in front of her. "If you're here, then I'm not dreaming. I'm dead."

"Not quite," Celeste replied. "Although I am sorry to say that your mana is now balanced on the razor's edge, and more than a trivial amount has dissipated into the Void, which was how I found you. Despite your desperate state, I must selfishly admit that I am very thankful for it. I've missed you terribly."

Thorne smiled sadly, "I've missed you too, Celeste."

The dragon made a motion to embrace him, but quickly drew back and said, "We don't have much time like this, so I must tell you right now that you need to get to the Engine."

A gust of wind whipped around them and Thorne felt a chill start at his sodden boots and work its way into his wet hair. Rubbing his arms in an attempt to get warmer, he said sullenly, "If I'm close to death, then I don't need to worry about having you erase this memory any longer." He made a small circular gesture to indicate their immediate surroundings.

This time Celeste did not check herself and reached out to caress Thorne's cheek. "Don't say such terrible things. Thorne, there are so many reasons that I want you in the Void with me, but perhaps the most important now is that the Iron Bane holds no dominion there."

Remembering his conversation with the pixie at the Archive, Thorne's brow creased as he said, "You sent Barrow to spur me on, but she also said you were preoccupied with something important. Is that finished?"

"No, but my work would be completed much quicker if you were able to destroy the Engine after you passed through," Celeste answered.

"What is the purpose of these Engines?" Thorne asked, now suspicious. "I found pixie dust more than once in the past few weeks and every time it has been connected to something about physical transport into the Void. If you have been attending to other matters, I wonder how Barrow has been spending her time."

Celeste looked slightly surprised and took a step back from Thorne. Her expression grew serious as she said, "Barrow has been acting strictly according to my instructions. I need you to believe me that despite our time apart, I haven't forgotten my promise to you." She paused and looked towards the river and her expression changed to something more thoughtful. "Are you sure you really want all of your memories of her gone?" she said with a hint of sadness.

"I don't need them anymore," Thorne said firmly.

"What about your adopted name?" Celeste asked. "You won't recognize yourself as 'Thorne' any longer, and you'll likely forget your birth name as well."

"It would be an easy thing to be known by a new name," the mage replied with indifference.

Celeste gave a tight-lipped smile and then said, "Your resolve never ceases to amaze me. Please, hurry. The Engine is not far away, but time grows very short."

"Once in the Void, how will I find you?" Thorne asked.

From Celeste's dress, skin, and hair a painfully bright, white radiance flared. Threatening to fill his vision and blind him, Thorne closed his eyes and shielded his face with a forearm. Unable to see, he only heard Celeste's reply, which sounded as if it came from a distance, "Go towards the light."

Thorne lowered his arm and opened his eyes, then grunted in surprise. Turning around in a full circle he found that he was completely alone and in an abruptly foreign environment. Thorne now stood in an empty black space that seemed to replicate the Void. Celeste had left before answering his question about her connection to the Engines, or why she had sent Barrow to lead him down this particular path.

An empty feeling of abandonment assaulted Thorne, which ignited a tumult of other emotions. At first there was loneliness from being apart from the one person who he thought understood him. This was followed by shame from countless small wrongs committed over his life, which now would include the prospect of deserting Trinity and the others after leading them far from home. Finally, Thorne was weighed down with a weary sadness accompanied by a dull ache in his chest that came from a lifetime of ripping open the emotional scars from his sister's death.

The churning feelings in him were too much to bear. Thorne dropped to his knees and wept.

CHAPTER THIRTY

CARLION

The march down the tunnel was in silence save for the occasional grunt from Carlion or Trinity as they carried Thorne on the only bedroll that had not been lost in their flight from Masters Hall. Amos, in the lead, used his glow globe to light the path ahead, with Metauk, using Shara for support, following closely behind. Trinity was ahead of Carlion as they carried Thorne, and the mercenary had made it clear that the Darkman should consider himself lucky to be tolerated at all at this point.

When he finally reached the end of the tunnel, Carlion realized that he had lost track of time after leaving the Yaboon Archive, as he now saw that it was still night. Just before the tunnel's exit was a large grate that might have originally kept the passageway secure, but the thick metal bars had been cut and the resulting gap let them pass unimpeded to the outside.

Pointing up to one of the iron bar fragments, Amos said, "Something very hot melted through these bars, and did so with some speed. You can tell by the way the metal stretched here at the end. That would have been enough to make me suspicious, but look down there."

Carlion jostled past the others and stepped out of the tunnel onto a small exposed ledge. He looked down a series of steep switchbacks that eventually emptied into an old rock quarry. All along the perimeter were glow spheres that cast a pale yellow radiance along the quarry floor. The artificial light allowed the Darkman to see a series of switchbacks running up the cliff face on the opposite end of the crater, eventually disappearing into the trees.

Off center, at the bottom of the quarry, was a gigantic stone and metal archway, and Carlion surmised this must be the Engine. At opposite ends of the huge device stood two men. They were pressing their hands on large protrusions and seemed oblivious to their surroundings, which astounded Carlion because also at the bottom of the quarry was a writhing mass of insectoid figures.

"A B'nisct swarm!" Metauk exclaimed. "What is going on here?"

"Look," Shara said and pointed to a large stone block a short distance from the Engine. On top of the block was another B'nisct, but this one looked much bigger than the others. The armor this B'nisct wore was colored red and yellow, which contrasted sharply with the dark blue and green armor of the swarm fighters, even in the weak light of the glow spheres.

Waving a rod decorated with an odd assortment of artifacts, the elevated B'nisct somehow selected two fighters from the swarm and directed them to the front of the Engine. The fighters moved towards the aperture and paused, seemingly wary of the device. The large B'nisct slammed the rod against the stone block and a shower of sparks erupted. The sparks seemed to hang in the air and glow an unnaturally fierce red before fading.

"A shaman!" Shara said amazed.

"What does that mean?" Trinity asked, not taking his eyes off of the scene below.

"It's what the B'nisct call those who are Aware," Shara answered. "They don't have any formal training like we do, but in a crude manner they still can command the arcane elements in powerful ways."

The entire swarm reacted to the shaman's display and seemed to swell and shift around the Engine. One of the selected fighters appeared to be spurred on by an unseen force and immediately passed through the Engine. The aperture of the Engine was a film of absolute blackness that appeared to swallow up the light from the glow spheres and reflect nothing back.

The second fighter watched the other B'nisct enter and then, after a pause, attempted to pass through the film in pursuit. However, as the fighter reached out and touched the aperture a ripple ran down the film and the fighter exploded into a sticky mass of chitin and hemolymph.

"What the fuck?" Amos exclaimed, but the swarm below barely reacted to the fighter's messy death.

"The aperture isn't stable," Metauk said, pointing at the men on either side of the Engine. "Look, the mages are having a hard time maintaining a charge because it's so big. They must be exhausted from expending so much mana, even in tandem."

"It looks like the swarm is here to test it," Shara guessed aloud. "Or guard it. Maybe both."

"That's not important right now," Trinity said. "We need to get Thorne out of here, and Nanock is a half-day walk. We'll have to be careful on the switchbacks and find the path that leads out of this quarry. If we do it now, while it's still dark, then we'll have the best chance to avoid attracting the swarm's attention."

"Wait a minute," Shara said. "We came here to find the Engine and destroy it if possible."

"It's not possible," Amos quickly interjected. "It took a deluge of sea water to collapse the Engine in Uksyo's secret lab. This one looks to be triple in size."

Shara ignored him and said, "This is an arcane device of incredible power and no one knows why it was built. And thanks to the Darkman," she turned and gave Carlion a withering look, "The Yaboon military will be here in a matter of days to take it. For that reason alone, we need to make sure it's completely unusable before they get here."

Trinity pointed down to the B'nisct fighters and said, "We're not equipped to fight off an entire swarm, especially with Thorne hurt. The best we can do now is get to Nanock as fast as we can and get help. With the bribe money from Thorne's satchel we could hire at least a half dozen mercenaries from the guild. That still might not be enough, but we'd have a better chance than we do now."

Amos nodded his head and replied, "Even so, but as much as I hate to admit it, this might be one time when we do want the Sovereignty military involved. They would have the armaments and numbers to overtake the swarm and dismantle the Engine, but we can't warn anyone if we all die here."

"What if they don't destroy it, but try to keep it for themselves?" Metauk countered. "The military would finally have Archive technology, something they've been after for as long as I can remember. We need to stay here and try to find a way to destroy the Engine."

"I agree," Carlion said. When everyone remained silent the Darkman licked his dry lips and continued, "It's too dangerous. The military can't get it. If we keep close to the edges at the bottom, I think we can sneak around to the far end of the site and get to the Engine. If you need two mages to power it, then even killing one should shut it down, right?"

"Most likely," Metauk said, though her voice lacked confidence. "We'll have a better chance of success if we target both mages simultaneously and try to take them by surprise."

"How are we going to avoid the swarm?" Amos asked, still

watching the action below. "They're surrounding the Engine."

"We'll need a diversion," Shara said thoughtfully. She shouldered her way back into the tunnel and bent over the pack she had left along the wall opposite Thorne. Carlion followed her and was quickly joined by the others in time to see Shara hold up a flask in each hand. Sloshing the liquid, she turned to them and said, "I only have two flasks of lamp oil with me." Looking at Trinity she commanded, "Get me Thorne's satchel. Let's see what he's got in there."

"Thorne doesn't carry anything like that in his bag," Trinity said. "It's too heavy."

"Then he might have something else that's useful," Shara answered, annoyed. When Trinity gave her a questioning look, she added angrily, "He's not using any of it now. Just give it to me."

Carlion reached down and grabbed the satchel at Thorne's feet and thrust it into Shara's hands. When Trinity gave him a threatening look, the Darkman said in a clipped manner, "We're wasting time."

"It's not yours I'm worried about," Trinity said before kneeling down next to Thorne's head to check the mage's condition.

Carlion looked back at Shara, who had opened the satchel and was rummaging inside. She pulled out a small flask and read the label before saying quietly, "Papaver extract? Thorne, what skullduggery have you been up to with this in your bag?" Dropping the flask back in the satchel, she eventually pulled out a pair of glass spheres and gave a grunt of satisfaction. "These will work fine," she said to herself and set the bag next to hers on the tunnel floor.

"It sounds like you have plan," Amos said. "Let's hear it."

Shara led everyone outside again and pointed down to where the switchbacks emptied onto the quarry floor. "Unless we find another path on the way down, we'll end up there," the

Venhadar said. "Even with the glow spheres, it's dark enough that we shouldn't be seen. I'll hug the left edge and get around the shaman. I've got enough lamp oil to cover one of those piles of rubble. When I light it, I bet the shaman will direct the swarm to investigate the fire."

"Why don't you just ignite the shaman?" Carlion asked. "It worked back on Uksyo's island with those creatures."

Shara shook her head, "The swarm would still follow the last command from the shaman. Only a strong biological urge, like getting food or sleep, would make them stop following a previous order, and even then only temporarily."

"That isn't enough of a distraction to pull the whole swarm away from the Engine," Amos said.

"That's what these are for," Shara said holding up the glass spheres she took from Thorne's satchel. "Once the lamp oil is lit, I'll climb up the switchbacks on the opposite side of the quarry. In two places I'll charge one of these and then send it rolling back down. It'll be two more targets for the swarm to chase. Once I get to the top, I'll find a place to hide. After you kill one, or optimally both mages, you come up the other side and I'll meet you. We'll work our way around the ridge here and get Thorne."

"Or we could take that same ridge, circumvent the entire mess down there and be at Nanock by early morning," Trinity argued. "Nothing you said changed my mind. The best way to help both Thorne and ourselves is to get to the city."

Shara scowled and waved the mercenary's suggestion away. "No. We need to do this now. Too much is at stake."

"This is insane," Trinity said with a raised voice. "You're more concerned with the Archive's reputation than Thorne's life."

"We understand that Thorne is your friend," Metauk said as she stepped to Shara's side and rested a hand on her shoulder. "But I agree with Shara. As callous as it may sound, getting control of that Engine right now, tonight, is more important than one mage." Trinity was about to protest, but the empath quickly held up a hand and added, "You are not abandoning him, Trinity. Thorne has a reputation at the Archive for being a fighter, in more ways than one. He set out to destroy this Engine and asked for your help. Please continue to do so. The second this is done we will take him straight to Nanock. You have my word."

Trinity stood still for a long moment with his jaw set and his eyebrows lowered. Finally, his faced relaxed and he nodded silently once. "I'll go scout out a way to the bottom," he said in a weak voice before quickly leaving the tunnel.

When Metauk looked at Amos, the corsair made a brushing motion with an outstretched hand and said, "You won't need to be so persuasive with me. As soon as Trinity said yes, then so did I. I'm not the most enthusiastic about doing this without Thorne, but maybe this is what he would have wanted anyway. Let's organize what gear we've got left and make our move."

After following Amos' suggestion, Shara and Metauk left the tunnel and waited for Trinity's return on the short ledge. Amos knelt down and grumbled something into Thorne's ear and then grasped the mage's shoulder before also leaving. Left alone with the mage, Carlion cast one final look at Thorne. He could not see the mage well, but the Darkman hoped that they found him still breathing when they returned.

"It's not an oath, but know we'll get it done. The Engine won't be a threat much longer," he murmured quickly, before exiting the tunnel and joining the others.

Once assembled on the small ledge, they moved as a group and carefully descended down the switchbacks. At the quarry bottom everyone crouched behind a large pile of rubble to stay hidden from the B'nisct swarm. The yellow light from the glow spheres seemed to wrap around the boulders as Trinity carefully peered out and quickly drew back. "It looks like things haven't changed since we left the tunnel," the mercenary said.

"That's good," Shara answered. "Sneaking around them shouldn't a problem, but I don't know how much time you'll have once I start a fire. You need to get as close to the Engine as possible."

Metauk reached out and grabbed Shara's hand and looked at her intensely. "Be careful," the empath said before letting go.

Shara opened her mouth to say something, but then looked at Carlion and mashed her lips tight. The Darkman watched her adjust the pouches on her belt before she turned and snuck away. Carlion stared at the spot where she had stood until he felt a hand shake his shoulder. Turning around, he saw only Trinity was still with him behind the rock pile.

"Come on, we need to get closer," the mercenary said, pulling the sword from his belt. "Metauk and Amos already left. We drew the short straw, the mage on the far side of the Engine is ours."

Carlion and Trinity tried to stay low and in the shadows as they moved between rubble and rock piles. They had covered nearly half the distance to the Engine when the Darkman stopped Trinity's movement and brought a finger to his lips. With a subtle gesture, Carlion pointed at a lone B'nisct fighter that had wandered from the swarm and blocked their way forward. The fighter had not noticed them and was facing the Engine.

"I'll do it," Carlion whispered, drawing the steel sword he had recovered earlier.

While Trinity crouched low near a boulder to conceal himself, the Darkman silently advanced toward the B'nisct fighter. When he was a step away Carlion abandoned stealth and rushed forward and wrapped one arm around the fighter's neck and savagely stabbed his sword into a gap between chitinous armor plates. The fighter's back arched from the blade's impact and then went limp. Carlion jerked his sword free and eased the body to the ground.

"Let's hope that there aren't too many more that decided not to be part of the swarm," he said when Trinity came to his side.

"One or two shouldn't be a problem as long as we're quiet," Trinity replied, scanning the darkness in front of them.

They had only taken a few steps forward when a short column of flame sprang upwards at the opposite end of the quarry.

"There's the signal," Trinity said, surprised. His tone grew concerned when he added, "Shara's too early. We're not ready."

"Something's wrong," Carlion said and pointed with his sword. "That fire's on the ground, not on the rock pile."

A second column of flame erupted a short distance from the first and the Darkman saw a small figure running towards the back of the quarry. From atop the stone block, the shaman thrashed the rod frantically and sent a shower of sparks into the air. With a shriek that made Carlion's ears ache, the shaman dispersed the swarm, and the mass of B'nisct fighters spread in all directions with weapons drawn. With the swarm scattered and dashing madly around the quarry floor, it would be impossible to reach the Engine or retreat without having to fight every step of the way.

Amidst the chaos Carlion saw the mages pull their hands off the Engine charging pads and fumble to pull small bottles from pouches at their belts. Almost in unison they threw the containers on the ground, which shattered with small explosions. Thick smoke billowed up from the points of impact and any B'nisct fighter nearby was driven away by the fumes.

The routes the B'nisct fighters took seemed completely random to Carlion, but he saw that increasingly they were moving into the shadows at the edges of the quarry floor. When the

Darkman realized that the swarm was searching the entire area, his chest was gripped by a fear he had only felt once or twice in his life. He and Trinity were considerably outnumbered with only a matter of seconds before being discovered, and Carlion knew they had no hope of fighting their way to an escape.

CHAPTER THIRTYONE

THORNE

Thorne's eyes slowly opened and as his vision adjusted to the darkness the mage realized that he was looking up at the ceiling of an underground tunnel. It hurt to breathe and his throat burned from the iron dust he had inhaled. His skin was coated in an oily sweat from a fever. Thorne tried to sit up, but a wave of nausea brought him crashing onto one forearm and he vomited. Rolling over to rest on his hands and knees the mage retched again. Despite feeling terrible, Thorne was at least thankful he didn't have to taste what he knew would have been a disgusting sourness in his mouth. It was a small comfort, given his current circumstances.

After a few deliberate breaths the mage felt a little better and rose to his knees. Scanning his surroundings, Thorne saw that he was near a tunnel exit, but there was no sign of Metauk, Shara, or the mercenaries.

"Hey," he called out weakly in a raspy voice. When it was clear that no reply was coming, Thorne used the tunnel wall as support to rise to his feet.

Being careful to avoid the remnants of an iron gate, the mage left the tunnel and stepped onto a small ledge and looked down at the quarry below. Still fighting disorientation from waking up alone in an unfamiliar tunnel, it took Thorne a few minutes to process all that he saw. The bottom of an abandoned quarry seemed a reasonable place to build an Engine, but the presence of the B'nisct swarm baffled him.

Behind the shaman Thorne watched a pair of small fires flare into existence. The explosions were clearly unexpected, as the shaman sent the swarm darting across the entire area, and it was then that Thorne realized Trinity and the others must be down on the quarry floor. He had no idea what their plan was, but from his vantage point on the upper rim of the surface mine, Thorne could see that his companions would be quickly overwhelmed. Looking back at the Engine, the mage knew that in his current condition he had only enough strength either to make it to the aperture or to rescue his comrades.

The frustration of the dire situation before him was mere tinder as it quickly ignited into anger. That anger expanded into rage as the mage saw the parallels between the tumult of action on the quarry floor with the fast moving waters of the river where Rose died. Inaction now would surely result in the deaths of those who willingly accompanied him on this dangerous endeavor.

Thorne bent down and tucked his trousers into his boots, and then tightly knotted the laces. Slowly standing, the mage removed his canvas shirt so his torso was covered in only a snug vest. In the scant light from the quarry floor Thorne could see hard black veins bulging under the taut skin of his arms. He quickly went back to the tunnel and took the resin knife from his satchel. Securing the blade in the waistband of his pants, Thorne returned to the ledge. His body felt heavy and the mage knew there was not much time before the Iron Bane sapped him of his mana and ultimately his life.

The mage reached behind him and charged his hand with mana to feel the air on his fingertips. With a powerful sweep of his arm, Thorne pulled the surrounding air forward and generated a jet of wind that burst from the tunnel. The sweat on his bare skin quickly dried as the wind rushed past him and tore at his pants.

Standing at the edge, Thorne steeled his nerves and tried to take a deep breath, but the attempt ended in a choking cough that brought blood to his lips. Trying again with a deliberate and slow movement, Thorne took in a single deep breath and held it. Then flinging his arms backwards the mage jumped off the ledge. Guided by his mana, the air current bent into a chute that Thorne slid down in a descent that was little more than a controlled free-fall that sloped slightly as he neared the bottom. The instant he skidded on the quarry floor Thorne maintained his momentum by breaking into a run.

With another forward sweep of his hand, Thorne produced a column of wind that ran parallel to the slope of a large rock pile. As he entered the jet of wind he was pushed forward, which allowed him to accelerate up the rubble. As he ran, Thorne saw the B'nisct shaman directing the swarm to scour the entire quarry floor. Beyond the swarm he saw the Engine and a pair of mages seemingly positioned to protect it.

Thorne did not see any sign of Shara, Metauk, or the mercenaries, and in that instant, he made his decision. The mage's powerful shout was magically amplified as he dashed up the rock pile. As he ran, ribbons of magenta light snaked down Thorne's arms and past his fingers until a pair of whip-like tendrils of raw mana flowed alongside him. In that moment, Thorne allowed himself to be taken over by The Beast.

The bright light emitted from Thorne's tendrils attracted a cluster of B'nisct fighters. The mage jumped and rose unnaturally high into the air, as if he were lifted by an unseen platform. Thorne then slammed back down to the ground, landing hard on one knee. The mage's impact with the ground sent a visible shockwave into the group of B'nisct fighters. As the crescent of arcane energy ripped through them, the bodies of the fighters shuddered violently and then toppled over dead.

A shriek from the shaman drew Thorne's attention and he saw a shower of red sparks spray from the stone block where the B'nisct leader was standing. From around the quarry floor the swarm stopped searching and converged on the mage with a frightening quickness. Thorne flicked the energy ribbons like whips over his head, which briefly expanded the bubble of space around him. It seemed that the B'nisct fighters did not know what to make of the mage's brightly glowing weapons.

Another shower of sparks from the shaman finally drove the swarm to action. The fragile pocket of space around the mage collapsed as the swarm rushed to cut him down. At the last instant, Thorne whirled in place and extended his arms. The energy ribbons at the ends of his hands twirled around him and sliced into the fighters. Slabs of chitin armor and flesh peeled away until the B'nisct fighters nearest to the mage were slimy, unrecognizable masses on the ground.

The few fighters that had not been killed pulled away and encircled the shaman's stone block. It appeared that the shaman was now fearful of Thorne and was using the swarm as a shield. Pairs of fighters continued to rush across the quarry floor in search of something, but none approached Thorne.

Only the mages at the Engine now stood between Thorne and the aperture. Turning to face the Engine, Thorne saw one of the mages throw a bottle at him, the projectile flying through the air with surprising speed and accuracy. Thorne lashed out with one of his arcane whips and snatched the bottle in mid-flight. Spinning in a complete circle, he slung it back at the mage who had thrown it. The bottle was returned with blurring speed and its impact blew the mage off his feet. Smoke and an occasional flickering flame rose from the torso of the dead mage's garment as it slowly caught fire.

Before the other mage could react, Thorne reached out with one hand and made a violent pulling motion. The ground underneath the mage's feet collapsed. Staggering, the man fell into the hole with a cry of surprise. Thorne clenched his fist and the cavity filled in from the sides, which crushed and entombed the mage underground instantly.

Now with a clear path to the Engine, Thorne sprinted towards it. The mage flung his energy ribbons around the base supports of the Engine and catapulted into the aperture. After he passed through the film Thorne pulled on the energy ribbons and felt them cut through the archway of the Engine. The aperture instantly contracted into nothing and sheared the energy ribbons.

The now shortened tendrils that Thorne held dissipated and he found himself in complete darkness. The mage was alarmed when he saw that his body did not generate any luminescence, and for a terrifying moment Thorne thought that he had not survived the transition into the Void. The mage had not conjured any platforms, but he felt gravity pull on him and he stood as if supported on something substantial.

Feeling a powerful presence behind him, Thorne slowly turned around and saw a pinpoint of light. At first, he thought the bright mote was distant, but then it slowly oscillated a short distance in front of Thorne's face and the mage realized it wasn't far away but extremely close.

"I am not normally one to grant second chances, but here we are again, Thorne," a voice reverberated around him.

The mage wasn't sure if the words were spoken aloud or heard only in his mind. "Who are you?" Thorne asked. In the absolute silence it sounded like he was shouting.

The mote of light brightened and morphed into a humanoid shape. Indistinct at first, but when the light dimmed, a heavy-set human woman wearing grey alchemist robes stood in front of Thorne. Her round face was framed by shoulder-length black hair and luminescent blue eyes cut right through the mage. "Perhaps you recognize me now, Thorne," she said with a voice that dripped venom.

"Reihana," Thorne said the name like it was an accusation.

She looked back at the mage and while Thorne did not feel afraid, his body tensed instinctively. As Reihana walked a slow circle around Thorne, he noticed her pallid skin had a waxy sheen. The mage wondered if the years had been as transformative for her as they had been for him.

There was no love lost between them. Thorne had not made it a secret that he thought Reihana conceited and power-hungry. In turn, she had denounced his idealism and mocked his efforts to prove himself amongst the more powerful Paragons. It wasn't a surprise when the council put them on opposite sides of the continent when the Paragon program was abruptly ended.

"Despite the fact that you destroyed my Engine," she said behind Thorne's right shoulder, "I'm still willing to extend my offer to you again. Work with me and I will reverse time and bring Rose back to you."

"Work with you?" Thorne echoed as Reihana completed her circuit and stood in front of him again. "Your purpose still eludes me."

"I need soldiers," Reihana replied.

"What for?" Thorne countered.

"A coup d'état," Reihana spoke the words with a savage gleam in her eye.

"Against who?" Thorne asked.

"Who do you think?" Reihana snapped sarcastically. "The Archive council has kept its mages from fulfilling their potential for generations. They got scared once they saw what Paragons were capable of and they snuffed out the program before their little experiment could exert real change on the continent. We were discarded, Thorne! Thrown away to rot once they saw us as a threat to how the Archive was run."

"You're throwing a tantrum like a spoiled child. Your rhetoric puts forth the illusion of noble intentions, but I think the real reason is that you want revenge for having your Awareness bound," the mage accused.

Reihana pulled down the neck of her robes to expose the top of her chest. Thorne saw blue veins crisscrossing her pale, translucent skin, but the binding mark that should have been there was completely erased. Her puffy face grew red in anger as she said, "It's gone here, as is your little slap on the wrist. You can't imagine how terrible it feels to lose the one thing that defines you. That's what it's like to have your Awareness bound."

"Am I supposed to feel sorry for you?" Thorne said, growing angry. "You used the Paragon program for your own selfish ends. Even after your Awareness was bound, you found a way to manipulate Torstein and Skevald to kill an entire Sovereignty garrison. You set Paragon against Paragon. What did you think would happen?"

"You would have done the same thing, perhaps even worse." Reihana shot back. "Do you think I did not mourn Mirtans' death the same as you? We were special, Thorne, all of us." She seemed to have a thought and her expression softened. She gave a close-lipped smile that pushed her cheeks up to nearly obscure her eyes and looked more pained than welcoming. "I find your resistance to the idea of liberating our fellow mages very strange," she said. "Why don't you want to join me?"

The mage looked at her disapprovingly. "If for no other reason than I don't want to be your pawn," he said with a scowl. "Never again."

Reihana looked at him with genuine surprise. "No, not a pawn, but a general," she said. Taking a step towards the mage she continued, "You see, Thorne, here in the Void you could train a multitude of mages to wield their mana as a weapon. As a Paragon you would be the perfect leader, and here you have no limitations, no restrictions."

"Then why haven't you done it yet?" Thorne asked.

"The dragon conclave has been trying to stop me, so I have to work in secret, even in the vastness of the Void," Reihana replied.

Something clicked in the back of Thorne's mind. This was an important admission, but the immediacy of an unbound and obviously unhinged Paragon made Thorne focus on Reihana.

"How did you even get here?" Thorne asked, trying to stall for time. "Let alone recruit Uksyo and Nion?"

Reihana tut-tutted and replied, "A lady doesn't reveal all of her secrets, especially to someone who hasn't agreed to join me and train my army."

Thorne made a show of looking around and said, "Even if I were to agree, there is no one here to train. First of all, both Engines are now destroyed. Second, the B'nisct swarm I cut my way through to get here would never obey me, never mind that none of them were Aware."

Giving the mage a smug smile, Reihana said, "You are wrong that I have no one ready to be trained. Here, let me show you."

Reihana turned her back to Thorne and languidly swept her arm out, and dozens of glowing ellipsoids winked into existence a wide semicircle. The mage saw that the shapes were pulsing rhythmically at different cadences, which to Thorne looked like heartbeats or breathing.

Turning back to Thorne, Reihana looked at the mage with a very self-satisfied expression. "As you can see," she said, "I have all the recruits I need right now. These are all of the mages in the midst of their Transformation as astral projections. I have been holding them here to be trained."

A visceral anger erupted inside Thorne as he looked at the host of trapped mages. "Not a minute ago you spoke of letting mages be free, but here you are holding them prisoner when they are most vulnerable. Let them go, now," he demanded.

Reihana looked at him sternly and replied, "No, I need them."

With a growl, Thorne simultaneously charged and released a burst of mana through his hand and shot out an energy ribbon that wrapped around Reihana's neck. The mage pulled the glowing magenta tendril taut and seethed, "Release them."

Reihana slowly reached up and gently plucked the ribbon like a lute string. She then grasped the ribbon with both hands and with a gentle pull snapped the tendril in two. It was an effortless movement and she watched with a detached expression as the remnants of the ribbon dissipated in a glimmering red light.

"The years have made you weak," she said. "Without someone to challenge you, push you beyond your limits, you've stagnated, Thorne. Stop this foolishness and I will give you an opportunity to lead fighting mages once again."

Reihana spread her arms out wide and the astral projects began to emit a low thrum. The sound then increased in pitch and threads of light slowly started to stream from them. The sparkling strands spiraled and undulated lazily towards Reihana. As they approached her outstretched hands, the threads began to weave together, increasing in brightness as they interlaced into a pair of shimmering braids. "Perhaps leaving you here alone to contemplate what I am offering will make you change your mind," Reihana said. "For now, I'm taking these mages with me."

Just as Reihana reached out to grasp the radiant plaits, Thorne darted forward and shoved her. The blow knocked

Reihana down, and before she could recover Thorne snatched the braided threads of light. The mage felt a familiar charge of energy, and he realized the braid was mana drawn from the astral projections.

Straining, the mage pulled the two ropes of light and the astral projections rapidly drew towards him. As they converged on Thorne, the mage became the epicenter of a sphere with the brightness of a star. Thorne felt his mind splintering, and each shard traveled down an individual thread and then beyond the astral projection to the mage that was housed in a chrysalis at one of the provincial Archives. Nearly instantaneously, there was a return from the astral projections with their own memories. Thorne reveled in the overwhelming collected experiences of the mages to whom he was connected.

Thorne faintly registered hearing Reihana's scream, but the mage couldn't see anything save the blinding white light surrounding him. His exposed skin tingled and the mage somehow knew that the sphere was expanding, seemingly unrestrained, and he was the epicenter. Unable to stop what was happening, Thorne's last conscious thought was of Celeste. He hadn't gone toward the light, but brought it to him. Would she still be there at the end?

CHAPTER THIRTYTWO

CARLION

"I can't believe it," Carlion whispered to Trinity after it was over.

Just when the Darkman was certain he was going to spend the last few frantic minutes of his life trying to cut his way out of a B'nisct swarm, he saw Thorne dash down a pile of rubble like a man possessed. The mage was wielding glowing whips the likes of which Carlion had never seen before and slashed through the swarm with little effort. Carlion then watched Thorne move with a singular purpose towards the Engine and catapult into the aperture. The instant Thorne disappeared the entire structure collapsed with a groan of metal and crunch of stone.

"I thought I'd never see those weapons again. They were the hallmark of a Paragon," Trinity said, still watching the tangled mass that was the Engine.

Before Carlion could ask if all Paragons fought in a similar manner his attention was drawn to the shower of red sparks that the B'nisct shaman sprayed into the air. The remaining fighters of the swarm returned from the outer edges of the quarry and converged on the twin pillars of flame that were distant from the remains of the Engine.

"He could have at least stayed and finished the job," Carlion said, though it wasn't a genuine complaint. The Darkman had quickly counted about twenty B'nisct fighters remaining in the swarm, which were odds much more to his liking. He rolled his shoulders to force them to relax and adjusted the grip on his sword. "Since he collapsed the aperture we can't follow him now, so I guess he wasn't planning on coming back," he said.

"Or he was keeping whatever is on the other side from reaching us," Trinity said as he scanned the quarry perimeter.

Carlion contemplated that idea as one of the fire pillars across the quarry flared. In the momentary brightness he was able to see two figures, one tall and one short, standing between the blazes. Recognizing Amos' profile, Carlion pointed and said, "There they are. If we skirt the border, we should be able to make it to them without too much trouble."

The two mercenaries kept low and moved quickly between piles of rubble. As they passed what remained of the Engine, Carlion could smell hot metal and ash. Giving the ruined device a wide berth, they approached the twin pillars of fire from behind. Periodically, one of the pillars sent gouts of flame outwards at unnatural angles and drove any nearby fighters back into the interior of the quarry. However, once the fires calmed down, small clusters of fighters from the swarm darted in again, though they were hard to find in the darkness.

As they got closer Carlion saw that Metauk and Amos had positioned themselves directly between the two blazes in an attempt to limit where the B'nisct fighters could attack. The empath was facing the center of the quarry and holding her small fist dagger at her side while her other arm was outstretched with the fingers on her hand splayed widely. Amos was facing the opposite direction and using wide sweeping swings with his daggers to keep any attackers away. The B'nisct fighters that were harassing him were dashing into and then out of range, testing the Venhadar's ability to track multiple attackers.

When the corsair saw Carlion and Trinity approaching from the edge of the quarry he shouted, "Get over here! Shara's hurt!"

Rushing towards their companions, Trinity moved up to support Metauk while Carlion joined Amos. With a quick glance at the ground behind him, Carlion saw that Shara was doubled over and clutching one of her arms. Her eyes were clenched closed and her eyelids were coated in blood seeping from a series of cuts on her forehead. The hat she had been wearing was gone and Shara's shaved head was covered in dirty sweat.

"We were able to drag her here just before that damn shaman sent the whole fucking swarm down on us," Amos said, quickly followed by, "Watch out!"

A pair of fighters rushed towards them, each armed with short-hafted spears. The Darkman was able to easily deflect a weak thrust and countered with a stab of his own. He felt the blade slide between chitinous armor plates and the fighter cried out piercingly before falling over dead.

The second B'nisct had dodged Amos' initial set of slashes and had reared back for a forward charge when the nearest fire pillar seemed to lurch forward, almost as if the flames had a will of their own, and tried engulf the fighter. The erratic motion of the fire staggered the B'nisct back and Amos took advantage of the distraction and quickly cut down the fighter.

"How did you do that?" Trinity said behind Carlion. The Darkman turned and saw Metauk facing them with her hand seemingly pushing the flames out from their source. "I thought mages couldn't control fire," the mercenary added.

Metauk looked fatigued as she lowered her hand. "I can't," she replied. "I'm manipulating the air around it, creating pockets of vacuum and then collapsing them. The burnable gasses rush in to fill the empty space and create the flame bursts."

She looked at Trinity and shook her head, then said, "It's nothing more sophisticated than a bellows, but I can't keep it up much longer. I'm taxing my mana and it's only a matter of time before the fuel for the fire is exhausted. We need to find a way to escape."

"There's still too many of them," Amos said, scanning the darkness. "And we're not going to be moving quickly carrying Shara."

Carlion looked past the fires to the stone blocks where the shaman was commanding the swarm. The B'nisct leader paced the length of the raised stone platform and occasionally sprayed bright red sparks out by thrashing a thick rod onto the edge. "We need to kill that one," he said, pointing his sword towards the shaman. "That should pull enough of the swarm away from us to get up the switchbacks at the back of the quarry."

Trinity gave an angry yell and the Darkman whirled around in time to help drive back three fighters. The B'nisct appeared to be using hit and run tactics and rotating fighters to wear them down. Carlion stood shoulder to shoulder with Trinity as Metauk crouched down next to Shara. "She's not going to make it through the night if we don't get someplace safe to treat her wounds. I'm not strong enough to carry her, so I'll get the shaman."

"No," barked Trinity with a fierce look over his shoulder. "You and Shara need to get back to the Archive and tell them what is going on here. Thorne brought us here to fight, and whether he's here or not that's what we're going to do." The mercenary glanced at Amos and said, "Amos, you carry Shara out of here as soon you get an opening. Try to watch for us on those stone blocks."

"What are you planning?" Carlion asked with a confused look at the mercenary.

"Follow me!" Trinity shouted in reply and dashed toward a

pile of rubble in the shaman's direction.

The Darkman gave Amos a nod and said, "Good luck," before chasing after Trinity. After catching up, he knelt down next to the mercenary and asked, "Now what?"

"We climb up opposite ends of those blocks and start hacking away," the mercenary said. "The platform is narrow, so that shaman won't be able to defend both directions at once."

"Good enough for me," Carlion said and pointed towards the end of the platform that was facing the interior of the quarry. "We'll both wrap around the back so we're not seen and then I'll run down to the interior end. You climb up and draw the shaman towards you, then I'll climb up and attack from behind."

Carlion got a thumbs up in reply from Trinity before the Darkman tucked his head low and ran along the perimeter of the quarry floor, just outside the reach of the firelight. When he approached the end of the platform furthest away from the center of the quarry, Carlion could hear Trinity's footfalls and heavy breathing behind him. With a quick look over his shoulder, the Darkman saw Trinity motion for him to move to the other end of the platform.

Pressing against a stone block and with his eyes upwards to keep watch on the position of the shaman, the Darkman carefully made his way to the opposite end of the platform. The shaman's back was to Carlion as he passed and for a moment he had the impulse to lunge upwards and pull the B'nisct off the stone block. While such an attack might have worked, Carlion didn't want to risk the one chance they had to kill the shaman. He moved to the end of the stone block and tried to stay low and in the long shadow of the platform.

Carlion felt very vulnerable waiting that tense minute before Trinity's attack. The Darkman twitched in a combination of fear and surprise when he heard Trinity's hoarse yell from the opposite end of the platform. The Darkman stood up and peered over the stone block to see Trinity already on top of the platform and brandishing his resin short sword at the shaman.

Quickly the Darkman hoisted himself up onto the stone block and now had a clear view as the shaman sprinted down the length of the block to engage Trinity. Thinking his attack from behind would bring the encounter quickly to an end, Carlion was not prepared for what the shaman did next.

Just before being in range of Trinity's short sword, the shaman struck the stone block with the rod. The entire platform shook violently and Carlion fell to his knees. Stumbling to his feet, he saw that Trinity had fallen as well but managed to keep his short sword pointed at the shaman. The B'nisct raised the rod in preparation to strike and Trinity stabbed weakly upward in an attempt to push the shaman back.

Shock turned to horror as Carlion watched the shaman easily knock the haphazard thrust aside. With a vicious quickness, the shaman took a step towards the prone mercenary and slammed the rod down into the mercenary's back. Trinity screamed in pain as the shaman lifted the rod again and raked it across the entire length of the platform and over the mercenary. A cascade of red sparks burst from the rod and ignited and the mercenary's clothes. Trinity's screams became inhuman as he flailed his arms in an attempt to escape the flames.

Carlion felt queasy and his knees wavered at the sight of Trinity burning. His grip loosened and he almost dropped his sword as it hung limply at his side. "Trinity!" he called out.

The shaman spun around and shouted something in the buzzing B'nisct dialect then pointed the rod at Carlion, its tip still glowing red. With a frenzied scream, Carlion drove his feet forward and charged. He thrust his sword into the shaman's torso and slammed his body into the B'nisct. The shaman had enough strength to twist when Carlion's shoulder hit, and both tumbled off the platform. When the Darkman struck the ground the impact filled his vision with starbursts and his ears rung as he rolled onto his hand and knees.

Carlion had let go of his sword during the fall and now groped around on all fours trying to find it. Sweeping his hand in front of him the only thing that Carlion felt was the dry dirt of the quarry floor. His vision started to clear when he heard a hiss in front of him and the Darkman looked up to find a B'nisct fighter looming over him. The fighter lifted a spear for a fatal strike, when suddenly the B'nisct shuddered and then collapsed.

Standing over the now dead fighter was Metauk. Hemolymph coated the blade of the empath's fist dagger, which she held in a sure and unwavering grip. The vertical pupils of her eyes shone luminescent, which made her calm expression unsettling as she looked down at Carlion. She moved to the Darkman's side and helped him to his feet. "The swarm is in disarray," she said. "Amos has Shara and is carrying her up the switchbacks. We need to hurry and catch up to them."

"Trinity's dead," Carlion said. He wanted to say something more meaningful, but he didn't have the words.

"I know," Metauk replied as she reached out and grasped Carlion's shoulder in a gesture of comfort. "I felt his passing. It was the only thing I could do for him." She looked towards the stone block where Trinity's body rested for a moment before returning to the Darkman. "We have to go now so that we can mourn him properly."

"We can't just leave him here!" Carlion protested. The nausea he felt before attacking the shaman was returning and he felt his back and neck begin to sweat.

"The spark of life, the energy, that was Trinity is gone," Metauk replied. "Do not lament leaving behind his physical remains. We carry within us who Trinity really was now."

A sudden shifting of the shadows accompanied by humming

fragments of B'nisct speech made Carlion understand that they still were not safe. While Metauk's words were not exactly convincing, they brought enough comfort for him to nod wearily in agreement. "Let's go," he whispered hoarsely.

They kept low and ran towards the rapidly dwindling twin fires near the back of the quarry. Around them B'nisct fighters raced the length of the crater in a directionless frenzy. With the shaman dead, it seemed that the fighters were left confused as to where they were and what they should be doing. With the power of the swarm dispersed and no commands coming from the shaman, the fighters had no interest in them.

Reaching the ramp at the back of the quarry without incident, Carlion and Metauk found Amos waiting for them at the top of the switchbacks. Despite the grimace on his face, the corsair was holding a seemingly unconscious Shara in his thick arms easily. As Carlion passed Amos, the corsair said, "We did what we set out to do, but he deserved better."

The Darkman turned and looked down to the bottom of the quarry. The glow spheres that lined the perimeter were no longer active, and Shara's fires were now only smoldering spots of orange in the darkness. Somewhere down there was Trinity and the destroyed Engine. The Darkman never thought things would have ended this way. He had been in battles where victory had come at a heavy cost, but this time it felt different somehow. Carlion knew he wasn't going to sort out his feelings on the edge of the quarry, so he slowly turned and followed behind the others on a subdued and lonely walk to Nanock.

• • •

The City Watchman who gave them entry to Nanock after seeing Amos' guilder suggested a quiet boarding house that would welcome late night travelers. The empath paid for a single room and after getting Shara settled on the sole straw pallet told Amos and Carlion to wait in the adjacent tavern until she came for them. They got nothing but sour looks when they entered the pub, but were left alone after sitting down at the end of a long communal table.

"What're you drinking?" the barkeep asked lazily when he eventually made his way to them.

"Rum, and bring the bottle," Amos answered.

The tired-looking man did as he was told and after he had retreated back behind the bar Amos filled two clay mugs with the dark liquor. The corsair just barely lifted a cup off the table and held it there for a moment while studying the contents. Slowly looking up at Carlion and staring at him with an almost confrontational intensity, Amos said, "To Trinity, a better man than either of us miserable fucks."

The Darkman held Amos' gaze and took the remaining cup from the table. "May his star ever bring a light to the darkness," he replied with the words spoken by Sovereignty cavaliers when a comrade was mourned. Carlion closed his eyes and took a drink and felt the rum sear a path down his throat. He held his breath a moment while the liquor warmed his chest and then slowly exhaled before opening his eyes just in time to see Amos putting his empty mug on the table.

"How do you manage it? The guilt," Carlion said, not looking Amos in the eye. "It was easy when I was a cavalier. They died for a cause, for the betterment of the Sovereignty, for the glory of the prince, something." He brushed a few fingers mindlessly on the table and added, "Trinity burned alive, and for what?"

Amos grabbed the bottle and filled his mug again. "It's a noxious mix, survivor's guilt and disappointment. I reckon you spent that long walk here thinking about what you could have done differently so that we all of came out of that quarry."

"Why would you say that?" Carlion asked, still poking at

the cracks in the table.

"Because that's what I was doing," the corsair replied. His voice softened when he added, "I've lived a long time, mate, and I can tell you with all honesty, it doesn't get any easier when you lose a friend."

"So how do you move on?"

"I don't want to move on," Amos growled, suddenly angry. "I want this to hurt."

"What? Why?" Carlion looked up in surprise at the Venhadar's response. He clutched his mug and moved it closer to his chest like it was a shield.

"So you and I never forget him," Amos said. "Our memories of Trinity are all that we have left. Metauk shouldn't have to shoulder the burden alone."

"I don't understand," Carlion said.

"Metauk told me she witnessed Trinity's passing. Do you know what that means for a Sehenryu?"

Carlion shook his head.

"It means she used her empathy to imprint his emotional state, his final feelings, to her memory. Until the day she dies, Metauk will perfectly remember Trinity's final moments. It's something that's done for family, lovers, only those that are closest to you. To carry that weight, and for essentially a stranger, is unheard of."

"Then why'd she do it?" Carlion asked.

Amos relaxed and leaned back in his chair. He blew a long breath out of his nose and replied thoughtfully, "For Thorne."

Carlion did not know how to respond, so he remained silent while Amos quickly drained his second mug of rum. They said nothing more for a time and the murmur of quiet conversations and the clunk of cups hitting the table filled in the silence. Finally, the Darkman relaxed the grip on his mug and set it on the table. "I'm not going back with you," he said.

"Why would you?" Amos answered. "There's nothing for you in Yaboon."

"I need to get to Deccern as fast as I can," Carlion said as if he were trying to convince Amos to let him go that instant. "I have to protect Julia and Natty from that cavalier."

Amos nodded slowly and replied, "Then you best sneak out just before daybreak while we're all still asleep. It will be better that way."

Carlion nodded. He retrieved his mug and took another long drink. "Yeah," he said absently.

CHAPTER THIRTYTHREE

THORNE

Thorne woke to the sound of ocean waves rolling along a beach. His face was pressed deep into the ground, and he grimaced when his teeth crunched down on sand. Rubbing the remaining sand off his face, Thorne sat up and tried to get his bearings. He was on an empty beach of black sand that ran as far as he could see in either direction. Behind him the beach eventually transitioned into prairie with clusters of woody bushes rising over the tall brown and gray grasses. The breeze that came off the ocean was warm. Overhead, the cloudless sky was the type of brilliant blue that was only found in the early afternoon.

Taking a moment to watch the white surf run up the black sand and feel the sun on his face, Thorne suddenly realized that this place was familiar to him. The volcanic islands far to the south of the continent had beaches like this one and the mage had been there twice, once on his protracted traveling education and once on assignment as a Paragon. During the latter time, he had come with Celeste.

Thinking about the dragon made Thorne stop his introspection and start searching the ground around him. Finding the footprints he was looking for, the mage followed them down the beach and eventually saw a lone figure staring out at the ocean. As he got closer, he saw the woman wore white linen trousers and a matching tunic with bell-shaped sleeves. Long grey hair was tied up in a bun, but a few strands had come loose and were being pulled by the breeze.

Even when Thorne approached and finally stopped right at her side, Celeste did not turn to look at him but continued to look out across the ocean. Learning a long time ago not to rush her into conversation, the mage knew Celeste would share with him how he got here and for what purpose when it suited her. Thorne tried to follow her gaze and find what she was looking at amongst the ocean waves. He did not see anything of note other than a stubborn seagull that rode the swells seemingly unperturbed.

"This place is one of my fondest memories of us," Celeste said finally, though still without looking at him. "Barrow told me you still have the hourglass in your apartment at the Archive."

"Not my best craftsmanship," Thorne replied with the hint of a smile.

"You're not a builder, Thorne," Celeste said. "You never have been."

The ghost of a smile evaporated from Thorne's face upon hearing what sounded to him like an unnecessary critique. "What am I then?" the mage asked.

Celeste turned and looked at him with a surprising intensity. "Perhaps something unique," the dragon replied. Her expression softened when she said, "You can't go back. Your metabolism is in stasis here, but the Iron Bane will kill you almost instantly if you leave."

Thorne started in surprise. "This is the Void?" he asked in disbelief.

Celeste nodded slowly. "I made all this," she said with a gesture indicating the beach. "The level of detail is far greater than what a mage is normally capable of creating as an astral projection."

"It all seems so real," Thorne said looking around with a new admiration for his surroundings. Celeste's curious statement from before filtered back into the mage's mind and he asked, "What did you mean before that my body is in stasis?"

"Since you were here physically for only brief periods before you might not have noticed, but here in the Void you no longer need food, water, or even air. I'm not certain, but you might not even age."

"So, I'm trapped here in the Void, but now immortal?" Thorne said with a frown. "That sounds like the worst type of prison."

"Would that be so bad, now that we're together?" Celeste replied, the hurt obvious in her voice.

"No, of course not," Thorne said, trying to save himself from his previous careless comment. "I think I was just lamenting that I'll be lonely after you leave. Am I correct to assume that you'll need to go back to the conclave to complete whatever it was that made you leave in the first place?"

"I'm not sure," Celeste said. "Reihana was distressingly good at concealing her whereabouts in the Void. But that doesn't matter now. I doubt she survived the merger of all those astral projections. The amount of mana she absorbed was the same as you, but she didn't have me to act as a siphon."

"Wait, she was the reason why you left?" Thorne asked in disbelief.

"I suppose I can't deny it anymore," Celeste said. "Once the conclave figured out what she was planning and how far along she had actually gotten, the few remaining free dragons were rallied to find and stop her. However, she has proven to be more cunning and powerful than even we had anticipated."

"Why didn't you tell me any of this before you left?" Thorne asked with an edge of exasperation in his voice.

Celeste sighed heavily and then said, "Because you would have insisted on coming with me and I wasn't going to put you in that kind of danger. That's why I left the way I did, but I always intended on keeping my promise to you about Rose's memories." She gestured out to the ocean. "I created all of this so that you'd feel something akin to happiness when you woke up. I wanted you to remember something good from your past."

"I appreciate the kindness," Thorne said, though his voice held little gratitude.

"If I erase your memories of Rose, you will never get them back," Celeste said in a serious tone. "This is ancient magic and it can't be undone."

The mage took in a deep breath and held it. Now that what he had been chasing was finally within his reach, he didn't feel exultation, but instead relief. After slowly exhaling Thorne said, "I've said my good-byes to Rose. It's time for me to move on."

"What will you do afterwards?"

The mage thought for a moment and then replied, "I'm not sure, but it appears I have no shortage of time to make a decision. For now, I will be satisfied just being free."

Celeste gave him the briefest of smiles and took a few steps backwards. Once she decided the distance between them was enough Celeste stopped and slowly spread out her arms. From the center of her chest emerged a sphere of white light that scintillated for a moment before slowly growing in size. The globe grew and Celeste disappeared inside. Thorne heard what sounded like the chime of slender bells or the breaking of thin glass as the sphere shimmered and then began to contract.

When the light receded, the dignified looking woman was gone and in her place was a dragon. In her true form, Celeste had the size and musculature of a large jungle cat but with pearlescent scales instead of fur. A mane of bristling whiskers framed her face, and coupled with huge blue eyes she had expressive and animated facial features. Tucked along her back were membranous wings so pale that they neared transparency.

As the dragon padded casually towards him, Thorne heard Celeste say, "Would you like me to change the surroundings?" Her mouth hadn't moved, but the mage heard the question clearly.

Looking down at Celeste, Thorne shook his head. He became acutely aware of the surf rolling onto the beach. The rhythmic sound of the ocean waves was almost hypnotic and the mage found himself counting the oscillations until he realized that some time had passed and Celeste was still watching him.

"What happens now?" Thorne asked.

"You forget," Celeste answered.

CHAPTER THIRTYFOUR

CARLION

Carlion handed the partially folded tabard of the Deccern City Watch to a page as the barrack's quartermaster scratched a series of notes in a thick ledger. With his shift ending, Carlion was required to relinquish all City Watch regalia such that he wasn't tempted to use it for unofficial business during his leave time. The notion still made him inwardly smile to think that such a strict set of protocols was actually employed in a frontier mining town. Still, he appreciated the return to something that resembled military discipline, and Carlion gave a polite nod to the quartermaster as he left the barracks.

The Darkman had only taken a few steps into the street when he passed another pair of City Watchmen also returning from patrol. As they passed, one gave Carlion as mock salute and said with a smile, "Not long until you'll be running the show here, right Sir Cantra?"

Carlion gave the man a rude gesture, but also a genuine smile. Despite being the newest recruit, he had been immediately granted a daytime shift, which by-passed the usual hazing of working during the night until the first service evaluation. He had been getting a hard time from some of the other City Watchmen because they surmised, correctly as it turned out, that it was his connection to Julia's uncle that got him the preferential treatment. It also didn't take long for his status as a Darkman to be known, though it seemed to matter little in Deccern. There was no love for the Sovereignty military out on the frontier, and despite the ribbing, Carlion was slowly building friendships with the other City Watchmen.

The sun was nearly to the horizon and Carlion heard the ring of fourteen high bells when he passed a cart full of ore being pulled by two oxen. Watching the beasts lumber by reminded him of the last request he gave Amos. Since he hadn't returned to Yaboon, Carlion asked Amos to tell Oskar that he could rent out the barn loft to someone else. The corsair grumbled that he wasn't Carlion's messenger, but ultimately agreed after the Darkman promised a hot meal and a warm place to sleep the next time Amos' travels brought him up north.

The Darkman turned a corner and walked down the wide paved street where a small number of guildhalls were all clustered. Not all towns were large enough to have complete guild representation, so often other guilds acted as proxies for the absent guild and as a point of contact with the closest relevant guildhall. Carlion went to the blacksmith guild and pushed the heavy iron-banded door open. Before he could return home, he had one final bit of business here.

Carlion was assailed by the smell of soot and sweat when he entered the blacksmith guildhall. On the walls hung a display of tools and metalwork, while one long table flanked by a series of benches dominated the floor. As there was still a bit of daylight left in the sky, though fading quickly, the guildhall was mostly empty and populated by a few apprentices, judging by the looks of their soft physiques. A brief exchange with one of them brought the Darkman to an office in the back where he found himself standing in front of the guild historian's desk who, as the record keeper of this guild chapter, was the person

Carlion came to see.

The historian waited until the apprentice had left before addressing Carlion. "What business do you have with us?" he asked between puffs on a pipe.

"Not the smiths' guild, but your proxy with the mercenary guild," Carlion replied. He reached inside his vest pocket and pulled out his mercenary guild medallion. Laying it on the table he continued, "I was a mercenary registered in Yaboon and I'm here to pay the fee to be released from working in that region."

"Pretty sure that more than a few of your fellow City Watchmen still have their mercenary guilders. Shit, probably most of the former miners still have theirs, too," the historian said with a laugh. "Things aren't so formal up here, Sir Cantra."

Carlion gave the man a surprised look, "You know who I am?"

The historian took a big puff from his pipe and blew out a billowing cloud of smoke before he said, "Of course I do. Don't you think the guilds talk to one another? You've only been here a few days, but I would imagine anyone that pays attention to the comings and goings of Deccern knows that you're here."

"Then I'm surprised that the governor doesn't have me in custody, given how I left last time," Carlion replied.

"What for?" the historian asked. He took the pipe out of his mouth and used it to point out the now dark window. "Governor's daughter has recovered from her fever, and her care had been taking up much of his time. There's still the business with the town's healer gone missing, but you didn't have anything to do with that, right?"

Carlion ignored the question and instead asked, "No word from the capital about a replacement healer?"

With a grunt the historian jammed the pipe back into this mouth, "Not likely to happen with the Sovereignty military running a blockade on the Archive. I have no idea what those fools were thinking."

The Darkman didn't know if the guild historian was referring to the Archive or the Sovereignty, but didn't press the issue. From what he could gather from the conversations in the City Watch barracks, opinions were mixed about the recent military activity in Yaboon. Some of the younger men thought the Sovereignty had overstepped their authority, while the old campaigners enjoyed speculating what the Archive had done to earn the prince's wrath.

Digging in the small coin purse at his belt, Carlion pulled out five coins and placed them carefully as a neat stack next to his guild medallion. "Resignation tax and paperwork fee," he said as way of explanation. Having a new thought, the Darkman retrieved one more and set it gently on top of the short column of coins and added, "Plus one for your service as proxy."

The historian took the pipe out of his mouth again, "It is appreciated. Give me a few minutes to draft the documents."

Resting his pipe on a small tray, but leaving it still smoldering, the historian pulled a few pages of coarse paper from his desk drawer and then uncapped a small inkwell. Taking the stylus that had been resting behind his ear, the historian began scratching a letter. When he was finished, he spun the papers around for Carlion to examine.

Down at the bottom of one page was a large X where the Darkman was to sign. Taking the offered stylus, Carlion's hand hesitated over the mark on the paper as he felt a strange sense of déjà vu. When he signed a similar set of documents to get his mercenary guild credentials, Carlion thought that selling his sword would be how he would spend the rest of his days. He now considered himself lucky that Trinity had been standing right behind him on unrelated business and helped him feel less of an outcast those first few months.

Carlion drew in a deep breath at the painful memory of

Trinity's death. He mourned the mercenary, and strangely enough, Thorne as well. It was the mage, after all, that had put him on the path that reunited him with his family. Though he didn't want to admit it, Carlion knew that he would have probably wasted his life being a coward, sending money and excuses to Julia, if it wasn't for the mage.

"Getting cold feet?" the historian asked.

The Darkman shook his head to clear it and then looked at the man behind the desk. "Not in the least," Carlion replied. He looked back down at the desk and signed his name in clear bold strokes.

Leaving the blacksmith guildhall, Carlion felt the tension that had been with him since returning to Deccern finally diminish. Not only was it unlikely that he'd suffer any repercussions from his involvement abducting Nion, he was now free from any obligations he had with Yaboon and the mercenary guild. There was still the risk that the cavalier running the blockade would make good on her threat to do Julia and Natty harm, but now that he was here, Carlion liked his odds much better. In the end, the Darkman wasn't sure what the future would hold, but as he quickly made his way home he did know that he was finally someplace where he could belong.

When Carlion opened the door to Julia's house and was warmly greeted by her and Natty, he looked at them both and was struck with an emotion that he hadn't hoped to feel in a long time. He was content.

EPILOGUE

METAUK

Metauk stood on the second-floor balcony of the Yaboon Archive, and under a clear morning sky watched the soldiers milling lazily about the front gardens. She could feel the listlessness and boredom of the men below, but carefully scanned them all anyway in case she was able to detect any betraying emotion that would hint at a change in the status of the civil siege. If the soldiers had noticed the regularity that Sehenryu mages had come to the balcony and watched the patrol changes, they gave no indication that it mattered to them.

Unable to feel any emotion of interest, she disengaged her empathy and turned her attention to the distant rooftops of the city center. Shara was down there somewhere amongst the guildhalls, taverns, shops, and other places of business. A few days after Shara's strength returned they began to plot their return to Yaboon and how to best aid the Archive. They both agreed that only one of them should return, with the other hiding in the city to exchange messages with Archive allies. Metauk said that Shara should be the one to return to the Archive so she could make use of the infirmary to ensure a complete recovery, but the Venhadar outright refused. Shara had insisted that Metauk be the one to return, because she would be better able to explain how she had used the eggshell fragment to locate the Momontre Archive, which had been a priority for their expedition.

Metauk had given Shara all of her possessions save her guilder, which granted her entry to the Archive after a few minutes of harassment from the Sovereignty soldiers. She had immediately given her report to the few council members that were present, and afterwards was contacted by one of Olaf's agents that she was to meet with him this morning to further discuss recent events. Metauk didn't like the cryptic wording of the message, but figured that Olaf would reveal his true intentions soon enough.

The ringing of three high bells heralded the start of the workday down in the city center and Metauk quickly left the balcony, as she did not want to be late to her meeting. The corridors of the residence and laboratory wings had considerably more traffic than when she had left with Thorne and the mercenaries. It appeared that the initial shock of the blockade had worn off, and most mages had resumed relatively normal activities within the Archive.

When she arrived at the council conference room, Metauk found no scribe posted outside and the door ajar. She slowly pushed it open to see Olaf and Erma Kent inside, both looking out the window, past the blockade to the cityscape beyond. When the Sehenryu entered, she was greeted with smiles from both, though the major-domo's was the only one with genuine warmth.

"Master Metauk," Olaf said taking a step away from the window and towards her. "Thank you for joining us during your convalescence. I don't think this should take too much of your time."

"It is no trouble," the empath replied graciously, though she wondered why the councilman addressed her by a rank she had not yet earned. She looked past him and out the window and added, "However, I must admit that I wish it was Shara here and I was down in the city. She healed incredibly fast, but I still think a visit to the infirmary would have been a better option."

"While I agree that our facilities are superior, I know that church medical aid is still more than adequate," Erma said. "The military and most of the citizenry prefer their services over ours, anyway." The major-domo seemed to be struck by a thought and then said, "Unless Shara thought she'd be recognized as an Archive mage and forced to return here if she strayed from the sanctuary."

Metauk smiled and replied, "I wouldn't worry about that too much, Erma. Despite not being a mage, on the way home our mercenary escort taught us a spell that could make us invisible." Metauk raised her hand close to her face and then rubbed a finger and thumb together.

"Even without exploiting the avarice of the common Sovereignty soldier, I think that Shara is perfectly capable of taking care of herself," Olaf said confidently. "Wouldn't you agree?"

Metauk inclined her head in silent assent. Wanting to change the subject, and to confirm the rumors she had heard around the Archive, the empath then asked, "Have you determined what we've done to incur the wrath of the farm guild?"

Erma scoffed and then said in a disgusted tone, "All of this over a pile of manure." She gestured towards the window and the soldiers loitering in the Archive gardens.

A rare frown momentarily creased Olaf's face as he looked at the major-domo. Quickly recovering, the councilman answered, "Given that they consider time on the scale of crop growth and harvest, the farm guild is not known for their vision or patience. Despite our best efforts, the superior fertilizer we promised them hasn't materialized yet and they felt their trust was betrayed. All it took was a few unsubstantiated stories of wilted crops and whispers of wrongdoing into the ears of those who hold the prince's confidence for the blockade order to be issued."

"That's rather short-sighted," Metauk said. "A simple investigation of their fields cross-referenced to our own gardens would make their lie apparent. In fact, this could be seen as a ploy to avoid taxes if they claimed a poor harvest."

"An excellent point, Master Metauk," Olaf said. "And one we have done our best to communicate to the prince. This is a rather clumsy attempt to bully us, and I have no doubt that the farm guild will regret it in time. However, the prince needed to make a show to appease them. The farm guild does feed the Sovereignty after all, so they are powerful, to a point."

Now that Olaf had called her a Master twice, Metauk became wary. He was a man of deliberate word and deed, and not known to use ostentatious or unnecessary flattery. A sense of self-preservation overrode any guilt she felt about scanning Olaf, but Metauk detected no emotions that would betray a deception on the part of the councilor. Deciding to now address the issue directly, Metauk said, "That's twice you've addressed me as 'Master,' however I have not completed the prerequisites to earn that rank."

"Oh, but you have," Olaf replied. "To be a Master one must successfully astral project into the Void and safely return. You've physically entered the Void twice and astral projected from the Void to the physical plane, which is more than sufficient to be promoted. Furthermore, your recent journey, though short in duration, is more than adequate to count as your traveling education. Since the council is separated given the current circumstances, we cannot make it official, but I have no doubt the vote will be unanimous."

"If only we could travel to them through the Void as Master Metauk did to the ruined Archive," Erma said, giving Olaf a sidelong glance.

Metauk felt a sudden excitement from Olaf that surprised her. The normally unflappable councilor rarely projected anything more than a pleasantly neutral aura, but now his emotions were unabashedly eager. However, outwardly he still appeared to be composed and Olaf slowly rested his hands on the conference table and leaned forward.

"Yes, a pity that nothing was salvageable," Olaf said, but it was clear that the empty statement was uttered without any thought.

Trying again to engage Olaf, Erma asked, "And how do you think that will affect the civil siege and the accusations of the Sovereignty?"

"Well, the dead Momontrian soldiers in the ruined Archive won't help ease any tensions," Olaf admitted and then pushed back from the table. The light streaming in from the tall windows gave the impression of a halo as it filtered through his wispy crown of white hair. "And I imagine that by now their prince has dispatched another patrol to recover the dead and refresh those stationed at the ruined Archive." The councilor shook his head in disappointment and finished, "I should have anticipated that they'd have regular patrols, even after all this time. It was a costly mistake."

"In more ways than one," Erma added. "The resin weapons and armor loaned to the mercenaries weren't returned. Aside from being extremely costly alchemic artifacts, those items could be dangerous in the wrong hands." Giving a pointed look at Olaf, she added, "Given the circumstances, I don't think we need any more rumors of Archive martial development. Wouldn't you agree, councilor?"

Metauk did not need her empathy to sense the undercurrent of agitation from the major-domo. However, Olaf seemed unperturbed and replied, "Given that in actuality, the cuirass and daggers are in our mercenary friends' possession, I consider them still on loan and safe. The two other resin blades were both lost in the vicinity of the ruined Archive, so I highly doubt anything could be traced back to us to further aggravate the prince. That being said, I agree that we must make an effort to recover them if possible."

"It will be some time before any Archive mage could approach the ruins and not be stopped by a military patrol," Metauk said. "Especially when they find what remains of the Engine and B'nisct swarm. Neither of those will be easy to explain away."

"The decimation of both should be evidence enough that any imminent threat is over," Olaf said with certainty in his voice. "I think a story about a B'nisct swarm that uncovered a long-abandoned research project that was buried in the ruined Archive quarry would satisfy any Sovereignty inquest."

"Would that story actually placate the prince?" Metauk asked.

"Given the location and the complete absence of any Archive activity there, I believe so," Olaf replied. "More importantly, we need to have that issue resolved quickly so we can focus our attention on this squabble with the farm guild. We want both matters resolved, not only for the obvious reasons, but also to give us the breathing room to accelerate the research field you just founded."

"I'm not sure I follow you," the empath said.

Olaf pantomimed holding something in front of him. "Think about it," he said, staring at whatever invisible object was in his hands. "What you have achieved Master Metauk is unprecedented. Physical transport of biological matter through the Void, something that has only been theorized up to this point, is actually possible. Using the modified chrysalis that you used as a template, and generating beacons of analogous material, in less than a generation, any Archive mage will be able to travel across the continent via a chrysalis. Think of the opportunities for communication and commerce! This is an epoch-defining technology!"

"But not without dangers," Metauk said. "I agree the implications of physical Void transport could be immense, but this is a technology in its infancy. There still needs to be significantly more research before we could even consider using it routinely."

"Which brings us to the point of my wanting to talk to you this morning," Olaf said. "I've taken it upon myself to organize a very small group of mages to begin a project to standardize Uksyo's chrysalis modification. I want you to lead the research team."

Metauk drew back in surprise. In addition to the field promotion, now it seemed that she was going to be the principal investigator for an area of research that had previously been extremely restricted. With Archive support however, the empath knew that some measure of success was assured.

Once the initial shock passed over her, Metauk still felt a mixture of suspicion and caution. "It will be some time before we, as the Archive, will be able to share any of this with the wider world," she said in a measured tone. "And how we do it will be as important as when. You can be certain that the Sovereignties will want to control access to this technology, and probably find a way to tax it once the guilds figure out how to exploit continent-wide transport. And let's not even begin to discuss how the military would want to use this technology. Now, I agree that the risks are acceptable and I certainly will lead your group, but I want to be clear with my misgivings. We need to exercise extreme caution. We are playing with fire."

"I agree completely," Olaf said. "That is why the group is very small and will be taking the upmost precautions to prevent knowledge of their work from being known to the wider Archive. The fewer people who know right now the better. What I'm more concerned about at the moment are the few others outside of these walls that know about what you've done."

"I think the risk is acceptable. There are only three people outside that know anything about this," Erma said. "I have every confidence that Shara will show discretion, but I worry that the mercenaries that accompanied you will be less restrained."

"Carlion has abandoned the mercenary guild to be a family man," Metauk said. "And I get the feeling that for Amos, this was just one more weird adventure in a life filled with them." Her voice was weaker when she added, "I'm sure Trinity would have acted with integrity as he had the entire journey. I know it is not a common thing to mourn a mercenary, but I continue to think of him as something more. He was Thorne's friend."

Erma tried to give a consoling smile, "My father told me in the old knighthood they believed that when one of their comrades fell in battle, a dragon would turn their soul into a star. Then they would be able to light the way for the others when it was dark."

"A fine romantic notion," Metauk said, after taking a calming breath. "We Sehenryu believe that death releases a being's mana to disperse through the whole world, becoming both everything and nothing. That gives me solace, knowing that Trinity is part of me now. And you."

"Thorne, too?" Erma asked.

The empath shook her head and replied, "No, Thorne will return to us in time."

Olaf raised his eyebrows, "You think he's still alive somewhere in the Void?"

Metauk looked at the councilman, "I'm sure of it."

"How?" asked Erma.

Metauk was silent for a time, and then said, "It's just a feeling."

Erma made a show to look out the window and said, "If our business is concluded councilor, then I really must return to the atrium."

"Of course, Erma," Olaf said. "I have other matters to attend to as well." Turning to Metauk, he said, "Master Metauk, I will be in touch with you shortly to make introductions with your new research group. Until then, please try to rest and recover."

"I was planning on spending a few quiet hours in my apartment," the Sehenryu said. "This whole ordeal has inadvertently given me the time to finally transcribe a few of my older laboratory notebooks."

"If you are heading back to the residence wing, might I ask a small favor of you?" Olaf asked. Without waiting for an answer, he reached into his pocket and pulled out an Archive guild medallion. "This is the guilder that Thorne took from Nion, which originally belonged to Erza. Since she no longer has any official quarters here I thought the best place to store this would be in Thorne's apartment. His room is unlocked at the moment, so if you would, please put this in a drawer."

As Olaf offered the medallion to Metauk, she felt a hint of guilt from the councilor. Not wanting to press the issue, she silently took the guilder and left the conference room. A short time later when she entered Thorne's apartment, despite knowing the mage was gone, Metauk couldn't shake the feeling that she was intruding into someone's private space.

Quickly sliding the guild medallion into the top drawer of Thorne's writing desk, Metauk was ready to make a quick retreat when she noticed the hourglass on the tabletop. All of the black sand was at the bottom and something she could not explain compelled her to flip the timepiece over. The empath inverted the hourglass and was surprised to find that the sand didn't fall. She bent over to examine the hourglass more closely and she saw the design flaw that prevented the sand from falling. Straightening, Metauk solemnly left Thorne's room and as she closed the door, she caught a final glimpse of the curious hourglass on the table.

Time was standing still.

Acknowledgements

While there is just one name on the cover of this novel, it took a team of people to make it a reality. I first want to thank the Director of Apprentice House Press, Dr. Kevin Atticks, for his oversight and education on the entire publishing process. My Developmental Editor, Samantha Dickson, did a fantastic job helping to revise the novel and file down the rough edges of the submitted manuscript. The cover design and internal manuscript typesetting was done by my Design Editor, April Hartman. To ensure that the novel had the best chance for being seen in a very crowded marketplace my Promotion Editor, Shanley Honarvar, put together a marketing plan. Thank you to my Managing Editor, Claire Marino, and the entire Apprentice House staff for their part in my novel publishing journey.

On a more personal level, my family is deserving of the most thanks, but I fear they didn't hear it often enough. I'll put here just a few of the many memories that had an impact on me when I was younger, and therefore also on this novel.

Growing up my father, Tim, would make up words and then try to get away with using them in conversations with my family. He would also sing short impromptu songs that didn't really make any sense. He still does both of these things today (mostly for the grandkids), and I now understand that my enjoyment of words and their use to convey an emotion actually comes from him.

When I got a particularly blunt rejection letter as a teenager I went to my mother, Sue, for advice. She said to me, "So what now, quit?" It was a challenge, a dare, and ultimately a lesson about resiliency, perseverance, and self-belief. Even when I was unable to write consistently because life kept getting in the way, I never forgot that conversation and it helped me keep alive the dream of writing a novel.

When my brother, Kevin, and I were little, he always let me have the "good" garbage can lid to be a shield when we pretended to be knights, fighting dragons and monsters in the woods surrounding our rural house. We spent a lot of time building forts, making spears, and generally getting banged up before dinner in the summer. His willingness to go on adventures, even when we ended up fighting each other instead of the monsters, taught me a lot about being a good brother and also a good friend.

This novel exists in no small part because of my wife, Laura. With the birth of our daughters I found that paternity leave let my mind wander during the repetitive nature of infant childcare, and during that time I started thinking about my old stories again. During baby naps I would work on "the book." Once I had a complete manuscript draft Laura was the first to read it, and she was brutally honest in all the ways she didn't like it. But she knew how important the book was to me, and helped with revisions to make it better (including drawing the map).

I would be remiss not to acknowledge the part my daughters, Genevieve and Alexandria, played in the writing of this novel. Experiencing things as they do has inspired me to imagine a world full of pixies and dragons, and reminded me that it is OK to do things just for fun.

Finally, I want to thank you, the reader. Time is one of the most precious things a person has, and I am deeply appreciative that you have given me yours to read this novel.

About the Author

J.G. Gardner has a Ph.D. in Microbiology and is currently a researcher working on new ways to generate renewable energy using bacteria. While having published many technical papers on genetics and biochemistry, he has always wanted to write a novel about magic, wizards, and dragons. After the birth of his children, he was inspired to fulfill that dream and used spare moments on nights and weekends to write his debut high fantasy novel, *The Path From Regret*. To learn more about his writing, visit jgardnerauthor.com.

Apprentice
House Press
Loyola University Maryland

Apprentice House is the country's only campus-based, student-staffed book publishing company. Directed by professors and industry professionals, it is a nonprofit activity of the Communication Department at Loyola University Maryland.

Using state-of-the-art technology and an experiential learning model of education, Apprentice House publishes books in untraditional ways. This dual responsibility as publishers and educators creates an unprecedented collaborative environment among faculty and students, while teaching tomorrow's editors, designers, and marketers.

Eclectic and provocative, Apprentice House titles intend to entertain as well as spark dialogue on a variety of topics. Financial contributions to sustain the press's work are welcomed. Contributions are tax deductible to the fullest extent allowed by the IRS.

To learn more about Apprentice House books or to obtain submission guidelines, please visit www.apprenticehouse.com.

Apprentice House
Communication Department
Loyola University Maryland
4501 N. Charles Street
Baltimore, MD 21210
410-617-5265
info@apprenticehouse.com
www.apprenticehouse.com

CPSIA information can be obtained
at www.ICGtesting.com
Printed in the USA
LVHW052332210523
747631LV00002B/95